Yuri Smirnov

About the Author

DENNIS COOPER is the author of the George Miles Cycle, an inter-connected sequence of five novels that includes *Closer*, *Frisk*, *Try*, *Guide*, and *Period*, as well as *My Loose Thread*, *The Sluts*, and his most recent novel, *God, Jr.* He is a contributing editor of *Artforum* and editor in chief of Little House on the Bowery/Akashic Press, a book imprint focusing on collections of fiction by emerging North American authors. Cooper spends his time between Los Angeles and Paris.

SMOTHERED IN HUGS

ALSO BY DENNIS COOPER

SMOTHERED IN HUGS

Essays, Interviews, Feedback, and Obituaries

Dennis Cooper

HARPER PERENNIAL

NEW YORK • LONDON • TORONTO • SYDNEY • NEW DELHI • AUCKLAND

HARPER ● PERENNIAL

HarperCollins books may be purchased for educational, business, or sales promotional use. For information please write: Special Markets Department, HarperCollins Publishers, 10 East 53rd Street, New York, NY 10022.

FIRST EDITION

Designed by Justin Dodd

Library of Congress Cataloging-in-Publication Data is available upon request.

ISBN 978-0-06-171561-7

10 11 12 13 14   OV/RRD   10 9 8 7 6 5 4 3 2 1

For
Craig Marks
Jack Bankowsky
Andrew Hultkrans
Tom Christie
Judith Lewis
Joy Press
M. Mark

CONTENTS

PREFACE

I published my first piece of nonfiction when I was about a year out of high school, meaning in 1972 more or less. A friend of mine—who liked my poems and short stories and who thought I talked intelligently about music—knew an editor of a small Pasadena, California, newspaper, whose moniker I've since forgotten, and somehow she talked this higher-up into naming me, an inexperienced Rimbaud wannabe who thought every linear sentence was a lie, as the paper's official music critic. My initial assignment was to critique Leonard Cohen's then brand-new *Songs of Love and Hate* album, and while I thought I had plenty to say, I found putting my thoughts into prose completely torturous. One, I had almost no chops as a stylist, and, two, I seem to suffer from a lifelong disconnect between my very opinionated side and the side of me that seems to need to write stuff down. I was so embarrassed by the review I turned in that I never even cracked that issue of the newspaper. After I similarly botched a second task to review a Neil Young concert, the editor canned me.

The next time I braved a nonfiction assignment was about ten years later, also at the behest of a small Pasadena newspaper, in this case a short-lived alternative free monthly called *Gosh!* They offered me a regular column in which I could write about virtually anything I wanted, and that freedom made the opportunity feel more alluring and safe enough. What I wrote for *Gosh!* and for other publications (*Advocate, LA Reader, New York Native, Art in America, a.o.*) over the next few years was not as absolutely terrible as my initial forays had been, but you'll notice that nothing from that era has survived the cut. Honestly, I still think nonfiction and my particular writing ability do not make a natural couple. And every time I take on a journalistic gig to this very day, it feels as though I've embarked on a difficult formal experiment as much as set out to make a valid case about something or someone. I'm guessing that if the pieces in this book have a value outside of the inherent charisma of their subjects, it's probably due to some effect caused by my writing's struggle to fulfill the formal requirements of the assignments I was given.

Otherwise, I just want to say that in the early 1980s, the critic and poet Peter Schjeldahl told me I had a sensibility that might make me a good critic, and without his encouragement and support, I'm not sure any of the pieces in this book would have existed. Also, I feel like I should note that my opinions have changed since I wrote certain of these articles and reviews. I now think Samuel Delaney's *Hogg* is a great novel, and I don't know why I didn't realize that upon first reading. When *The Violet Quill Reader* was published, I felt it was part of an attempt to create a kind of hierarchy within so-called gay literature whereby the writers in that group were to be seen as the high standard, and I think in my great dislike of this proposal, I was too harsh on the work of the writers in the volume. Lastly, while I stand by my low opinion of Brion Gysin's writings, I wish I had made a stronger case for the brilliance and quality of his visual art.

Dennis Cooper
2010

SMOTHERED IN HUGS

HOMOCORE RULES
(March 1985)

Punk has always had a contingent of lesbian and gay bands, critics, fans, and general scene-makers. Out of fear of skinheads and the like, they remained a relatively silent subminority until the rise of Reaganism, then AIDS, and the gradual realization that silence under the circumstances meant, well, death. Bolstered by the popularity of bands like the Smiths and Bronski Beat, as well as by the support of cool, straight upstarts like Jello Biafra, Lydia Lunch, and Henry Rollins, these punks began to think out loud, meet, organize. Trouble was, the gay community at large, giddied and a little spooked by its growing political power, seemed to meet calls for anarchy with a collective finger to the lips. To punks' horror, many gays in the early '80s had gotten as lazy as the heterosexual mainstream who sought to oppress them. "Problem children" (punks, activists, women in general) were marginalized via an unspoken but entrenched class structure that effectively alienated all but the most "privileged."

Homocore is pretty much a direct result of that schism. The term was coined a few years back by Bruce LaBruce and G. B. Jones, the editors of Toronto's seminal lesbian/gay punk minimagazine (or "zine"), *J.D.s*, and later adopted by the San Francisco zine *Homocore*. There are about twenty Xeroxed and/or cheaply offset-printed publications like them across North America, constituting a network of sub-desktop alternatives to established, large-circulation periodicals like the *Advocate* and *Outlook*. Mutually supportive for the most part, but individualistic in outlook and design, these zines share a hatred for political correctness, yuppification, and all things bourgeois, especially within gay culture. In fact, for many of these young editors, the enemy is less heterosexuals than, in the words of Johnny Noxzema of *Bimbox*, "cryptofascist clones and dykes . . . telling us how and what to think." Or as Tom Jennings describes his zine *Homocore*, "One thing everyone in here has in common is that we're all *social mutants*; we've outgrown or never were part of any of the 'socially acceptable' categories. You don't have to be gay . . . any personal decision that makes you an outcast is enough."

Homocore (c/o World Power Systems, P.O. Box 77731, San Francisco, California 94107; $1, cash only) is the most generous and info-packed of the zines. Produced on the kind of cheap newsprint that seems to yellow before your eyes, it consists of letters from readers, reports on anarchist goings-on, pics of partying local scenesters, and lots of opinions from Tom Jennings and assistant Deke Nihilson. Though he'd probably deny it, Jennings's motormouthed editorializing makes him the unofficial conscience of the movement, and his pronouncements, even when couched in who-the-fuck-am-I-to-say-ism, give this zine the hyper-earnest tone of classic punk periodicals like *Flipside* and *Maximumrocknroll*. In a recent issue he seems to speak for all when he bemoans the scarcity of lesbian-edited zines, and declares himself pro-drugs (or certain drugs anyway—LSD, mushrooms, cocaine). But occasionally he distinguishes *Homocore* from the pack by taking a rather old-school liberationist stance, as in his recent dismissal of one of the more self-consciously abject gay zines, *Carnifex Network*, whose provocatively unopinionated debate on the pros and cons of intentionally spreading sexual diseases brought out the traditionalist beneath the mohawk. "If you hate yourself," he responded, "and wanna indulge that, fine, but I am not gonna support it. The world-at-large does enough of this for us, thank you, without 'us' doing it to ourselves."

Also out of San Francisco is the tiny and stylish *Milquetoast* (c/o Kennedy, 3491 17th Street, San Francisco, California 94110; send SASE). Editor Jeffery Kennedy is a pioneer in the field, having given the world the legendary (in these quarters), defunct *Boysville U.S.A.*, sometimes called the thinking person's *Tiger Beat*. If there were a church for sensitive, easily love-struck gay punks, *Milquetoast* is what they'd consult instead of the Bible. One sheet of pink paper folded like a girl's party napkin, its surface is a pristine collage of cute boys, beauty tips, and found items with a homosexual subtext. The zine's considerable charm can be traced to the tensions between Kennedy's transcendent goals and the realities of low-tech publishing. Even one more smidgen of professionalism and the project would be something much blander and less sweetly pitiful.

Traditions are exploded in the utterly amazing *Fertile La Toyah Jackson Magazine* (7850 Sunset Boulevard, Penthouse Suite 110, Los Angeles, California 90046; $4, cash or checks payable to C. D. Sanders). Jackson, an LA drag-queen-about-town, is the namesake, guru, and perennial cover girl of this lawsuit-defying zine, edited by writer/"Blactress" Vaginal Creme Davis. Davis and staff spend most of each issue fantasizing about the sexual preferences of the famous with an abandon that makes *OutWeek*'s Michelangelo Signorile seem like a heterosexual apologist.

Here are some flights of fancy from recent issues: "Oh I went to one of THOSE parties. . . . Beautiful Billy Idol was harking back to his Generation X sissy days by slobbering all over model ex-Wasted Youther Jeff Dahlgren. . . . Mickey Rourke seemed to have an even better time as he was rimming and fudgepacking *Head of the Class*'s Michael DeLorenzo. . . . Later I personally . . . watched [Jason Bateman] fudgepack cute jewishy teen heartthrob Rob Stone from ABC's sitcom *Mr. Belvedere*." *FLTJM*'s genius lies less in such details than in the stylish violence with which Davis gives white-bread celebrities the lifestyles we demand of true Stars, at least since *Hollywood Babylon* came out. Wish it were [can't read] . . . some divulgences (Tom Cruise getting fist-fucked in John Schlesinger's dungeon, for instance) would strain the gullibility of the mentally challenged.

Toronto's *Bimbox* (282 Parliament Street, #68, Toronto, Ontario, Canada M5A 3A4; "free to those who deserve it") is a relative newcomer. According to the coeditors Rex Boy and Johnny Noxzema, their project is a "forum to reach a secret network of lesbians and gay men across the globe who can barely ride a bus without vomiting out of disgust and contempt for the walking heterosexual abortion sitting across the aisle." *Bimbox*'s wild layout pits typewritten rants/fiction against a quilty Xeroxed collage of imagery both found and invented, as well as plenty of those zine regulars, comics and porn. Highlights of the first issue include TaBorah's account of fist-fucking the well-known lesbian writer Pat Califia, a complete Nancy Sinatra discography, and the column "Clone Watch" by Jo-Jo Price-Morgan, which all but suggests that the mustachioed among us be targeted for assassination. Throughout, *Bimbox* reworks images originally created to titillate heterosexual libidos into *fiercely* gay graphics, as if attempting to hallucinate the enemy away.

Most unusual is the undifferentiated array of male and female voices, a rare occurrence even in this determinedly nonsexist scene.

Gentler in spirit but no less incendiary, Laurence Roberts's *Holy Titclamps* (Boxholder, P.O. Box 3054, Minneapolis, Minnesota 55403; $1, cash only) is a quarterly zine made up of whatever readers mail in. In the latest issue, Roberts answers complaints that *HT* "lacks focus and vision" by accepting the blame. To him a hands-off policy is the natural end product of anarchism. In fact, one of the zine's lures is a slight overall haziness, magnified by a lackadaisical if neat layout, where anything photocopiable, whatever the intent or degree of sophistication, fits snugly. Number 4 gathers romantic poetry, a B-52s review, comics, letters, and Roberts's smart, poetic daydream of a gay punk utopia. *HT* is also inordinately literary, with regular dollops of writing by and/or reviews of faves like Sarah Schulman, Robert Glück, and Kathy Acker. Astute, as well as relatively ego-free, Roberts is one of the gay anarchist movement's clearest thinkers. His practical twist on the Andy Warhol chestnut—"In the future we'll all be famous to fifteen people"—could easily become the motto at large.

Robert Ford, Trent Adkins, and Lawrence Warren's *Thing* (1516 North Sedgwick, Chicago, Illinois 60610; $1, cash or checks payable to Robert Ford) is the first zine directed primarily, though not exclusively, at black lesbians and gay men, to whom the more extreme Acid House is punk. Ford's gorgeous layout is complicated and multiplicitous without seeming either overfed (à la *Spy*) or overcompensating (à la *Egg*). Recent features have ranged from an interview with DJ/producer Riley Evans to a Monopoly-like game board, "House Hayride (just add dice and spin)," to profiles on the artists Keith Haring, Louis Walker, and

David Wojnarowicz. (*Thing*'s been known to appropriate material—I was surprised to find a piece of mine from an old art catalogue here.) Each issue has four or five separate gossip columns, most only a shade less wittily libelous than *FLTJM*'s. Plus there's an up-to-the-second taste-making chart called "Thing/No Thing." In the most recent issue Pat Stevens, Bobby Short, "Fuck Me," and *One Nation Under a Groove* are among those rated as "Thing," while Pat Buckley, Harry Connick Jr., "Fuck You," and *Rhythm Nation* are deemed "No Thing." If there was ever a zine that begged for the backing of a gutsy billionaire, it's *Thing*, though it looks plenty resplendent in simple Xerox.

Chicago is also "house" to perhaps the most underground zine, *Gentlewomen of California* (the address is a well-kept secret). Editor Steve Lafreniere is one of the city's best-known entrepreneurs (for lack of a better word), and his occasional Xeroxed publication is founded on the principle that "everybody owns everything." Therefore it's a highly discriminating repository of images, fiction, quotes, and essays swiped from other places. Lafreniere crops, enlarges, defaces, prints them on various colored and textured papers to create what might be considered an (ugh) Artist's Book, if he wasn't such a terrorist. "Say No to Democracy" and "Homosexual Men Arm Yourselves" read two of the messages masked into the zine's topsy-turvy design. The latest issue involves texts by Jacques Attali, Gary Indiana (on Mapplethorpe), Angela Carter, Paul Bowles, and New Narrative writers David Sedaris and Kevin Killian, plus doctored erotica galore, including an actual page ripped from some porn magazine and scratched with the slogan "Where's your mind now?"

J.D.s (P.O. Box 1110, Adelaide Street Station, Toronto, Ontario, Canada M5C 2K5; $4, cash only) is pretty much everybody's favorite, the zine whose style of combustible romanticism triggered the onslaught. Bruce LaBruce and G. B. Jones are roommates (and a fag and dyke respectively; they hate the terms "gay" and "lesbian"). They manage what's quickly becoming a J.D.s empire. In addition to the zine, they produce compilation cassettes of "Queercore" (music by gay punk musicians, including their own band, Fifth Column), direct and star in videos, host a popular film series at a Toronto nightclub, and head a clique of anarchists called the New Lavender Panthers. *J.D.s* the zine organizes news, porn, whimsy, transgressive diatribes, letters, and drawing into an intricate supermess of a "look" so fresh I wouldn't be surprised if it affected magazine design the way Neville Brody's the *Face* did in the early '80s. The current issue's subheading could be the "Nazi Skinhead Special," since a slew of pages are devoted to the pros (and a few cons) of punks "worshipping the oppressor." LaBruce offers an autobiographical-sounding sex story, as well as some teasers for his just-released video, *No Skin off My Ass*, "the tender love story of a punk ex-hairdresser obsessed with a young, silent, baby-faced skinhead." Jones contributes a smoky photospread of Jena von Brucker, "Human Ashtray," and some Vermeeresque sketches of tight-jeaned dyke punks. Fleshing out the subject are LaBruce's awe-struck interview with porn icon Peter Berlin, a picture of Sid Vicious in bed with a boyfriend, and Vaginal Davis's history of closeted homosexuals in the Los Angeles rock scene. Significantly, and this could apply to the other zines, too, *J.D.s* is free of the simplistic anti-Helmsesque rhetoric that suffocates much gay product these days. In classic anarchist fashion, they just invent a world for themselves in and around the givens of the big fucked-up one, and say, "Join or leave it alone."

PLACEBOMANIA
The World Wrestling Federation
(April 1989)

My family used to summer in Hawaii. Its popular culture was wa-a-ay behind the rest of the United States, with hit songs from up to ten years before just entering local playlists. When John Lennon made his remark about the Beatles being more popular than Christ, people in so-called uncivilized regions of the country tossed 45s onto bonfires. Hawaii was such an outpost in those days that few locals even knew the name Beatles. Word. I was there. Imagine the peep of response if Throwing Muses made the same remark now. This was the late sixties, when professional wrestling was professional in name only. You could watch the sport in my hometown of LA, maybe, if you were lucky, late at night on some static-infested TV channel. I remember stopping briefly at its embarrassing spectacle. A handful of fat, middle-aged guys would be sitting on folding chairs around a raised platform where two fatter guys dressed in Halloween costumes knocked each other around on a floor as springy as a trampoline. I think one of my friends' dads was into it. But in Hawaii, pro wrestling was big, mega, "more popular than Christ," even. The little town of Lahaina, Maui, where we stayed was eternally plastered with posters of scarred, scowling, ludicrously named men soon to be locked in combat at the local high school gymnasium.

One summer I happened to wind up on a small, interislands plane with a troop of these wrestlers. People around me gasped in recognition and lined up for autographs, but the wrestlers were horrifying to the point of hallucination, if you ask me. For one thing, they each took up two or more normal-sized seats. Most of them had to turn sideways to enter the cabin. Weirdest of all was how foreign their system of values seemed, at least to someone in his early teens. I mean, you could tell which of the wrestlers were supposed to be handsome and/or signify "hunkiness" because of the quasi-handsome neatness of their features and their dyed-blond pompadours, but the supposed charmers were really no less alien than the supposed monsters among them with green hair and dried lava skin. Certainly there was nothing particularly regal or starlike about any of them. They just seemed lonely, dangerous, cliquish, victimized . . . *something*. They must all be dead by now.

When, almost twenty years later, professional wrestling suddenly became a national pastime of sorts, I was living in another so-to-speak cultural outpost, Amsterdam, Holland. There's a TV station over there that covers most of Europe called Sky. Its programming, as of the mid-eighties anyway, consisted of MTV-styled blocks of rock videos, reruns of *Charlie's Angels*, *The A-Team*, et al., and sports coverage. Owned by the Australian tycoon Rupert Murdoch, Sky siphons its contents from whatever's new and popular in the United States, and inexpensive to rebroadcast. When the wrestling fad began, Sky was immediately on the case. While a segment of Dutch society got pretty caught up in the spectacle, it wasn't the same yahoo-type audience that embraced it over here. Sure, a few louts ran around wearing "Hulk" Hogan fashion gear, but in general Dutch louts are a little more sophisticated than ours.

Their favorite sport is soccer, a far, far more graceful time waster than football or basketball. Maybe for that reason, they seemed to think wrestling was just too crude, not to mention fake. In fact, the fakeness is exactly what attracted wrestling's real European audience—artists, intellectuals, cultural theoreticians. It wasn't unusual to read lengthy essays in literary journals about the possible meanings of flamboyant wrestlers like Iron Sheik, the evil Iranian, or the chained, snorting black man, Junkyard Dog, or the lisping, wrist-flapping "Adorable" Adrian Adonis. I, an American, found myself agreeing with the theorists that these character constructions represented a kind of extreme distillation, a visual readout of the childish American system of value and belief.

Now I'm back in New York and I haven't completely changed my mind. Maybe I would change it if I had somebody to argue about wrestling with, but no one I know can stomach more than a couple of seconds of the stuff. Sure, there are a few wrestling fanzines edited by people with reasonably high IQs. But am I really the only World Wrestling Federation addict who sees in the "sport" a fascinating, ever-changing, and highly structured microcosmic system of signifiers for the way our society limps along? The WWF is like an update of the fucking Greek myths, I'm sorry. Embodiments of good versus embodiments of evil—saintly Hulk Hogan against freakish Andre the Giant, hunky Ultimate Warrior against the snide and elitist Million Dollar Man, friendly dunce "Hacksaw" Jim Duggan against the self-absorbed "Ravishing" Rick Rude. . . . The former win by playing fair, period; the latter win strictly by cheating. It's been remarked before that pro wrestling is like a live-action cartoon or comic book. That's true, and it's a compliment, but that doesn't take into account the growing complexity of the "sport" on all levels. Once wrestlers waddled into the ring, obese slobs with bad makeup jobs, low parodies of our worst fears. Nowadays wrestlers are not only physically fine-tuned; they're introduced to the viewing audience via elaborate, Olympics-styled pseudo-documentary footage showing them in their "natural" surroundings, sometimes months before they finally appear in the flesh. In addition there are characters who never actually wrestle, such as Brother Love, a broad and rather evil parody of televangelists like Jimmy Swaggart. Love merely interviews and goads opponents on a small, pulpitlike set. In the last year or two pro wrestling has been further complicated by the introduction of characters whose weird combination of heroic and evil qualities test and manipulate viewers' loyalties, most extremely in the case of the current WWF champion, Randy "Macho Man" Savage.

The Savage character began life as a bad guy. With his dark glasses, scraggly long hair, sawed-off voice, and little fey mannerisms, he was an assembly-line WWF villain. To top it all off, he had a co-character, an attractive female "manager" named the Lovely Elizabeth, with whom he acted out his blatant misogyny. There are always a few wrestling aficionados who perversely and routinely throw their support behind the thugs and liars, but Savage's mixed-up machismo held an unusual fascination for a lot of fans. So, a couple of years ago, his image was gradually sweetened, detail by detail, until he was no longer the archenemy of aging champion Hulk Hogan, but the character who would ultimately replace him as benevolent top dog and even join together with him in an occasional, Elizabeth-managed tag-team combination called the Mega Powers. Recently, however, the powers that be at the WWF decided to shake things up for whatever reason, and a rift was introduced between Savage and Hogan. It began with great subtlety (by WWF standards) when Savage could be spotted cringing at Hogan's rather more intense postmatch ovations. Next Hogan's energetic personality was revved up a notch too high so that he could possibly be interpreted as being a bit of a bully. Savage's behavior grew increasingly erratic. He'd sneak up behind his partner, fists clenched, ready to kick butt. Manager Elizabeth, while obviously distressed by the undercurrents of tension between her two "clients," remained, nevertheless, rather noncommittal considering she's supposed to be Savage's girlfriend. So Savage began to suspect hanky-panky. The feud escalated until one night in the dressing room, where a cameraman just happened to be poised, Savage flipped out, beat up Hogan, knocked Elizabeth around, and had to be restrained by a couple of other good-guy wrestlers, Brutus "the Barber" Beefcake and Tito Santana. A bandaged, confused Hogan challenged Savage to a fight. Savage thought it over for a few suspenseful weeks then accepted. The two will meet (or will have met by the time you read this) at Trump Plaza in Atlantic City in early April.

What's interesting about this little narrative, and WWF goings-on in general, is the degree to which the machinations of the spectacle are exposed, and the degree to which they are cloaked in standard mythological costuming. Back in the days when wrestlers merely rolled around in silly outfits, the tawdriness and fakeness of the venture was so blatant it was mind-boggling that anyone could train their eyes on the show for more than a few seconds. The WWF, a multi-multi-million-dollar entertainment corporation, is less a direct descendent of that "sport" than its Reagan-era-infected mutation. Pro wrestling's original simplistic set of values—good/tough versus bad/weak—remains, but it is entangled in a deceptive system of narratives and cross-narratives that has a lot more in common with, say, the films of Jacques Tati or the Bush administration or *It's Garry Shandling's Show* than it does with a street fight. Like Tati's Monsieur Hulot or Bush or Shandling, Hogan, Savage, Elizabeth, et al. are simple, flexible directives whose construction is based not on real people per se, but on certain media precedents, in wrestling's case the history of superheroes, which includes everything from elected officials to cartoon stars. Introduced with elaborate, authoritative fanfares, à la politicians, wrestlers engage viewers' sympathy or disdain based entirely on who they choose to fight. If the opponent is a designated scumbag, the new character is a god, and vice versa. But if the opponent's character is as blurry as Hogan's or Savage's is at the moment, you have a confrontation not unlike the recent presidential election where you can't quite tell the angels from the devils, with or without inside information. Ultimately it may be this increasingly valueless surface that makes pro wrestling so fascinating to esthete wimps like myself, who can't take our eyes off American culture but are also dead tired of the ennui-inducing content of the real struggle.

THE KEANU REEVES INTERVIEW
(September 1990)

Equal parts sex symbol, madman, oaf, and overgrown kid, Keanu Reeves is unique among younger actors in his ability to fill movies with a specific, contentious energy, no matter how small his role. His is a presence that lies somewhere between Crispin Glover's manic self-involvement and Jimmy Stewart's gentle remove, with maybe a dash of Jacques Tati tossed in. Reeves—a walking explosion of misbehaved limbs—would have been great in the silent film era. In his bigger roles—especially in flawed movies like *Permanent Record, Prince of Pennsylvania*, and *I Love You to Death*— he's capable of literally wrenching plots loose from their flimsy foundations when need be, making them tag along after his characters' wild quests for sensation. In his best movies, *River's Edge, Bill & Ted's Excellent Adventure*, and *Dangerous Liaisons*, he seems to embody the sensitive soul of all disenfranchised youth. Two upcoming projects match him with suitably maverick directors, Kathryn Bigelow's *Riders on the Storm* [ultimately released as *Point Break*] and, especially, Gus Van Sant's *My Own Private Idaho*. His next movie in release will be *Aunt Julia and the Scriptwriter* [ultimately released as *Tune in Tomorrow . . .*] later this year. I met with the tanned, newly muscular Reeves at one of his occasional hangouts, Linda's, a restaurant-cum-jazz-club located in the nether reaches of the Melrose strip.

Dennis Cooper: Is it true you're playing a male prostitute in Gus Van Sant's new film?

Keanu Reeves: Yeah, I play Scottie, who's based on . . . Hal? Prince Hal? From, um—Shakespeare. I come from a wealthy background and I've denied that. And I've been on the streets for three years.

"The streets" meaning Santa Monica Boulevard?

Yeah, yeah. But in Seattle. It's not quite au courant. It's more about family. I call it "Where's Dad?" Hopefully River Phoenix will be doing it with me. And if that happens, then who knows what's going to happen.

You'd both be prostitutes?

Yeah!

What a funny idea.

Yes. He plays a character called Mike, who has an extreme case of narcolepsy. So he'll pass out and awaken and the film follows him around. I'm more like a side character.

Sounds cool. Any relationship between this and *Wolfboy*, that gay play you did in Toronto early on in your career?

[*laughing*] Um—wow. No. The guy that I played in *Wolfboy* was a jock, who just lost it. He was under so much pressure, he didn't know what was goin' on. Then he fell in love with this guy who gave him back his sense of power. And even then I dumped the guy. [*chuckling*] And he killed me. Cut me.

Yeah, I heard.

He sucked my blood.

Friends of mine in Toronto sent me some yellowed clippings.

Really? What did they—I don't recall.

Oh, um—just that it was disgusting. The play was revolting, et cetera.

Oh, yeah!

And there should never have been anything like it perpetrated on a stage.

Really! Well, that's kind of cool. The poster was the cast in white T-shirts, kind of wetted down. I had my eyes closed and this guy is almost kissing me with this like grin? So the first couple of performances, we had leather boys comin' out. You know, caps and the whole deal. And they were walking out at intermission because there weren't enough shoes flying.

You grew up in Toronto. Wildly, innocently?

When I see stuff in LA now I realize how safe and sheltered my upbringing was. We didn't even do graffiti, you know? We'd build go-karts called "Fireball 500." I mean we did sling chestnuts at teachers' heads, and in grade eight hash started to come around, and LSD kinda. But Toronto's become like a shopping center now. Under all those banks you can actually go shopping fourteen city blocks underground. You can buy lotto tickets every five hundred feet.

In Tokyo they're about to begin construction on these sixty-story underground buildings. Combination apartment complex, shopping mall, business office.

Wow! Do they have floors or are they gonna be like spirals going down or something?

I saw computer-animated mock-ups of them on CNN. They look like silos connected by a futuristic subway system. The point is, you'll never have to leave them. There'll be parks, museums—

What kind of light?

The Japanese have figured out a way to reflect light down via a series of mirrors or something, so that its quality is better than direct sunlight. Sounds a little suspicious to me. But the die is cast.

Who knows what the human beast is gonna do under there!

You play bass guitar, right?

Do I play it? You know, it's all relative.

You're not starting a band à la River Phoenix?

Um—I wouldn't mind doing bar band shit, I guess.

What kind of music do you listen to?

Okay, where to begin, where to begin. Let's see, Hüsker Dü, Joy Division. . . . The Ramones changed my life. Oh, and what's that band? It's like an industrial band.

British, or Canadian, or—

American. Black—Black—Big Black.

Oh, they're great! Do you know their song "Kerosene," about these kids who are so bored they light each other on fire just to have something to do? Someone should buy the film rights to that song. Maybe you?

Yeah. Who else do I like? There's the Pixies, but I mean I don't know if I love 'em. I was telling some guy in a frat in San Diego what bands I like and he says, "Oh, so you like slightly alternative music." [*laughing*]

Were you into punk when it started? I guess you must have been pretty young.

I'm like second-circle punk. But yeah, man!! [*clapping*] Totally!! GBH and the Exploited are my two hardcore bands of choice. I love playing them, too.

Actually, I've always thought there was something very punk about your acting, not only your erratic energy, but the way you seem incapable of

conveying dishonesty, no matter who you're playing. Which I guess is why you have this punk cult following.

Oh yeah. King Punk.

No, really. For instance, I know these punks in Toronto who adore you so much that they invented a dance called "The Keanu Stomp" based on the way you walked in *Prince of Pennsylvania*.

No!!!

Yeah. Apparently it's turning into a bit of a fad. There are slam pits full of punks doing "The Keanu Stomp" even as we speak. In fact, two of these punks, Bruce LaBruce and Candy, who head up this gay and lesbian anarchist group called the New Lavender Panthers, begged me to ask you some questions for them. Is that okay?

The New Lavender Panthers! Whoa!! Sure, it's okay.

All right—"Why haven't you made a movie with Drew Barrymore yet?"

Oh ho ho! They're not up on their Keanu lore because I did work with Drew on a Xmas TV special. This was after she got off drugs.

"Was Rob Lowe gross to work with on *Youngblood*?"

What?! No, Rob's okay.

"Why haven't you worked with Molly Ringwald yet?"

I want to! I want to! I want to!

"Would you rather be murdered by John Wayne Gacy, Richard Speck, Martha Beck, or Gertrude Baniszewski?"

I don't know what their specialties were.

Gacy molested and tortured teenage boys. Speck raped and killed nurses. I forget what the others did.

Hard to decide, man.

"Any inside info on the two Coreys?"

Hm. I know exactly how much heroin Corey Feldman was arrested with to the decimal point!

"Why haven't you made a European art film yet? (Might we suggest Dario Argento, Michelangelo Antonioni, or Lothar Lambert?)"

Oh, yeah. I'll just send them a tape of me going, "Whoa! Bodacious!" Sure.

And finally, "Are you gay or what?" Come on, make it official.

No. [*long pause*] But ya never know.

Cool. So are you a very politically aware person?

No, I'm an ignorant pig. I'm makin' movies in Hollywood, you know? The things that I'm doing are pretty sheltered. For me, with acting and the parts and all, it's very self-involved, especially between projects. Once you get a part, you're liberated. You can find out what that character thinks.

Your character in *Parenthood* was kind of weird politically.

Yeeesss?

Well, initially he was an outsider in every way. He even had a different energy level than anyone else in the movie. But by the end he's happily ensconced in that big family portrait with all the other characters, holding a newborn infant.

Yeah. I dug that guy, man. He was trying.

Well, at one point your character does this monologue about how his father used to wake him up by flicking lit cigarettes at his head. It concluded with a statement that could be interpreted as vaguely homophobic.

Really! Like what?

He says, "They'll let any butt-reaming asshole be a father these days," which seems to imply that "father" is some kind of godlike state, and "butt-reaming asshole," i.e., gay male, isn't.

Oh, that is homophobic. It's weird.

Your character does this fantastic double take right after that. Some friends of mine interpreted that as you trying to express your discomfort as an actor at having to say that line.

Right. Yeah. "Butt-reaming asshole" was a weird line. But no. The character's just dismissing his past. He understands it, he's beyond it, it was ugly and he doesn't want any part of it. That double take's like him going: Fuck that shit.

Do you want to have a family?

Yeah.

Do you have a serious girlfriend?

Um—not—not that heavy. I want kids.

How many?

Three.

What sexes?

Whatever comes out.

Do you read much? Books, I mean.

How about if I said I don't read as much as I'd like to.

Nothing recently?

Um—yeah. I've been rereading *Letters to a Young Poet* and *The Autobiography of Malcolm X*. And some John Rechy novels as research for the Gus Van Sant film. Oh, I love Philip K. Dick.

Me, too. I just saw *Total Recall*.

How is it?

Disappointing. Everything's in the trailer. The K. Dick story it's based on gets avalanched about an hour in. Then it just turns into an excuse to blow seventy million dollars.

Explosion movie.

Yeah.

Have you read Dick's short stories? He'd begin writing by having like a fantasy, like—he would take a glass and go, "Hm, that's ironic." And write a story, you know?

Well, he was on speed all the time.

I want to be on speed! I've never been on speed. I want to be a speed freak for a while.

It's really—

Is that a stupid thing to say?

No, no. I love speed. I mean, I used to do speed all the time. Trouble is, you do get really depressed for three days afterward.

It burns you out?

Yeah. It's ultimately not worth it. I used to do crystal meth, which is scary. I'd snort it.

Yummmm! Wild!!!

I know. It's yum indeed. Speaking of speed, you do a lot of films. Do you like it that way?

Yeah, definitely. Like recently *Aunt Julia and the Scriptwriter* has been having reshoots. In between them I did a couple of parts in student films.

Didn't you do a Shakespeare play in Massachusetts last year?

Yeah, *The Tempest.* Played Trinculo, and it was a blast. Andre Gregory played Prospero. His daughter Marina played Miranda.

Gregory must be intense.

He was *very* intense. Anyway, my next half a year is pretty much set. With Gus Van Sant, and I'm doing *Bill & Ted's Excellent Adventure, Part Two*, or *Bill & Ted Go to Hell,* or *Bill & Ted's Bogus Journey.* We're also doing a

Bill & Ted Saturday morning cartoon, and that's kind of trippy. And *Riders on the Storm* with Kathryn Bigelow.

Based on the Doors song of the same name?

No, or—I don't think so. I play an FBI agent who has to infiltrate some surfers who are bank robbers. The character is a kind of adrenaline junkie, and there's this other adrenaline junkie, and they push each other into jumping out of airplanes, shooting guns, shit like that.

Is he a classic Keanu Reevesian character—sweet, confused, distracted, awkward?

I call it victim acting.

Do you make a point of seeking out roles like that?

Well, I don't know about manifest destiny and all. You get what you put out and all that shit? I guess it's just been my lot so far.

Even your creepy characters are so sympathetic. In *I Love You to Death* you were supposed to be a thief, but—

No, my guy was just harmless. Larry Kasdan wanted this guy to be beat up by the world. Just kind of in a daze. Harmless and drugged. So they hired me. [*laughing*]

That daze is one of the things I really love about what you do. You're always kind of talking around what you actually want to say.

Right, right.

Most actors just manufacture emotion and expect audiences to match it. With your characters, it's their inability to produce that's the key. They're often, if not perpetually, distressed, spooked, weirded out by the world. They're always fighting with their contexts.

Always, man! Always.

Granted most of them are teenagers, but they're not exactly future stockbrokers, which seems like the teen norm nowadays.

No, not at all. Actually, the futures of most of my characters are pretty bleak. [*laughing*] You know, Matt, Ted, Rupert—who knows what they're gonna do.

Do you research your characters?

Definitely. Definitely. Right now with this film *Riders on the Storm* I've been hanging out with athletes, FBI agents, police, people in college fraternities. I'm seein' a whole other part of the world, you know? When I did Ted I took stuff from cartoons. Stuff comes up that you never thought of. I look for physical things, background, and emotionally where he's at for every second. I'm pretty flexible. I've studied some of the Uta Hagen techniques and Stanislavsky, and I've done some—you know, some basic physical Grotowski exercises, and I've read some Artaud. A lot of times you get tired, 'cause you're seventeen and you got a certain kind of energy that they dig. You know? In some of the character stuff, I've got a chance to explore more, working with a whole new caliber of people like Stephen Frears, Tim Hunter. *River's Edge*! That's a movie, man. American cinema!

Yeah, a great movie. I keep waiting for Tim Hunter to do another movie. It's been years now. I guess he did a *Twin Peaks*.

He did? Did you see it?

Yeah.

What was it like?

It was nice. It was sparer than the others. Not quite as surrealistic. So, where do you think you fit into the Brat Pack, if at all?

The *Brat* Pack? I have nothing to do with them.

Do you think your acting style's fundamentally different from theirs?

Jeesh! What?! *No!!!* Agggghhh! I really respect those guys, man. Emilio Estevez, Judd Nelson, Kiefer, Rob Lowe, all those guys. They've really set a path for us. Who would have thought that you'd give a development deal to a twenty-three-year-old actor?

Well, unlike them, you don't seem like a career socializer. I never see your mug in *Details*, *Vanity Fair*, etc.

Right. I guess 'cause I'm a nerd.

You don't avoid trendy photo ops?

No, I dig going out, but—you know, I have *fun.* I don't get many invitations and stuff—it's just kind of whatever happens. Once in a while I'll ask my friends, "What're you doing? Where are you going? What's going on?" I'll go see art, I'll do whatever—buy a drink, dance, play. All that shit. Sometimes I go to clubs. I dig the blues, man. The blues have always had some of the *best* times, *best* feelings I've ever had. The last person I saw was Buddy Guy, but it was in a bad space. Just bummed me out. Everyone was sittin' down, and they had candles in the middle of the tables! So it's like, "Bababawawa!" [*He mimes a frenetic guitar player.*] And everyone's like [*claps politely*], "Excellent music."

Do your friends tend to be actors?

Some of 'em. Yeah. Alex Winter, John Cullan, Dean Feiffer. Alan Boyce I don't see much of, but I love his guts.

It must be weird making films, seeing a smallish group of people constantly for four or five months, then never seeing them again.

Yeah, right. "How ya doin', man?" "Bye." "Good to see you at the Academy Awards."

Do you want to say something about your motorcycle? I saw it parked out front.

My motorcycle. My 1974, 850 Norton Commando, high-performance English touring motorcycle. Yaaggghhhhhh!!!

Didn't you have a semi-serious accident?

I've fucked up a couple of times.

I thought so. When you took your shirt off in *Prince of Pennsylvania* you had this porcelain upper body. But when you had your shirt off in *Parenthood*, it looked all gnarly.

[*laughing*] I love that bike, man.

Well, not to be too parental or anything, but don't kill yourself. You've got a pretty love-struck cult of fans to think about. And you're getting more and more famous. I mean that's—

Yeah, I'm pseudo-quasi.

Pseudo-quasi-famous?

Pseudo-quasi. Yeah. I mean, why is *Interview* even doing this?

I asked to. I think you're one of those guys who's like—they don't think of you until someone suggests it, then they go, "Of course!"

Right, right. I'm not really around. I'm around. Yeah.

So where *are* you, if you know what I mean?

Um—lately?

Okay.

Lately. Training, surfing. On the weekends I've been kind of cruising the boulevards. LA is so trippy. Chhww. It becomes like a small town really quick. On those weekend nights the prostitutes are out, and the kids from school, and people cruising, and in the clubs all that stuff is going on? I ride my bike sometimes. I'll just go out, say, around one? Midnight? And I'll ride until four? Goin' through the city to see who's doin' what where, you know? Going downtown, riding around and just—I care, you know?

About—

Yeah. Just to look around. Great.

NO MO' POMO
(October 1991)

What's strange to me, though not particularly surprising, is the number of critics who seem to feel they have a stake in a postmodernist eternity. I don't know how else to explain their labeling as "pomo" any new literary work that even nods in the direction of such accepted "cutting-edge" techniques as appropriation and pastiche. Actually, defining postmodern the way it's most commonly used (i.e., as a catchall term for the here and now), every current American writer, no matter how old-fashioned, could be contextualized simply by being in the vicinity. And if it *has* reached that ubiquitous stage, what good is it except as a way for intellectuals to practice some weird form of nationalism with regards to history and the future? Obviously, I don't think we have to choose between the status quo and the "good old days" so lusted after by reactionaries like Camille Paglia. And I'm hardly the first to suggest the jettisoning of this term in future symposia just as a way of clearing our heads.

The seriousness with which bores like Paul Auster, T. Coraghessan Boyle, and Michael Chabon are studied by the arbiters of postmodernism has got to signal its death rattle. For as helpful as these critics' openness has been in encouraging deconstruction of the Eurocentric, patriarchal culture perpetuated by modernism, there's a point at which even great things go stagnant; only a bankrupted sensibility could accommodate, much less promote, the avant-bland fiction of the aforementioned people just because it juggles literature's tropes with a degree of class. Meanwhile such radical writers as William T. Vollmann, David Wojnarowicz, Kevin Killian, and Kathy Acker tend to be marginalized by these same critics when their work should really be studied for signs of a possible "post-postmodernism."

It's counterproductive to imagine a special post-postmodernism, since any attempt to establish parameters for future writing would crimp its style before it even exists, thereby precluding an unexpected move. Me, I'm a great believer in maintaining a certain amount of naïveté as a way of escaping period formalities without necessarily abandoning them outright. That's the secret of solitary obsessives like Cormac McCarthy, Jean Rhys, Anna Kavan, Denton Welch, and Thomas Bernhard, whose fiction hasn't and probably won't date an iota, nor, I gather, build much more than a cult audience since it will never be comfortably categorized. And that's why new writers whose work doesn't fraternize aesthetically with that of their peers will take a frustratingly long time to be understood.

I no longer consider postmodernism a useful filter for new writing because scribes roughly my age and younger grew up when it was already the well-worn fringe of contemporary literature. Its preferred techniques are just there now, demystified, givens. As utilized by the more rebellious younger writers—many of whom display a fresh belief in the mysteries of history, sex, violence, horror, politics, love, etc.—these techniques tend to become submerged to the point of insignificance or else tarnished to the point where they have no more bearing on the work than realism, surrealism, and other former trends had on the work of scavenging postmodernists. Point is, there are all sorts of interesting things being written that aren't clarified in any way by being seen in relationship to some saggy banner.

THE QUEER KING
Derek Jarman
(April 1992)

I was going to say, "The first time I heard the name Derek Jarman . . ."
Honestly, I tripped and fell on Jarman's work in the mid-'70s, thanks to
an eye-catching *LA Times* ad. It starred a seminude male, wrists tied to
a pole. He was crisscrossed by text that read, in huge letters, *Soundtrack
by Brian Eno*; then, in tiny letters, *Derek Jarman's Sebastiane.* Now that
Eno's best known as a producer of U2's *The Joshua Tree* LP, it's hard to
remember that there was a time when his own artsy-fartsy LPs struck
certain of us as holding the key to rock music's immediate future. A time
when we would've dropped everything and torn to a theater, incapable
of imagining a movie adventurous enough to be scored by our favorite
genius.

Disappointment doesn't begin to describe it. My friends and I
positively groaned through an hour or so before storming out. Ultra-
leisurely paced, with humorless Latin (?!) dialogue, *Sebastiane* seemed
at once incompetent and aesthetically overbearing. For years afterward
the term "Sebastiane" doubled for doggerel in our casual conversation.

For me, Jarman's star only sunk lower with the stateside release of
his second film, *Jubilee* (I missed—or avoided—his third, *The Tempest*).

A "piss take," as the British say, on punk culture, it seemed—at least in the days before the marauding Sex Pistols were exposed as Malcolm McLaren's situationist theater piece—both inauthentic in its fashion-centrism and cynical in its prediction of punk gentrification.

The first time I heard the name Derek Jarman pronounced respectfully, I was living in Amsterdam in the mid-'80s. My friend the late filmmaker Howard Brookner (*Burroughs, The Movie; The Bloodhounds of Broadway*) had stopped through town for a visit. He'd just been in London to see Jarman, who, unbeknownst to me, was one of his heroes. While there, Howard had managed to see an almost-completed cut of Jarman's film in progress, *The Last of England*, which he exuberantly declared the greatest piece of art he'd ever seen. I expressed huge reservations based on my experiences with Jarman's earlier work, so Howard sat me down and conducted a little tour through the guy's films, one by one, pointing out things I'd missed or misconstrued. The key, according to Howard, was to accept the films' strange imbalances and pretensions, lags and lurches, as what naturally happens when an artist has had to wrest his material from countless years of heterosexual ownership. There were moments when the liberation was complete and the picture in focus, and moments when Jarman's struggle became the point. It was a notion of distortion-as-beauty familiar to me from the rock music I knew, but less so from other media. So while I understood Howard's theory, it wasn't until I finally saw *The Last of England*—a staggering, hallucinatory meditation set in a desolated future London—that I began to see Jarman as an artist with specific, definable genius.

Now I find my earlier bafflement curious, explainable only by how idiosyncratic Jarman's openly gay, poetic, lowish-budgeted work seemed at a time when gay film meant porn, John Waters, and maybe Pasolini and Fassbinder. Those three, while hardly conventional artists, seem positively old-fashioned compared to Jarman, whose pre-mid-'80s oeuvre in particular is not only free of stylistic continuity but constructed to defy analysis by even the director's most devoted admirers. Where *Sebastiane* is faggy Antonioni, *Jubilee* is lurid spectacle à la early Ken Russell. *The Angelic Conversation* is a languid, homoerotic idyll weirdly fused to a prim recitation of Shakespeare's sonnets, while the short-story films he made to accompany *The Queen Is Dead*, an LP by the British rock band the Smiths, are jittery little acid flashbacks made flesh. And while these shifts from film to film may seem quaint next to, say, Gus Van Sant's *My Own Private Idaho*, which constantly changes gears within itself, back in the mid-'80s I had to recall Kenneth Anger to find a queer filmmaker both so honest and yet given to indulging in private rituals of time and imagery.

There's a special cult mystique that accrues to filmic poets like Jarman and Anger. It leaves them anathemas to mainstream audiences, but makes them fiercely important to a smaller, more discriminating subculture to whom visionary artists are the closest thing to gods. For a partial generation of younger, disenfranchised gay men—and, to a lesser extent, lesbians—Derek Jarman has become something of a deity. Like us, he is at once politically incorrect to his bones, steadfastly antiauthoritarian, brainy yet anti-intellectual, passionate almost to the point of embarrassing himself, and inspired by passion in others. In his most famous film, *Caravaggio*, it was the uncompromised artist's agenda that he lionized. In his new film, *Edward II* (based on the Christopher Marlowe play), his hero is, or rather *are*, queer activists, specifically the collective members of Outrage, a British group akin to America's Queer Nation. In Jarman's "improved" version, King Edward is targeted for an intragovernmental coup because of his flagrant homosexuality and is defended against a mutinous army—represented as riot-gear-clad police officers—by the real-life Outrage, whose contemporary chants and placards overwhelm his predicament in their call for queer rights and money for AIDS research. With their support, his execution—in Marlowe's version he's fucked with a hot poker—is averted, becoming a brief bad dream. It's a deeply moving conceit, and—as far as I can tell—the first time this crucial social movement has been ennobled within fictional film.

Though it's possibly too formally esoteric to interest a mainstream audience, even a lesbian and gay one, *Edward II* may nevertheless provide some sort of solace to critics frustrated by the predominantly marginal, transgressive tone of most young queer filmmakers' product. Van Sant, Monika Treut, Gregg Araki, Todd Haynes, Tom Kalin, Chris Münch—some of the (coincidentally queer) cognoscenti of the much ballyhooed New American independent cinema—are not particularly interested in portraying lesbians and gays as conventionally heroic, at least relative to standard American culture. To wit, Tom Kalin's forthcoming *Swoon* is a version of the famous Leopold and Loeb "thrill kill" murder case in which the main characters are dominant in, but not transcendent of, an icily elegant love story. Monika Treut's recent *My Father Is Coming* unapologetically foregrounds a kinky, mostly heterosexual relationship. Gregg Araki's forthcoming *The Living End*, a tale of death-obsessed, HIV-positive male lovers, calls itself "an irresponsible movie" and will be promoted in part by buttons that feature a line from the film, "When I start to come, choke me." *My Own Private Idaho* angered many in gay, activist circles with its self-destructive, drug-taking hustler protagonists. Earlier, *Poison* had struck some of the same people as arcane and debauched. Chris Münch's *The Hours and Times*—apparently the queer hit of this spring's Sundance Film Festival, whence *Poison* had previously sprung—has as its protagonists the closeted Brian Epstein and the "desirable," straight John Lennon.

Gay & Lesbian Alliance Against Defamation (GLAAD), the self-appointed arbiters of political correctness in and for the lesbian and gay world, have yet to launch a serious attack on the work of an openly queer artist, but one senses much teeth grinding among the organization's ranks. *Idaho*, for one, put some activists in the weird position of having to defend the film against the attacks of homophobic reviewers while privately nursing doubts about the morality of the film's gay characters. GLAAD's call for positive lesbian and gay images—that is, assimilationist characters whose goals are as conventional as average heterosexual Americans'—is understandable since many if not most lesbians and gays lead relatively conventional (if ghettoized) lives at this point. But it's the extremely rare film of note that merely portrays so-called average lives without exploring the spiritual sacrifices that averageness involves. And while the symbolic positioning of any oppressed minority in a secure environment is bracing, the kinds of films that have tended to result when filmmakers emphasize gays' user-friendliness are sobby TV movies, such as *Our Sons*, *An Early Frost*, and *Doing Time on Maple Drive*, or else quasi-TV-movie-like feature films, such as *Longtime Companion*, which, well intentioned as it obviously was, had little aesthetic vigor and inadvertently angered activists by focusing on the AIDS crisis without addressing the work of ACT UP.

There are those for whom an intensely watered-down yet positive portrayal of lesbian and gay life—a brief scene of two men in the same bed (*thirtysomething*); a peripheral, nice-guy gay neighbor (*Coach*)—seems a greater victory than the appearance in the world of unapologetic, gorgeously intransigent art that happens to be queer, like Van Sant's, Jarman's, or Araki's. These conservative critics won't be happy until they can switch on a popular TV sitcom built around two "well-adjusted" female or male lovers, and enjoy a mild, unchallenging half hour of entertainment. It's hard to argue with anyone who makes education their priority, and it's certainly possible that a queer-owned-and-operated TV series would mellow out the masses on the subject of homosexuality (although I defy anyone to prove that *The Cosby Show* has curtailed ongoing governmentally sanctioned racism against blacks in this country; on the contrary, by portraying them in upper-middle-class whites' goofier image, *The Cosby Show* may have inadvertently fed on the culture's antagonism toward those blacks too oppressed on every level that "counts" to even consider assimilating).

Similarly, a lesbian or gay sitcom with hopes of seducing straights would surely either edit out or somehow neutralize foreign substances: anarchist politics, the sexual experimentation that is a basis of our identity, our sometimes heavily coded humor—in other words, the kinds of details that make a subculture several times more interesting than its wishy-washier surroundings. Maybe a more attainable goal, and one that might begin to fulfill GLAAD's daydreams, would be something on the order of a queer *Grapes of Wrath*—that is, an artful populist film that romanticizes lesbians and gays' struggle for rights without reducing us to saintly stick figures mired in standardized plot twists. In John Ford's film, we not only recognize our own struggles in those of the poverty-stricken protagonists, we're seduced by the film's aesthetic design, in which a strong socialist message is greased with a little sentimentality and blurred into an impeccably measured narrative.

Obviously a substantial amount of money (not to mention talent) is involved in making a film like this, and major studios seem unwilling to commit to the queer audience, to put it mildly (although the Oliver Stone–produced Harvey Milk biopic supposedly in progress is worth keeping an eye out for). Anyway, for the moment we can (and certainly should) pat ourselves on the back about *My Own Private Idaho, My*

Beautiful Laundrette, and *Edward II*, which, in terms of quality and the precedents they set, are probably the *Five Easy Pieces*, *Taxi Driver*, and *Blue Velvet* of the young queer film history.

Back to Jarman in particular . . . While *Edward II* indicates an artist with amazing energy and spirit, it's no secret that Jarman has had a real struggle with AIDS, including a couple of hospitalizations. His previous film, a luminous diatribe called *The Garden*, had revolved around his own bedridden, daydreamy form. So, as I'm knocking on his hotel room door at the appointed interview time, I wonder how happy he'll be to see yet another microcassette-recorder-wielding admirer. When the door opens, I'm ushered inside by a stern, trendily coiffed young man—barely recognizable as the henchman from *Edward*—who leaves in a hurry. The room is too full of sunlight; I extend my hand, wince, and out of the glare, Jarman positively bounds over, giddily waving the fax of *Edward*'s great *New York Times* review, his first from that paper. During our subsequent visit, he almost dances in his chair he's so energetic. Jarman has a sweet, elastic, bug-eyed, thick-lipped face that sort of juts out from his neck and shoulders, as though fifty years of mile-a-second thinking and speaking have somehow eroded the air in front of him. Tall, thin but fit, he spins out gossip and anecdotes as he sits on one crossed leg like a teenager.

Under all his perkiness and enthusiasm, however, Jarman's an aesthete of the old school. And like other eccentric British film directors of a slightly-older-yet school—say, Lindsay Anderson, Richard Lester, and Ken Russell (for whom Jarman once worked as a set designer)—he approaches the art of cinema with an oddball, highbrow, boat-rocking playfulness.

Jarman was a painter when he got the idea to make *Sebastiane*, and he believes his fine-arts background is the mulch from which his films arose. When pressed for influential filmmakers, he avoids the afore-mentioned Brits and instead name-checks the experimental elite of the '50s and '60s—namely, Anger, Maya Deren, Stan Brakhage, Michael Snow, and Warhol, all of whose works he'd become familiar with in college. Jarman's come to narrative "the hard way," as he puts it, which perhaps explains why forward movement in his films can seem so, well, roundabout. He sees *The Last of England*, his least narrative and most personal film, as the work that explains his oeuvre. Its mutating, ob-sessive, repetitive iconography—self-destructive beauties, soulless power-mongers, artists gone insane, uninhabitable landscapes—is the buried treasure in all his films, whatever their ostensible subject. Lo-cate and concentrate on these dream elements, he says, and each nar-rative becomes a mere current, transportation. "And this is a kind of activism in the name of art, don't you see?" Jarman explains. "I can't reinvent film. No one can. But I can disrupt it. I can reconfigure it in my mind's image. Queer activists aren't saying we should go live on an island somewhere to be truly queer, nor are they willing to accept the standard idea of a decent life. They're saying an honest world is a fair but shaken one. And I'm saying something similar about film. An hon-est film, like an honest life, makes just enough sense on the surface to survive in a largely idiotic world, while remaining free and complicated and original underneath."

It's this belief that narrative can be transcended that unites queer filmmakers, young, old, and dead. As one of the most visible openly gay filmmakers of his generation, Jarman—along with John Waters, the late Curt McDowell, and Paul Bartel—has inadvertently spear-headed a movement. He personally knows and has counseled most of the aforementioned queer directors, and talk of a "queer cinema" makes him even more manic with delight than usual. Because apart from long-term support from the Berlin Film Festival, where most of his films have premiered, he has remained a mystery, even to film buffs, and especially here in the United States, where all the film repertory houses prevalent in the '70s and early '80s have dwindled to a struggling handful. It's really only recently, thanks in part to the successes of *Poison* and *Idaho*, that Jarman has begun to be regarded as something more than a fag kook, at least among establishment opinion-makers like those at the *New York Times*. *Edward II* will easily be his most widely distributed and reviewed film since 1986's *Caravaggio*, and in the course of our conversation he discusses several possible future projects (including a version of Wilde's *The Picture of Dorian Gray*) with the confidence of someone who has financial backing at or very near his fingertips. (Although the film he really wants to make—an original story that would treat the subject of man-boy love sympathetically—has had to be abandoned for numerous obvious reasons.)

The one thing that should be a stumbling block to Jarman is the precariousness of his own health, but to hear him talk, he's either bored with the subject or trying not to think about it. In fact, his only real mention of any illness comes late in our conversation, amid his lengthy description of one of his possible projects in the works—a John Waters–style black comedy about queers conquering AIDS. The aside he throws in about his condition is so offhand I don't even notice it until I play back the interview later. "Because," he said, "*I've* conquered HIV, so why not make a film about *that*." It's an astonishing thing to say because, obviously, all of us who are either concerned about the spread of the disease or infected ourselves would love to believe him. But knowing the way his films are attracted to the passions of others, it's significant that his favorite topic—one I almost had to drag him away from at times—is not his own health, but queer/AIDS activism in general. In fact, less than a month before our meeting, he'd been arrested demonstrating with Outrage in London, and not for the first time.

It's hard not to think that in finding activism, and in seeing a queer cinema rise before him, Jarman has now reimagined his own ending, just as he did for Marlowe's King Edward, as if knowing that his death, whenever it comes and whatever the cause, will ultimately dissolve meaningfully into the actions and art of others, not unlike a single body into a demonstration.

BURDEN OF URBAN DREAMS
Gary Indiana's *Gone Tomorrow*
(April 1993)
Gary Indiana's fiction swoops, stalls, freaks out, and dazzles

Gary Indiana, the name invokes an age when eccentric young Midwesterners traded in their nondescript given names for glittery, self-devised monikers, hitchhiked to New York, and, if they were really lucky, flounced around for Andy Warhol's staring camera for a reel or two. They became movie stars strictly because of their skewed personalities. In the traditional sense, most of them couldn't *do* anything. A few wound up writing memoirs (Viva, Ultra Violet, Holly Woodlawn so far). For the most part, they were just *fabulous*, as we fags say—people who, unlike most capital-A artists, didn't feel the urge to compensate for inherently bland identities. Gathered together under Warhol's aegis, they formed a star system of lovable mutants whose "performances" continue to throw under-forty film buffs into adoring conniptions.

Indiana, who's a little too young to have gone the Warhol/Factory route, is nevertheless one of the guys who exudes style. A wee, bratty, extravagant man, Gary Indiana could probably get through life making appearances at the right clubs and parties, popping up in odd movie roles, and still end up on a million nerds' mental lists of the holy. In fact,

Indiana *has* appeared in a slew of mostly avant-garde films, radiating fucked-up charm alongside the likes of Taylor Mead, Udo Kier, and Cookie Mueller. A lucky few Angelenos even caught his sweet cameo as Jim Morrison in Raymond Pettibon's recent play *Jim and a Groupie in UCLA's Sculpture Garden* at LACE. Anyway, as a result of all this activity, there's a popular misconception that Indiana—a prolific journalist/critic as well as a novelist—is just another charismatic weirdo growing too big for his writerly britches.

For almost a decade, Indiana has been a critic-at-large at the *Village Voice*. Thanks to his notoriety, tons of readers who might otherwise flip immediately to the gossip and fashion columns devour his articles—if only to lift bons mots for their own coffeehouse confabs. Even when he tackles such non-cocktail-chatty subjects as AIDS research, child abuse, and, recently, the Rodney King trial, Indiana's writing is a crackling read, equal parts bitchy sideswipes, hard facts, and intellectual asides—a gorgeous collision of mixed feelings that abuses and deconstructs contemporary cultural icons with none of the knee-jerk P.C. trappings that tend to homogenize the supposedly diverse voices of the alternative press. Even Indiana's detractors concede he's a treasure, although the more conservative among them can't get past the force of his personality, and the more airheaded can't see his analytical brilliance for the pleasures afforded by his wit.

Indiana's first novel, 1989's *Horse Crazy*, may have started the rehabilitation of his image. The story of one man's insanity-making desire for a careering young artist/junkie, *Horse Crazy* has a craggy, mock-transcribed structure that slowly divulges an evolved sense of what a novel can convey in secret. People rant and rave about the subtextual complexities of Spalding Gray's monotonous, digressive texts, but, hype aside, his determinedly bland if brainy fireside chats amount to little more than what Garrison Keillor might come up with after tea with Derrida. Indiana's fiction, on the other hand, swoops, stalls, throws tantrums and freaks out, all the while emitting a bright, fierce understanding of narrative's multiplicitous codes. This is the antithesis of the snooty, ironic, lipless, slum-lording fiction that many readers associate with downtown New York writing, a category that Indiana is usually lumped into along with the likes of Janowitz, McInerny, and Ellis.

Horse Crazy was a cult hit, but it did little to alter the picture of Indiana as an obsessive writer with certain stylistic gifts—an unrepentant idiosyncrat short on social responsibility, long on personal grievance. True, Indiana has earned his thorn-in-the-side reputation. Anyone who's ever read an interview with him knows that he has as little patience with the lesbi-gay community's attempts to police heterosexuals' attitudes as he has with the government's myriad crimes against minorities. But this is also a man who can write worshipfully of such bastions of refinement as Alexander Kluge, Thomas Bernhard, and Dirk Bogarde. Somehow, these crucial interests get lost in the shuffle.

Unlike *Horse Crazy*, which was a novel in the way a burning building is a building, *Gone Tomorrow*, Indiana's latest, is a Novel, albeit closer in form to the slippery European model than it is to the nuts-and-bolts American version. Told in Indiana's infamous first-person singular and set mostly in the wilds of Colombia, it tells of a young American actor/writer's involvement in the making of a German film entitled *The Laughter in the Next Room*. *Gone Tomorrow* describes a time in the not-so-distant past when European film directors were visionaries who, overfinanced by coked-out, artsy-fartsy billionaires, regularly made grueling treks into this or that remote part of the world, along with a slavishly devoted cast and crew, to get stoned out of their minds and shoot footage that might somehow, perhaps paranormally, capture the nature of the human soul. Think Werner Herzog—although he's not the model here.

It's interesting to note, while unnecessary to know, that Indiana was, for a time, friendly with the Fassbinder crowd, and *did* appear in just such a film, directed by the Fassbinder protégé/producer Dieter Schidor. Since *Gone Tomorrow* is dedicated in part to the memory of Schidor, it's not hard to deduce that what we have here is a roman à clef, which would hardly be a first in Indiana's ultrapersonal oeuvre. The novel features a peripheral (mostly because he's dead), omnipresent character named Rudolph, described as a great, fat, respected German director whose last picture was a "big homo wet dream called *Tarantella*." (*Querelle*, anyone?) But while all of this curious info makes the book even more of a page-turner than it already is, Indiana has immersed whatever nonfiction he's referencing in prose of such peculiar elegance, of such strangely tuned emotional nuance, that all the tattling—some of it pretty juicy—winds up swirling around under the novel's note-perfect surface.

In its most moving sections, the book returns us to a present in which many of the characters are dead—victims of excess, suicide, or AIDS. Ensconced in New York's Chelsea Hotel, the narrator and another survivor reminisce and fret, immobilized by anxiety about, well, everything. But unlike the majority of pointedly AIDS-era novels, *Gone Tomorrow* is neither an amoral nostalgia fest nor a thinly concealed wake-up call hyping the religion of sobriety. It's a philosophical work devised by a writer who's both too intelligent to buy into the popular notion that a successful future requires the compromise of collective decision, and too moral to accept bitterness as the consequence of an adventurous life. Like all the best recent novels, *Gone Tomorrow* sorts frantically through our culture and comes up solutionless—stumped in its politics but accurate and fresh in its aesthetic choices. As we veer toward the blur of our deaths, the most we can realistically ask of writers is to seduce us into a state of hopefulness, or, at the very least, to tend to our beleaguered curiosity. Gary Indiana, a tortured idealist if there ever was one, meets that criteria beautifully.

BEAUTY AND SADNESS
R.I.P. River Phoenix
(November 1993)

River Phoenix's death has startled and depressed everyone I know, even people who had previously dismissed movie stardom as a form of corporate-induced mass hypnosis. About seventy-two hours after his fatal collapse, a cynical friend and I happened on a recent television interview in which the earnest young actor was laying out his future plans, and we burst into horrified tears. Weird. That's what we keep saying: Weird that he's dead; weird that we care so much. Phoenix seems to have been admired by a whole lot of people in relative secrecy—an artist whose work insinuated itself into viewers' good graces, no matter how faltering a particular vehicle, nor how initially coldhearted his audience. To wit: As I write this, *Hard Copy*, hardly a show known for its moral fortitude, is heaping praise on a paparazzi photographer who couldn't bring himself to document the actor's dying convulsions.

The word on the streets, even in the gossip columns, had always had Phoenix living a pretty honorable and pristine existence relative to the goings-on of his peers—a poetry-reading, vegetarian, open-minded, Democratic life, free of Shannen Doherty's creepiness, Judd Nelson's self-destructiveness, Mickey Rourke's bombast. Occasionally you'd hear about him standing tensely and unsociably on the fringe of some art gallery opening: S/M performer Bob Flanagan, once a member of the improvisational comedy troupe the Groundlings, remembers Phoenix staggering drunkenly onto the stage during one of their skits. But big deal. He was a *kid*. Mostly he seemed, if anything, too serious, too incapable of relaxing into a benign mindlessness, even for a minute. In a recent issue of *Detour* magazine, he positively excoriated many of his fellow actors for being ego-driven, and spoke of wanting to move not just out of LA, but out of this wretched country entirely. Nonetheless, he did continue to live here, and he did die under the influence of drugs at a trendy local nightspot. So it's hard to know what to think right now.

Death always focuses people, even if the demystification process takes years in some cases. It shouldn't with Phoenix, since his sincerity and forthrightness have never been in question. Ultimately, barring unforeseen revelations, his name, his work, will acquire that particular cult holiness that people naturally create to fill in the blanks around the prematurely taken. Phoenix will be our James Dean, just like so many pundits are predicting. Meanwhile, by default, his fellow "outsider" types, like Keanu Reeves, Matt Dillon, et al., are stuck being our Marlon Brando, if they're lucky. And that's because actors can't compete with their fans' imaginations, and the accomplishments we'll fantasize for a hypothetical mature Phoenix can't help but outstrip the potential feats of the bona fide middle-aged Phoenix. Life's funny, and even a little disgusting, that way.

Comparisons between Phoenix and James Dean are lazy, not to mention ubiquitous at this point, though they did share several of the qualities that separate great actors from mere signifiers of glamour. Both were extremely attentive to detail yet seemingly incapable of submerging their actual emotions under an artificial personality. No matter how peripheral Phoenix's role—the scatterbrained junior hippie in *I Love You to Death*, the poet/Casanova in *A Night in the Life of Jimmy Reardon*, the loyal spooked son of Harrison Ford's megalomaniac in *The Mosquito Coast*—he was always a little more perceptive and soulful—more real—than anyone else on-screen. Even in as offbeat and dislocated a milieu as the Portland street-hustler scene of *My Own Private Idaho*, Phoenix's Mike stood out as unusually lonesome—someone who was afraid of, and simultaneously astonished by, his squalid conditions, who desperately sought affection from others while at the same time avoiding sympathizers like the plague. It was a performance that, like most of Dean's, seemed to distill the confused melancholy of an emerging generation.

Phoenix was the son of hippie parents. He sometimes described his acting style as an attempt to represent how he felt upon trading his family's blanket humanism for the film industry's hatred of the unrepentant individual. The actress/performer Ann Magnuson, who costarred with Phoenix in *Jimmy Reardon*, once remarked to me with a kind of amazement how solid and unspoiled he seemed even then, in the teen-idol phase of his career. As someone who entered showbiz with her own mixed feelings, she wondered how or even *if* he'd survive its multifarious forms of corruption. Maybe that very struggle explains why, as he aged, his performances exuded ever more sadness and pointed discomfort. His best recent work found him playing overgrown kids who clung for their lives to youthful notions of a perfect romantic and/or familial love.

In a profession that divides its young into marginalized wackos with integrity, like Crispin Glover and John Lurie, or hipster sellouts, like Christian Slater and Robert Downey Jr., Phoenix was that once-in-a-decade actor honest enough to connect powerfully with people his own age, and skillful enough to remind members of an older generation of the intensity they'd lost.

LOVE CONQUERS ALL
Courtney Love
(April 1994)

Our story begins where it ends, at five AM, in a parking lot in Seattle's warehouse district. Hole is huddled together against the side of some huge delivery truck, forcing expressions at once eager and snarly onto their spaced-out faces, while a photographer snap, snap, snaps. For most of the night, the guitarist Eric Erlandson, the drummer Patty Schemel, and the bassist Kristen Pfaff, a.k.a. Hole's lesser-known three-fourths, have been inside a photo studio's office area, hypnotized by a crappy TV, flipping aimlessly between infotainment and the late, late news. Meanwhile, their leader, an elaborately lit and costumed Courtney Love, is in the next room vamping her way through what seems like a hundred rolls of film. Occasionally, she rushes in, changes clothes, then rushes out, joking guiltily with her cohorts. "You'd better behave yourselves," she announces with a motherly chirp.

Love is a curious superstar. She's amazing-looking, even weirdly gorgeous: fit, paler than pale, her features both soft and blunt, with a big wad of lipsticked lips, and huge, perpetually startled blue eyes capable of great ferocity. But she lacks the spartan androgyny required of '90s sex symbols. With her soft, recently slimmed waist, big bones, and shock-tactical makeup, she seems slightly out of date, more a time-traveling silent film siren than any kind of direct competition for Kate Moss or Winona Ryder. Watching her strike the prerequisite "bad girl" poses for the photographer, I can't help wondering if this hellishly beautiful, punk-derived image—an image she has carefully maintained with some refinements since her career's earliest beginnings—honestly suits the woman.

The previous afternoon, dressed in a simple blouse and slacks, roots showing, talking animatedly about her life, her band, and its new album, *Live Through This*, Love had reminded me a bit of the late, great Simone de Beauvoir. Like de Beauvoir, Love is very intelligent, kind of a workaholic, and full of curious, knowledgeable takes on her culture. She's also inherently charismatic, albeit in a strange, almost "anti-" way. So while this public image—the vengeful female—may be useful to Love as a feminist tool, it simplifies her as well, coloring her natural sensuality into something wacky. I've seen people point at her picture, then roll their eyes and lick their lips, like she was some comic-book character with big tits, the punk-rock Cyndi Lauper. But if Love is a cartoon, then she's drawn more in the style of Peter Bagge's fiercely bratty Girly Girl than Betty or Veronica. Who else but Love would have the smarts and audacity, after the horrific accusations leveled against her maternal qualifications, to write a song about her tabloid pregnancy featuring the barbed lines "And I don't do the dishes / I throw them in the crib"?

Let's get this out of the way. When Love talks about husband Kurt Cobain, which she does with some frequency, it's with affection and slight amusement. Mostly he shows up in benign little anecdotes. Like how she keeps finding him dolled up in women's sweaters from the '50s. Or how, at her urging, he recently agreed to buy them a Lexus. But, after one relatively brief spin around town, and the catcalls of virtually all of their old friends, Cobain insisted they take it back. So they did. Now they're back to his scuzzy old Valiant. If you only knew Cobain by Love's descriptions, you'd think he was an adorable, antic-prone young lug, more Ozzie Nelson than Ozzy Osbourne. And maybe that's exactly who he is. Point is, her love for him, and for their daughter, Frances Bean, is obvious.

I'd been forewarned by Geffen's publicist, by friends of hers, even by the rest of Hole that Courtney Love doesn't trust journalists. Not since *Vanity Fair*'s Lynn Hirschberg, whose infamous 1992 profile portrayed Love as little more than Cobain's heroin-addicted, gold-digging girlfriend. The article contained a particularly scandalous quote, attributed to a "business associate." "Courtney was pregnant and she was shooting up," it said. What followed was an approximately yearlong trashing of the couple, chronicled rather exhaustively in Michael Azerrad's Nirvana bio, *Come As You Are*.

"Yeah, Lynn," Love sighs when the subject is broached. "I did a little private investigating on her, you know, and she has no friends. None. None!" For the next, oh, forty minutes or so, Love's conversation keeps veering back to Hirschberg, usually with disclaimers. As much as she may wish Hirschberg dead, Love admits she continues to read *Vanity Fair*. "Shit," she says at the end of one particularly lengthy diatribe. "Why can't I just fucking shut up about the bitch? Okay, that's it. Zip." She raises one hand and makes a slash across her lips. (When asked to comment, Hirschberg laughed and said, "I thought Courtney was my friend.")

So what about the actual charges? "Innocent," Love says, smiling mysteriously. "Isn't that obvious?" Okay, how about claims that you punched out four people last year, including K records–Beat Happening's Calvin Johnson, the British writer Victoria Clarke, and a young female Nirvana fan who called her "Courtney Whore" in a Seattle 7-Eleven? "There's a lot more to those stories, but I don't intend to go into it." Several journalists told me they'd received threatening phone messages after criticizing her in print. "So?" When I mention Cobain's interest in guns, she cuts me off with a glower. Bringing up last year's legal battle to keep custody of Frances Bean (a result of the *Vanity Fair* drug implications) only magnifies the glower. On a lighter note, Lydia Lunch recently accused Love of ripping off her persona. "That's too bad, because I admire her a lot." Well, how about the fact that a lot of people just think you're a mean, horrible person?

"Look," Love says. "Years ago in a certain town, my reputation had gotten so bad that every time I went to a party, I was expected to burn the place down and knock out every window. So I would go into social situations and try my best to be really graceful and quiet and aloof. But sometimes when people are bearing down on you so hard, and want you to behave in a certain way, you just do it because you know you can.

"I'm so busy these days pleading with everyone that I'm lucid, that I'm educated, that I'm middle-class," she continues. "It's stupid. If you ask me, why aren't people on the cases of the real assholes of this world, like Axl Rose and Steve Albini, both of whom should be exterminated. Really, they should leave on a shuttle to the sun. They shouldn't be on the earth. Because they're not good for anything."

I'd been told by a mutual friend that Love tends to feel comfortable around gay men "as long as they don't like disco." Hoping to warm up the atmosphere a little, I drop the names of a few famous actors I bedded when younger, and sure enough she giddily spills some beans herself. She practically begs me to "out" a notoriously homophobic music producer. Sorry. We move on. She has a few less-than-flattering adjectives for Evan Dando's physique. "I'm the one that got him to stop taking off his shirt all the time," she says. Then there's the sad tale of her arch-enemy Axl Rose's rapidly receding hairline, and his crazed search for a cure. "That's what happens when you mix Prozac and heroin." Finally, she regales me with a long, hilarious story about how Eddie Van Halen showed up backstage at a recent Nirvana show and practically begged to join them onstage for the encore, completely oblivious to the fact that bands like Nirvana exist partly to destroy dinosaurs like himself.

"I was talking to Sophie Mueller, the director of our new video," Love says. It's a few minutes later. She's chummier now, curled up in her chair, gazing contentedly out a tinted hotel window at Seattle's ugly harbor. "And she asked, 'What do you want to project?' Well, it's kind of pomp-ous to do this, but I thought, 'What is my public image?' I kind of as-sessed my character flaws, and what I need to work on, what's good and bad about me, what my unknown qualities are. And . . . it's so hard to know.

"Because there are people like this journalist who interviewed us one night. He really believed that I was like him. You know, that I grew up in a trailer park, that I'm a drunk full of incest stories. I kept trying to calm him down. And the only thing that shut him up was when I read his astrological chart out loud, and even then he was hanging all over me, drooling. It was like being stuck in a room with a drunk Rupert Pupkin [the pathetic stand-up comedian portrayed by Robert De Niro in *The King of Comedy*]. And I love Rupert Pupkin. There's a Rupert Pupkin in all of us, but I killed mine a long time ago. And that guy should, too."

A long time ago may or may not mean Eugene, Oregon, where Love grew up the bookish, overweight kid of well-educated, upper-middle-class parents. She doesn't really like to talk about them, but from what slips out, you don't get the feeling that they were or are particularly monstrous. Mom's a "New Age therapist," as Love describes her. In fact, Linda Carol is a respected psychologist, whose celebrity clients include '60s radical-turned-jailbird Katherine Anne Power. The name Hole is partly inspired by a saying of her mother's: "You can't walk around with a big hole inside yourself." (It's also inspired by a line in Euripides's *Medea*: "There's a hole that pierces right through me.") Love is no longer in contact with her father, Hank Harrison, the author of *The Dead Book: A Social History of the Haight-Ashbury Experience*, and would only say of him that his single claim to fame was his long-ago, peripheral involvement with the Grateful Dead. Harrison's ties with the Dead were tight enough, however, that you can find a young Courtney Love in the extended family group photo on the back of *Aoxomoxoa*, the Dead's third LP.

Eugene is a university town, woodsy, relatively un-fucked-over by gentrification, with decent book and CD stores. Nevertheless, it's a dullish place if your ambitions are huge and culturally based like Love's were. So, after suffering through the usual peer shit that befalls rebellious smarties, she took off. From her contacts in nearby Portland, she went to work informally for Bob Pitchland, a street person raconteur who's become quasi-famous as Gus Van Sant's model for one of the central characters in *My Own Private Idaho*. Under Pitchland's auspices, and with off-and-on financial support from her folks, she traveled the world, living for brief periods in such places as Taiwan and Tokyo, and taking care of her mentor's spurious business.

In the early '80s, she settled in Liverpool for a couple of years, attending school and making her first serious contact with the world of rock stars. As an adolescent, Love had adored sensitive singer-poet types such as Joni Mitchell, Laura Nyro, and Leonard Cohen, while taking note of the condescending way they were portrayed by the rock press, "like ethereal little fairies." Now she fell for equally poetic but noisier bands like Echo and the Bunnymen and the Teardrop Explodes. She worshipped Bunnymen front man Ian McCulloch and claims to have copped most of her stage moves from him. When she wasn't in class, she followed his band around England. "I ran into Ian again not too long ago at this hotel," she says. "He walked in dressed in his tennis whites, and, you know, he'd aged a lot, like great beauties do. And he saw me and he gave me this look like, 'What the fuck are *you* doing here?' He didn't like me at all."

Through Love's connections in the British rock scene, she met the film director Alex Cox, who was revered at the time for the punkish cult film *Repo Man*. Cox came very close to casting her as the lead in *Sid and Nancy*, the project he was then developing around Nancy Spungen's mother's memoir, *And I Don't Want to Live This Life*. Luckily for Love, she lost the part to Chloe Webb, winding up instead with a tiny role as one of Nancy's bereaved friends. "Can you imagine?" she says, shaking her head at the thought of living down that particular portrayal on her résumé. But at the time she was crestfallen. Fighting suicidal depression, she signed on with a small acting/modeling agency, and wound up working as a stripper in the Far East for the next year or so. "Stripping's all right," she says. "It's better than prostitution. I was lucky, because I was fat. So nobody paid attention to me."

It was in the late '80s that Love met one of her closest friends, the Los Angeles artist Joe Mama, who says, "She was the same then as now. She had this attitude like 'I'm a freak, but I know what I'm doing.' It wasn't calculating, it was scary." He remembers that she moved around a lot, living for brief periods in LA, San Francisco, and Minneapolis. It was in Minneapolis that, along with Kat Bjelland and L7's Jennifer Finch, she formed an early version of Babes in Toyland, described by one friend as sounding like an "atonal Roches." For maybe a week she was a member of Faith No More, and remains friendly with the band's Roddy Bottum. One night she met the guitarist and begrudging Capitol Records' employee Eric Erlandson. They hit it off, started to pal around, and eventually, with the help of a classified ad in *Flipside*, scraped together the first incarnation of Hole.

Love's proud of the band's early work, especially its first LP, *Pretty on the Inside*, coproduced by Sonic Youth's Kim Gordon, a hero of Love's, and Gumball's Don Fleming. Still, she says, "That record was me posing in a lot of ways. It was the truth, but it was also me catching up with all my hip peers who'd gone all indie on me, and who made fun of me for liking R.E.M. and the Smiths. I'd done the whole punk thing, sleeping on floors in piss and beer, and waking up with the guy with the fucking mohawk and the skateboards and the speed and the whole goddamned thing. But I hated it. I'd outgrown it by the time I was seventeen." She pauses, grabs a glass of fizzy water, and takes a huge gulp. "But fuck people if they didn't guess it the first time around," she continues, eyes blurring with anger. "If they didn't get the lucidity. If it's one thing I am, it's lucid. I know that's not a very heavy word like 'intellectual' or whatever, but still, to take away my lucidity, that pisses me off."

Live Through This is both a scruffier and more commercial record than *Pretty on the Inside*. The angsty rants of yore remain, but they're decorated with a lot more poetry. Milk (as in mother's) is a recurring motif, as is dismemberment. Female victimization remains the overall theme, this time depersonalized into odd, accusatory mini-narratives in which a variety of female characters receive the protection of Love's tense, manic-depressive singing. Hers is a natural songwriting talent, full of excellent instincts and yet wildly unsophisticated. All of which makes Love, in some ways, a more intriguing figure than, say, Polly Harvey, Tanya Donelly, or Liz Phair, each of whom, idiosyncrasies aside, is a traditional talent with an inordinate knack for the pop tune. It's not inconceivable that Love might have ended up some kind of peroxided Joni Mitchell if it weren't for the musical gifts of the diligent, like-minded Erlandson, and her unstoppable need to fuck with rock music's male-heavy history.

"Like I was talking to Sophie . . ." It's a few minutes later, and Love's relaxing again. "Sophie's done a bunch of Björk's videos. And Björk is seen as the Icelandic elf child-woman. But Björk wants to be seen as more erotic. And I'm like, 'Why?' Elf child-woman is a *good* job. And my job as rock's bad girl is good, too. I should just stop trying to correct people's impressions."

I understand, I say, but it's strange that you're written off as one-dimensional and didactic when your lyrics, if anything, tend to err on the side of the abstract.

"That's because I'm not intelligent enough to write direct narratives," she says sarcastically. "I've always worked really hard on my lyrics, even when my playing was for shit. So it's weird that when I try to work in different styles, to juxtapose ideas in a careful way that isn't pompous and Byronic, it's just taken as vulgar. The whole cliché of women being cathartic really pisses me off. You know, 'Oh, this is therapy for me. I'd die if I didn't write this.' Eddie Vedder says shit like that. Fuck you."

Misogyny's been a big shock to Love. After all, her parents were '60s quasi-liberals bent on showing their daughter life's brightest profile. The first record she owned was *Free to Be You and Me*. There was a copy of *Our Bodies, Our Selves* sitting on the family toilet for years. She grew up thinking books and records like these were the culture's official textbooks. And she remains an avid reader of feminist theorists, like Susan

Faludi, Judith Butler, Camille Paglia, and Naomi Wolf, though her face crinkles up at the mention of the latter's newest book. "Ugh. Wimp," she crows.

I mention a riot grrrl show she'd helped organize in London last year. Rumor had it the show was a critical and financial disaster, despite the participation of name acts like Huggy Bear, Bratmobile, and Hole. Since the fiasco, the riot grrrl phenomenon has been treated a lot less reverentially in the British music papers. "Yeah, it didn't work," she says, echoing the opinion of other Hole members, male and female. "But then the whole riot grrrl thing is so . . . well, for one thing, the Women's Studies program at Evergreen State College, Olympia, where a lot of these bands come from, is notorious for being one of the worst programs in the country. It's man-hating, and it doesn't produce very intelligent people in that field. So you've got these girls starting bands, saying, 'Well, they printed our picture in the *Melody Maker*, why aren't we getting any royalties?'

"I tried to start a riot grrrl chapter in LA at one point. I called a bunch of people to try to set up a meeting, and they were like, 'But the place will be bugged! *A Current Affair* will be there!' And I'm like, 'Listen, nobody cares, girls. Interest is on the wane in this little fad.'"

No surprise then that Hole's tentative spring tour couples the band not with a "look-alike" band like L7 or Bikini Kill but with those great bicoastal idiosyncrats Pavement. Love likes them a lot, in part because they're fellow unrepentant Echo and the Bunnymen fans. Still, I sense that there's more than aesthetic compatibility to the pairing. "Remember when Madonna was making the rounds of the clubs scouting bands for her label?" she asks. "Sniffing around people like us and Cell and whoever? Well, a friend and I decided back then that the only cool thing Madonna could do at this point in her career would be to go out with

Steve Malkmus." Her eyes get uncharacteristically dreamy. "He's great. It's the Stockton part of him, you know? If it was just the East Coast thing he'd be gross. And he's so well-bred. He's like the Grace Kelly of indie rock."

Our story ends where it began, at three PM that same day. Jim Merlis, the genial publicist whom Geffen has assigned to the Hole beat, has just deposited me at the apartment of bassist Pfaff, and is on his way to pick up Love, who doesn't drive. Pfaff's place is stuffed with records, all neatly if unartfully organized along the walls, and there are posters everywhere of her former band Janitor Joe, as well as a few of her favorite band, the Cows.

Eric Erlandson does most of the talking, since Pfaff and Schemel are newcomers. He, like Love, is still reeling from the recent encounter with the drunken journalist. When I turn down a beer, the band's relief is tangible. They seem a pretty sober bunch, if speculation is allowed based on relatively skimpy knowledge. Not to say they spout twelve-step rhetoric or anything. But I wait and wait for the drug stories, and when they finally do enter the conversation, it's in a manner so casual and yawny I barely take notice. "Oh, I was so fucked up that night," one of them will say with a bemused wag of the head. Or, "[unnameable celebrity] is such a mess." Later, Love will surprise me even more. Discussing a fellow alternative rock star and Seattle resident's severe heroin problem, she'll chastise the local needle exchange program's home delivery policy, which she thinks only contributes to the severity of the poor guy's habit.

In Lynn Hirschberg's *Vanity Fair* piece, the hard evidence on Love the junked-out monster came via worried quotes from anonymous "friends" and "associates." Having talked to some equally anonymous, long-term friends of hers, what I surmised was that, yeah, like a few of us, she's done some serious drugging in her twenty-eight years. She's been out of control, fucked-up, a complete and utter asshole. She herself refers to periods when "chemicals," as she puts it, were both her major pleasure and obstacle. These mentions may be glancing, but their tone is rich with horror. Partway through the marathon photo shoot, Love spotted Pfaff spacing out on a couch, and rushed over, asking her in this frightened, accusatory voice, "Are you high?!" (She wasn't.) At another point, when I told Love how amused I'd been watching her and Kim Gordon humiliate Dave Kendall on an old episode of *120 Minutes*, she shook her head and said, in this sad, self-incriminating way, "Oh, I was so out of it," then looked grimly off into space.

Maybe the problem is contextual. In *Vanity Fair*'s world, there are two ways to attain power: by leading a glamorous, amoral lifestyle, or by becoming an embittered, subservient, morally superior chronicler of this kind of life. To the latter, Courtney Love is no different than the Barbara Huttons, Demi Moores, and other eccentrics and beauties for whom the bourgeoisie spill their collective saliva. Naïvely, mistakenly, Love threw her and Kurt Cobain's rough-hewn but essentially moral lives on the mercy of that amoral court because she thought it would be cool. And it was, for those of us who joked about it and rolled our eyes at the subsequent hubbub. If, for one moment, Love thought she could subvert *VF*'s intentions and prove to the world that she wasn't the grunge Valerie Bertinelli or Bianca Jagger, big deal. Nice try. The real question isn't why Love got savaged in the process, or what drugs she did, but rather why we care in the first place.

Is it just that we're starry-eyed misogynists? Twenty or so years ago, our alternative-rock-fan foreparents blamed Yoko Ono and Linda Eastman for the breakup of the very obviously tired and burned-out Beatles.

Before meeting the aging moptops, Ono had been a serious Fluxus artist, and Eastman had been an active photojournalist. Back in the '70s, people shredded these two women in print and conversation with the same lazy cattiness we now use to crucify Love, and with even less reason: Nirvana is intact, Cobain is still writing cool shit, Hole is making better and better music, Frances Bean is healthy. The amount of energy expended trying to track and clarify Love's personal quirks is bizarre. Is she really that important?

Me, I like her a lot. And I keep thinking you would, too, but then I don't know. Others might tell you different, but I get the impression that, assuming even half of what's been written about Love is true, she's changed. "Changed?" she asks, blinking at my suggestion. She regards me suspiciously for a moment, then squints off into the distance, wondering. "Well, I'm jaded. I've faced every situation for many years with a certain naïveté and innocence. But I've somehow become a cynic. Cynicism is a good thing to have on the outside, but it's a terrible thing to have on the inside. All I ever wanted, ever, was to make rock music. Whether it was in the back of a Camaro smoking pot and listening to Journey with some guy who was trying to make out with me, or whether it was the first time I heard the Pretenders. Fuck, Chrissie Hynde really saved me, you know, because she manifested it. She was a pragmatist. Pragmatism is what makes a good songwriter. Pragmatism or drugs. And drug-influenced songs are great, I agree. But I write songs that are clean. Songs that come from here." Love slugs her heart.

GRAIN OF THE VOICE
R.I.P. Kurt Cobain
(April 1994)

In John Lydon's autobiography, *Rotten: No Irish, No Blacks, No Dogs*, he compares Nirvana to Eddie and the Hot Rods, a late-'70s R&B bar band who'd lucked into a little popularity and acclaim during the dawn of British punk, when any group with short hair and short songs were temporarily mistaken for revolutionaries. "It really annoys me," Lydon writes, ". . . when [Nirvana] say they were influenced by the Sex Pistols. They clearly can't be. They missed the point somewhere." My first thought on reading this passage was *Jesus, what a clueless fool*. But thinking more about it, I realized he had a point, however reductive and however inadvertently self-indicting.

Lydon, who likes to characterize himself as a talented troublemaker, can't see Nirvana for the darkness and length of his own shadow. To him, the members of Nirvana can only be protégés, and so their very admiration of his work becomes an embarrassment, an admission of weakness. A classic prefeminist bully, Lydon all but calls them fags and wussies. But of course, the very qualities that made him and other punk hard-liners suspicious of Nirvana—sincerity, overemotionalism, formal conservatism, intellectual spazziness—are at the center of why they're a great band.

The Sex Pistols predated AIDS, homelessness, MTV. Not to say life was easy in the mid-'70s, but Nirvana didn't have the luxury, nor the megalomaniacal naïveté, to attempt a coup of popular culture. In this world, it's hard enough just to get an absolutely honest song on the airwaves. Nirvana, like most interesting current bands, just wanted to represent their exact feelings appropriately. Luckily, in their case, they were guided by Kurt Cobain, a gifted if obviously tormented man with high ideals, original ideas, and a beautifully erratic way of expressing himself.

Kurt Cobain may have loved John Lydon, but I suspect that it was in the way a kid loves his or her abusive father. Unlike that cynical old fuck, Cobain wasn't a monster, ever. At his worst, he was a mess, but so are most of us, only we get to act out our shit among friends, and not in front of people who think our every woe is a generational signifier. I mean, Cobain's idea of media manipulation was to wear a Daniel Johnston T-shirt during photo sessions. He may have been rich, but he thought like an anarchist. He wanted to share. He wrote consistently great lyrics about not being able to express himself adequately, he sang like God with a dog's mouth, and he believed in the communicative powers of popular music. And precisely because he believed, Nirvana wound up doing what the Pistols could only masturbate thinking about.

Cobain's work nailed how a ton of people feel. There are few moments in rock as bewilderingly moving as when he mumbled, "I found it hard / It's hard to find / Oh well, whatever / Nevermind." There's that bizarre, agonized, and devastating promise he keeps making throughout "Heart-Shaped Box": "Wish that I could eat your cancer when you turn black." Take a look in his eyes the next time MTV runs the "Heart-Shaped Box" video, and see if you can sort out the pain from the ironic detachment from the horror from the defensiveness.

American culture has reached a strange impasse, which is largely the fault of our pathetic educational system. It's left us intellectually undernourished, emotionally confused, and way, way too vulnerable. That imbalance may have produced artists like Cobain, but it has also softened our brains to the point where we just let political and corporate higher-ups of various sorts manipulate our very ways of receiving information. Instead of being encouraged to expand imaginatively on the music we listen to, we're told to reduce everything in our world into simple rights and wrongs, effectives and ineffectives, yeses and nos. We comply because the world is scary and because we understandably want to be coddled by the things that interest us. Kurt Cobain, so conflicted in his attitude toward success, and so complex in his ideas about love and politics, was a classic beneficiary and victim of this dilemma.

What's amazing is that after all that interference, he won. Well, he didn't, but Nirvana did. Nirvana, a band that embodied every important quality that punk had ever championed, managed for a brief period to flip off power-mongers and signal believers with the very same gesture. And, in succeeding so spectacularly, and so cleanly, Cobain and crew showed what was possible, even in this ugly and demoralized culture. Unfortunately, with his stupid, infuriating death, he also showed us what our belief costs.

PURPLISH PROSE
The Violet Quill Reader
(May 1994)
The Emergence of Gay Writing After Stonewall

Historians place Gay Liberation's launch date in late June 1969, the time of the Stonewall Riots, a small but retrospectively significant confrontation between vice cops and patrons of a New York gay bar. As legend rosily has it, the ensuing ruckus marked the first time that American gay men banded together to assert their inalienable rights. Within a few years, Gay Literature was an official subcultural movement with enough product to its name to warrant a shelf or two in the chain stores. Now, literature is not generally known as a trendy, up-to-the-second form. In terms of innovation, it lags behind film, pop music, visual art, and performance art, beating out only ballet, opera, and sometimes theater. But it does have a history of being one of the best forms in which to express the personal effects of social change. And it remains the medium wherein our particular minority most likes to unburden itself.

Before Stonewall, homosexuality was a kind of flotsam that occasionally washed up on fiction's cutting edges, along with such topics as drug use and criminal activity. With one steamy reference to the homosexual underworld, any writer transformed his or her novel, no matter how conventional its shape, into something outré and avant-garde. But with liberation, the subject was effectively normalized. So began the age of the traditionally plotted, realistic, worldly gay novel in which likeable gay characters dealt likeably with traditional everyday traumas like mortgage payments, job stress, prostrate cancer, and relationships gone sour.

Then this was a true political victory, no question. But this normalization also made the work of gay men more, well, pigeonholeable. *Myra Breckinridge*, *City of Night*, *Naked Lunch*, *Our Lady of the Flowers* had been scandalous best-sellers, devoured by rebels, intellectuals, art farts, and pervs of all orientations. The closest thing to a crossover smash that post-Stonewall literature has produced is David Leavitt's *The Lost Language of Cranes* (1986), a novelty hit of a novel that created a heterosexual market for user-friendly gay fiction and then all but sated this audience's curiosity in one swoop.

The Violet Quill Reader is the first attempt to make a mountain out of the molehill that was a small, informal, very occasional writing workshop that took place in New York circa 1980–81. Consisting of the novelists Edmund White, Andrew Holleran, Robert Ferro, Michael Grumley, Felice Picano, and the critic/photographer Christopher Cox, the Violet Quill—one of several jokey nicknames this social set gave themselves—is a legend of convenience that may provide a Plymouth Rock for gay studies courses, but it's a relative if harmless sham. As the editor David Bergman's introduction accidentally makes clear, there's not much *there* there. Yeah, they sat around in one another's living rooms on eight occasions sharing works in progress. But the most talented of these men had distinctive voices long before they started bumping into each other at Fire Island soirees. If anything, it might be argued that the Violet Quill did as much harm as good, however fortuitous this salon may seem to academics, and however happy it may have made the participants.

By 1980, Edmund White had already published maybe his two best novels, *Forgetting Elena* (1973) and *Nocturnes for the King of Naples* (1978). They'd been blurbed and praised in print by the likes of Gore Vidal, Susan Sontag, and Vladimir Nabokov. Because of White's talent, his connections, his growing fame, and his considerable personal charm, the Quill revolved around him, fueled by the other men's awe, envy, and/or desire for a contact high. He is clearly the most gifted of the six, as well as the only Quillee whose fiction has a snowball's chance at immortality. (This is a group positively stoned on the notion of a literary pantheon.) Where lesser-known members of the Quill sincerely sought advice and criticism from the group, White used the occasions to entertain friends with his latest efforts. From what I can gather, the Quill was something of a lark for White. He may have basked in and benefited from his colleagues' strokes, but there's no evidence that his work was affected by their comments or their writings in one way or another.

Andrew Holleran, probably the second most gifted member of the Quill, is a far better essayist and social critic than he is a novelist. His most famous novel, *Dancer from the Dance* (1978), is a Gay Lit classic. But its reputation rises from how cleverly he documents gay men's lifestyle pre-AIDS, not from his style. In fact, his second and only other novel, *Nights in Aruba* (1983), written during the period of the Quill's existence, is prissy, self-absorbed, and irritatingly disconnected from the social context within which his writing clicks. Like most Quill members, his fiction has a tendency to read like cheap aftershave lotion smells. And *Nights in Aruba* does stink intriguingly of late-'70s discos and backrooms, but it's all pretense. Compared to the heavyweight stylists Holleran so admires—Flaubert, James, Nabokov—he's nothing but a preener. Still, when he sticks to writing factually about the behavioral patterns, tastes, and fears of his own fortysomething generation, as in the essay collection *Ground Zero* (1988), he's rather fun to curl up with.

Robert Ferro, like White, published a couple of books prior to meeting the men who would form the Quill. A deeply conventional writer, he was also the most seriously afflicted with the delusion that he was Henry James's openly gay heir. His four novels are models of how not to go about achieving greatness. Gertrude Stein's famous assessment of the work of Glenway Wescott—"His writing is syrup which will not pour"—applies to Ferro's as well. But, unlike in the case of Wescott, whose absurdly ornate fiction has an inadvertent camp appeal, Ferro's writing is both overwritten and bland, elegantly wrought but as beige as a leisure suit. His novels achieve neither the impassioned fanciness of White's best work nor function as valuable, if slightly contrived, period pieces, à la *Dancer from the Dance* or Larry Kramer's *Faggots*. Only in his final novel, *Second Son* (1988), is there even a shimmer of animation, and that ironically in its lush, poisoned depiction of a character dying of AIDS, which Ferro succumbed to shortly after the book's publication.

Michael Grumley, Ferro's lover, wrote a number of nonfiction books during his life, most famously *Atlantis: The Autobiography of a Search* (1970), which he coauthored with Ferro. But he longed to be a serious writer, and his involvement in the Quill reinforced this longing in a sick way. Later, in the final stages of AIDS, he kept a diary, from which Bergman has pulled some effective excerpts. It chronicles both his physical decline and his last, desperate attempts to find a publisher for *Life Drawings*, a novel he wrote with encouragement from the workshop. It's grim stuff. Even Picano, who headed a small gay publishing house, rejected the manuscript. *Life Drawings* was eventually issued by Grove Press in

1991, accompanied by two peculiar, telling essays in which Holleran and the late editor/scholar George Stambolian spend more time gossiping about Grumley's sexual attraction to Afro-American men than defending his work.

George Whitmore is a great example of the Violet Quill's downside. During its existence, Whitmore published his first novel, *The Confessions of Danny Slocum* (1980), and began a second novel about homosexual pirates that he ultimately abandoned. *Danny Slocum* is an odd book. At times Whitmore's neorealistic bent makes it seem like a homelier *Dancer from the Dance*. At other times he loses himself in parochial high style, and his prose just kind of wends from page to page with a slightly uncomfortable sashaying and nothing on its mind. If the Quill had been a real workshop, and not just an amusement overinflated by legend-mongers, Whitmore, being the least developed of its members, might have benefited. But his work was treated dismissively by the others, which made him bitter, and helped induce a lengthy writer's block. It wasn't until years after the workshop members had gone their separate ways that he managed to finish a second, far superior novel, *Nebraska* (1987), whose rough, tense, minimalist voice had absolutely nothing to do with the Quill's.

Felice Picano is a resilient, plucky, prolific scribe, but he too has suffered from the occasional delusion of grandeur. At the dawn of the Quill, he was an established author of thriller novels, notably *Eyes* (1976), *The Mesmerist* (1977), and *The Lure* (1979). But even this most unpretentious Quillee got swept up in the group's Bloomsbury-esque antics. His works from '80, '81, mainly the semiautobiographical novel *Ambidextrous* and a collection of short fiction, *Slashed to Ribbons in Defense of Love*, subsume his workmanlike skills in a cheesy, pompous tone that sounds like Minnie Pearl trying to imitate Jeremy Irons. Still, the main reason to buy this *Reader*, and not just pick up a book or two by White and Holleran, is a previously unpublished chunk from the diary Picano kept during the Quill's brief existence. Full of odd historical detail, giddy, self-important, catty, and completely honest, these passages are the snazziest work of Picano's career. They also tell you everything you need to know about the Quill's ins and outs, and with far less bluster than in Bergman's introduction.

Obviously, there's nothing wrong with publishing a Best of the Violet Quill, but let's not go insane. Attaching too much significance to this particular group's place in history narrowly defines the origins of so-called Gay Literature, upgrading minor figures like Ferro, Grumley, Picano, and Whitmore, while ignoring other writers of their generation who were grappling just as fortuitously with ways to express homosexual identity, but who happened to move in different social circles. One of them, Ethan Mordden, the editor of the forthcoming gay fiction anthology *Waves*, presents a savage, revisionist take on White and co. in that book's spunky introduction. "The Violet Quill," he writes, "seemed more like the last era of old Gay Lit than the beginnings of new Gay Lit—all that faded European prestige. . . . Most of what came out of [it] was more clever than wise, more self-regarding than perceptive. . . . [It was] a movement that was less about good writing than about vanity." Certainly this opinion reflects that of many younger queers, for whom these mustachioed, upper-middle-class white men must seem like very suspicious forerunners.

Maybe for gay writers to outmaneuver the reductive and stigmatizing label "Gay Lit," these kinds of canonizations are necessary, or at least karmic. If we can specify exactly which works are about their authors' sexual identity, it may free people who happen to be gay from the pressures of having to represent some imaginary collective viewpoint. The incredible and controversial success last year of Dorothy Allison's *Bastard Out of Carolina*, a lesbian's novel as opposed to a Lesbian Novel, has annoyed some in the establishment—for instance, the Lammys, a yearly awards program for lesbian/gay books, refused to nominate *Bastard* because its content wasn't gay enough—but it's made a whole lot of queer writers beam like prisoners at the news of a fellow inmate's bust out. But still, if academics like David Bergman insist on distorting history to support their definition of Gay Literature by creating hierarchical models where there are none, then it's up to us writers to dismantle these lies or risk laboring under them. The Violet Quill is bullshit.

LARRY CLARK'S *PERFECT CHILDHOOD*
(June 1994)

Acclaimed as it was, *Tulsa* got Larry Clark's career off on a curious foot. For it seemed not the work of an artist versed in post-Conceptualism but of a documentarian—a more subculturally directed Robert Frank, a subtler Weegee. Although intensely beautiful, the images were disguised by their settings' unfamiliarity and sexual heat. Initially, it was only those of us who actually haunted such locales who could feel the extraordinary, indescribable aestheticism radiating off them. That's my guess. Back when crystal meth ran my daily affairs, when each day's goal involved fierce, disorganized sex with a broke, drug-addicted white-trash teenager who wouldn't or couldn't possibly read my elaborate interest in his body as anything but one of the more confusing aspects of his job, I used to see this one young guy, Mike, on a regular basis. Mike was a scrawny hippie type with a pretty, pockmarked face and lost-seeming eyes that I believe were pale blue. Very much like the type you see in early Larry Clarks. I forget how we met. He'd come over a lot, hang out. We would drug ourselves into an insane mental and physical state, then have sex, if you want to call it that. To Mike, I was a representative of the real, normal world. He thought that if he could keep men like me interested in his body, then his life would have a conventional purpose. That was important to him, same as it's important to you and me. Because, yeah, when Mike wasn't trading the use of his orifices for drugs or petty cash, he was just one more manic-depressive layabout. Or that's how he described himself, in so many words. My interest in him was intense but specific, and even kind of worshipful within limits. Anyway, one day when our sex had been especially great, and we thought we were in love or something, Mike hung around afterward for a few hours, and, over their course, he happened to pull my copy of Larry Clark's second book, *Teenage Lust*, off the shelf. He sat in the middle of my bedroom, looking and relooking through the pictures. I was just lying around in bed snorting crystal and watching him, thinking who remembers what thoughts? Eventually Mike glanced up from the pages, all astonished, and asked me, "What is this?" Really, like *Teenage Lust* was some bizarre new invention. So I explained what I knew about Larry Clark, his work, his world, etc. Mike nodded along, growing increasingly excited. He couldn't seem to believe that the desperate, extreme way in which he conducted his life—Mike's life closely resembled the lives chronicled in Clark's work—could be contextualized as art, for one thing, and, more important, that somebody in the real, normal world had been impressed enough by guys like him to "upgrade" their lives into works of art, to use his term. Because to Mike, art was the ultimate sign that something was significant. If there was art about something, that thing had earned its keep in the world. I don't know where he got this idea. So I gave him the book, and he managed not to sell it for drug money longer than almost anything else among his belongings. Eventually he died, at twenty-four. OD'd, from what I hear. I don't mean to sound cold, but it's been years now, and my life is so different. By the time Mike died, he'd become a mental and physical wreck who could do nothing but annoy everyone he knew. Still, there were a couple of years when he was weirdly beautiful, and unconventionally intelligent, and I thought he'd wind up okay. He wanted to be a rodeo star, whatever that entails. I've stopped befriending and sleeping with guys like Mike. For one thing, it's too painful to watch them try to exist in so much pain. And it's scary to objectify white-trash street-hustler types to the degree to which you must in order to find them beautiful enough to go to bed with. Luckily there are works of art that explore guys like Mike, because photographing someone nails him down but leaves him free. In a way, I wish I'd never had sex with Mike, because I still get these tastes of him, meaning his body, on the people I do go to bed with, even though they're nothing like him. And then that makes me think of Mike, which is a mixed blessing. Sometimes, as stupid as it sounds, I feel like my mouth is Mike's fossil, which wouldn't be so terrible, except that his memory hurts, and I'm not into pain anymore, or not in the way I was. In Larry Clark's *Perfect Childhood*, he has taken the most sublime pictures of his career, and there's no one like Mike anywhere in them.

TOO COOL FOR SCHOOL
(July 1994)

It's a breezy, lukewarm Friday evening on a nondescript stretch of East Melrose. Brent Petersen, a graduate student in UCLA's Fine Arts program, is inaugurating his tiny storefront gallery with an exhibit by one of his classmates. A crowd of fellow artists-in-training and faculty members are doing what people usually do at openings: chatting nervously about anything but the art. They're a noisy, dressed-down, twentysomething-heavy crowd. Rumor has it that Petersen, a cherubic if slightly deranged twenty-five-year-old whose artwork involves stalking the Ronald McDonald clown with a video camera, might be playing jokey tribute to the Heaven's Gate mass suicide of the past week by serving Ecstasy-laced applesauce and vodka at the opening. That could explain the healthy turnout.

For most of these students, this is their last year of grad school. In less than two months, they'll do a final group exhibition in one of UCLA's on-campus museums, the faculty will grade them on the fruit of their schooling, and worst-case scenario, they'll be on the street, fast-tracking for day jobs, dropping their slides off at local galleries, and repaying student loans. If that isn't stressful enough, UCLA just happens to be the hottest art school in the country. The art world is watching their every move, and right now could be their one chance to make it. Put another way, if UCLA were a rock scene, it would be Seattle right after *Nevermind* went platinum.

Evan Holloway, twenty-eight, and the cause célèbre this evening, is inside one of his artworks, an immense plywood box that takes up most of the gallery. The box houses a soundproofed room just large enough to hold a drum kit, a couple of Evian bottles, and a ventilation tube. Inside, Holloway plays a loose, amateurish drum solo for as long as he can stand it, which causes the box to emit a faint, muffled rhythm. Like most of the work being created by UCLA students, it's a strange and trippy thing, a kind of special effect masquerading as an art object that appears to be haunted. Or, as someone in the crowd puts it, "This is giving me an acid flashback. And I've never taken acid."

A handful of teenage boys, maybe curious neighborhood intruders, just tried unsuccessfully to snag themselves beers (Petersen opted for a keg rather than the vodka-Ex potion) and have resorted to pressing their ears to the box.

"I think it's playing . . . what's that Tad song, their MTV hit?" says a floppy-haired kid in a Soundgarden T-shirt.

" 'Natural One,' " says his ravey-looking chum.

"No, *Tad*," the boy repeats.

"It's playing 'Natural One,' listen," the second boy insists. "Duh-duh-sh-sh-duh-duh-sh-sh . . ."

Three of Holloway's school friends, the sculptor Tim Rogeberg and the painters/musicians Casey Cook and Francesca Gabbiani, have been studying this little scene with knowing grins.

"I like things that when you try to figure them out, your mind snaps," Rogeberg says. He's an affable twenty-five-year-old from Virginia who just this week got snagged by a big local gallery. "I think that's what Evan and a lot of us are doing, trying to make things that are ungraspable. You can't see the content, you can't see the form. You only see the flip-flop."

"I think it must be hard for people who aren't our age to get our work," adds Cook, twenty-six, a mildly punked-out young blond with a cool if slightly frazzled demeanor. The most successful of the students, she just had her first New York show this past spring. "It comes from our world. You know, the music we listen to, the clubs, the things we talk about."

All of a sudden, the box goes silent. The teenage boys scrunch up their faces. Holloway's friends get a slightly panicked look. Then a secret door in the box's side pops open and the artist crawls out, dressed in a sweat-soaked gold thrift-store suit. It's not the kind of moment you're supposed to applaud, but Holloway does get a few laconic back slaps as he stumbles toward the gallery's entrance and fresh air.

The artist Charles Ray, a faculty member and one of Holloway's biggest supporters, stops him long enough for a compliment, and wonders aloud if the box will be a part of his final review show.

"Sort of," Holloway says. "I'm going to make a forty-five. The A side will be the sound of the drums outside the box, and the B side will be the sound of the drums inside the box. And the picture sleeve will have a photo of the exterior of the box on one side, and the interior of the box on the other."

Ray, who claims never to have listened to music, popular or otherwise, when he was growing up, and only figured out what the term "rock music" meant a year ago when a student made him a Jesus Lizard tape, looks perplexed.

"Trust me," Holloway says, too exhausted to deconstruct the whole indie-rock aesthetic at the moment. "It'll be cool."

The Warner Building is a former factory located in a light industrial area of Culver City, ten miles south of the UCLA campus. The university bought the property in the mid-'80s, and had its interior converted into a maze of studio spaces for graduate students. It looks something like an indoor swap meet crossed with a Halloween spook house; you can get seriously lost in here. Students tell stories of friends, a little stoned or drunk, wandering into the building and getting so confused by the intricate, illogical layout, and so flipped out by the bizarre spread of art, that they're found cowering in the bathroom. Lately, thanks to the buzz around UCLA, the place is swarming with gallery dealers, curators, and collectors from as far away as Europe.

On a basic level, UCLA's success is rather simple to explain: Its teaching staff is a veritable supergroup of well-known artists who, to quote the art critic Peter Schjeldahl, "aim to hit the wrong note squarely." Plus, thanks to UCLA's shockingly low tuition, its students are a blur of social backgrounds, rather than the rich-white-kid hordes that populate most other art schools. And while faculty-student interactions are precious and few, the teachers' clout lets them bring art-world honchos right into their favorite kids' studios. It's just a happy accident that the result is probably the world's top artist-producing machine.

The biggest indicator of UCLA's newfound status may have been this spring's Whitney Biennial, the vast exhibition of sculpture, painting, photography, video, and film held every two years at New York's Whitney Museum of American Art. Always controversial, it's also the most important single gig in any young artist's life. The 1997 edition—dubbed "the UCLA Biennial" by the art critic Christopher Knight—exhibited a remarkable number of artists associated with the school, either as graduates or teachers. "The art coming out of UCLA is very individualistic," says Lisa Phillips, one of the show's chief curators. "It's refreshingly free of dogma and academic approach. Let's face it, it's hard to make iconoclasm an academy." She doesn't see the work as something entirely new, but rather "something very peculiar. It's amazing how strange the work is to the New York audience in particular." At the same time, "so many people who aren't in the art world have told me that this Biennial has been easier to enter," she says. "It's a very interesting moment."

It's worth pointing out that while a number of UCLA students could soon hit art stardom, it's still nothing like being a rock star. Consider Matthew Barney, arguably the most famous younger artist of the '90s. Ever heard of him? Probably not. The art world is a very small, rarefied place, so invisible to the average person's eye that it's practically a fifth dimension. Occasionally an artist might sneak into popular culture, like Mike Kelley, whose work popped up on the cover of Sonic Youth's *Dirty*. But more often, only an insider could understand the art that's shown in galleries, much less love it. The UCLA crowd hopes to change that. "We don't get our ideas from other art, and that makes a difference," explains Rogeberg. "I think we sense that all that codified, secret-society art you see in most galleries is over."

This afternoon, Liz Craft, a sculpture student, is in the Warner Building's lumber-strewn lobby saying good-bye to a local art dealer named Richard Telles, who recently lured her into his stable of what he calls "younger, experimental, hands-on artists." She has a weird look on her face, which I just assume is the usual pre-career pressures.

"No, I just found out this morning that I live next door to a cop," she tells me. "He's always been really suspicious and weird, but I never imagined he was *that* weird. It kind of puts a new spin on my home life."

Raised in the tiny town of Mammoth Lakes, a ski resort situated on the side of a semi-active volcano in the eastern Sierra Nevadas, Craft is a shy, spacey twenty-seven-year-old with huge, anxious eyes. Initially, she enrolled in the undergraduate program of another local university,

Otis, majoring in fashion design. "When I was a kid I made weird outfits for myself," she says, leading me through the Warner maze. "So I just figured I'd be a designer. But when I got to school, I realized how crass fashion was." At the encouragement of her painter boyfriend, she switched majors to fine art, and "took a lot of mushrooms, which helped me unlearn a few things." She arrived at UCLA two years ago, and has pretty much been wowing everyone here since.

We sidle past two students fighting over a chain saw, then squeeze through a pack of young curators from the Museum of Contemporary Art. We happen by Francesca Gabbiani's studio, and I can see her inside, anxiously describing her mystical abstract paintings to two Italian collectors. There's Casey Cook boxing up a painting for her show in New York. A little farther along, the instructor/artist Paul McCarthy is having Gregg Einhorn demonstrate his latest sculpture to a New York dealer. The piece is a handmade Colonial dollhouse suspended from the ceiling by invisible wires. The dealer slips his head inside the dollhouse and watches an extremely disorienting nature video through the back windows. "Yeah, it's sort of David Lynchian," I hear Einhorn say as we pass.

"It can turn into such a soap opera here," Craft mumbles. "All these people are always here looking around, and we all get so sick of each other. I just hide out in my little world."

Craft unlatches the door of her studio and leads me inside. Her boom box is blasting the Orb, which turns the hammering, drilling, and yelling outside into a faint, tolerable crackle. Most of her studio is taken up by the sculpture she's been working on for the last six months. Part of Craft's brilliance is that her work is so visually discombobulating that it reduces commentary to a stammer. All I can say is it looks sort of like a cross between a giant Rubik's Cube and an IKEA display.

"God, I don't know what to say about this," Craft says, blinking at the piece. "You know how at raves there are so many things going on at once? The music's superprimal, but the visuals are so future. You get lost in all that trippy, fun space, all the levels and layers. I'm sort of going for that, I guess. But that sounds so lame."

She flops down on a folding chair, swigs from an Evian bottle, and gives her piece a sad, defeated look. While everyone at UCLA thinks Craft is an unstoppable genius, she's easily as uncertain as any student here, if not more so, especially when it comes to career stuff. Truth is, she finds almost everything outside her art to be kind of bewildering.

"The whole gallery thing kind of sucks," she says. "It's so private, and everything gets treated like it's the Crown Jewels or something. I think my parents could understand my art, and get something out of it, but they'd never go to a gallery in a billion years. I don't even go to them very much. Honestly I think the art world is gross-looking."

Charles Ray—Charley to the students—is in the backyard of his small West Los Angeles home, working on his newest piece. It's a full-scale fiberglass replica of a severely totaled '91 Pontiac Grand Am, realistic down to the tiniest motor parts, upholstery flaws, and bits of broken windshield. A year ago he bought the original car from a police garage. Ray has this idea that the replica will somehow retain the horrific aura of the accident and, at the same time, create the impeccable formal confusion that his work's famous for. It's costing him roughly $120,000 to fabricate. Luckily, he sells everything he makes, so he'll undoubtedly recoup when it's exhibited at an LA gallery this fall.

An extremely youthful forty-four-year-old with the spazzy energy of an adolescent boy and the unpredictable, free-associative speaking patterns of a more together David Helfgott, Ray takes his teaching duties way beyond the classroom. He invites students out on his sailboat, lets them hang out at his studio while he's working, and organizes spontaneous field trips to such un-museum-like places as the Nixon Library, funny-car shows, and amusement parks, all to get them to think about art's relationship to the non-art-world world. What he's not too crazy about is the media's need to put a label on art, whether it's his or his students'. In other words, he's not at all that wild about me at the moment.

"For a long time, UCLA was like an ivory tower school, very out of touch," he says, kicking one tire after another. "I got here in 1981. Chris Burden [the infamous sculptor and self-destructive performance artist] was already here at the same time, and we were big exceptions to what was a very retro, old-guard group. Around '87, a group of us kind of took over. We dechaired the Chair, pushed out the old farts, and started to fill the department with working artists. Then the school got a lot better."

So what exactly is UCLA's secret?

"None," he says. "Most art schools are about teachers and students. UCLA is about artists working as artists. And UCLA isn't conceptually oriented. You don't have to write a fifty-page thesis. You just have to make things. The reason the kids here are getting all this early success is because they're not art students, they're young artists. Young artists get galleries. Students study. Simple as that."

A phone rings in the house. When it stops after two rings, Ray guesses that his girlfriend, the artist and UCLA alumna Jennifer Pastor, is home. The kitchen door opens, and Pastor comes out toting their portable phone. She's a sweet-faced, compact thirty-year-old. "It's Liz," she says.

Ray grabs the phone. "Yeah, Liz . . . Have you looked in the gallery where your piece is going to go? . . . Yeah? . . . What's nice about that stuff is that it's like the inside of a jellyfish, because it has a linear structure to it. . . . Yeah, just light the trash bag on fire in the kitchen, and say you smelled smoke, because the cops will take ten minutes to get there. . . . No, there's this two-part primer that'll work perfectly. Here, talk to Jennifer. She knows about it." He hands the phone back to her.

"Liz?" Pastor says. "What are you trying to paint?"

Ray heads into the kitchen, tears a banana from its bunch, and puts some water on for coffee. He peels the banana, and shuffles back and forth in the room in a slouchy moonwalk, casting desperate glances at the stove.

"You know what somebody asked me the other day?" He adopts a pinched, European-esque accent. "He said, 'Is UCLA art a new kind of art that is hemorrhaging into the art world?' And I told him, 'Art hemorrhages into the art world and dies from lack of blood.' You think I like being in the art world? You think any of us do? No. We're there because we have to be there. If we teach the students anything, it's to not let the art world bleed their work to death."

But does he think they're doing something totally new?

"No," he says, obviously frustrated. "Nobody is. But there's something unfamiliar about it, and that's saying a lot."

I tell him how a number of the students I've talked to say mushrooms and acid have helped them see the world more complexly, and how that complexity shows in their work. Could that somehow be the key to their . . . ?

"Oh, Jesus. Every youth culture is druggy," Ray says, and gives me a look like, Why are you telling me this? "That isn't something . . . look, all I can say is their work isn't about the psychedelic. That's too easy." He walks over to the stove and watches water boil for a few seconds. "To me, what the students are doing is reenchanting the world."

Evan Holloway and his friend Amy Sarkisian, a twenty-seven-year-old sculptor, are doing the Friday evening traffic in his dad's '85 Nissan 200SX. They're on a steam-releasing trip to Universal City Walk, a gargantuan theme-park-like outdoor mall in the Hollywood Hills. If anything in the world is the antithesis of fine art, they figure it's this consumer-absorbing monstrosity, and besides, they've heard it has a great "3-D vampire ride or something."

The son of hard-core Christian, working-class parents, Holloway grew up in the Los Angeles suburb of Whittier. He left home young, drifted in and out of several universities, and lived for a time in Tacoma, Washington, basically to be near the then burgeoning grunge scene. If he hadn't been accepted into UCLA, he planned to go to trade school and become a refrigerator repairman. When he first arrived at school he was making messy, charming junk assemblage sculpture that the faculty found "troubling." But in the last year, he's found his voice, as they say. The teachers are more supportive, and Holloway's studio is a regular stop for the invading art honchos. Things look good, but he's "maxing out" his student loans, and most of his work, like the drum box, is too grand and unwieldy to sell. Still, he's easily UCLA's most improved graduate student this year, and for now, that means a lot.

"When I came to UCLA I had no idea what was going on," he says. "I mean, I'd heard about Chris Burden's piece where he had a friend shoot him with a rifle and said it was art, and I thought that was cool. But my friends in Tacoma were just guys in bands, and they were completely bewildered by what I was doing. For me, this is the first time in my life that I've been in the right place at the right time."

Holloway parks and we work our way up to Universal City Walk, which looks like the entire Vegas Strip squashed onto a plot of land the size of a small high school campus. After a while we spot a street performer dressed in Hawaiian drag doing a marionette show based on dead rock stars. Dangling from his fingers is a tiny, loose-limbed Kurt Cobain puppet, complete with face-obscuring bangs, painted-on stubble, and a plastic guitar-ette. It proceeds to rock out, stage dive, and knock over a miniature amp.

"Oh, my God." Holloway laughs, and they go into hysterics, less about the Kurt marionette than the weird puppeteer, who's doing this kind of freaky, ultra-serious ballet. "Do you think he has a girlfriend?"

"And if so, is she proud of him?" Sarkisian adds.

They make it through the little Jimi Hendrix and Jim Morrison numbers, but when Janis Joplin struts on, they're giggled out. Holloway finds them a vacant bench, and they crash there, studying the shoppers and garish storefronts until they're either dead tired or slightly depressed.

"I already miss the Warner Building," Sarkisian says under her breath.

"I've got to get off my ass," Holloway mumbles. "Or I guess I should. All I want to do is get loaded, go in my studio, and let things happen. My peers and I are really talented, but realistically, we're not all going to get grabbed."

"Yeah, but sometimes I feel like a lot of people at UCLA think showing is more important than the work," Sarkisian says. "I can't see that. Maybe I'm just naïve."

"Paul McCarthy talks a lot about making things happen for yourself," Holloway says. "That's what he did, that's what Charley did. But fuck if I know what to do. At least I've got the band."

A guitarist as well as an artist, Holloway recently formed a group, Ovaltone, with fellow students Francesca Gabbiani and Gregg Einhorn. A softly noisy, song-oriented outfit, they've played a few campus gigs, and are angling for a show at Spaceland, LA's grooviest rock club.

"Did I tell you, Amy?" Holloway says. "Brian McMahon, you know of Slint and the For Carnation, saw that last show we did at Warner, and he's going to put in a good word with Spaceland's booker."

"Cool." Sarkisian grins absentmindedly.

Holloway grins, too, but it crumbles. Suddenly he's just one tiny figure in a throng of people looking for something extraordinary to do.

"Even if nothing happens, at least I can repair refrigerators," he says. "That's something I learned while working at Starbucks in Tacoma—when refrigerators go down, the world falls apart."

It's four AM, a few days later. The Warner studios are packed with frazzled students working overtime to get their pieces in shape for the final review show, now less than three weeks away. Tim Rogeberg is polishing off his contribution, a mobile-like mini-solar-system of planetesque sculptures that, fingers crossed, will resemble an extremely fucked-up astronomical science demonstration. Having waterproofed his studio's floor, he's about to flood the space with a pool of chemicals when he yells to Holloway in the studio next door. "We need a blowout or something," he tells me. "Everybody's bickering over tools and things. I'm thinking about throwing a party that's more like a collaboration, kind of a performance piece. Something to get us all working together." Holloway arrives, and he's happy to help. By the time they crash on the couches that litter the building, it's dawn, and there's an announcement chalked out on the Warner blackboard. PARTY HERE TONIGHT, it reads. BLOOD WRESTLING. KEG. MUST WEAR COSTUME.

By ten the next evening, the place is a zoo, maybe thirty students, each one overdressed to freak. Holloway is wearing a gigantic, upside-down Christmas stocking with holes cut out for the face and the arms. It takes everyone a weirdly long time to recognize Craft beneath her Afro wig, feather boa, fishnet stockings, and stilettos. Gregg Einhorn has gone the Dada route with a pointed paper hat, oversized beak, and angel's wings. Rogeberg's character is called Trippy Longstocking, which I suppose is self-explanatory. Francesca Gabbiani is a "pregnant '70s chick." And Sarkisian keeps disappearing into her studio to change costumes, from the Unabomber to the Zodiac Killer and back again, because "I think they're the same person."

In the middle of the floor is an inflatable plastic kiddie pool, which Rogeberg has filled with a mixture of stage blood, jelly, Kool-Aid, and chocolate. Students have been shoving each other in its direction all night, but no one's taken the plunge. Then someone knocks Holloway into the gory liquid, and a free-for-all erupts. Two messy hours later, it's down to a wrestling match between Craft and Holloway. Most of the students have gone home by now, but a hard-core "blood"-soaked handful remain, cheering hoarsely for their favorite. Craft may wind up the most celebrated artist of her generation, and Holloway may spend his life fixing refrigerators and making weird contraptions in his basement, but tonight they're just interchangeable pieces of a wacky extravaganza that has UCLA stamped all over it. It's no big deal necessarily. Still, it's not quite like anything I've ever seen, and I can understand what Ray meant. I'm entranced. It's hard to say if this is an apt metaphor for the whole UCLA aesthetic, or just a bunch of drunken weirdos having fun the only way they know how. Anyway, if I asked them which, they'd probably just push me into the pool.

REAL PERSONAL
Bob Mould
(September 1994)

From the air, Austin, Texas, looks like a toy train set, but without the train. The trees are a little too pretty, too . . . organized. Buildings, most of them the color of fresh sandcastles, poke cutely through the foliage. The landscape is beige and very flat in all directions. Everything looks faded, I guess on account of the sunlight, which is fierce. It's early July. Texas is in the middle of an unusually long heat wave. One hundred degrees, according to a flight attendant. No joke. Waiting outside the airport a few minutes later, eyes peeled for Bob Mould's silver Subaru, I'm forced to do a little war dance to keep the soles of my tennis shoes from merging with the sidewalk.

Last time I saw Mould, his band, Sugar, was whizzing through Los Angeles on its *Beaster* mini-tour. He and I had recently become friendly, and I was hanging out backstage at the Palladium, trying to act cool, as a succession of alternative-rock gods—Michael Stipe, Evan Dando, and Frank Black among them—dropped by the dressing room to pay their respects. Mould is one of the most honest, bullshit-free, unpretentious people you'll ever meet, but it's hard not to feel humbled around him. I'm not sure why. I mean, it's totally natural to feel indebted to someone whose work helped define your belief and emotions, like Mould and Hüsker Dü did mine. But even Stipe, who's known the guy for more than a decade and is no artistic slouch himself, acted all shy and fidgety, crouching before Mould's folding chair like an acolyte, asking sweet fan-style questions. And Frank Black, who looks a little like Mould crossed with a character out of *Peanuts*, literally toed the floor and blushed as the two compared touring horror stories.

"Hey!" It's Mould's slightly twangy Midwestern accent. He waves me inside his car, then steers for the 'burbs. "How about this heat, huh?" Wearing his usual faded, untucked T-shirt and loose jeans, Mould is a kind of ageless everyman. He's over six feet tall, with a pale, round face, blue eyes, and short, fine, reddish blond hair.

"Do you know them?" It takes me a few seconds to recognize the wheezy, ironic, heartbroken tones of Sebadoh issuing from his tape deck.

Great band, I say, nodding at a speaker.

"Yeah, I'm hoping maybe we can hook up with them for a West Coast tour this fall."

Makes sense.

"Yeah," he says, maybe with a slight uncertainty.

You should produce a record for them, I say.

"Oh, I don't know. Producing is okay, but think about it this way. Pick out an album that you liked marginally when it came out, then got totally sick of. Imagine having to listen to nothing but that record for two months. You have to be pretty selective."

Turn a lot of people down?

"I get a lot of offers. From Crosby, Stills and Nash to—I was supposed to do the latest Lush album. But I had to back out because they sent me a tape of all the material, and I kept choosing the wrong girl's songs." He laughs. "I had to get out before I broke up the band. No, I think I'll stick around here for a while, thanks."

Mould has lived in Austin for a little over a year now, after a couple of years in Brooklyn and Jersey City. With his friend Kevin O'Neill, he cohabits a roomy Mission-style brick house in central Austin, north of the university. Once this house formed the centerpiece of a gargantuan ranch, complete with lake, crops, horses. Long ago subdivided into a woodsy neighborhood, the property is still substantial enough to hold, in addition to the main house, a two-story guest quarters wherein Mould is building a recording studio, and a small pond, recently dug by O'Neill and packed with belching bullfrogs. The main house's interior is dark and cozy, a stained-wood maze with large rooms and high-ceilinged hallways. The furniture is elegantly nondescript. The stereo is no great shakes, and its turntable is busted. There are a few very un-trendy figurative paintings on the walls, some of them by friends, like the singer-songwriter Vic Chesnutt, others selected from O'Neill's modest collection of works by Southern "outsider" artists.

We plop down at the dining room table, absorbing the first icy tickles from a rattling AC. Mould leans way over, rubbing the stomach of their scruffy dog, Domino. O'Neill, a slender, handsome, preppily dressed blond, appears with coffee and samples of the cover art for Sugar's new album, which have just arrived via FedEx. We pass them around. Mould and O'Neill are bemused by the eccentric, knick-knacky design—a soft, cartoony pattern that wouldn't look inappropriate on the walls of some hipster's kitchen. Mould chose it precisely because it's the last thing people will expect from Sugar, especially after *Beaster*'s sinister cover shot of a bloody, coiled rope.

Strangely enough, it suits the new album just fine. *File Under: Easy Listening*, Sugar's third LP, sounds positively cheery. It may be the happy-go-luckiest batch of songs Mould has penned since Hüsker Dü's *Flip Your Wig* in the mid-'80s. After the tormented beauty of *Copper Blue* and *Beaster*, the lightness of the new songs, such as "Granny Cool" and "Gee Angel," feels victorious, not to mention hard-won. Does it follow, I wonder, that Mould's feeling A-OK these days?

"Well, I felt pretty good when I wrote those songs." Mould, who laughs easily, gives a tense chuckle. And his hands knot together in his lap.

But not anymore?

He shoots O'Neill a very complicated glance. Maybe O'Neill shoots back an equally complicated glance. "Nope," says Mould. And they both laugh.

Turns out that *FU:EL* almost didn't happen. The first recording sessions last spring at an Atlanta studio were so unsatisfactory that Mould broke them off, flew back to Austin, and half considered disbanding Sugar. He's still not sure what went wrong. But after a couple of intercontinental phone powwows, the trio reconvened in another studio, and this time everything clicked. Still, Mould remains unnerved and often depressed by this first serious stumbling block in Sugar's short history.

And there's been some fallout. A recent solo appearance at London's Royal Albert Hall—part of a celebration of ten years of Alan McGee's maverick Creation label, which puts out Sugar's records in Britain—turned into something of a psychodrama when Mould's low spirits clashed with the event's pressures to party down, leading to a performance so intense and erratic that some English critics fretted about the state of his mental health in print. This "funk," as he describes it, has yet to lift. Rykodisc, Sugar's American label, thinks *FU:EL* could be a commercial breakthrough, but Mould reports this bit of good news with a shrug. *Copper Blue*, which sold extremely well, achieved success over such a long period of time that it never actually entered Billboard's Top 200, and things never got too crazy on a publicity-fame level. But *FU:EL* could easily enter the charts in the Top 50, if not higher, and Mould can only imagine the hell that could result. All that promotion, all those overtly personal questions, etc. . . . Does it make him think about Kurt Cobain?

"Yeah," he says, spacing out into a sad, sad look. "I wonder if Kurt ever wanted the fame. Or whether he wasn't just caught in this industry that feeds on frail, emotional people."

Did he know Cobain well?

"No, not really. We talked. But his death was definitely a shock, a big letdown. God, that was rough." And Mould looks at O'Neill. "Did I ever tell you that I was originally approached to produce *Nevermind*?" And he looks at me.

No way.

"Mm-hmm." Mould laughs. "Obviously, it didn't happen. But had it happened, well, *Nevermind* would have been a very different sounding record, I'll tell you."

Less clean?

"A lot less clean."

Things might have gone a lot more sanely for Nirvana.

"Maybe. Who knows? But anyway, back to what you were saying about people confusing an artist's work with his life . . ." He smiles thinly. "Are you referring to the Hüsker Dü shit?"

"Partly." Like a lot of other Mould fans I know, I had mistakenly assumed that the songs on *Copper Blue* were about the ex–Hüsker Dü drummer, Grant Hart. That assumption was contingent on another rather common assumption that Hart and he had been lovers at the time of Hüsker Dü's breakup. But that was before I knew Mould very well, and when I finally got around to testing this interpretation on him, he'd been completely astonished.

"Yeah, that's fucking bizarre," Mould says, remembering our conversation. "That's one I'd never heard before. Not even on the Internet."

Everybody I know thinks you were an item.

"Nope, not at all. Grant wishes." He laughs uproariously. "I'm kidding. Look, I've always wanted people to have the freedom to make the ultimate interpretation of my songs, whether it's something as bizarre as, 'Oh, Bob is writing songs about Grant because he's still upset about the breakup of Hüsker Dü,' or whether it's the people who come up to Kevin and say, 'I saw you having coffee with Bob. Are his songs about you?' " Mould lets out another huge laugh. "Kevin always says, 'Hey, do you think I'd be having coffee with Bob if those songs were about me?'"

I guess that's one of the pitfalls of keeping your mouth shut.

"Maybe. When Hüsker Dü broke up, I just stayed out of it. I let Grant say what he was going to say, and I didn't weigh in. I had a lot of personal stuff to figure out. Ultimately, who knows what happened? I'd gotten sober, someone else in the band hadn't. There were a lot of things. But the only song I had ever written that's had anything directly to do with the breakup of Hüsker Dü is 'The Poison Years.' At least that I know of. But . . . Grant and I as lovers? That's too much."

And while we're demystifying you, you weren't a junkie either?

"I wasn't a junkie," he repeats. "Heroin wasn't my problem. Drinking and speed. Speed really ate a hole in me, and it's still there. It's permanent." He raises his hand and looks at the back, the palm. "You can see right through it."

Mould knows that I'm going to get around to the issue of his sexual preference. In the last year especially, he's begun to be outed in print—in zines, in gay periodicals, and even in a few mainstream magazines. Just two days earlier, I'd questioned a British journalist friend's plan to mention Mould's homosexuality in a forthcoming magazine article. She just rolled her eyes, saying he was already out in England.

Last fall, Mould and I had discussed how I might handle the topic if I ever got the opportunity to write about him. Well, here we are, and it's a far more difficult and complex moment than gay activists would have you believe. Like Mould, I have doubts about both the importance of these kinds of self-labeling pronouncements and the public's right to know. But there's fierce external pressure on Mould to acknowledge his sexuality in a clear way, and he wants to get it over with so that Sugar and he can do what they do. So, since we're already on the topic of demystification, I wonder aloud if it's time to make the leap.

"Yeah, I guess we can. But let's eat first." He looks at O'Neill, who has been watching Mould with his usual tender concern. "You hungry?"

O'Neill nods furiously.

We hop in the Subaru, blast the AC, crank the Sebadoh, and head to Threadgill's, a legendary local eatery with an eccentric, faux-Americana decor and a menu huge enough to accommodate both O'Neill's vegetarianism and Mould's meaty diet. Some of the younger patrons recognize Mould as soon as we walk in. Their mouths stop moving and one or two people point, but no one approaches, and he seems oblivious and relaxed.

As serious as Mould can be, he's also a lot of fun, not to mention a great storehouse of (unconfirmed) information and gossip about the rock world. Over the course of our roughly hour-long meal he: (1) breaks the bad news that his brilliant, finicky friend Kevin Shields of My Bloody Valentine has just scrapped MBV's long-awaited, nearly completed new album; (2) acknowledges the existence of secret sound recordings, made by an acquaintance, on which Kurt Cobain and Courtney Love allegedly are heard having intense, unflattering (to her) shouting matches; and (3) describes recording studio troubles on the Butthole Surfers front that make *FU:EL*'s difficult birth seem trivial.

But before you deduce that deep down, under all that integrity, Mould is just another excitable rumormonger, you need to hear the horrified tone of his gossiping. One of Mould's favorite words is "information." He talks a lot about the importance of the complete picture, and how the media amorally distort and eroticize information under the guise of telling all. Another of his favorite words, at least during this visit, is "freak." He uses it to describe self-imposed victims of culture's information mania. Specifically some of his peers—the Farrells, Dandos, Loves, et al.—are intelligent folk and true artists whom he sees as behaving like rock 'n' roll cartoons in a desperate attempt to snag the media's limited attention span. "Freak" is what he's afraid of becoming, should the media discover some reducible, exploitable part of his personality. And homosexuality appears to be their idea of that long-awaited hook.

But, well, Mould can explain all this far better than I can. And after a quick stop at his favorite local record store to buy the new Guided by Voices EP, we streak home so he can do just that. O'Neill, who handles Sugar's business affairs, retires to a room just off the kitchen. Mould gives Domino a few stomach rubs. Then he and I head to the den, pull up two chairs to the coffee table, and warily study the tiny skyscraper of my microcassette recorder.

"Okay, let's go for it." Mould blinks at the recorder's red light, then sits back in his chair, and looks off into the distance. "Well," he says, "it seems that a lot of publications are hovering around, expecting some kind of grand statement about my sexuality. I don't think it's any kind of secret within the music industry and within the fan base at large what my sexual preference is. But this year it seems to be a gigantic issue. You know, 'Bob, it's time for you to come out and represent the gay community.' Or, 'Bob, it's time for you to be a role model because you are a successful artist who has transcended your "affliction," your "stigma," your . . .' something that I had fucking nothing to do with. I was born with it. My life is no different than anyone else's. People are going to have to get over the fact that I prefer not to talk about my sexual preference, nor do I really care about reading about anyone else's sexual preference. Because everybody on this earth, as far as I know, has a sexual preference. And if people are going to continually come to me looking for some kind of description, whether it be philosophical or sordid in nature, well . . ." And his eyes kind of charge.

"I am not a fucking freak." He looks at me. "I'm not going to be paraded around like a freak. I don't like the word 'gay' because I don't know what the word really means. The fact that I'm supposed to make outrageous statements to gain more column space in music publications is insulting. And if the gay community doesn't like it, then too fucking bad. I'm not your spokesperson, because I don't know what you're about. I'm a person, a human being. I'm an artist. I write songs. I'm a storyteller. I don't think, 'Hey, is it time to write a happy gay pop song, or is it time to write a depressing gay pop song?' Who the fuck sits down to think about that shit? Who in their right mind thinks like that? I don't. I expect to be judged on how I treat other people and how I carry myself as a human being. I do not flaunt my sexuality. I do not deny my sexuality. It is my sexuality. It is not the public's sexuality. It is none of their fucking business. I don't do what I do for some flag that I'm supposed to wave, I do it for Bob. People better get over that. I'm not a fucking freak. Or at least not because of that. I might be a freak for other reasons, because I'm a control freak, because of my compulsive behavior, because of my character flaws. But not because of that."

Anybody who really knows his work, I say, won't be surprised by his discomfort at the idea of being labeled.

"I am an island." Mould laughs. "And I like it that way."

I'd argue that the really oppressed people in American society circa 1994 are individuals like Mould who feel confined by the notion of collective identity.

"I'm not questioning my sexuality," Mould says. "That's never been a question in my whole life, for as long as I can remember. What I'm questioning is, am I supposed to be the cause célèbre for something I don't understand? And I know there are a lot of conflicts in what I'm saying. I know there are a lot of people who are going to hate this and say, 'Oh Bob, what a fucking loser. This is such bullshit. What a cop-out.' Well, I've been writing songs since I was nine years old. And I don't feel like I have to turn a very unimportant sidebar in my life into a headline just to compete with all the other freaks. And listen, if people don't like it, ultimately, they can fuck off. They can rot in hell."

Does he think the fascination with his sexuality is part of the larger trend of people substituting intense, mythical, media-controlled relationships with troubled celebrities for, well, real relationships?

"Sure. Kerrigan and Harding, O. J. Simpson, the Menendezes . . . none of these stories really speak to anyone, do they? They don't speak to me anyway. All these alleged tragic figures. What are people really absorbing from these spectacles? What's the information here? If this is what the world's coming to, then everything is just about a freak alert."

He shakes his head. "Society is losing its grip. It's like, we don't have the circus anymore. We don't have the He-She, the Dog Boy. Instead we have a bunch of people trying to cop this psychotherapy babble to sell records. Like this 'I'm clean when I'm really using dope' concept. Issue after issue of every magazine is just thriving on it. Magazines are in the industry of supporting the industry, let's not kid ourselves. It's not about the value of your work anymore, it's about the sordid details of your private life. There's no sanctity. Well, listen, I've got nothing to hide, but there are some things that are mine and only mine. I think I give people more than enough of my things. But there are some things that belong just to me."

PHONER
The Sonic Youth Liner Notes
(November 1994)

Click.

"Yeah?"

"Thurston Moore?" Cubby drops a pencil's nub onto the paper stack in his lap.

"Yeah. And you're . . . ?"

"Uh, my name's Cubby Branch." He starts doodling a skull. "Can I . . . interview you? Just for, like, a minute?" Doodle, doodle.

Thurston breathes out, an irritated-sounding rattle made kind of supernatural by the cheapo speaker in Cubby's greasy receiver. "It'll have to be quick."

"God, *thanks.*" Cubby clears his throat. He focuses on the almost imperceptible, eye-deadening grain in the top sheet of paper, so as not to let any rapport, good or bad, start with one of his four total idols, because . . . well, just because. "So I want to know why Sonic Youth does what it . . . *does.*"

"Meaning?"

Cubby looks around his room until his eyes hit a mirror, him in it. His eyes are so burnt-out and bloodshot they seem one-dimensional, like peephole views of an American flag. Otherwise he's just him, i.e., stoned, too thin, fucked-up hair, needy-looking. . . . Shit. He refocuses on the blurry pattern of ground-up, processed, bleached wood in his lap, which neutralizes his thoughts a little. Cool. "Meaning . . . ," he says. "Uh, *I* don't know. To understand how you think, I guess."

Deep in the cave of the earpiece, Thurston . . . snickers?

"Like . . . what was the difference between doing the, uh, *Dirty* album and doing the earlier stuff from, you know, way back in the, uh . . . eighties?"

"The eighties, huh?" Thurston sounds kind of . . . pissed, which would sound really great on a record, but, like, one on one, is a little nerve-racking, obviously. "Well," he adds. "We're better at what we do now."

"Right. Of course. Duh." Cubby's transcribing wildly, not that he's actually going to print this in a magazine or anything. "And what do you think of . . . fans like me? How differently do you feel now from . . . the way you used to think of us? You know, before you got famous and everything?"

"You're the reason we happen, dude."

"Then you're glad we worship you? 'Cos we *do*. I'm in this phase of playing *'Sister' all the time.* Check this out." Cubby reaches over and cranks up his stereo. The song "Cotton Crown" happens to be playing. He holds the receiver into that spacey onslaught. . . . *I'm wasted in time and you're never ready.* . . . After a minute, he turns down the volume and slams the earpiece into his ear again. "See?"

"Yeah . . . thanks." Thurston emits this noise that's the auditory equivalent of a shrug.

"But, uh . . . back to the worshipping question?" Cubby waits, listens, filling in blanks, etc., but it's taking Thurston for-fucking-ever to answer. "So," he continues tentatively. "You're saying, uh . . . ultimately . . .

that you're not . . . sure? Wait, wait. Give me a sec. I'm . . . writing this down . . . uh . . . Okay, ready."

"Ultimately?" Thurston's back to sort of snickering again. "Sure. Worship away."

"Thanks, ha ha." Cubby's scribbling. "Does us being, uh . . . male or female make any difference to you?"

There's this weird lull.

"Uh . . . you still there, Thurston?"

"Yeah. Is that a trick question?"

Cubby casts a little glance at his bedroom door. It's reassuringly shut. In the way, way distance he can hear his girlfriend tidying herself in the bathroom. "Sort of."

"Hm . . ."

Cubby quits writing and shakes his cramped hand a bit, worrying about that *hm*.

"So you're a male, I'm guessing," says Thurston.

"Yeah." Cubby snorts up some wobbly nose-goo and swallows it.

"And you're how old?"

"Uh . . . thirteen."

"And . . . why do you want to know?" Thurston's mouth's started making this, like, impatient clicking sound.

" 'Cos . . . Shit. Don't, like, hate me, but . . . your music gives me a boner, ha ha ha. Always. It's weird. Especially the, uh, *Sister* album, and . . . *especially* when *you're* singing. And *especially especially* on . . . You know in 'Schizophrenia' when you sing that line about, uh, 'Her brother says she's just a bitch with a golden chain'? Well, when you sing that, I'm thinking, 'Yeah, I *am* a bitch, Thurston,' you know? And I guess I'm worried whether you think I'm weird for interpreting that that way. Does it freak you out to know there's a kid in the world who gets a boner from your music . . . but especially from *you*? *You know what I mean?*"

"Gee." Thurston chuckles. In the earpiece there's this very faint *ding dong*. "Can you hold on, Cubby?" There's a clunk as Thurston's receiver's laid down on a table or something. While his idol's away, Cubby fills in blanks, crosses t's, etc. Out of decency, he tries not to take in what Thurston's and some other voice are discussing, but it's a chore to tune out since every other word's something interesting like "Geffen Records" or "tour" or "video shoot." "I have to cut this short," Thurston says suddenly. His voice is so loud and distorted that Cubby wrenches the receiver away from his ear for a second.

"Who's . . . there?" Cubby asks, wincing.

"A friend."

"Is he or she someone I might've heard of, ha ha ha?"

"Could be." Thurston's breaths have speeded up for some reason. Probably from, like, moving around or whatever. Duh. "You ever heard of Kim Gordon?" Thurston chuckles. "But seriously . . . " He has *such a beautiful fucking surferish way of talking.* Wow! There *is* a God. "I'm kind of busy at the moment."

"Kim Gordon!" Cubby punches himself in the head, albeit gently. "Tell her hi for me."

"Okay." Thurston clears his throat. "Hi from Cubby."

Now, from deep in the phone, a very faint voice, obviously Kim's, says, "Hi, Cubby," in a, uh, sullen-type way that could either sound totally sincere or bored to death depending on the level of a listener's paranoia, intelligence, etc. Such is her genius, thinks Cubby daydreamily. Then his ears catch the way-spooky creaking floor sounds that undoubtedly signal his girlfriend's return. Shi-i-i-it.

"Shit, uh . . . I'm gonna go now, Thurston, and, uh, hopefully get another boner thanks to you, ha ha ha, and you can, uh, go fuck Kim or whatever you guys want to do." Cubby stares, horrified, at his bedroom door.

Creak, creak, creak . . .

"Later, Cubby."

"Yeah, uh . . . Thanks a billion, Thurston."

Click.

JUNKIE SEE, JUNKIE DO
(March 1995)

When an Alice in Chains video comes on MTV, most of us either crank the volume or immediately change channels. But heroin addicts and struggling former addicts hear something in Layne Staley's grade-school junkie poetry that we can't: a kind of siren. As someone who has had several close friends who were strung out on heroin in the past two years, I think I have a sense of how this private call-and-response works, even if I can't understand the mechanisms. According to my friends, just the mention of the word "heroin" in a lyric, or a photograph of a hypodermic on a CD cover, or the sight of junkie musicians all wrapped up in some glamorous video, and they go crazy with longing for the stuff, even when, as in the case of Alice in Chains, they know full well that what they are hearing and seeing is silly and contrived. Recently, I saw one of the most intelligent people I know absolutely freak out watching the old Thompson Twins video "Don't Mess With Doctor Dream." One minute we were guffawing at its cheesy imagery—spinning needles, screaming skulls, sanctimonious antidrug captions—and the next minute he was a jittery wreck begging me to drive him downtown so he could buy a few bags.

Can I blame MTV? Maybe, at least according to Michigan's Institute for Social Research (ISR). It recently conducted a survey in which fifty thousand high school students around the United States were asked about drugs. According to the study, drug use is on the rise again. Big surprise. And Dr. Lloyd D. Johnston, the program director of ISR, thinks the problem lies in the representation of drug use in contemporary music, films, and rock videos. Like generations of academics before him, he sees teenagers as a kind of intellectually passive, easily seduced herd in need of strict parental guidance. Never mind that this conclusion is pure speculation, and not based on data actually unearthed by the survey. In this confused world of ours, even the appearance of fact attains a kind of godlike status, and statisticians, those great cultural simplifiers, are considered something on the order of gods. Thus, when the *New York Times* reported the results of this survey, Johnston's ruminations were treated as though they were the story, and the teens' statements were lost in the shuffle. It's all spurious, but coming on the heels of the aforementioned Thompson Twins fiasco it got me to wondering whether Johnston has a point.

Donna Gaines, a sociologist and the author of *Teenage Wasteland: Suburbia's Dead End Kids*, doesn't think so. She sees youth culture and drug use as historically enmeshed. "With MTV, drug use has just taken on the status of a commodity," she says. "When I was younger and some actress was wearing a really cool miniskirt in a movie, I wanted that miniskirt. Now when you see some guy getting fucked up on MTV, you want to get fucked up. But videos are expressive rather than coercive. I don't see it as a causal relationship. Anyway, most hard-core drug users don't watch MTV. Its audience is mainstream. And I don't think it's such a great cultural force anyway. Maybe for twelve-year-olds."

The video director Samuel Bayer, who has worked with Nirvana and Hole among others, gives MTV more credit, but thinks the network is sufficiently prudent in its policies. "I grew up in the seventies, when there were drug references all over the place," he says. "Kids are smart enough to read between the lines. Something like Kurt Cobain dying—that's what happens when your life is fucked up. If anything, videos have the opposite effect."

In the same *New York Times* article that reported Johnston's findings, Carole Robinson, a senior vice president at MTV, said that the network's guidelines call for programming that does not "promote, glamorize, or show as socially acceptable the use of illegal drugs or the abuse of legal drugs." And anyone who watches MTV regularly has noticed those little Tinkerbell-like digital blurs clinging to the pot leaves on hip-hop artists' caps. In the current Tom Petty video, a line about rolling a joint has been auditorially altered into a nonsensical slur. Especially since Cobain's death, the network's nonmusic programming has been nearly didactic in its cautionary tone regarding hard drug use. Still, you don't need a degree in deconstruction to see the signs of drugginess all over MTV, whether it's Alice in Chains's elegant little travelogues of junkie life, or Ministry's "Just One Fix" clip, in which heroin withdrawal is given a snazzy, action-packed movie-trailer look, or even Tori Amos's clip for "God," in which a character simulates "tying off." If kids are smart enough to know what's fiction and what's not, then they are smart enough to decode these kinds of messages, too.

If MTV has a drug policy, it's a confused one. It is as if the network had chosen to approach drug-related videos the way a makeup artist might approach crow's-feet on an aging actress. Pot leaves, pills, and hypodermic needles are successfully smudged beyond recognition, but the subtleties remain. Maybe this kind of approach works with drugs such as pot, cocaine, and acid, although I doubt it. But heroin is a complicated beast with a very subtle system of signifiers, most of which are invisible to nonusers' eyes. Take the aforementioned Ministry clip. To

MTV, it must read as an anti-heroin statement, with a surface narrative in which two young junkies detox in a shabby hotel room intercut with shots of heroin icon William S. Burroughs waving his hands in a cautionary manner à la the giant alien in *Twin Peaks*. But look closer and there's old Al Jourgensen himself slouched in the hotel's lobby. In one telling close-up, he looks at the camera and rubs his nose with one finger. It's a nervous tic common to junkies, and a signal to knowledgeable viewers that Jourgensen, or rather his character, is loaded on the stuff. So later when the boys leave the hotel, supposedly detoxed and ready for the world, and Jourgensen picks them up hitchhiking, there's a definite subtext, i.e., they'll be shooting up again any minute.

A few weeks ago, I happened to catch Primal Scream's "Rocks" video on MTV's *Alternative Nation*. Primal Scream is a U.K. band whose work flaunts the meagerness of its members' imagination and technical ability. Its records are affectionate pastiches of other, more talented bands' music, past and present. It's all very postmodern. In its current incarnation, Primal Scream is pretending to be junkie rock. Keith Richards, Johnny Thunders, and Gram Parsons are the obvious models. Last year, the band even caused a little scandal in the British rock music press by jokily referring to the late River Phoenix as a "lightweight." In the "Rocks" clip, front man Bobby Gillespie stumbles around slurring about the joys of unmitigated hedonism. His hair is long and filthy, his skin has the hue of a corpse, and his mouth hangs partway open in an imitation of someone nodding out on his feet. I think you're supposed to be bemused. But all I could think about while watching this freak show was what my troubled friend would do when he saw him.

Because heroin withdrawal is such an agonizing process, and the recovery period so long and psychologically disruptive, it doesn't take much to make former addicts slip. Heroin may be a nasty business on a day-to-day basis, but the drug's immediate effect is profoundly pleasurable. My friends say it is like the ultimate orgasm, elongated and unattached to the rest of the world. Its intensity, they tell me, makes life's relatively sober comforts like friendship, romance, and sex seem petty. So reentering the world in which these things are generally held as sacred can feel, I'm told, like a compromise, especially in the first year or so, when your body's gradual reconstruction causes almost continual discomfort. Thus even something like Kurt Cobain's suicide, which most of us interpret as the ultimate anti-heroin statement, has a double meaning. For instance, the morning I heard the news, I phoned up a Nirvana fan I knew who was struggling to stay off dope, and begged her to please fucking quit before she ends up like him. "No," she said, her voice edgy with a hunger and anger I couldn't decode. "You don't understand." And she explained how Cobain's inability to stay clean only reinforced her feeling that sobriety wasn't worth the trouble. When I hung up the phone I knew she was going to run out and score. And she did.

When I was a young teen listening to the Velvet Underground and John Lennon's "Cold Turkey," and reading William S. Burroughs and Alex Trocchi, I never—and I think I can include my former friends in this—thought, "Hey, I should try this heroin stuff." Presumably most kids are the same way now. But a number of young rock fans have started shooting heroin because one or more of their heroes has made light of the subject. I know a handful of them myself. I'm talking about talented, smart people who just want to experience everything that there is to experience. To them, River Phoenix convulsing on the sidewalk, or Kristen Pfaff nodding out in a lukewarm bath—these things are as faraway, unreal, and mythical as the song lyrics that render heroin use a profound, sensual voyage into the mysteries of the self. Some people will always choose to do extreme things. Others, maybe most of us, will choose to learn by listening to songs about extreme activities, or by reading nonfictional accounts. So how do those of us who don't really understand what it means to shoot heroin tell users to stop what they're doing because it's scaring us? Well, we can't. But we can air our fears and presumptions and hope for the best.

A former member of several prominent alternative rock bands, who requested anonymity, spoke to me about his own confusion around the representation of heroin in videos. A former junkie, he has been clean for several years. "I can see both sides," he says. "When you're doing dope, it permeates everything you do and think. It feels like enlightenment, and you also feel really alone at the same time, so you want to network. It's not even a conscious thing. I can't even watch MTV anymore, it's so full of junkies. I can spot them in an instant, and I feel like they're calling to me from this terrible and fascinating place in my past. The thing is, they're some of the most interesting musicians around, so it would be crazy to shut them up. So it's just this tortuous paradox." So the only option he sees is looking the other way?

"What other way?" he says. "That's what heroin does, removes you from the scariness in the world. I found out that doesn't work either. If there is an option, it's being strong, and believing in your loved ones. Because everything else, including drugs, is just meaningless entertainment."

Point is, even if MTV could eliminate every shred of every drug reference in every video, it wouldn't make any difference, and it would only cause the network to seem even more untrustworthy than it already is. Why should MTV be self-censorious when the record, television, and film industries are expected to support artistic freedom of expression? Pop culture is a mishmash of images of every type of behavior and attitude. It presents a chaotic, multitudinous portrait of life that becomes a kind of collective truth, which we are then responsible for decoding and using according to our own personal needs at any given moment. For every positive portrayal of drug use, you can be sure there's a negative one somewhere else. It's a balance, and that's fine, because, as painful as it may be to watch friends suffer because of some irresponsible rock star's posey bullshit, we have no control over one another's lives. We choose people to love according to psychological systems that are nobody's business but our own. And if we suffer as a consequence of our love, them's the breaks.

MINOR MAGIC
Quentin Tarantino
(March 1995)

There should be a dozen youngish American filmmakers as inspired as Quentin Tarantino. Then it would be easier to designate him a quirkily brilliant minor director, which is what he is. But even with his rather glaring limitations—stagey archetypal characters, short- and long-term memory problems, a lazy visual sense—there's so much finely tuned energy in his films compared to those of most of his contemporaries. Tarantino really is one of the few post–Martin Scorsese directors capable of bona fide cinematic magic. He isn't in a class with, say, *serioso* experimentalists like Jon Jost and James Benning, but, like them, he is fascinated by Scorsese and *his* obsessions (the intricacies of male angst). Scorsese is deep, and his best films are girded with emotional and spiritual scars. Tarantino gives terrific surface, but in a Ted Kennedy kind of way—he makes you feel like you're in the presence of greatness, even if the charisma is essentially inherited.

Tarantino can do great scenes, and his films' residual narrative drift is busy and clever enough to keep the momentum going. His forte is exquisitely rendered horror: the young drug dealers blown away and Uma Thurman's OD and lifesaving adrenaline shot in *Pulp Fiction*; the cop torture scene in *Reservoir Dogs* (1992); Dennis Hopper's execution by Christopher Walken in the Tarantino-scripted (but not directed) *True Romance* (1993); the slaughter in the diner that opens Oliver Stone's semi-Tarantino-scripted *Natural Born Killers* (1994). Before he became overly enamored of emptily gorgeous spectacle, Bernardo Bertolucci constructed similarly mind-boggling mid-film epiphanies, albeit scenes less triggered by literary games than by massively repressed homosexual longing, almost always by a man for a boy: the adolescent junkie's seduction by a father look-alike in *Luna* (1979); a child's spontaneous shooting of his pedophile suitor in *The Conformist* (1971); the upper-class boy's horrendous murder by his working-class molester in *1900* (1977). Bertolucci's films have a strong political outlook, are versed in twentieth-century philosophy, and are obsessively concerned with and painfully befuddled by their characters' hidden motivations. By comparison, Tarantino's films are pointedly thrill-seeking and apsychological.

Tarantino does one thing with absolute brilliance: he boxes talky, neurotic, bright but half-articulate, schlumpy characters into parallel orbits around an agreeable, slightly flammable, usually trendy topic—Madonna, TV chat shows, kinky sex, etc. The conversations he constructs are so superficially systematic that when one character grows frightened of a commitment to the interchange, separates, and unleashes some private insanity on his or her companion, the effect is nightmarish. In Tarantino's view, contemporary humans are something on the order of walking, talking issues of *Details* magazine, addicted to MTV chat and tabloid trivia. A verbal scrim unites his characters but quarantines the aspects of their psyches they cannot articulate—sexual attraction, emotional involvement, spiritual interests, etc. As a result, his characters are continually jittery, but the psychological reasons for their jitters are never specified, probably because Tarantino is afraid to know them.

While it's easy to recognize his characters' transgressive impulses—which are more savvily up to the minute than authentically personalized—their transgressions have no resonance. In fact, the violence in his films would have a pornographic effect if it weren't for the way he manipulates the viewers' morality. This moralistic fascination with the amoral, which is shared by David Lynch, among others, may be the main reason why, apart from their poetic gift of the gab, Tarantino's films are more compelling than, say, neorealistic "streetwise" TV series like *NYPD Blue*, but less absorbing than a docu-action series like *Cops*, which focuses, with similar irony but less agenda, on a similar social register (disenfranchised lower middle class).

The thing is, Tarantino is such a talented writer, and his neuroses feel unusually emblematic of the general cultural malaise circa the early '90s. His POV, frequently attacked for its cheap shots at the powerless, is actually, albeit *selectively*, compassionate—strangely innocent and guileless. Tarantino tends to rescue and recontextualize unintentionally sublime scenes from the skid row of B-movie history, like some postmodern Florence Nightingale with a soft spot re cultural trash.

Tarantino's writing is so pure in its own weird way that it misfires when he isn't in the director's chair. If it weren't for the prettiness of its script, *True Romance* would be a misshapen and aimless action flick for the MTV set. Its ugliness is too ugly, its cleverness too paved over by technical competence, its POV too blandly disapproving of its protagonists. *Natural Born Killers*, which Tarantino partially scripted and now disowns, has its technical charms, but Stone's cinematographic overdrive flattens the dialogue's obsessive machinations. Tarantino isn't such a great director either (or not yet anyway)—he's just a carefully skillful, sincere one. But it's hard to imagine a better look to go along with his scripts. He may be an artist on the order of the songwriter and fellow ironist Randy Newman, whose complex yet simply crafted songs function only in his own clunky, amateurish renditions. Both men's talents are just a little too idiosyncratic and fueled by unconscious drives to survive an out-of-body experience.

Tarantino's possibly doomed to be an imperfect maverick filmmaker, not what some would like him to be—the new Robert Towne or Paul Schrader, pre-directorial pretensions. While the hype around his skimpy, samey output may strike some as too much too soon, it's not especially surprising. Two or three films down the road, Tarantino's little tricks could well be shtick; in fact, I'd lay money on it. For now, though, his peculiar talent feels real, and obviously life is short.

AIDS
Words from the Front
(April 1995)
(The names of the people in this article have been changed.)

I'm sitting at a table in the Onyx, a dimly lit East Hollywood coffee-house decorated with clumsy neo-Expressionist paintings and half full of book-reading trendoids. Jason, the client of an acquaintance who works with HIV-positive street kids, has agreed to share a couple of days of his endangered life if I promise to plug his band. They're called the Rambo Dolls, and more on them later. That's Jason storming through the entrance. I can just tell.

With his wild blond hair, bony face, huge blue eyes, and grunge garb—ripped jeans, Sandy Duncan's Eye T-shirt, untucked flannels, scuffed Docs—Jason looks like a rock star, specifically Soul Asylum's Dave Pirner. But once he joins me at my table, and I get a closer look, his face is almost scary, just a little too perfectly constructed. It's weird to think someone this conventionally cute could be homeless.

"How did you get infected?" I ask.

"Well, it was either from sharing needles with people I didn't know," he says, staring at his lap, "or from letting guys fuck me without a condom, or from fucking girls I knew had AIDS without a condom. I could've been infected a hundred times, you know?" He pauses, and his stare grows extremely forlorn. "Do you think that makes a difference?" He looks up at me for a second. "I mean, that I could've gotten infected a lot?"

I just sort of stammer that he should, like, be careful.

"Yeah, obviously! I mean, I already should've been . . . more . . ." Suddenly he twists around in his chair, and yells toward the Onyx's door, "Go away! Do something!"

Every head turns. A scrawny young redheaded woman, maybe twenty-six years old, is standing outside on the sidewalk. "All right, all right," she yells back, and blurs out of sight to the right.

His . . . girlfriend?

Jason untwists. "Yeah," he says. "Katie. I'm crashing at her place right now. She's all right, she's just—she wants me to love her and I told her I can't because I'm going to die, but she still wants me to, so . . ." He cringes.

"That's a tough one."

He nods violently. "And she's a heroin junkie, too," he continues, slumping down in his chair. "That's fucked up because I'm off everything now since the HIV thing. So I have to watch her shoot up all the time and it's fucked. But I never liked heroin, so it's easier than if she was doing crystal or something I liked. But it makes her hard to deal with, you know?" He's growing increasingly hangdog, his gaze caught on what looks like a petrified muffin crumb on the table between us.

"I'm sure," I say. Anyway, what's this about his rock band?

"Oh, fuck." He tenses, kicks his chair back away from the table, and makes a face as if he has just been shot. "Now I have to live up to it, right? Maybe you should just come see us rehearse later, like I said. Then you can decide if . . ." He shrugs.

With such organizations as Covenant House, Angel's Flight, the Gay and Lesbian Center, and others all concentrating their efforts on the plight of young runaways, you'd think the situation would be under control, to some degree at least. I did. Not according to Jason. But then he's made a point of avoiding, whenever humanly possible, every aspect of the available support services, though he can't really explain his aversion. He doesn't want to be "controlled" is the short and long of it. According to him, even the most religion-free outreach program has some sort of freedom-obliterating agenda. He prefers to have floating parental figures. In the past, he relied on a series of older men who paid him for sex and whose concern for his welfare was just authentic enough to provide a little comfort, just suspicious enough to be rejected guilt-free whenever he felt like it. Now he counts on his immediate friends, several of whom I will meet later this day, and all of whom seem to be what therapists call "caretaker types"—people devoted to Jason's well-being, often to a slightly hysterical degree. And, yeah, even in our brief contact, I distinctly feel an intense, father-and-son-ish psychological push-pull.

We're leaning on a parked car outside the Onyx. Half a block up the street, Katie keeps yo-yoing in and out of a bookshop, neck craned, checking our status, I guess. I let Jason blab about whatever he wants. Mostly he rags on the Onyx clientele, and how, well, artsy-fartsiness is the opiate of the new bourgeoisie, basically. Classic punk stuff.

Jason may be an emotional wreck, but he's sharp, albeit in a knee-jerk, self-taught kind of way. For instance, his politics and musical tastes were formed by the brainy punk magazine *Maximumrocknroll*, which he's been reading religiously since he was a kid. Now that we're in the daylight, I can see that he has a freshly shoplifted book by the cultural theorist Noam Chomsky shoved between his belt and jeans. He's been meaning to dip into Chomsky since his pre-diagnosis, pre-homeless days, meaning four months ago.

Back then he lived with a bunch of other quasi-anarchistic teen squatters in an abandoned building just off Hollywood Boulevard. He'll talk about that year of his life in great detail, but the time before then—in other words, his entire childhood and adolescence—is off-limits. When he accidentally lets a detail slip—that he grew up in the San Fernando Valley, or that his father is a doctor, for instance—it's accompanied by a kind of physical explosion. The air is punched; the sidewalk stomped. When I press him, all Jason will admit about his past is that whatever happened, which is none of my business, it made him realize how people don't give a shit for each other, no matter what they say.

What about his friends?

"Right," Jason says. "Well, I don't keep them very long. Most of my friends aren't real friends, they're just guys who are into me sexually. But when they realize what an asshole I am, and that I'm never going to let them fuck me, they're gone."

Why doesn't he just let them fuck him? I mean, he's a hustler, so—

"Because they're my friends," he yells. Then he looks down at his scuffed-up Doc Martens, smiles, and clears his throat. "You're into me too, aren't you?"

"No," I say. And I'm not, actually.

Jason glances up. And his smile grows all weird and flirtatious. "Oh yeah, right," he mumbles.

I know that smile. My first boyfriend was a call boy, as were most of his friends. And in the days before AIDS, I used to hang around hustler bars, mostly because I liked the tension in the air. I've been given the hard sell by hustlers on hundreds of occasions, and Jason is obviously . . . well, if not an expert, then a veteran. Add that semi-expertise to his beauty, and he must do pretty well in that world. True?

"True," he agrees, and laughs uproariously. "But it's not like I'm spending my last days on earth in some rich scumbag's mansion." According to him, he's had innumerable chances to "sell out," as he puts it, particularly with "a famous record company executive," who he won't name, partially because the guy still rents him out on occasion and partially because he respects people's right to privacy. "But I guess if I was really considerate," he says, "I'd still be living in the squat and not with a fucking junkie." He shoots a murderous glare up the sidewalk. "Katie! Get your ass down here! Let's go!"

I'm driving Jason and Katie to her downtown apartment, where the Rambo Dolls have arranged a rehearsal. At my request, Jason directs us along Hollywood Boulevard, pointing out haunts from his days in the squat. In a spot near Mann's Chinese Theater that he has just called "the world's greatest panhandling area," he sees one of his friends, a former squat-mate, now the lead singer in their band.

Bouncer is a tall, skinny, sweet-faced late teen with a long, floppy blond mohawk. He's accosting passersby with his hand out when Jason orders me over to the curb.

"Hey, shit sack!" Jason yells, shoving his head and shoulders through the open passenger window. He topples out onto the sidewalk. Bouncer helps him up, and they half hug, half wrestle for a few minutes, while tourists veer around them.

Katie and I watch from inside the car, trading bemused smiles. Assuming Jason is telling me the truth about her addiction, she's jonesing pretty badly. Her face is greenish white. Her pupils are gigantic. Her skinny arms are practically strangling her upper torso. "Jason's . . . such a . . . liar," she says, teeth chattering, watching the boys mock-battle.

"How so?"

"Like when he says he doesn't love me," she says. "I'm sure he told you that. But I put up with his bullshit. Nobody else ever did. He's a lot sicker than he says he is. You can't see it that much at first, but he's really underweight, and he has diarrhea all the time now. That's why he doesn't hustle very much anymore. So when—"

Suddenly Jason swings open the passenger door. He hurls himself inside, squashing Katie against me, and me against my door. Bouncer joins us, slamming the door shut behind him.

"Howdy," the new boy says.

"Two things. First, you can give Bouncer a ride, right?" Jason's face is about an inch from mine. I can smell AZT on his breath. It's kind of a sour chemical stink that doesn't fit with his being at all. "And, okay, secondly he wants to know if, after you drop me and Katie off, you feel like fucking him for not very much money at all. Then you guys can meet us at Katie's later for the rehearsal. Because I told him you're a . . ." Jason's eyes get confused. "Queer? Is that what you guys want to be called now? Because he's queer too, and he's a nice guy, and he's broke, right?"

After we drop off Jason and Katie, I buy Bouncer a meal, and he tells me his story, which is as heavily censored as Jason's. As for the present, he mostly panhandles, smokes a lot of pot, and hustles occasionally on Santa Monica Boulevard, although hustling depresses him, maybe because he's queer and expects too much affection from his johns or something. Unlike Jason, he's happy to utilize support organizations for runaways when need be. To him, it's worth a little lecturing and "group encounter bullshit" to sleep in a warm bed. At the time of our conversation, he was still commandeering a room in the Hollywood squat where Jason used to live. After lunch, he walks me there.

We enter a faded Victorian mansion that has clearly been through several subsequent lives as an apartment building. Its fanciness is so smashed and dirtied that it looks like a baroque cave. Most of the squatters are away at the moment, hanging out on the boulevard, panhandling for fast food and drug cash, but there's a young heterosexual couple, maybe fourteen years old, playing cards in the former mansion's large, bare, filthy living room. They have angelic faces, dated punk haircuts, wear several layers of threadbare clothes, and I can smell their body odor all the way up to the second floor, where Bouncer is showing me his bedroom, a former walk-in closet: mattress, tangled blanket, small hill of clothing. He plops down in the middle, rests his eyes on his own crotch for a second, then looks up at me and smiles. One of those smiles.

"So who gets to live in the squat?" I ask.

"Anybody," he says. "You just have to be honest, and not too strung out. And you can't fuck around with our stuff."

"I take it Jason broke the rules."

"Every one of them. I fought for him. And we almost let him stay, because he's so fucking beautiful."

"My mind works like this," Jason is saying. We're standing in the narrow hallway outside Katie's apartment. She's inside, shooting up. Bouncer is at the corner store stealing us a six-pack. "Usually I don't think about having AIDS. I mean about having HIV. I always forget that it's not technically AIDS yet. But then when I do remember, this is what happens: It's usually right after I've had sex with somebody, not Katie so much, but with men who pay me. I think, 'I have HIV, okay, but it'll be fine.' The doctor says I have maybe ten years from the time I got infected before I die if I take care of myself. But then I think, 'Well, I could've gotten infected seven years ago, because I've been letting guys fuck me since I was twelve, as weird as that sounds. Then I think how many drugs I've done, and what that's probably done to my immune system. And I start to get really scared, and I think, 'Fuck it. I'm going to kill myself now before I get sick.' Because it's too much, you know? Then I think, 'I hate everybody. Somebody gave this to me. You can't trust anyone.' And I get so tense that I want to kill people, and my friends get shit from me because they're there. And then I get really guilty about treating my friends shitty, so I apologize to them and they're usually okay about it. And that's a relief. So I feel better and I've sort of forgotten about the AIDS. So my mind's made this weird journey to get me away from thinking I have AIDS, I mean HIV. Do you think it does that consciously?"

Jason always asks these impossible questions. Luckily his attention span sucks, and he immediately turns to Katie's door, pounding. "Wake up, you fucking pincushion!"

Minutes later, the rest of the Rambo Dolls show up. Brian is a tall, polite African-American in his early twenties. Six months ago, a friend bought him an hour with Jason as a joke birthday gift, and the two became friends. A bass player, he's the only member of the band with even a smidgen of technical prowess. Bart, the guitarist, is a hippie-esque sixteen-year-old, newly off drugs and a born-again Christian. He doesn't say much. He's brought along a crappy little amp into which he and Brian both plug their instruments. Jason, the drummer, can't afford a kit, so he perches on the edge of Katie's bed with a coffee-table art book in his lap and an unsharpened pencil in each fist.

Over the next, oh, hour and a half, Jason thwacks the book's covers so violently that he manages to spar with the general din. As much as I can tell from the Rambo Dolls' lurching sketch of a sound, the music is a parochial variation on hardcore. Sort of like if the Shaggs had grown up listening to the Melvins maybe. Bouncer, pogoing around mid-room with a humongous grin, sings/yells some artsy-fartsy lyrics that evince standard punky politics regarding racism, drug use, misogyny, etc. Watching these Little Rascal–style antics, I feel kind of sad, truth be told. Fortunately the boys are oblivious. It's only after Bart and Brian have left, and Bouncer is napping in a corner, that Jason nervously asks me what I think, by which time I'm mentally prepared to lie a little, offer encouragement. "Very cool," I say.

"Thanks," Jason says happily. Katie's sprawled in his lap, nodding out. "Yeah, I think in a year we'll be famous. That's my goal."

"How famous?"

"As famous as . . . and as good as . . . Sandy Duncan's Eye."

"But they're not very famous," I say. I'm beginning to see what Katie means. In the sharp window light, Jason's body does seem sort of under-inflated, his facial skin bunched a little too tightly around the bones.

"They're famous enough," he says.

"Why not as famous as U2?"

Jason goggles at me. "Because they suck."

"Okay, but why not be in a great band that happens to be really famous?"

He looks horrified. "Impossible, man."

"Then what else? Other life goals, I mean."

"To not die. Not for a long time." He glances at Katie, then smiles conspiratorially at me. "And . . . have a great girlfriend," he half whispers, then checks to see if she's awake. Nope. "And be rich . . . somehow."

Now he's crowing again. "And never see my parents again. Uh . . . be a great drummer."

"Like who?"

"Adam Pfahler."

"Who's in . . . ?"

"Jawbreaker. Fuck, they're great. Okay, I want my band to be as famous as Jawbreaker. And as good as them."

"Jawbreaker's more famous than Sandy Duncan's Eye?"

"Well, Jawbreaker's known for being so brilliant. Sandy Duncan's Eye is more known for their weird name. So it would be better to be like Jawbreaker." And he shoots me a grin that makes him look about seven years old. Suddenly it decays into a grimace, and he punches the air. "But I'm going to die soon anyway, so . . . who cares!" He glares into space for a second, then shoves Katie off of him. She hits the floor, thwack, not too far away from Bouncer, rolls slowly onto her side, and winces up at Jason with this deep if very foggy concern.

"Shit," she slurs, "are you . . . crying, Jason?"

And, yeah, fuck, he is.

Fast-forward. This day with Jason was supposed to be the first of a handful of visits, but, soon thereafter, he just sort of disappeared. I called Katie's to set up a meeting, and she screamed at me that she didn't know or care where he was. My friend, the part-time counselor who'd led me to Jason, hadn't seen him in months. He had a dozen other kids to worry about. It took quite a few drives up and down Hollywood Boulevard to locate the panhandling Bouncer. He said he hadn't heard from Jason either, and was worried, not that his friend was in trouble but that Jason had gone home to his parents' house rather than staying with his "real family"—his friends. It wasn't many days later that LA had its earthquake. It severely damaged the squat building, whose inhabitants, including Bouncer, scattered to who knows where.

To this day, I'll go out of my way to drive down Santa Monica Boulevard's hustler strip, looking for Jason's silhouette. Not that I know what I'd say to him. Get some help, blah blah blah. Maybe six months ago I ran into Brian, the bassist of the now-defunct Rambo Dolls, at a club. Yeah, he said, Jason was still missing. He just shrugged, but his eyes looked pretty distraught. Maybe, he said, some beautiful rich woman had taken Jason in. Right. This is a world where people come and go, and you rarely learn why or how. You have to use your imagination. You love your friends and lovers intensely, but you're always prepared to shut down. Maybe Jason really did luck out. Who's to know? But is it wrong to half hope that he went home after all? Because I half do. Because, as physically destructive as that setup might be, at least it's real. It would mean Jason was somewhere, not nowhere. But then it's easy for me to say since I don't even know him.

Flashback. Post-rehearsal. I'm driving Jason and Bouncer to the hustler strip, where they've decided to spend the night earning some quick cash. Jason's freaked out, ranting, mostly about whether or not he's going to tell the men who buy him that he has AIDS. I've been trying to convince him that not telling would be sort of evil. Bouncer has been mumbling his agreement with me. The more I argue, the more extreme Jason's opinions become, which makes me wonder if his obnoxiousness isn't just some kind of self-hating yowl for sympathy. Anyway, the atmosphere in the car is really confused. It's getting dark, so the sidewalks are starting to fill with teenage male loiterers, mostly shirtless, their eyes scanning each passing windshield. We've stopped at a light just west of La Brea. Without a word, Jason reaches across Bouncer, opens the passenger door, pushes his friend outside, then basically steps over him and stomps out of sight. After a second, Bouncer struggles to his feet, closes my car door, and leans way in through the window, shooting me what I guess is an apologetic grin, although it's so full of worry and confusion that I don't know how to respond. So maybe I seem worried, too, I can't tell. And maybe that's why Bouncer bends over close enough to me that I can smell his breath, which is as thick with AZT as Jason's. "We'll be okay," he says, and kisses my cheek. Then he withdraws, and chases his friend into . . . wherever.

THE BALLAD OF NAN GOLDIN
(May 1995)

I inadvertently stumbled into Nan Goldin's world in 1986. Hopelessly
in love with a young Dutch playwright, I'd left New York for Amsterdam to be near him and to finish my first novel, which had crapped out
thanks to a nasty cocaine habit and a last pre-safe-sex stampede of promiscuity. A year later, my boyfriend and I were enemies. I'd replaced
coke with crystal meth, and barely cracked the lid on my laptop.

When I wasn't storming in and out of my boyfriend's apartment, I was
hanging out in Amsterdam's slew of boy brothels, doing drugs with the
hustlers and copping the occasional freebie. I'd hoped to purify my life
with love and isolation-induced hard work. But all I'd done was graft my
bad habits into a lonelier, more exotic locale. Like all addicts, I wasn't particularly happy or miserable. I was just sort of there, cornered, one more
American expatriate who thought he was Rimbaud, treating chemicals as
though they were alchemical, with no will or energy to make my dazed
explorations into anything resembling art. One day I read in the newspaper that something called *The Ballad of Sexual Dependency* was being
shown at the local art museum, and, intrigued by the title—not to mention titillated by the accompanying illustration of a cute young hipster
with a needle in his arm—I stumbled into the theater.

The Ballad of Sexual Dependency is a slide show. Rather, it's a kind of documentary film in the guise of a slide show, incorporating forty-five or so minutes of slowly cross-fading images of Goldin and her friends through the years, accompanied by a rough medley of sad love songs past and present, from Marlene Dietrich's "Falling in Love Again" to Television's "Venus de Milo." Organized by subject, it depicts with loving attentiveness and absolute amorality the day-to-day lives of smallish gangs of reasonably hip young people—male, female, straight, gay, drag queens, artists, punks—as they party, drink, do drugs, suffer hangovers, fuck, fight, and fall in and out of love. Some of the images are as casual as any snapshot taken at any social gathering. Others are as dramatic and lushly beautiful as noir film stills. Together they tell a story that has no story per se, but is rather an intimate ebb and flow of bodies, especially faces, lost in private drug and/or endorphin-fueled utopias. It's hard to imagine in light of recent films like *Kids* and *Trainspotting* how astonishing it felt to be given such a careful, intimate, unqualified view of so personal a world, but at the time there was nothing like it.

"I remember being in a club, upstairs somewhere, when I first saw *Ballad*," says the writer/critic Lynne Tillman, a longtime friend of Goldin's. "A lot of people had been making Super-8 sound films, and Nan's slide show seemed connected to that. But you felt immediately that the concept was different. It was about being exhaustive; including everything she knew. It's like the way she takes notes about everything. She used to do that when we met, wrote things down as we said them." The novelist Linda Yablonsky, a friend of Goldin's since the early 1980s, concurs. "When I saw *Ballad*, the accumulated power of images hurt me, all that beauty and pain, and I cried," she says. "I knew those people, and she really captured it. In most photographs, people don't really look like themselves. In *Ballad*, they looked absolutely like themselves."

As for me, I . . . "You felt like that was your life up there?" Goldin says, completing my sentence. "Yeah, I hear that a lot." Goldin is in Berlin, putting the finishing touches on the catalog that will accompany "I'll Be Your Mirror," her fall mid-career retrospective at New York's Whitney Museum of American Art. I'm in Los Angeles, finishing my fourth novel. I feel like I owe her something, and I try to tell her so. Somehow, after I saw *Ballad* that day in Amsterdam, I never quite lost myself in drugging and promiscuity with the same intensity or lack of composure again. It was as if, through her pictures of lives so much like mine, my own fucked-up behavior acquired a look, a narrative coherency, an aesthetic. Even now when I think back on some of the shit I pulled, at some of the bottoms I hit, the memories are distinctly Goldinesque. I can see the rooms where I snorted drugs, fucked hustlers, screamed at my boyfriend; I keep thinking that if I'd had the wherewithal to approach her that day, I might have cleaned up a little sooner. "It's just as well you didn't bother me," she says. "I'm sure all I was thinking about was how I could cop. I was definitely hitting bottom in those days."

Nan Goldin was born on September 12, 1953, in Washington, D.C., and grew up in Silver Spring, Maryland, the youngest of four children in a "defiantly middle-class" family. She was especially close to her older sister Barbara, an intelligent, rebellious girl who played piano brilliantly. When Nan was eleven, Barbara killed herself by lying down on some railroad tracks just outside Washington. Devastated, Nan ran away from home several times that year, and was eventually placed in foster care by her parents. "I basically got farmed out to rich people," she says. "But eventually they threw me out because I was growing pot in their greenhouse, and because I had a black boyfriend."

By 1972, she'd found a "new family," seven fellow artsy, androgynous teenagers with whom she shared a railroad apartment in Boston. Her favorite among them was David Armstrong, a skinny, effeminate gay boy just beginning to experiment with drag. He became Goldin's life-long best friend, most frequent subject, and, as she puts it, "the eye of my storm." Now a respected photographer himself, Armstrong remembers those days as "just a really wonderful time. Nobody had any money. I was occasionally turning tricks. That summer of '72, Nan really started photographing a lot, and our lives revolved around that." "I started tak-ing pictures because of my sister's suicide," Goldin says. "I'd lost her. And I became obsessed with never losing the memory of anyone ever again."

For teenagers who were keyed into rock 'n' roll culture of the early '70s, art and life seemed gorgeously indistinguishable. It was a time of glam rock, surely the strangest and headiest subculture to have splin-tered from late-'60s hippiedom. Hippies might have talked stylistic and sexual freedom, but with the exception of period freaks like the Velvet Underground, Andy Warhol, and Iggy Pop, that movement's drift was in fact antistyle, grubby even, and comfortably heterosexist. But by 1973, thanks to the influence of Warhol, the director John Waters, and gender-bending rockers like David Bowie and the New York Dolls, gays and other sexual outlaws had a scene of their own, a modus operandi with which to flirt publicly if surreptitiously with the youth of America. For Goldin, it was enough to document the goings-on. She harbored dreams of being a fashion photographer, and of putting her drag queen friends on the cover of *Vogue*. "I just didn't see how I could make it as an artist at that point," she says. The idea of producing little glam souvenirs for New York gallery-goers bemused her, but it was out of the question, like wanting to get your parents stoned.

As a result, that era from the dawn of glam to the incursion of punk is remembered the way a party is remembered, through random snapshots of besotted, campily dressed, mugging participants. The genius of *The Ballad of Sexual Dependency*, perhaps the deepest visual record of that period, is almost accidental. Goldin snapped her trendy friends out of love and fear, purely to preserve their essence, to prevent them from leaving her without a trace. In one of those lucky, mysterious coincidences that distinguish artists from artistes, Goldin happened to possess an incredible eye for the multidimensionality of her surroundings. Her pictures not only did justice to whatever poses her friends wished to strike, they nailed the sometimes incongruous emotions that inspired the poses. Freed from the issues of commerce that qualify the work of career artists, Goldin could be the girl with the camera, the friend whom everyone instinctively turned to at moments of bliss, sadness, lust, et cetera, knowing they'd get a trustworthy record. If they'd thought their mugs would wind up on gallery walls, maybe they wouldn't have given themselves up so resolutely. But they knew that a few days later they'd be sitting around Goldin's apartment, stoned and guffawing as she clicked off the slides, and the Stooges played on the stereo.

This is not to say that Goldin didn't take her photography seriously even then. In the mid-'70s she enrolled in the School of the Museum of Fine Arts in Boston. While she considers the work she did there "the worst I'd ever done," too clouded with bourgeois polish, too sapped of intimacy, she did learn to make color prints and use a wide-angle lens. Also attending the school were some like-minded young artists who were equally cowed by the idea of art-world careers. There was Mark Morrisroe, whose punky, invasive, homoerotic self-portraits are only now being appreciated, ten years after his AIDS-related death. And there was Jack Pierson, later Morrisroe's lover, whom Goldin would meet in New York in 1985. Pierson's fey, melancholic, mock-bland snapshots of modelly hunks would later make him one of the biggest art stars of the early '90s. They, Goldin, and Armstrong would later be seen as a kind of movement, the so-called Boston School, early and influential progenitors of an artful, aggressive casualness that is currently de rigueur in the art world. But at the time they were just a bunch of druggies and fags who wanted to be artists, and their camaraderie wasn't enough to prevent Goldin, Armstrong, and his lover Bruce Balboni from fleeing to New York and its famous Downtown scene of artsy punk rockers and punky young artists.

When Goldin arrived in 1978, punk had already gobbled up what was left of glam. Androgyny and, to a certain extent, fagginess were still relatively cool, thanks to crossover veterans like the Dolls and Wayne County, but it was really, *really* cool to make a show of displaying your pain, boredom, rage, and disaffection. These were exactly the depths that Goldin had always been interested in recording, and people began to pick up on her work. Goldin and her friends became denizens of the legendary Mudd Club, where, as part of a celebration of Frank Zappa's birthday, she gave her first public slide show. By then she had gathered most of the coterie of pals who would make up the cast of *Ballad*—Armstrong, Balboni, the writer/underground film star Cookie Mueller, Mueller's lover Sharon Niesp, the transsexual artist Greer Lankton, and others. Emboldened by her Mudd Club success, Goldin photographed her friends and herself ever more obsessively, and worked on the slide show, adding its soundtrack and eventually giving it a name.

Soon, *The Ballad of Sexual Dependency* began to attract attention both in and outside the art world. Critics compared the work to the early films of Warhol and John Cassavetes. Screenings were events. *Aperture* published a best-selling collection of the slide show's images. Museums, nightclubs, and alternative art spaces around the world flew Goldin in to present *Ballad*. The high-powered gallery Pace/MacGill added her to its blue-chip roster. But in her life, and in the lives of many of her friends/subjects, the innocent drug play of what Goldin calls "the party years" had escalated into full-scale, horror-show-like addiction. Her photographs recorded the downward swing, even if she was too doped up to see the change. Armstrong, whose androgynous, bewitching face dominates Goldin's early images, became a sweaty, disheveled junkie sprawled on a couch. "All that glamour that had been attached to getting high," he remembers, "was hard to hold on to. Then there was no glamour left at all." Even Goldin began to avoid her best friend. "I hated to pity him," she says. Vibrant, wacky Lankton grew scrawny and zizzed. Balboni, an early modern-primitive type, started to look like some homeless guy who accidentally wandered into the frame. Across the board, people either packed on the pounds or deflated, their kingdoms no longer the latest clubs and cafés but rather the shadowy depths of their messy drug dependencies.

Goldin, meanwhile, had fallen in love. The relationship, which she describes as "intense, jealous, sexual, and bonded by drugs," became the center of her work. In pictures at least, Brian was a fearsome-looking character who seems to have two emotions, sullenness and rage. "No one could understand what she saw in him," says an acquaintance from the period. "They did nothing but fight." "Nan was way out there," adds another friend of this period. "She looked crazy. She got in a lot of fights with people, physical fights, and she alienated a lot of friends. It was very hurtful." At the time, Goldin was too gone to care. "Brian was really gorgeous for a while, and emotionally we fit," she says. "It was kind of like being in a wild three-way—me, my lover, and the drugs. I'd started shooting dope when I was eighteen, and I'd been able to stop, put it down with no problem. I just thought, 'Nothing can get me,' you know?"

One night in Berlin in 1984, where Goldin had come to show *Ballad*, she and Brian had a particularly nasty blowout, during which he beat her so badly that she had to be hospitalized. "The guy hit her in the face, in the eyes, which seemed particularly cruel considering she's a photographer," says someone formerly associated with the couple in Berlin. "She was really hurt, and it didn't seem like her friends knew how to deal, probably because of the drugs and all that. She seemed very alone." Goldin shot a series of photographs of her battered face, "so I would never go back to him." Still, her drug addiction worsened, and she began to hole up in her New York loft. Armstrong, who'd gotten clean by that point and was living back in Boston, accepted her request to move in and take care of her, but things were too squalid and he bailed after one day. Goldin's only self-portrait from this time is a blurry, haphazard-looking shot of her sitting on her bed, talking on the phone, dead-eyed, obese, and surrounded by ashtrays.

"It was pathetic," she says. "All I did was lie in bed and watch *I Love Lucy* reruns. There was no day or night. Nobody would deal with me. I guess that's what did it, the loneliness. But even so, I went into rehab not as a decision to get clean but as a decision to get methadone. But when I got there I was so disoriented I realized that I couldn't go on, and I gave in."

"Nan wrote me a letter when she was in rehab," remembers Yablonsky, who had herself cleaned up after a six-year-long drug addiction. "She said they had taken her camera away, and she didn't know what to do. Her work was her life. She had a hard time separating the two." When she was well enough to go to a halfway house, her camera was returned to her. She began taking simple self-portraits, sitting on her bed, standing by a tree. "It was during this time that I rediscovered daylight," she says. "I needed to relearn my face." By 1990, she felt strong enough to move back to New York. Armstrong accompanied her, and together they tried to reform their extended family, or what was left of it.

Where once Goldin had photographed her friends to keep them alive, to prevent anyone she knew from disappearing, now it was all about savoring the last drops: Cookie Mueller thinning, thinning, glazing over, and finally lying in her coffin. Her German friend Alf, spooky-eyed but otherwise fit, then suddenly bandaged and dead in a hospital bed. Her French art dealer Gilles transforming from a suave, tattooed hunk into a concave, expressionless skeleton. David Armstrong, Bruce Balboni, Sharon Niesp, et al., grimly dealing with it all.

A lot of photographers have explored AIDS and its consequences in their work. There's an undeniable power to all these photos, whatever their maker's skills or purity of intention. You take a picture of someone sick or unhappy, it's going to function, if for no other reason than it triggers compassion. It was Andy Warhol who said, "People are so great, you can't take a bad photograph." But the force of Goldin's work is more than coincidence. She knew her friends when they were beautiful and crazy, and she knew them now when they were fucking her over by dying, proving her to be powerless after all. Somehow, her pictures radiate that knowledge.

Still, too much knowledge can be a dangerous thing. So as a way of shaking off all that death, Goldin returned to square one. In 1991, she started shooting New York's drag queen renaissance, the hyperactive nightlife that had sprouted around clubs like Jackie 60 and Squeezebox, and the Wigstock Festival. "I really hadn't been around the queens for twenty years," she says, "and it had changed so much. Drag had become completely accepted. I saw it as probably the most hopeful, positive part of the gay world at that point."

Around the same time, she began a collaboration with the Japanese photographer Nobuyoshi Araki, documenting Tokyo's youth culture. The results, collectively titled *Tokyo Love*, were published in book form in the United States last year. It's perhaps her sweetest, most tender-hearted body of work. Paradoxically, it's also been her most controversial, causing some critics to claim she had merely simplified and exoticized a foreign culture. "Yeah, the PC police," she says. "No, I was just fascinated by the beauty and wildness of those kids. It was like going back to my adolescence. I saw Japan as this country where there was a simulation of wildness, without drugs, without AIDS, neither of which were much of an issue there. For them, it seemed to be more about style, and the appropriation of style, with no real understanding of what it all means. It seemed like a return to paradise. Those kids weren't self-destructive like my friends and I were."

In a week, Nan Goldin will leave Berlin and return to New York, then spend the next two months dealing with the minutiae around the retrospective. After all that's over, she'd like to think about making a film. She recently codirected a BBC documentary on her life, also titled *I'll Be Your Mirror*, and found the experience curious. "The thing about film versus the slide show is that in film everything's stuck," she says. For example, she tells me, since the BBC documentary was made, "David has lost thirty pounds and looks gorgeous. Sharon lost thirty pounds and broke up with her girlfriend. Bruce started shooting up again, but he's clean now. . . ." Otherwise, her agenda includes more photographing, probably landscapes and portraits of children and "hopefully more pleasure." The latter has something to do with the fact that, after six years of sobriety, Goldin started drinking again a year and a half ago while in Japan, a decision that concerns some of her sober friends. "I love being sober," she says, "I just wish I could be sober *and* drink. It hasn't been a big crisis for me. It's more a problem for people who are still in the program. When I was sober I was a total workaholic. I had an absolute vision of things, and everything was too compartmentalized. Now I have more tolerance of the variations. It's not all light, and it's not all dark. Not that I have anything against the program at all. It saved my life. I think I just outgrew it."

Like I said, when I saw *The Ballad of Sexual Dependency* back in 1986, I saw eerie parallels between Goldin's chaotic world and my own. From what I can gather, the parallels continue. Like me, and like most of the people that we both know, she seems to have gotten her shit together by becoming an artist first and a fun-seeker second. Not to sound like John Tesh at the Summer Olympics, but I can't help but wonder what, if anything in particular, is on the artist's mind at this, her proverbial moment of triumph. In the art world, a Whitney retrospective is the closest you get to a gold medal.

"Well, I guess I think about my sister," says Goldin, sounding not unlike an Olympic athlete for a moment. "Her death completely changed my life. I'm constantly looking for the intimacy I had with her, in my life and my work. And I think about the deaths of my friends. My sister's death is more abstract to me, more symbolic. Their deaths are real, and that's left behind this immense legacy. That's why I photograph. I miss so many people so badly."

HIPPER THAN THOU
Ryu Murakami
(May 1995)

Ryu Murakami isn't anything like his novels. *Almost Transparent Blue* (1977), *69* (1993), and *Coin Locker Babies* (1995) feature disaffected young Japanese androgynes whose eyes are permanently tweaked by the latest designer drugs, and whose conversations consist almost entirely of pop cultural CliffsNotes. Having just this week plowed through all three novels in a row, I knock on their author's hotel room door expecting... I don't know, some intimidatingly hipper than thou human buzzword? But the fellow who answers the door is ... well, he looks like a guy who sits around on his butt writing novels. Murakami's in his early forties, but seems older, with a dense, underexercised body, '70s helmet hair, a pricey but ultra-square suit, and a continually befuddled look on his face, like some grandpa who's been dragged to a rock concert. He also doesn't speak English very well.

We're sitting in a suite high up in LA's Century Plaza Hotel, trying to communicate through his bilingual traveling companion, Ralph McCarthy, the translator of one of his novels. McCarthy is a thin, nervous American academic with frazzly red hair and huge worried blue eyes. He's having a tough time keeping up with us.

Me (to Murakami): Your novels are very savvy about contemporary youth culture. Do you make it a point to keep up with its goings-on?

McCarthy (to me): Uh . . . I don't know how to say that in Japanese.

Me (to McCarthy): Okay. Does he go out to clubs a lot, see bands, hang out with younger people, that sort of thing?

McCarthy (to Murakami): Uh . . . hm. Do you understand, Ryu?

Murakami (to McCarthy): [*Japanese stuff*]

McCarthy (to me): Well, he didn't really answer your question.

Me (to McCarthy): That's all right. What did he say?

McCarthy (to me): He said, "Why is it that there has never been another rock band as good as the Rolling Stones?"

It's the day after the Kobe earthquake. I've been half expecting Murakami to cancel our interview at the last minute, either out of personal grief or to prevent himself from having to wax bereaved in print. But that was back when I imagined him as Mr. Cool. When I do ask him for his reaction to the tragedy, he just shrugs, says (through McCarthy, obviously) that he doesn't know anyone in that part of Japan, and can't think of anything interesting to tell me about it. So I guess he *is* disaffected at least. Still, his English is so rocky, his energy so lackluster, and his translator so unprepared to volley our repartee that I'm having a very hard time putting two and two together, i.e., those hyperactive books and this couch potato. It doesn't help that I'm being reduced to asking threadbare questions in grade-school English.

Me (to McCarthy): Are his novels autobiographical?

McCarthy, Murakami: [*a lengthy exchange in Japanese*]

McCarthy (to me): He said that he wrote *Coin Locker Babies* a long time ago.

Me (to Murakami): No. I'm asking if your books resemble your life in any way? Do you understand what I mean?

Murakami (to me): Yes.

Murakami (to McCarthy): [*Japanese stuff*]

McCarthy (to me): Uh . . . he's talking about the Rolling Stones again. Do you want me to translate it?

Murakami (to me): Yes, the Rolling Stones! Why is that?

Anyway, the interview's basically a bust, in the traditional sense anyway. I do manage to learn that, contrary to publicists' claims, Murakami was never a rock video VJ in Japan. He did host a semi-highbrow TV chat show years ago, and that's what made him famous back home. He goes out of his way to disparage Oliver Stone, for reasons neither he nor McCarthy can quite explain, which is curious since his new novel prominently features Stone's glowing blurb. Murakami doesn't feel like he's part of any literary tradition or movement, either in Japan or internationally, although, as best as I can decode from his facial expressions, that seems more like a statement designed to separate him from other trendyish, youngish Japanese writers like Banana Yamamoto and Haruki Murakami than the sincere clarification of a literary idiosyncrat.

The American artist whom Murakami would most like to meet is Quentin Tarantino, since he imagines they share some kind of affinity. And it's true that they're both quasi-amoralists with slight sentimental streaks and great technical instincts. The mention of Tarantino's name is pretty much the only time during the interview that Murakami energizes even a little. Well, Tarantino's name and that of the Rolling Stones, who definitely seem like the biggest bee in his aesthetic bonnet at the moment.

From what I can gather, the Stones also seem to be the last rock band he paid any kind of attention to. Even my mention of punk buckles his forehead and fills his eyes with horror, although it's a movement he regularly references in his later books. All he'll say to me about punk is that punks admire his work. Needless to say, youth culture of the '90s is a blur to him. Sure, he's heard of MTV. He knows what Ecstasy is. But the only thing he's willing to say specifically to or about today's young people is that he thinks technology has destroyed their spirit. "Based on what?" I ask. He looks confused. "Okay, how do you think it has destroyed their spirit?" Well, of course his answer has something to do with the Rolling Stones, whom he apparently considers the first and last word on rebellious passion. Still, unless I'm the object of some hoax, this is the man who writes those up-to-the-second novels. So, thinking he might be interested, I take a few minutes and tell him what I know about rave culture, specifically about its radical strategy to ignore the traditionally lefty, antigovernment/anticorporation tactics of previous countercultural youth movements, and instead embrace high technology, and explore its elaborate musical and graphic capabilities for signs of a new kind of spiritual meaning. Murakami listens to my spiel politely enough, but his expression tells me I'm wasting precious time that could be spent carving up the meat of his oeuvre.

Me (to Murakami): So perhaps young people's spirits aren't destroyed, they're just differently configured.

Murakami (to McCarthy): [*Japanese stuff*]

McCarthy (to me): Ryu says that such a thing as rave would not be possible in Japan.

Me (to Murakami): Well, correct me if I'm wrong, but I understand that rave culture already exists in Japan.

Murakami, McCarthy: [*a lengthy exchange in Japanese*]

McCarthy (to me): Uh . . . Maybe it would be best if we moved on to other topics.

American culture and Japanese culture have a notoriously strange relationship. On the surface, America would seem to be the dominant, influential half of this mutually fascinated duo, and Japan the clueless admirer, enthusiastically mimicking our ideas in a charming if slightly annoying fashion. But that's probably just our massively ego-invested reading of the exchange. If you believe cultural deconstructors like Barthes and Baudrillard, our culture is less Japan's idea of the ultimately awe-inspiring aesthetic machine than a kind of clearinghouse for recyclable art products. Maybe the Japanese can't quite grasp where we're coming from—check out Japanese heavy metal if you haven't already—but at least they know how to reinvent what we produce, whereas we're essentially agog at their creations.

Ryu Murakami's novels can seem like sleeker, more enigmatic, slightly silly rewrites of our Brat Pack novels of the 1980s, but with the angsty undercurrents taken out. He utilizes the same basic setting(s): nightclubs, rock concerts, chic apartments, etc. But there's something both calmer and more theatrical about his fictional world. Take *Coin Locker Babies*, written fifteen years ago but only now appearing stateside. The main characters, Hashi and Kiku, are orphans who have grown up to be, respectively, a bisexual rock star and a heterosexual pole vaulter. Hashi veers through Tokyo's nightlife, drugged, performing with his band, seducing or being seduced by members of his rabid fan base. Kiku, meanwhile, struggles to prove himself as an athlete, and puts up with a wacky girlfriend who has transformed her condo into a swamp in order to accommodate her pet alligator. These boys' lives, which move in and out of each other's orbits, are illuminated by spunky, clever prose that renders the characters irresistible but rarely transgresses their psychology. This is probably fortunate since, on the occasions when Murakami does attempt to elucidate a character's motivation, his revelations are pretty stock.

At his best, Murakami writes unusually spot-on teen-oriented word movies. *Coin Locker Babies*, easily his finest work, is so unliterary that it's more like a novelization than like an actual novel. And that's its beauty. It completely lacks pretense, or at least the sort we're accustomed to. You can pick up a Murakami tome looking for a cheap but elegantly feisty thrill, without fear that you're going to have to read around some wannabe genius's half-baked, quasi-serious stab at cowing the editorial staff of the *New York Review of Books*.

Me (to Murakami): Are your novels taken seriously by the Japanese literary establishment?

Murakami (to me): No.

McCarthy (to me): That's not what Ryu means. Wait.

McCarthy, Murakami: [*a lengthy exchange in Japanese*]

McCarthy (to me): Well, I don't know how to translate what he said. From my understanding, he used to be taken seriously in Japan, but now he isn't so much anymore.

Me (to McCarthy): So he's more of a popular novelist?

Murakami (to me): No.

McCarthy (to me): What Ryu means to say is that his audience is specialized because of his subject matter. For instance, he recently published a novel in Japan that includes the most brilliant, accurate description of what it's like to take Ecstasy that I have ever read. I mean, I've never personally taken Ecstasy, but . . .

There you have the four most lucid exchanges of our conversation. Frankly, there's not much more to report. Near the end of our visit, we do sort of get around to "discussing" Murakami's work as a movie director, a subject I had half hoped to avoid. Again from what I can gather, Murakami has focused most of his efforts in recent years on writing and directing films. He has four to his credit, but only the most recent, *Tokyo Decadence* (1991), has been released in the States.

Like his novels, *Tokyo Decadence* is stylish, glib, and easy to sit through, assuming you have a basic fascination with drugs and sex. Unlike his novels, which also include numerous scenes of fetishistic, soft-porn S/M-y rolls in the sack, *Tokyo Decadence* feels almost a little too revealing of Murakami's personal mind-set. It's like a weirdly overbudgeted homemade porn video, and while this gives it a mesmerizing car-wreck-style quality, you can't help feeling a bit embarrassed for the guy, what with all the leather-clad, spike-heeled babes and schlumpy middle-aged grovelers on display. It does, however, begin to explain his Rolling Stones obsession, since, like most of that band's post-'70s work, the film's idea of heterosexual love seems to have been conceived during masturbation.

Tokyo Decadence is also the only work of Murakami's that doesn't focus almost exclusively on the young. So, I ask him, is this what he foresees for the hedonistic young revelers in his novels? Are Hashi, Kiku, et al. fated to become jaded, sex-obsessed, overgrown adolescents acting out their fantasies in pseudo-medieval basements? For the first time, Murakami looks not just confused but uncomfortable. No, he says, rising to his feet. McCarthy immediately leaps to his. I guess this means my time is up. I know it's stupid to confuse an artist's work with his life, but it's equally stupid to pretend that by reading some guy's novel or movie you haven't just read his mind. So on the way to the door I ask McCarthy to ask Murakami if, taking into consideration the relative ineffectualness of our interview, I might venture an interpretation of him based on what I've read and seen. But of course something appears to get lost in the translation. So by the time Murakami's "yes" gets back to me, who knows if he understands what I was getting at. And it's anyone's guess what he means.

FLANAGAN'S WAKE
R.I.P. Bob Flanagan
(April 1996)

Bob Flanagan and I met in the late '70s. At the time he'd published one thin book of gentle, Charles Bukowski–influenced poetry entitled *The Kid Is a Man* (Bombshelter Press, 1978). We were both in our mid-twenties, born less than a month apart. I was sporting a modified punk/bohemian look and hated all things hippie-esque. Bob looked like one of the Allman Brothers: thin, junkie pale, with shoulder-length hair, a handlebar mustache, and an ever-present acoustic guitar that he'd occasionally strum while belting out parodies of Bob Dylan songs. His style put me off initially, as mine did him, but I found his poetry amusing, edgy, and odd, and his clownish, sarcastic personality belied a deeply submissive nature.

There was a new, upstart literary community forming around Los Angeles's Beyond Baroque Center, where Bob was leading a poetry workshop. I had met the poet Amy Gerstler in college, and she and I began to hang out at Beyond Baroque in hopes of meeting other young writers. After a few months of hunting and pecking through the crowds, a small, tight gang of us had begun to form, including, in addition to Bob, Amy, and myself, the poets Jack Skelley, David Trinidad, Kim Rosenfield, and

Ed Smith, the artist/fiction writer Benjamin Weissman, and a number of other artists, filmmakers, and the like. We partied together, showed one another our works in progress, and generally caused a ruckus in the then dormant local arts scene.

Very early on, Bob told us he had cystic fibrosis, and that it was an incurable disease that would probably kill him in his early thirties—if he were lucky. But apart from his scrawniness, his persistent and terrible cough, and the high-protein liquids he constantly drank to keep his weight up, he was, if anything, the most energetic and pointedly reckless of us all. At that stage, Bob's poetry only obliquely described his illness, and barely touched on his masochistic sexual tendencies. In fact, it took him a while to reveal the details of his sex life to his new chums. I think the fact that my work dealt explicitly with my own rather dark sexual fantasies made it relatively easy in my case, and I remember his surprise and relief when I responded to his confession with wide-eyed fascination.

Bob was working on the densely lyrical, mock-humanist poems that would later be collected in his second book, *The Wedding of Everything* (Sherwood Press, 1983). He began to encode within his poetry little clues and carefully offhand references to S/M practices, and gradually, as his vocabulary became more direct, the sex, and in particular his unabashed enjoyment of submission, humiliation, and pain, were revealed as the true subjects of his work.

Writing was difficult for Bob. One, he was a perfectionist. Two, with his sexual preferences finally out in the open, he was more interested in talking about and enacting fantasies that had already played themselves out in daydreams and in private autoerotic practices. It was around this time that Bob met Sheree Levin, a.k.a. Sheree Rose, a housewife-turned-punk-scenester with a master's degree in psychology. They fell in love, and, profoundly influenced both by her feminism and her interest in Wilhelm Reich's notions of "body therapy," Bob changed his work instantaneously and radically. For the rest of his life, Bob, usually working in collaboration with Sheree, used his writing, art, video, and performance works to chronicle their relationship with Rimbaudian lyricism and abandon.

Bob began to live part-time at Sheree's house in West Los Angeles, along with her two kids, Matthew and Jennifer. Bob was an exhibitionist, and Sheree loved to shock people, so their rampant sexual experimentation became very much a public spectacle. It wasn't unusual to drop by and find the place full of writers, artists, and people from the S/M community, all flying on acid and/or speed, Bob naked and happily enacting orders from the leather-clad Sheree. During this period Bob published two books, *Slave Sonnets* (Cold Calm Press, 1986) and the notorious *Fuck Journal* (Hanuman Books, 1987). He also began an ambitious book-length prose poem called *The Book of Medicine*, which he hoped would explore the relationship between his illness and his fascination with pain. At his death, the work remained incomplete, though sections had been used in his performances and have appeared in anthologies.

I was programming events at Beyond Baroque in those days and, as we were all interested in performance art, I organized a night called "Poets in Performance," in which we tried our hands at the medium. Bob and Sheree's piece involved Bob, clad only in a leather mask, improvising poetry while Sheree pelted him with every imaginable food item. It was such a hit, and Bob was so thrilled by this successful merging of his fetishes, his art, and his exhibitionist tendencies, that he and Sheree began doing similar, increasingly extreme performances around town. Perhaps the most famous and influential of these works, *Nailed*

(1989), began with a gory slide show by Rose and concluded, after various highly stylized S/M acts, with Bob nailing his penis to a wooden board. The performance made Bob infamous, and he was subsequently asked to perform in rock videos by Nine Inch Nails, Danzig, and Godflesh, as well as being offered a role in Michael Tolkin's film *The New Age*. *Nailed* also interested Mike Kelley, who later used Bob and Sheree as models in one of his pieces and wound up doing several collaborations with the duo.

Coincidentally, interest in S/M and body modification was growing in youth culture, especially after the publication of *Modern Primitives* (RE/Search), which profiled Sheree's life as a dominatrix. Bob was a hero and model to the denizens of this subculture, even as he found much of their interest to be superficial and trendy. Bob was always and only an artist. He never cloaked his masochism in pretentious symbolism, nor did he use his work to perpetuate the fashionable idea that S/M is a new, pagan religious practice. His performances, while exceedingly graphic and visceral, involved a highly aestheticized, personal, pragmatic challenge to accepted notions of violence, illness, and death. For all the obsessive specificity of his interests, Bob was a complex man who wanted simultaneously to be Andy Kaufman, Houdini, David Letterman, John Keats, and a character out of a de Sade novel. So his performances were as wacky and endearing as they were disturbing and moving. For example, at the same time he was making a name for himself as a shockmeister, he was performing on Sundays with the improvisational comedy troupe the Groundlings, in hopes of fulfilling his lifelong ambition to be a stand-up comedian.

By the early '90s, Bob's physical condition was worsening. He was having to hospitalize himself before and after performances just to get through them. He and Sheree proposed a performance/installation piece to the Santa Monica Museum of Art, which was accepted and became *Visiting Hours*, a multimedia presentation comprising sculpture, video, photography, text, and Bob himself poised in a hospital bed acting as the work's amiable host and information center. *Visiting Hours* was popular and critically well received, eventually traveling to the New Museum in New York and the School of the Museum of Fine Arts in Boston. In 1993, RE/Search published *Supermasochist*, a book entirely devoted to Bob's life and work. Also that year, the filmmaker Kirby Dick began to shoot a feature-length documentary film about Bob and Sheree entitled *Sick*, which will be released this fall.

There was some hope during this period that Bob might be able to have a lifesaving heart and lung transplant, but after months of tests it was determined that his lungs had deteriorated too much to allow him to survive the operation, and he began to accept that he had maybe a year yet to live. He and Sheree concentrated on visual art pieces, some of which were exhibited at Galerie Analix in Geneva and at NGBK Gallery in Berlin. The duo collaborated on a last installation work, *Dust to Dust*, which Sheree is currently completing, and Bob kept a yearlong diary of his physical deterioration, *Pain Journal*, which will be published in the future. Even as most of Bob's life began to be taken up with stints in the hospital and painful physical therapy, he was still on the scene, frail but good-natured, using his omnipresent oxygen tank as a comical prop just as he had once used his acoustic guitar. Right after Christmas, Bob went into the hospital one final time and died on January 4, 1996. In the fifteen years I knew him, Bob grew from a minor poet into a unique and profoundly original artist who accomplished more than he ever imagined he could, and whose loss, predictable or not, is one of the greatest difficulties those of us who knew and loved him have ever had to face.

KING OF THE JUMBLE
Stephen Malkmus
(July 1996)

Dennis Cooper: What's your writing process like?

Stephen Malkmus: Well, unfortunately I sometimes feel a little guilty. I know some people. . . . For instance, Robert Pollard of Guided by Voices is writing down stuff all the time. I tried to do that. I went to Malaysia by myself before we recorded *Brighten the Corners*, and I brought my computer, and I tried to write about what was happening there, and about the people I saw, like I guess writers do. But I couldn't really write until we were done with the music.

The music comes first?

I'll have a first line maybe, off the top of my head, and I'll kind of build off that. Usually I'll be thinking of what I've read lately. Like I'd been reading John Ashbery before we did the album. He's brilliant, and I took his work as like, Okay, I can do something like that. It's not against the rules. I don't have to do something that's really formal.

I read that you appropriated lines from Ashbery's "The Tennis Court Oaths."

[*laughing*] No, no.

I tried to compare your lyrics to the poems, and the only thing I could find in common was the word "concierge."

Mm-hm. That could well be. But I was thinking of *The Tenant*, that Roman Polanski movie, too. That always reminds me of a concierge. I love that movie. It's so sick.

I can see the Ashbery connection in the sense that your songs seem personal, but, at the same time, they adopt a kind of omniscient, everyman stance.

That's true. Say in "Type Slowly," the line "Sherry, you smell different." I was thinking about how if you haven't seen an old girlfriend in a while, she'll still smell the same. People generally smell a recognizable way, even if you haven't seen them in years. I thought it would be strange and sort of disorienting and sad to say, You smell different. I mean, that sounds personal, but it's so distanced, and then the lyrics go off in this sort of . . . hallucinatory way, I guess.

Do you write in song form, or in paragraphs, or . . . ?

This time we did this thing where I sang the songs right before we mixed them, which is very radical. I don't think bands normally do that. We recorded all the music in North Carolina. Then I had a month before we mixed and sang in which to think about what I wanted to do. I like to give myself a deadline and just hope that something comes out. I have to force myself. So say in "Shady Lane," I had, like, [*singing*] "A shady lane, everybody wants one." And I had the first line. And I had, "recognize your heirs," because I just thought it was funny to have to recognize your heirs. Other than that, it was sort of mix and match at the last second.

The tones shift pretty intricately in the songs. I assumed they were very carefully composed.

It's hard to say where it comes from. I wanted the album to have a psychedelic edge, and have a hallucinogenic edge, but not have it be acid-based. Have it be a little bit weird, and a little bit creepy, but not self-consciously so. For me the third verse is always the big mystery verse. That's always last-minute. Because the third verse is, like, Okay, the story's been told. Now we can screw around. Everyone knows it's coming around again, because it's a song. We don't have to bang the dead horse by that point. The war's been won.

Your songs have a lot of room in them. It's almost like the music and the lyrics and the singing are on different planes.

Well, as a point of comparison, Sonic Youth, a band I love . . . Thurston tends to sing with the guitar line. For me, it's a battle to think in the fourth dimension—because I'm the guitarist, and sometimes the bass player—to think of how to have that extra person in there, the singer, contributing this additional element.

Do you write, apart from songwriting? I know you're a big reader.

Not that much. I have a pretty Protestant, pragmatist thing to my writing. I only do it when I have a goal. I love to read, and be a dumb reader of books, a fan, and think, This is so beautiful, and not compare it to what I do. The thing is, I don't generally like reading books by people my own age, for some reason. I gravitate toward fortysomething men, midlife-crisis writers like . . . um, Barry Hannah and Russell Banks or whoever. I guess I don't think I know enough to write a book. Maybe I should try, though. I could keep a journal.

Don't worry about it. You write great songs.

Yeah. That's enough . . . isn't it?

Of course.

I don't know . . . I'm sort of afraid of being a real good vocalist or lyricist. I mean, I try really hard, and when you weigh what's important about a great band, those are crucial things, but . . . I worry about it.

You used to work at the Whitney Museum in New York, didn't you?

Yeah, Steve West did, too. It was sort of an escape for me. Normally I like being idle. But in New York, it's so cold and lonely. I think, like most people, I thought that I needed to have something to do. Anyway, I was a guard. It just basically involved standing against a wall for thirty-five hours a week.

So were you interested in contemporary art? Did you read *Artforum* and all that?

Yeah. I mean, Steve and I were both outsiders there. We were both more into reading and music than art. It was an icing-on-the-cake type of thing. I developed an appreciation for things that I never would have otherwise. Postminimalist sculpture, you know. Eva Hesse, Barry Le Va, Charles Ray. Humans like to classify and name things. And just for my own satisfaction, it's fun to be able to go to a museum and say, Oh, that's a David Salle. Typical bourgeois thing, you know. "I know art." We were guards so we were invisible, and that was nice, especially at openings. It was the end of the '80s. So Ashley Bickerton would be there smoking nonfilter cigarettes and being daring. Those kinds of '80s guys were dying at that point, and Bruce Nauman, who I really like, was becoming the intellectual leader for all the younger artists.

Did the bad reaction to *Wowee Zowee* disappoint you a lot?

Not really. It's so blurry to me now. I think about it historically, about what it'll all mean eventually. That's the only way I can stand it. I mean, more people liked it than liked *Trout Mask Replica* when it came out. Not that *Wowee Zowee* is even close to being that kind of work of genius, but I mean in terms of sales and stuff like that.

Every Pavement fan I know, including myself, loved it and were excited by it. We all felt that after *Crooked Rain*, *Wowee Zowee* was exactly the kind of move we wanted you guys to make. It seemed like a challenge to yourselves and to us.

That's what I thought. It really polarized people. We sent out these bad, muddy advance tapes before it was mastered properly. That might have been part of the problem.

Do you think that things will be different or odder for Pavement in England now, what with you being perceived as the saviors of Blur?

It's hard to tell. We're going there tomorrow. When something like that happens, it just seems really artificial, because it's England, and anything you get from that is going to be so transitory. I think people genuinely like us there. And I just imagine that that guy Damon will move on to another influence next album. That's his style. Blur is all concept anyway. That would be a terrible thing, if that was your only claim to fame. That you influenced Blur.

It could have been worse. It could have been Cast.

[*laughing*] Totally.

Blur's a clever band. They always make me think that there's more there than meets the ear, and that's all you can really ask of English bands. Whereas Oasis seems so gentrified.

I have a soft spot for Oasis, and that kind of lunkheaded thing. Rock 'n' roll, man. Tunes. And just dumbness. I could never do that. It's like a Beatles-versus-Stones thing. The Beatles are more art-school boys, whereas the Stones were appropriating black music and trying to be rock. I'm more likely to be a Beatle than a Stone, because I just couldn't do that. I guess Jon Spencer would be a Stone.

What are you listening to?

I don't know. I haven't really gotten an informed opinion about new stuff yet. Like Tortoise. I approve of what they're doing. I'm on their side. I'm supportive, but I don't really listen to them in my house. I listen to a lot of jazz. I like noise bands, the absurdity and fun of it, but I mostly love bands that give songs, put the vocals up loud and go for it. It takes more guts to do that. In the end, I'd want to support those bands.

What's the most beautiful place you've ever been?

Well, we did this video shoot yesterday out in the Simi Valley. Very California suburban landscape. It wasn't the kitsch element that I liked. It was the light, the California weather that was relaxing and beautiful to me. The clichéd suburban sprawl. But then I'm the kind of person who loves to defend things that everyone else hates, especially in music. People say, Ugh, the Spice Girls, and I'll say, They're the greatest.

Well, I like Silverchair. What do you say to that?

Silverchair's good. I kind of like Alice in Chains. They have a lot of dumb songs, but they have a spooky psychedelic side that I like. Silverchair has this beautiful mix of that and '70s music. Their videos are always stupid marketing strategy ones, but I close my eyes, and I think they're cool. Generally bands that a lot of people like, they almost always do have something. There are some exceptions. I think Bush isn't very good.

You can't get much worse than Live.

Yeah, Live. I call them Live as a protest. They've asked us to support them twice, and we were like, No, thank you. Their new song is bad, scary bad. I'm sure it's going to be followed by some earnest ballad. It's funny how bands like Smashing Pumpkins do the same exact pattern for every album. They introduced a hard rocking song for their first single. Then they did "Today" and "1979" respectively, which I think are their best songs. And then came the string ballad. It works. Smashing Pumpkins. . . . More like Smashing Marketing Plan.

You mentioned the video shoot. Spike Jonze was the director, right?

Yeah. It's for "Shady Lane." It's bordering on *Logan's Run* meets Todd Haynes's *Safe.* We're out in this valley that's very antiseptic, and wearing all these color cottons, and we're kind of zoned. I could do that pretty well, because when I was younger my parents were into EST and stuff. They weren't into crystals or anything. It's pretty bourgeois New Age style, what they did. But they got touched by it.

You live in Portland now. Why?

My parents live in Sun Valley, the ski resort near there. And they'd had all my furniture since I moved east in 1990. Anyway, I moved to Portland partially because I'd split up with a girlfriend, and I wanted to start over. I wanted to go to the West Coast. I couldn't live in San Francisco because I was born near there, and that would be too much. To move to LA would be too audacious a step. And Seattle kind of sucks. The people there are so mean. Portland's nice, low-key. It's kind of small. I think I might move back to New York, though. I have friends there. You make your best friends in your twenties, I think. I thought I could start over and make new friends, but you get kind of set in your ways. The guys in Pavement are my best friends, and they're all out East basically.

Will you miss the West Coast?

Sure. It's so much more beautiful out here, the weather, the light, and it's so stunning visually. But the lack of history thing . . . it's all relative, but geologic time here is so intense, plates always moving, earthquakes. I guess I just want the comfort of New York's history, such as it is.

You guys are on the road a lot. Any interesting tour stories?

Well, Keanu Reeves came to our show in New York. He gave us a book on chess. He said, "I heard you're chess fans." He was really nervous and shy. A friend of mine saw him in a restaurant by himself the other day. It seemed kind of sad. Keanu eating by himself in a mid-scale restaurant on the Sunset Strip. Poor little guy.

Yeah, since he's put on weight, nobody likes him anymore.

I know. What's up with that?

Beats me. Okay, one last question. It's an odd one, but go with it, and I'll explain why I asked it in a second. Name your three favorite animals.

Hm. I'd pick a bird for my first choice, some sort of predator. A falcon or a hawk, because it seems like a pretty good life. Except killing little creatures would bum me out, I guess. Second, I think I'd go land. My land creature would be . . . maybe a lynx or a mountain lion. I'd want to be on top of the food chain. Lone creature, an outsider cruising around. Fast. Can't be fucked with. Third . . . well, I should pick something warm and open and loving. How about a nice otter, cracking clam shells, having fun, making children laugh.

Well, that was a psychological test question. There's some official validation for it in psychiatric circles. The first animal represents who you want to be. The second represents who you are. And the third represents what you want in a lover.

That's nice. That works really well. Yeah, I would like to be with the otter.

INSIDE THE HIGH
Irvine Welsh's *Ecstasy*
(September 1996)

Irvine Welsh is that rare thing, a serious writer who's also a youth-culture icon. Douglas Coupland writes like a groovy lawyer; the mind-bogglingly gifted, coincidentally hip David Foster Wallace is a couch-potato genius; William Burroughs has become so ubiquitous, he's practically the Beat Generation's Angelyne. Welsh, on the other hand, is (at least in theory) a hard-living idiot savant whose fictional world, with its rough-and-tumble Scottish setting and its glary, slang-encrusted prose, offers the purest transgressive escapism around.

Trainspotting is one of those first novels that tend to haunt a writer for the rest of his career, à la Hubert *Last Exit to Brooklyn* Selby Jr. and John *City of Night* Rechy. It's a piece of work so phenomenal that you half suspect Welsh made some kind of satanic pact to write it. You know, *Give me the speech patterns of an undereducated yob, the instincts of a great psychologist, and the chops of a William Faulkner, and I'll give you . . . whatever, a percentage of the gross?* But to re-reference old Burroughs for a second, *Trainspotting* is Welsh's *Junky,* not his *Naked Lunch,* and while none of his subsequent books is quite as raw and unself-conscious, his snowballing sophistication is easily as exciting as that first blast of his talent.

Welsh's fourth and latest book, *Ecstasy*, as the title implies, is a work in deep consultation with the drug and its surrounding youth culture. But it's not the book many expected: a headlong, inebriated, epic study of the drug's effects in the tradition of *Trainspotting* and heroin addiction. Instead, *Ecstasy* (the book) is a trio of mildly experimental novellas in which Ecstasy (the drug) reconfigures the psyches of pointedly cardboard protagonists, transforming them from hoary clichés into progressive clichés.

This is far and away the most English book that Welsh has ever written. Where his earlier books have about as much to do with the clever-clever mewlings of Martin Amis or Will Self as an unprovoked attack has to do with cocktail-party chatter, *Ecstasy* reads more like what Amis might have written had he been dosed, given an amnesia-inducing whack on the head, and abandoned in a working-class Edinburgh pub. This is especially true in "Lorraine Goes to Livingston," the story of a famous, elderly Barbara Cartland–like author of romance novels who suffers a mild stroke while correcting the galleys of her latest best seller. During her stay in the hospital, she's befriended by a young nurse who's into the rave scene, and allows herself to be reinvented into an Ecstasy-popping writer of cheesy, sub-Batailleian porn. It ruins her career, but it frees her soul, and she's last seen whirling like a dervish in a trendy London club.

Interwoven with peculiar subplots involving a necrophiliac TV chat-show host, the nurse's raver friends, and Lorraine's pervy, gold-digging husband, "Lorraine Goes to Livingston" is Welsh-lite, an easygoing, confident romp whose basic appeal lies in watching him throw his considerable voice around.

"Fortune's Always Hiding," novella number two, pits a young soccer hooligan and his armless girlfriend against the upper-class English corporate exec who marketed the drug that deformed her. Most of the story is told by the hooligan, and his voice is classic Welsh—a voluptuous, inarticulate, Scottish-sounding machinery of language that mysteriously manages to seem crude and impassioned while intelligently denoting complicated psychological states. Here it's spruced up very slightly in service of a serviceable plot, and the results feel a bit like Welsh line edited by Jim Thompson.

> ... there was always this one thing that Bruce Lee said, one bit of advice that he gave which has always stood me in good stead. He said: you don't bleedin' well punch some cunt, you punch through them. This geezer with the mouth, all I could see was that orange brick wall behind his face. That was what I was going for, what I wanted to demolish.

Ostensibly a love story wherein the laddish young druggie sacrifices himself to avenge his girlfriend's honor, "Fortune's Always Hiding" is really a comedy of a distinctly postmodern sort. For instance, the hooligan mentions early on in the story that his working-class accent is a fake, a ruse to disguise himself while committing petty robberies. So while readers are drawn into the novella's raucous play-by-play, they're really the narrator's little victims. It's a bit like being mugged by a strung-out Ren and Stimpy.

The third novella, "The Undefeated: An Acid House Romance," is so good that one suspects its predecessors are there strictly to give the book a marketable bulk. Here Welsh abandons the schematics and delivers a dazzling, over-the-top, intricate depiction of Ecstasy- and LSD-zonked club kids that only falls short of definitive because its brevity prevents him and his characters from going the distance, emotionally and philosophically. "The Undefeated" is reminiscent of those late-'60s drug novels by guys like Tom McGuane and Terry Southern. It's similarly breezy and wacked out, with just enough plot and character development to ground a plethora of druggy special effects.

A lot of writers have described the heroin high; some, including Welsh, extremely well. The Ecstasy high, with its strange combination of horniness and benevolence, has been harder to nail down, appearing in fiction most often in the form of a thin, Hallmark card–like gushiness or as a speedlike fuel for action scenes. Welsh catches all its lovey-doveyness, its absurdity, its adolescent profundity, and throws his take into the mouths of two puppety characters, Heather, a prim Londoner caught in a loveless relationship, and Lloyd, a crazed young Scottish DJ, whose love lives intersect—where else?—in a trendy club.

Heather: I took the pill in the club. It came on strong at first and I felt a bit sick in the stomach. . . . Then I felt it in my arms, through my body, up my back: a tingling, rushy sensation. I looked at Marie and she was beautiful. I'd always known that she was beautiful, but I had come, over the years, to look at her in terms of decline. . . .

Lloyd:—Aye, right . . . well, this bird thinks, cause she's E'd in aw, she's thinkin tae herself: this is a romantic cunt. So wir up oan Arthur's seat and ah looks at her in the eye and says: ah really want tae make love tae ye now. She's up for it, so it's oaf wi the fuckin gear n we starts gaun for it, cowpin away, looking doon oan the city, fuckin' great it wis. Thing is, about ten minutes intae it, ah started tae fell like shite. Ah goat aw that creepy, tense, sick wey; the comedoon's diggin in good style. They wir funny cunts for that, they flatliners. Anyhow, aw ah wanted tae dae was tae blaw ma muck and git the fuck oot ay thair. That's what ah did, eh? The bird wisnae pleased, but there ye go, needs must. So ye have tae watch oot before ye call it love. It's just another form ay entertainment.

See if the feelings transfer tae yir everyday life, then call it love. Love's no jist for weekenders.

Snazzy as it is, however, *Ecstasy* creates something of a dilemma for a reviewer. On the one hand, it's easily the most accessible of Welsh's books. On the other, its freaky, loose-limbed story lines turn his sometimes opaque prose into something like an acid-spiked literary candy—there's almost no depth here. In a funny way, *Ecstasy* has more in common with Danny Boyle's film version of *Trainspotting* than it does with Welsh's own work. It's a blast, top to bottom, but it feels like a book written specifically for people whose idea of going book shopping is to turn left when they walk into Tower Records.

Since it's the follow-up to Welsh's strenuous and serious novel *Marabou Stork Nightmares*, this makes sense. Welsh probably needed to relax and half concentrate, to amuse his immediate circle. And while the resulting insider quality gives *Ecstasy* a sexiness and glamour that's new to his work, it also threatens to divide readers into those thrilled to see their particular subculture legitimized in print, and those who admire the book's energy but can't relate. If Welsh weren't one of the two or three most exciting writers out there right now, it wouldn't matter. But *Ecstasy* is being published at the exact moment when most American readers are going to want to check him out, and this is the wrong place to start.

ICE NINE
The Many Lives of Experimental Fiction
(October 1996)

Something happened around about the early 1980s, a cultural shift of some sort, wherein younger and/or savvier readers lost interest in experimental fiction. Or should I say they lost interest in experimental style? The smart, densely fanciful prose of writers like John Barth, Alain Robbe-Grillet, John Hawkes, and Marguerite Duras lost its titillation and began to be seen as a kind of overelaborate façade that obscured rather than delineated what was interesting about the world. The new cool writing spoke clearly, energetically, and conventionally about daring things—drugs, kinky sex, violence, disaffection. Blame growing illiteracy, blame the Brat Pack, blame Raymond Carver. Whatever the reason, this sudden impatience with the explorative mirrored a new, across-the-board neoconservatism among artsy consumers. Fewer and fewer people rushed to see the new Godard film or buy the new Steve Reich recording, and young writers out for challenge were satisfied with cyberpunk, experimental gutter-mouths like Burroughs and Acker, and smooth-talking European intellectuals like Kundera and Eco. The aforementioned writers slowly retreated to smaller or academic presses—if they were lucky.

There are signs that experimental fiction is making a comeback—which is not to say that people are rushing back into the old crew's arms. William Gass's *The Tunnel*, a huge, legendary, decades-in-the-making avant-garde novel, thudded into bookstores this spring, years after anyone cared. Ditto the recent extravaganzas by William Gaddis and Harold Brodkey. But the daring young writers are doing pretty well. The success of David Foster Wallace's brilliant and difficult *Infinite Jest* is the most obvious sign. Wild novelists like Steven Wright, Mark Leyner, Jeff Noon, Richard Grossman, and William T. Vollmann are selling well and snagging respectful reviews in powerful, conservative contexts like the *New York Times*. Maybe most important, in terms of reviving avant-garde fiction's clout, these writers' books are considered to be groovy luggage among the college and coffeehouse crowds. And it's not just literature that's freaking out again. Techno and rave culture, which are entirely about experimental atmospheres and rhythms, are crossing over into the KROQ /*Spin* set as we speak; the Internet is nothing if not an invitingly chaotic space; and the popular notion of hypertext has given language a second life. All of this will seemingly benefit the vibrant if obscure scene of seriously underground writers who believe in the importance of the uncompromised, individual voice, and many of whom are published by a small press out of Boulder, Colorado, called Black Ice Books.

Black Ice is a subdivision of a larger, older, and more established press, the Fiction Collective. Founded by the novelist Ronald Sukenick, the Fiction Collective has been issuing heady, complex novels and story collections for a couple of decades now, irrespective of the famine of interest in these kinds of books. Black Ice, founded in the early '90s, is the wilder and more aggressive of the two houses. Its books are generally published in a hip-pocket-sized, paperback format à la the somewhat similar and better known Semiotext(e). Its distribution is crap, in Los Angeles at least, and you'll be lucky to find Black Ice titles in even more literary local bookstores like Book Soup and Midnight Special. (Best bets: the Outsider Bookstore in Hollywood, Vagabond Books in Brentwood, and Beyond Baroque in Venice.) Black Ice Books' designs look flat, utilitarian, and, unless you're preternaturally drawn to the underdog, uninviting. This may be one of the reasons they're anathema to booksellers, and it's a shame, since books as forbidding as these need all the help they can get.

Black Ice publishes both "name" writers—that is, better, if not necessarily well-known, cutting-edge writers like Mark Amerika (one of Black Ice's editors in chief), the cyberpunk veteran John Shirley, Curtis White, and Samuel Delany—as well as lesser-known writers. The typical Black Ice writer is a well-educated heterosexual white male in his thirties, which, to be fair, basically describes the prototypical avant-garde novelist of any era, although the press's roster has grown more diverse each year. Black Ice titles tend to feature hallucinatory narrative structures; fast-talking, poetic prose; blatant examinations of sex, drug states, and violence; and a terse pace that suggests the writers have spent more than a little quality time with noir detective and SF novels. The work displays little of the absurdist humor and exalted vocabulary that give the work of '60s-period meta-novelists a slightly icky modernist hangover. Instead, Black Ice authors are both punkily direct and almost insidiously refined.

Take Doug Rice's first novel, *Blood of Mugwump: A Tiresian Tale of Incest*. Like all explorative fiction worth its snuff, the book is extremely difficult to summarize, but here you go. *Blood of Mugwump*'s elaborate conceit is that it's a pseudo-autobiography written not by Doug Rice himself but by a fantasy figure, also named Doug Rice, who is a member of an ancient clan of Catholic, gender-mutating, incestuous vampires called the Mugwumps. He and they constantly shift from male to female without warning or logic. Their lives are pretty much a twenty-four-hour-a-day orgy as Rice's narrator fucks and gets fucked by his siblings, parents, and grandparents in constantly renewed configurations. Rice's prose is a wondrous thing, a kind of porn on acid as transcribed by J. R. R. Tolkien that wraps the virtually nonstop sex scenes in a lush, quirky, wide-eyed innocent poetry of elegantly bad manners. "Lightning of my eyes making fires in the hard muscles of Caddie's cunt. Her thighs flexed, my dress falling to the floor. Careful, Mom might hear the falling. She made me into stone, watching her turn away from my gaze. Buzzards flew out of some book and began undressing what little remained of my skin."

While *Blood of Mugwump* could not have existed without the examples of Acker and Burroughs, it's also not particularly derivative. If anything, it's as though Rice, in his high postmodernist fashion, set out to write a novel that their novels would want to have sex with. It shares their androgynous, bisexual, brainy, lustful bent, but it has a distinguishing fecklessness and a pleasant, slightly nerdy grace.

Curtis White is one of the most interesting and underrated contemporary novelists. *Anarcho-Hindu* is his fourth book, and his first Black Ice title after having published his last couple of novels with LA's Sun and Moon Press. White's writing is more subversive than Rice's. Relatively free of sexy razzmatazz, it's built almost but not quite conventionally around linear plots and reliable characters. But White's amazing and supple intelligence, his ability to layer multiple narrative strategies within deceptively clean sentences, his wickedly laconic sense of humor, and his quiet learnedness about things metaphysical is anything but standard. Best of all, his prose has a drop-dead beauty that you almost never find in experimental fiction, which tends to tear itself to shreds in search of newness.

Anarcho-Hindu concerns the travels and observations of a learned Midwesterner and his wife, Siva, a mysterious creature who seems part Hindu divinity, part porn goddess. Now living quietly in a suburb of Normal, Illinois, they recount their younger adventures in India and Europe, and use the idiosyncratic wisdom they've acquired along the way—which might be described as a kind of mystical Marxism—to critique a variety of archetypal contempo characters, from an odd antiques dealer to an earnest member of Queer Nation. By the novel's conclusion, the man and woman have transformed into White and his wife, May. It's not exactly a shocker, given the tendency among Black Ice authors to insert themselves into their novels as backseat tour guides, but White's point throughout is that the obvious in life is rarely made apparent, and he makes this twist seem not only fresh but almost old-fashionedly moving.

A completely different kind of book, and a good example of Black Ice's bravery and significance, is Samuel Delany's *Hogg*. Written more than twenty years ago by the famed, respected SF writer, this brutal, pointedly repellent, triple-X-rated, and very uncharacteristic novel was considered unpublishable until Black Ice came along. The Black Ice context, as it were—anything goes as long as it's rigorously devised—positions the novel as art, and emphasizes the scabrous critique of societal violence and racism that underlies Delany's thickly pornographic prose.

Unlike his usual grand, immense speculative novels, *Hogg* is virtually plotless. Its two main characters—an insanely slutty adolescent boy and an insanely horn-dog truck driver—basically drive around the backwoods of America having sex and raping, murdering, and/or having orgies with everyone they meet. The pace is molasses-slow. The story line is irrational and slapdash, rushing from sex scene to sex scene as though written in a masturbatory frenzy. At the same time the sex, which is absolutely relentless, tests readers' imaginative limits, involving as it does almost nothing but pedophilia, rape, urination, and coprophilia.

As pornography goes, *Hogg* is tiresome and indulgent. It establishes its fetishes very early on, then reiterates them hundreds of times, always with the same excitement and comically hokum diction. As a commentary on race relations—Hogg, like Delany, is black; the young boy is white—the novel makes a blatant and unsubtle point in a unique way that, again, goes relatively nowhere at great length. Read along either of these two lines, *Hogg* has a kind of car-wreck fascination. It's astonishing that a writer of Delany's stature would expose his sexual fantasies with such unqualified enthusiasm and with such a thin literary justification. The novel is most interesting as a historical curiosity. What would have happened if *Hogg* had been published back in the early '70s? My guess: not much, apart from big career problems for Delany. For his admirers, *Hogg* provides a great excuse to reread and rethink novels like *Dhalgren* and *Tales of Neveryon*, whose far more subtly perverse subtexts have generally gone unnoted. In any case, the book is a highly charged object, and in a world where readers are so easily shocked that a bourgeois horror novel like A. M. Homes's *The End of Alice* seems to signal the end of the world, that's reason enough to recommend it.

REBEL JUST BECAUSE
The Leonardo DiCaprio Interview
(November 1996)

Leonardo DiCaprio walks into the Dresden Room, a semilegendary bar and restaurant in the East Hollywood district of Los Feliz. He's here to promote two films, *William Shakespeare's Romeo + Juliet* and *Marvin's Room*, both in release this fall. That's two movies to add to a catalog of credits that grew from a mid-'80s TV stint on *Growing Pains* into an Oscar nomination for *What's Eating Gilbert Grape?* He's wearing a faded red T-shirt, loose blue jeans, running shoes, and has a girl's barrette in his hair. He's six feet tall, lanky, thin but fleshy, and moves rapidly with a wary, teenaged lope. He looks like a very large adolescent boy with weirdly knowing, nervous eyes. When I wave, he crashes down at my table, orders a 7-Up, and immediately bums a Camel Lite Wide off of me. He's friendly, reserved, and very focused. He has a flat, affectless LA accent and a mid-range crackly voice with a sardonic edge. He's talkative, easily bemused, and very well mannered. In other words, he is nothing like what I'd expected, i.e., a mischievous brat.

After spending two hours with DiCaprio, first doing the interview, then just hanging out talking about this and that, I wonder how all the wild rumors about him got started. For instance, just a month before the interview, a friend told me he'd heard that DiCaprio had raped a girl and it was being covered up. Then another friend told me he'd heard that the rape story was a plant to hide the fact that the actor is gay. He's supposedly been in and out of rehab, is a recent convert to Scientology, and I forget what else. People seem absolutely determined to make him into the new River Phoenix. You know, tormented, unstable, brilliant, self-destructive. When you meet him, all that seems so absurd. To me he seems like a sweet, canny, clear-headed, sane, young heterosexual guy—fun-loving but a little sad and anxious, intelligent and highly insecure about his intelligence—who likes going to art museums, loves his family, hated all the summer blockbuster movies, adores acting, and dreams of swimming with blue whales. Why people insist on projecting all the gloom and doom onto him, I don't know. But I was determined not to perpetuate the myths. So I began the interview at square one.

Dennis Cooper: In almost every article I've ever read about you, journalists ask the same questions, and make the same assumptions. You know, that you're a party animal, that you have drug problems, that you're gay and closeted, that you're a brat . . .

Leonardo DiCaprio: Yeah, they are all kind of the same.

It always seems like journalists treat you fair and square when they're with you, but then, when they actually write the articles, they start speculating and drooling all over you.

[*laughs*] Yeah.

I guess that *Details* cover story on you last year was the most notorious.

That guy . . . I was really nice to him. I brought him over to my house, and introduced him to my mom, and then he twisted things around to make me seem like a badass, when it wasn't like that at all.

Everyone I know thought the piece was creepy. Well, I'm going to try to not cover the same old ground, and if I get creepy, you can be a badass and throw your Coke in my face.

[*laughs*] Okay.

Supposedly one can tell a lot about someone by what they find funny, so tell me a joke.

I just heard some good ones. Let me think. [*pause*] Okay. A guy hears a knock on his door. He answers it. There's nobody there, but he looks down and sees a snail. So he picks up the snail and throws it as far as he can. Three years later there's a knock on the door. He answers it, and there's this snail. And the snail says, "What the fuck was that about?" [*both laugh*] You tell me one.

This one's kind of old, but . . . What were Kurt Cobain's last words?

I don't know.

Hole's gonna be big.

[*laughs*] That's pretty sick.

Well, something has just been revealed about you, but I'm not sure what it is. So, I just saw a chunk of *Romeo + Juliet*, sort of a montage of scenes. From what I could tell, it looked amazing. Have you seen the film?

I saw a rough cut. Yeah, it looks pretty wild.

Did you see *Trainspotting*?

That's a great movie. I loved that movie.

Both movies are based on literary works that are very dense and complex on the page, and they both make this savvy decision to neutralize the difficulties of the language by being incredibly stylized and energetic. It seemed like a great way to deal with Shakespeare.

Yeah. Some people have criticized the movie. You know, "You can't do that to Shakespeare. You shouldn't mess with Shakespeare like that." But Shakespeare was a genius. I'm sure if he was alive he would have been totally behind what [director] Baz [Luhrmann] is trying to do. And I see what you mean about the two movies. But Baz didn't see *Trainspotting* until a few weeks ago, so it's just a coincidence.

The movie has that wacky, surreal Australian feel, à la *Priscilla* or *Muriel's Wedding*.

But it's not like that, really. It's definitely surreal, but . . .

The black drag queen with the white Afro?

That's Mercutio. That's at the ball where Romeo meets Juliet. Romeo's on drugs, and that's him tripping out on Mercutio. Mercutio's wearing the Afro as part of his costume, but I trip out on him, and it grows about three feet. That's a wild scene. In this version, the ball takes place at a club, and everybody's on drugs and dancing. It's crazy. But the movie's very real, too. I don't know how to explain it. You just have to see it.

Romeo's a tricky one. He's so lovey-dovey. In the Zeffirelli version, the way Leonard Whiting played him, he was such a bland, wussy guy.

Yeah. Well, at first I wasn't sure about doing this. I didn't want to run around in tights swinging a sword, you know? But Baz convinced me to come to Australia and meet with him for a week, and while I was there he figured out what his vision was, and then I was really interested.

Is Romeo still a total innocent in this version?

He's pretty innocent. Well, in the first half he is. Then Mercutio dies and Tybalt dies, and everything just goes wrong. I'm crying all the time in the last half of the film. I cry a lot in this movie. That was hard.

You filmed in Mexico City. Is it as hellish a place as one hears?

Well, while we were making the movie, somebody on the crew got attacked, and somebody else got robbed, and somebody else got shot. And they say Mexico City has the worst smog of any city in the world. But it was nice, too, because it's not a place where tourists tend to go. It's kind of undiscovered in that sense. And some people I know from New York were down, so that was fun. There's a lot of poverty, and that was depressing, but there are parts of the city that are just like Beverly Hills.

Are there good clubs there?

There are some clubs. But we didn't do that so much. We were more into silver.

Silver?

[*grins*] Silver.

In what sense?

We got into buying silver. You can buy these bracelets and necklaces and things, and these guys will etch your name into them, or these skulls. We'd go out in the city wearing all this silver and people thought we were just ridiculous. [*laughs*] I haven't worn them out here, but they're nice to have, you know?

What kind of music do you like?

I like rap. Nas, Wu-Tang, that sort of thing.

Are you political?

Not really. I try to stay out of that because it's so damn confusing. I sort of want Clinton, because I don't think he's that bad. [*laughs*] He seems like a nice-guy president.

Are you religious?

Haven't been brought up that way. But I have a weird karma thing. Like I used to be able to steal bubble gum and stuff when I was younger, but I'm really ridiculous with it now. If someone gives me the wrong change, I can't deal with it, even if it's a gigantic department store. It's not because I'm getting money now. It's because I always think that when I go outside, something terrible is going to happen.

All that, and you're not interested in Buddhism?

My brother is, and he's constantly preaching to me. I'm curious about it. I want to get into it, but I want to know a lot more about it. But, yeah, I'd say it was the best religion. [*laughs*] There I go with my big thing: "Yeah, I'd say Buddhism is the best religion." [*laughs*] In bold print.

Here's a hypothetical for you. A friend posed this to me. Would you rather be really, really fat or really, really old?

You mean old-looking?

No, old. Either you're ninety-five years old or you're your age and weigh five hundred pounds.

I'd be really fat, and go out like Biggie Smalls every night, you know what I'm saying? I'd have people wheel me into places. I'd have a woman on each leg. I'd go out like a rock star if I was that big. Yeah, I'd rather be fat. I mean . . . really old? Man.

I found the question harder to answer than you did. Maybe because I'm older than you are.

Well, I did *Gilbert Grape*, and Mama was pretty big, but she was just the sweetest woman that I have ever met in my entire life. I still talk to her every once in a while. And I have a friend who's . . . pretty large, and who I hang out with every day, and he's the sweetest guy ever. I really like to have sweet people around me. I can't stand badasses. There's too many of them, especially my age in LA. I like to get to know people, and you have to peel away so many layers of those people. Just give me someone who's relaxed and cool to hang out with, even if they're not studs.

Well, you being you, a lot of people want to be your pal.

I have a good group of friends, people I've accumulated over the years. Some I've known since elementary school, some I've met recently. They're just a good group of guys and gals. And I think they like me, too.

But you're never sure.

You're never sure. No, I know they like me. Because it's not really about that, you know? Our friendships are completely separate from everything else. I hardly know anybody who's . . . in showbiz. It seems like I do through all the press, but I really don't.

So is it difficult for you when you attend, say, the Cannes Film Festival or something? You know, flash-flash-flash.

I'm great at avoiding press, too. [*laughs*] I've been handling this thing pretty well. I keep thinking something bad is going to happen, but it's been pretty cool so far. I've maintained the exact same home life that I've had for twenty years. All I see is more people looking at me than before, but, you know, who cares? You just can't obsess yourself with this fame stuff. I used to take everything to heart. When the things they said to me in the press were detrimental, I thought it would kill me. But stuff keeps changing all the time, and now I'm cool about it, and I just think it's weird to watch it all happen.

I get the feeling that *Total Eclipse*, about the relationship between the French poets Rimbaud and Verlaine, was a rather discomfiting experience for you. It wasn't very well liked.

People hated it.

I'm one of the only people I know who thought the film was interesting. But then I love Rimbaud. When I was a teenager, Rimbaud was my hero. He's still my hero, in a way.

Really? That's cool. Yeah, I wanted to do the part because Rimbaud was such a badass, but he was a genius, so he had the goods to back it up, you know? I think the only people who liked *Total Eclipse* were people who liked Rimbaud. But then, a lot of people who liked Rimbaud hated it, too. I don't really know what to say about *Total Eclipse*. The movie was made in France. Over there, Rimbaud's like James Dean, but over here people really don't know who he is. And I think maybe the film didn't explain enough.

The way people reacted to the film, you'd have thought the whole movie was just a frame around the scene where you and David Thewlis, who plays Verlaine, kiss.

I know, I know. It was crazy.

And *Total Eclipse* came right on the heels of *The Basketball Diaries*, another film nobody liked very much.

Yep. But you know what? It doesn't really bother me what people think.

Before those movies came out, you were seen as the brilliant young actor, the Academy Award nominee, and then suddenly you were the actor everybody gossiped about. You were supposedly a junkie, and you were gay. Assuming that neither one of those rumors is true, that had to have bothered you.

Sure. But I'm really glad I did those movies. I'm proud of my work in them. In five years nobody will remember any of that, or the bad reviews, and my work in them will be seen as part of all of my work. I'm not worried about that. I just think people expected me to go a certain way with my career, and I didn't do it. I didn't do the next John Grisham movie.

Did it make you gun-shy?

No. I want to keep doing different things. But I want to say this: I don't do drugs. I've never done drugs in my life. I'm just not interested. And if any of my friends start doing drugs, they're going to hear about it from me. What people don't realize is that half of the reason I did *The*

Basketball Diaries is because of the whole heroin craze, and . . . I'm not saying I was doing a "Say No to Drugs" special or anything, but I wanted to help make some kind of statement against heroin. But then, of course, people decide I'm into it, right? God damn. And I also want to say that I've had a girlfriend for a year coming up. I'm sure people will make something out of that.

It's amazing to me, what with all the rumors about you, that you trust people at all.

I don't, really. Like I had a friend who I did a short film with recently who slandered me. I was trying to do a favor for him. His name's R. D. Robb. It's scandalous. It was originally a short film, and then he tried to make it into a feature. I worked one night on it. He tried to make it into a feature. And I heard all this stuff about how he was going to pit the press against me if I didn't go along with him and do the feature. I just did it as a favor, you know? And then all this stuff happens and you ask why. Why be nice if that's going to happen?

The editor of *Detour* wanted me to ask you about something. Answer or not as you see fit.

Let me guess, sex and drugs.

Well, you tell me. In *Vanity Fair*, Alicia Silverstone is asked about you, and there's an implication that you and she were romantically involved at some point, and she says something on the order of, "I don't even want to talk about that guy," meaning you. So . . .

Right. [*sighs*] Alicia and I did our first movies at about the same time. We've known each other for years. We're not really good friends or anything, but we know each other. I'm sure she was asked that question, and she thought it was ridiculous, and she just said, "I'm not even going to answer that question," just like I would do.

You've played two brilliant young writers, Rimbaud and Jim Carroll. I'm wondering if the way you think about acting is in any way related to the way they thought about writing.

Hmm. I wish I could come up with a brilliant answer to that, but I can't.

An actor I know told me that for him, acting was like being in a trance.

I've heard people say that. I never took acting lessons, so I don't have a way to think about it like that. I know some actors get sort of lost in what they're doing. I'm not like that. I like to know everything that's going on around me. I guess when I'm acting, I think of myself as the camera. I'm watching myself act. I'm trying to see how what I'm doing looks from the outside.

That's interesting. It seems like it would make you feel really self-conscious.

I feel self-conscious all the time anyway.

After *Total Eclipse* and *The Basketball Diaries*, you're seen as a real risk-taker. You must get a lot of weird scripts.

You're right, I do. But I don't mind. I'm always looking for something different.

Did you know John Waters wrote a film thinking of you for the lead? It was called *Cecil B. DeMented*, and you would have played an avant-garde Super-8 filmmaker who kidnaps a major movie star and forces her to star in his Super-8 film. But the film didn't happen for whatever reason.

Yeah. I had dinner with John a couple of weeks ago at [photographer] Greg Gorman's. He's one of the people who's really doing it, and I admire him a lot. And he's just hilarious. He tells the best stories.

John's the best. So do you have any small, risky films in the works?

I have one thing in the works, but we'll see.

Is that *The Inside Man*? You initiated that project, didn't you?

It's not my project. It's just . . . this project came along, and I really liked it, and I took it to Michael Mann because I loved *Heat*. He's such an intelligent guy. He's like a computer, he knows so much. So he's interested, and it's in the works, and we'll see. I don't really want to talk too much about it right now. But I have this huge movie coming up.

James Cameron's *Titanic*.

Yeah.

You seem a little nervous about it.

No, I just . . . I've never done anything like this. I never planned to do a movie like this, but I agreed to do it, and . . . it should be interesting. It's a huge movie, like I said. Huge. One-hundred-twenty-million-dollar budget, and a six-month shoot. Jim Cameron says he wants it to be a *Doctor Zhivago* type of thing, and it'll be interesting to be part of that. It's an epic love story that goes backward and forward in time.

Do you go down with the ship?

[*nods*] Dead.

Cameron's films are generally amazing things, but I don't think of his films as places where actors get to shine very much. It's more like they become parts of the machinery. But maybe *Titanic* won't be so special-effects oriented.

Phew. It is. Huge special effects. I don't know, I'm just going to do it, and we'll see.

I've read that you love to travel.

I do. I just skydived recently. My 'chute didn't open. [*laughs*]

Well, you're here.

Yeah, I'm here. It was a tandem thing, and I jumped out of the plane, and I pulled the cord, and my 'chute didn't open. And the next thing I know, the guy with me pulls out a knife and cuts this cord and we start free-falling. And you know, it's not like a video game where if you mess up, you're okay, you lose a quarter. [*laughs*] This is your life. The whole trip down I didn't cry. I wasn't weirded out by it. I was just . . . depressed. [*laughs*] Let's see, this year I also went scuba diving in the Great Barrier Reef.

I've always wanted to do that.

Oh, God. It's like space. It's the best thing you could ever do. Better than anything.

I saw the IMAX film about it.

Yeah, the one Meryl Streep narrates. That was trippy. Did you see that ill sea creature that was at the bottom of the ocean that was about a mile long? How trippy was that, bro? [*laughs*] When I was young, I had this thing where I wanted to see everything. It's weird how that's sort of died down. I used to think, How can I die on this earth without seeing every inch of this world?

Have you been a lot of places?

I have. Madagascar is where I really want to go next. I went to Africa for *Total Eclipse*, but I didn't see any wildlife at all. It was depressing. We shot between Somalia and Ethiopia, which is where all the refugees go, so it was like . . . kids walking around on all fours from polio, literally like animals.

Do you ever pick films because they're going to be shot in exotic locales?

Nope. Otherwise I wouldn't have chosen Mexico twice. I'm going to be spending a year of my life in Mexico.

Isn't *Titanic* being filmed there?

Yeah. Rosarito Beach. There's garbage everywhere.

At least you're in a profession where you get incredible opportunities, like being able to travel a lot.

It is fucking cool. I really love acting. I love it when it's really about acting. I love it when you get to create stuff, and collaborate with a director. You feel like what you're doing is not going to waste. It's in the archives. It's going to be there for years. Pain is temporary, film is forever. That's my big quote that [*This Boy's Life* director] Michael Caton-Jones told me: "Pain is temporary, film is forever."

But then you'll get old and you'll have pain all the time.

Mm-hm. I don't know. [*pause*] My grandpa just died last year. That was a big depressing thing. And my dog died. Our household dog. Last year was like the year of . . . misery. But this year, so far, I have to say I'm liking it a lot.

No complaints?

No complaints.

LETTER BOMB
How Gordon Lish Became "Gordon Lish"
(December 1996)

Gordon Lish is one of the literary world's most curious figures. His reputation is so subdivided—as an editor, a mentor, a novelist—that it can be difficult to form an opinion of him. Many have formed opinions, however, and Lish generally inspires either protective loyalty among those he has supported or furious dislike among those he hasn't. To his champions, he is the former Knopf editorial kingpin who nurtured the work and careers of Raymond Carver, Don DeLillo, Gabriel García Márquez, and others. More important still, as the fiction editor of *Esquire*, he is among the chief architects of the minimalist fiction movement that dominated critical thought in the 1980s. To those who revile Lish, he is an arrogant fussbudget of an editor and writer, the man who launched an initially successful literary magazine, the *Quarterly*, then blew it all by packing its pages with the work of interchangeable anal-retentive young writers, and who occasionally writes irksome, refined novels designed only to infuriate the reader.

As a writer, Lish is definitely a noisemaker, a provocateur. His most famous novel, *Dear Mr. Capote*, takes the form of a letter to the famous writer from a deranged murderer. *Extravaganza*, another novel, is a sequence of interrelated, repetitive jokes. His short-story collections *What I Know So Far* and *Mourner at the Door* are like literary puzzle books full of brief, tricky prose poems and imitations/homages/parodies of favorite and/or hated writers like Salinger, Bellow, and Roth. What the books share are smooth, tight-assed prose, a kvetchy tone, and a near obsessive-compulsive tendency to cutesiness, generally whenever Lish feels called upon to represent an authentic emotion. Apart from *Dear Mr. Capote*, which some camps of the critical establishment consider a cult classic, his novels have each been subject to a few defensively swoony partisan reviews. But they've been more often received with nervous, backhandedly respectful silence, no doubt because Lish is regarded as too powerful and cranky a figure to risk pissing off.

Things have changed. Lish and Knopf parted ways a few years back, and he has not been in an editorial position since. The *Quarterly* lost the sponsorship of its publisher, Random House, and has become a marginal publication. Minimalism is no longer a tasty buzzword. Subsequently, Lish has become something of an outcast whose enemies outnumber and outpower his friends. His new novel, *Epigraph*, is being published not by a major house but by the admirable smaller press Four Walls Eight Windows, known for its careful, eccentric roster of experimental writers. Technically, this move makes complete sense, as Lish's weird novels have had a hard time establishing an identity in the mainstream. Many have seen them as the self-indulgent flights of fancy of a workaholic, and their publication as mere perks of his powerful position. In the context of Four Walls Eight Windows, Lish can be seen clearly for what he is at this point in his career—an iconoclastic fiction writer, period, a Gilbert Sorrentino– or Ronald Sukenick–type who publishes books not for the money or fame but for whatever it is that makes serious writers bother.

Epigraph is the most provocative novel Lish has ever written, which is not to say it's his best. Still, on the basis of its gumption alone, this short book is some kind of benchmark. Talk about your high concepts. *Epigraph* takes the form of a series of crazed letters written by one "Gordon Lish," whose wife, "Barbara," has just died after a lengthy degenerative disease. The letters are mostly addressed to the Christian caregiving women who took care of his wife in her final months, though there are also occasional missives to a "Clerk of the Court," remonstrating with him for continuing to send his deceased wife notices for jury duty, and to the church agency that lent the Lishes some sort of life-support device, a specially equipped bed he's grown sentimentally attached to and refuses to give up. All that is straightforward enough. The tricky part comes from the fact—much trumpeted in the publicity that accompanies the novel—that Lish's real-life wife, also named Barbara, died after a lengthy degenerative disease not long before he completed the novel.

Reading this novel is a challenge on a number of levels, the most obvious and consuming of these being the old "Is this real or is it Memorex?" question. It's Memorex, for sure, but rather than stabilizing the work, the pseudo-ness of Lish's memoir only adds to its difficulties. If it's not true, then how much of its mean-spirited, self-aggrandizing, accusatory ranting is Lish's and how much is "Lish's"? Are *Epigraph*'s implausibly obsessive attacks on his wife's caregivers' behavior a twisted catharsis on Lish's part, or are they as ironic as they seem? Or are they half-truths? If we dislike the narrator—and it's almost impossible not to find him boring and simplistic—are we disliking Lish? Or by judging Lish on his narrator's actions, have we fallen into his conceptual trap? And who are we to question the stylistic choices of someone so presumably deep in grief? In a funny way, reviewing *Epigraph* invokes some of the same problems that plague critics of science-fiction novels—i.e., if we haven't seen the future, how do we judge the success or failure of a writer's imagination? In that situation, a work lives or dies depending on the seductiveness of its prose. And that's what we're left with here.

This much is certain: Lish's prose is a drag. Sure, he can make fluid, complex, yet unassuming sentences and string them together with an impressive finesse, but none of that ultimately matters, because he has such a limited pitch—hysterical, paranoid, insistent, guilty—that all his subtle cadences and rhythmic flip-flops fuse together into something that would be hard to enjoy even if what he was writing about weren't simultaneously grim and phony. *Epigraph* starts out sincere, grows crazier and crazier—and Lish's idea of crazy is to rev up the vocal tics and name-check his own literary identities—then apologizes for itself for a few pages, and ends in a self-consciously literary flourish with a fake "Errata" and a quote by Julia Kristeva that basically evacuates readers from the novel's narrative premise and asks us to believe that *Epigraph*'s tedium is the point: Lish, pursuing the ineffable, has naturally grown antisocial, non-demonstrative, and uninteresting. He is at the mercy of literature and, more specifically, of language, which naturally fails all serious seekers of truth, or, as Kristeva has it, of "the invisible."

All great novels make that point in some way or another. But the truthfulness of Lish's/Kristeva's point doesn't justify what amounts to an unpleasurable, unenlightening, and predictable read. Lish wanted to write a novel as a series of letters, and he did so, by hook or by crook, and his unwavering dedication to this preset structure is his downfall. The novel goes nowhere precisely because he won't let it. He can blame literature, but the problem is his unwillingness to surrender to literature. He has tackled the subject of his wife's death with the exact same mannerisms and stylistic devices that he has used to tackle everything he has ever written about. So it's no surprise that the whole enterprise feels cheap and secondhand. Lish's idiosyncratic talent is a valued and underrated presence in contemporary fiction, but in this particular case, he just comes off like a freak.

WHY DOES HERR F. RUN AMOK?
Rainer Werner Fassbinder
(February 1997)

Twenty-five years ago, the term "foreign film" was shorthand for better-than-American film, and local buffs prowled repertory houses like the Nuart and the late, great Fox Venice looking for the new Godard/Bergman/Fellini. It was the early '70s. Movies were first and foremost an art form, specterlike and eventful, and the beautiful people were all atwitter about a sudden onslaught of them from, of all places, Germany. Sometimes called the German New Wave or the New German Cinema, these sharp and sharply varied films by a half dozen or so young, unknown directors were squarely in the tradition of earlier film waves from France and Italy—i.e., irrevocably personalized, narratively distressed, and capital-A aesthetic above everything else—but with a refreshing, hard-edged gloominess that seemed to nail youth culture's post-hippiedom depression of the time and predict the coming punk revolution.

There was the stern, spacey Werner Herzog, whose meandering tone poems were much adored by brainy young potheads. And Hans-Jurgen Syberberg, deviser of extremely long, stagy, curiously stiff-jointed films that were something like a shotgun wedding between Robert Wilson and Sid and Marty Krofft. Wim Wenders's work interestingly mistranslated Bob Rafelson and Nicholas Ray's off-kilter Americana into a kind of Teutonic slackerese. There were the sublime and delicate visual collages of Alexander Kluge, the artsy action films of Werner Schroeter. Most extravagantly of all, there was Rainer Werner Fassbinder, an insanely prolific avant-garde theater-director-turned-filmmaker whose work presented such a mind-boggling crosshatch of the intellectual, the crude, the old-fashioned, and the daredevil that they smacked of genius. "Genius" is a word you almost never hear anymore—with the rise of identity politics, the concept of know-it-all artists seems not only quaint but slightly fascist, though it was key to Fassbinder's legend, and that legend—based in part on behavior so extravagantly quixotic that it made Orson Welles seem like Rob Reiner—was inextricable from the work at hand.

In a career that spanned just under fifteen years, Fassbinder went from making fiercely thought-out, rocky-looking features like *Why Does Herr R. Run Amok?* (1969), a slapdash but mesmerizing paean to self-destruction that Fassbinder later declared one of the most disgusting German films ever made, and *Chinese Roulette* (1976), a high postmodernist puzzle of a film that Michel Foucault once credited with helping to inspire deconstructionist theory, to crafting the elegant trilogy of Sirkian melodramas that basically capped Fassbinder's voluminous output—*The Marriage of Maria Braun* (1978), *Lola* (1981), and *Veronika Voss* (1981). In between *Herr R.* and the trilogy, Fassbinder tried almost every filmmaking style under the sun: post-neorealism, as in the critically revered *Mother Küsters Goes to Heaven* (1975) and *Ali: Fear Eats the Soul* (1973); the borderline conventional *Fox and His Friends* (1975), a grimly poignant portrait of a doomed working-class gay hustler that hugely influenced Queer Cinema; the avant drawing-room comedies like *Beware of a Holy Whore* (1970), *Satan's Brew* (1976), and *Despair*

(1978), a much anticipated but weirdly misfiring English-language collaboration between Fassbinder, the screenwriter Tom Stoppard, and Dirk Bogarde in one of his last screen performances; political films like *Katzelmacher* (1969), *The Third Generation* (1979), and *Bremen Freedom* (1972), all thought to be among Fassbinder's trickiest, not surprising when you consider that in his lifetime he was denounced as both an anarchist and an anti-Semite; and even a television miniseries, *Berlin Alexanderplatz* (1980), whose deliriously sneaky ensemble acting and complicated, laconic narrative paved the way and suggested the visual language for *Twin Peaks*, *The Singing Detective*, Lars von Trier's *The Kingdom*, and pretty much any other quality television series you can think of.

All in all, Fassbinder seems to have been incapable of either perfection or disaster. Even when he's infuriating, say in the irritatingly passive-aggressive *Lili Marleen* (1981) or the knuckleheaded pseudo-gangster pic *Love Is Colder Than Death* (1969), the torture tends to linger meaningfully. His one almost-dud, *Querelle* (1982), a wildly overschematic and static take on Jean Genet's novel starring a hopeless Brad Davis, doesn't really count, since it was edited after Fassbinder's death, and has an inadvertent, between-the-lines appeal only if you understand it as Fassbinder's repressed mash note to Davis, whom he was often quoted drooling over in interviews. For every flawed Fassbinder work, there are several near masterpieces—the brutal downer *In a Year of Thirteen Moons* (1978), the densely layered soap operas *The Bitter Tears of Petra von Kant* (1972) and *The Merchant of Four Seasons* (1971), to name a handful. The worst that can be said about Fassbinder's work is that it overachieves as often as it achieves, but always with an intimidating stylishness that makes his glitches not only forgivable but possibly necessary.

As amazing as Fassbinder's work itself is the fact that he managed to do so much of it while simultaneously wrecking himself with alcohol and hard drugs. He died at thirty-seven of so-called natural causes, all very publicly and with obvious extracurricular consequences, such as the sadistic psychological games he was purported to have played with his bizarrely loyal and/or codependent actors, many of whom—Hanna Schygulla, Ulli Lommel, Kurt Raab, Ingrid Caven, and others—formed the regular population of his movies. There are several books currently in print that provide an unstinting chronicle of Fassbinder's short, furious life and the toll it took on everyone around him, and they're well worth a look. For a quick take on the majestic hideousness of his personality, check out *Germany in Autumn* (1978), a short documentary about Fassbinder's relationship with his then boyfriend, an unbelievably masochistic thirtysomething man whom Fassbinder berates, humiliates, rapes, and beats up in a drunken rage. If the man hadn't committed suicide not long after the film was completed, *Germany in Autumn* would seem a very dark act of fictional self-parody. Instead, as Fassbinder himself later described it, "It's a film which, for minutes at a time, strikes me as more terrible than terrible."

Fassbinder's films have been all but out of circulation for a decade, more invisible than unfashionable, for reasons known only to their distributors. It will be interesting to see how his work looks now after all that breathing space, since its original cachet was so involved in the fact that his films arrived and departed in such a flurry—in 1970 alone, he had five features in release, and followed such an unpredictable course, changing styles, subjects, and POVs seemingly at whim. The only contemporary director who comes close to matching Fassbinder's output is Woody Allen, but even he seems lazy and repetitious by comparison. In their time, in his rush, Fassbinder's films seemed less distinct, separable works than a series of progress reports from one man's rather violent struggle to master his medium. He couldn't, but he certainly made it seem infinitely pliable. Still, Fassbinder and his films are history now, as weird as that seems. There's nothing left to do but sort out the good, the bad, and the ugly.

A RAVER RUNS THROUGH IT
(March 1997)
Cowritten with Joel Westendorf

Even if you haven't read *On the Road*, you probably know the story of Jack Kerouac and Neal Cassady's semi-mythological road trip. If you don't know the story, suffice to say it took place in the 1950s, a time of political conservatism and pervasive emotional and sexual repression. These two future Beat icons set off in search of what they believed was the real, if temporarily confused, America, a place of unlimited hope and big, wild dreams.

Well, this is that kind of story. Except our wanderlust hasn't been fueled by jazz, booze, and the prismatic beauty of free verse poetry. Instead, it's stoked by rave's dreamy, experimental music and almost crazily sweet ideology. We're heading into a more fucked-up America, with even more blind faith than the Beats could ever imagine.

Our rental car is zipping through the huge blur of desert between Palm Springs and the eastern California border. Somewhere beyond the desert's bleak and scalding horizon is Flagstaff, Arizona, site of the World Unity Festival, billed as a weeklong United Nations–sponsored showcase for indigenous cultures from around the world. We're targeting one of the festival's sub-events, a four-day Mega-Rave that has been the talk of rave aficionados since it popped up on the Internet last spring. Supposedly organized by the Zippies, a relentlessly self-hyping gaggle of middle-aged English rave promoters, it promises to do for ravers what the original Woodstock did for the hippie set—namely, crystallize an underground movement, magnetize a thus far indifferent media, and give the already converted an incredible time.

The two of us are friends, but we come from very different backgrounds. One (Dennis) was rudely awakened from childhood when an older friend played him *The Velvet Underground & Nico*, and his musical taste has evolved along alternative rock lines ever since. The other (Joel), almost twenty years younger, grew up addicted to soul and R&B, but with enough interest in New Age music to spend his Sundays with a syndicated radio program called *Musical Starstreams*. Still, he only fell in love when electronics married tribal rhythms in the sprawling genre dubbed techno. To Dennis, dance music is little more than a form of mass hypnosis. To Joel, rock 'n' roll has grown unchallenging and obvious, and Stone Temple Pilots have a cuter feel than Sonic Youth. Point is, we're plunging into rave culture with mixed feelings.

To read published reports in such magazines as *Details* and *Options*, you'd think rave was already dead in its crib, a victim of its proponents' drug-induced befuddlement, and of inter-scene squabbles over what constitutes a pure rave experience. But that contradicts everything we've seen and felt over the past four months as we crisscrossed the western United States and visited rave's hothouse, London. Dennis, whose limited scene experience and indie-rock bent makes him something of a rave couch potato, is feeling a rumble of countercultural hope that he hasn't felt since the early days of punk. Joel's identity has already been shaped by his immersion in rave culture, and he talks excitedly about his and his friends' intentions to infect the world with their wide-eyed enthusiasm.

So what is rave exactly? Well, it's hard to explain. You might think back to the mid-'70s, or even further back to the late '60s, in the sense that, like punk and hippiedom, rave is a countercultural movement with specific musical tastes, a highly developed fashion sense, and a left-of-Democratic politics. But unlike punks or hippies, ravers are more interested in issues of spiritual growth and increased communication than they are in transgressing traditional political structures. To generalize—and with a movement this amorphous, you're forced to—ravers tend to see the government and its laws as besides the point. If ravers lionize anything, it's technology, which offers ways to circumvent the kinds of blockage that derailed countercultures of the past. Rave is not about destroying corrupt power structures; it's about general things like self-belief, open-mindedness, and faith. It's about seeking the limitless. Hippies and punks named their enemies, which helped the media define them. They had specific goals, and when these goals weren't met, their movements were easily debunked. Ravers have no particular enemies, so they're relatively invisible. And their invisibility is their strength.

Rave is nothing particularly new. In England, the movement has been barreling along since 1987 or before. But in America, where the media tends to grab, misread, and gentrify every passing trend at birth, rave has somehow managed to grow in popularity and mutate aesthetically for a number of years now, with only the occasional sidelong glance from MTV and the rock music press. *Wired* and *Mondo 2000* have done their share of profiles, but, even there, coverage has been light, slanted to suit the magazines' technological themes and bemusedly parental in tone. Then there are articles like the feature in *Details*, which quoted a few disgruntled fans and promoters, then declared the LA rave scene a dead duck.

It's kind of ironic that Los Angeles's Millennium I, which quickly sold out its eight thousand tickets, happened just about the time that *Details* ran its funeral oratory. Organized by local promoters to meet the speculations of the film director Kathryn Bigelow, whose movie *Strange Days* required a huge New Year's Eve 1999 party scene, Millennium I was the exact opposite of an illegal underground party. Heavily advertised on local radio, its location in the streets of downtown Los Angeles required governmental support and massive police protection, which in turn severely curtailed attendees' drug use. A blocked-off intersection at the base of the Bonaventure Hotel became an immense, cross-shaped dance floor, blindingly lit for the cameras, constantly sprayed with confetti, and surrounded by actors dressed as machine-gun-toting National Guardsmen. The rave itself could easily have been dwarfed or co-opted by the moviemakers' designs and equipment. Instead they just seemed surreal, a kind of visual drug substitute that meshes surprisingly well with the sound of techno echoing wildly through the skyscrapers. Millennium I felt like a raver invasion. The ecstatic quality of the dancing that night had nothing to do with Ecstasy per se, and everything to do with having finally won a long, uphill battle.

So we've made it to Flagstaff. Unlike the bulk of Arizona, which is culturally arid and politically inhospitable, Flagstaff is a pretty little college town buried in the woods about eighty miles from the Grand Canyon's southern rim. Deep in its historic downtown section, currently a scaffold-covered eyesore partway through a Disneyland-style "restoration" project, is the office of the World Unity Festival. Occupying a room on the second floor of an artists' co-op building, its puniness is the first sign that we might be in for a letdown. In the doorway stands a short, balding hippie type, clearly stoned and obviously more than a little stressed out. Behind him several phones ring, ring, ring. He's staring forlornly out a dusty window, but when he spots us, he simultaneously stiffens and breaks into a shit-eating grin.

It seems the festival, scheduled to begin today, is siteless at the moment, not to mention long abandoned by the United Nations. The original site, near the Canyon, was never officially okayed. The second site, on a nearby Indian reservation, was yanked just two days ago when tribal leaders realized the scale of the planned event. But there's a chance, he says, that a local hippie commune, the Turtle Family, might donate part of its property, although he's not advising people to head on up there just yet since the roads to the commune are currently blocked off by police and their drug-sniffing dogs. "Check back later this afternoon," he tells us. Uh, will do. But in the meantime, how do we get in touch with the Zippies? He looks at us blankly. You know, the people who are organizing the Mega-Rave? His bloodshot eyes widen. "The . . . what?"

On the street, we buy a local newspaper. Sure enough, its front page is a multipart article detailing the festival organizers' incompetence. There are several pictures of despondent out-of-towners slouched in front of local businesses and wandering the streets. We drive around the city, blasting techno, the place a sea of lost festivalgoers. Every once in a while, a car will pass ours, also blasting techno, and hopeful squints are exchanged. Plastikman is in the tape deck. Joel is dancing in his seat, head flicking back and forth, his hands raised, fingers slicing at the air. Dennis is constitutionally unsuited to dancing, but he's all ears. Plastikman, a project of a young Canadian named Richie Hawtin, uses a speedy, rolling tick-tock beat overlaid with spare, shredded-sounding synthesizer textures. It sounds a bit like straw feels. Crackly.

We stop into what appears to be Flagstaff's two hippest CD stores; neither of the shop's clerks have heard anything about a Mega-Rave, and don't seem particularly interested in the prospect. So we give up for the moment and check into a hotel, lug our clothes and tapes inside, and settle in for what looks to be a very long week. The Mega-Rave is scheduled to commence two days from now, so all is not lost quite yet. Still, when we call the festival office later in the afternoon, the phones have been disconnected, and we reluctantly begin studying the hotel's *Tourist Guide*.

Dennis is pissed. He's used to the rock world's professionalism. After all, rock 'n' roll has had decades to organize. But Joel is just a little bit disappointed. He scrunches his face up and glares into space for a couple of minutes. Then he's his cheery young self again, leaning over a road map, calculating the distance from here to the town of Sedona, supposedly a site of great spiritual energy. Apparently, fuckups like this aren't uncommon in rave culture. Maybe now just isn't the time for a Mega-Rave. Maybe the culture is still too chaotic and lively to get that in focus. So in a way it's a positive thing, eyes on the future and all that. Dennis wonders if Joel's in denial or something. Then he thinks about Woodstock, and how much more interesting '70s rock might have been without that overrated signpost. If nothing else, we might have been spared Ten Years After.

Earlier in the summer we separately attended two rave-related events, one of which piqued Dennis's interest, the other of which confirmed Joel's hopes.

Narnia is the closest thing rave culture has to Lollapalooza. This yearly rave, always held in some unannounced location in California, has a reputation for being the most elaborate and professional event in the country. Named after a series of novels by C. S. Lewis, it promises a veritable dream world: seven different "lands," one to suit attendees' every possible mood, from an ambient area for relaxing between dance spurts to a special-effects-thrashed area featuring the hardest techno beats. Dennis, being the novice of this duo, figured Narnia was the perfect place to begin.

Narnia, near San Diego, California: At first I don't know where I am. Then my eyes adjust and the place gets real. I'm at the entrance of an abandoned quarry. A dozen huge mounds of gravel and dirt have gradually weathered into a mini-mountain range, creating a series of isolated valleys connected by winding trails. The entirety is lit up in blurry purples, reds, and yellows, and crisscrossed by thousands of vibrating laser beams coming from all directions. They rise and fall every couple of seconds like a thatched lid. Passing through them, I'm bombarded by a confusion of sounds—a soft, meandering whir from a small gravel pit over to my left; some old-fashioned hip-hop blasting from a big tin shed over the hill to my right; acid jazz apparently being played live at some spot in the distance; and, overwhelming them all, the *thud-thud-thud* and *squeak-squeak-squeak* of techno pounding from the valley below me.

I wander around, following the little trails from gravel pit to gravel pit. The ambient area has a sleepy campfire atmosphere. People are scrunched up in sleeping bags, talking and passing joints. Up and over the hill is the acid jazz area. A band plays on an unlit stage, but most of the listeners are gathered at a series of booths along the pit's opposite wall. One booth offers face painting. Greenpeace mans another. Two booths sell legal faux Ecstasy pills made from ephedra root, ginseng, and other herbs. I buy a few, then take the first trail I find into a pit full of stuttering white light. The music sounds like a skipping CD. There are several hundred stiffened bodies of indeterminate gender vibrating on their feet in a clump. They look like they're being electrocuted. I'm out of here, and over the hill. Which brings me back to techno.

This is obviously Narnia's main attraction. It's easily four times larger than the other pits, and ringed by a long, narrow, curving stage full of drums, gongs, speaker cabinets, and several mixing decks. Above the stage hangs a five-story screen, upon which lasers, slides, and Super-8 movie loops battle it out at such a high speed that it's impossible to pick out the imagery. All around me, thousands of people dance, grin, and stare at the same time. Most of them look very high, but there's not a beer can or bottle to be seen, which may be the most disorienting detail of all. Teenagers and people in their twenties predominate, but there is a fair number of us older types, and, unlike at a rock gig, I can't immediately peg them as record company employees. The male-to-female ratio is about 60:40. Clothes are loose, colorful, and designer casual. Hairstyles vary from hippie-esque to shaved.

It's strange how seductive the music becomes in this setting, even to this rockist's ears. Songs parade by, cross-fading almost unnoticeably, like individual movements in some vast, nightlong symphony. I stand around for a while, kind of weak in the knees, craning my neck, trying to decide if it's the most otherworldly sight I've ever seen, off acid anyway. Everybody looks intensely self-involved. Their slack, unreadable expressions give the scene its only meaning, though I'm not exactly sure what it means. They just move around in tight little areas, mesmerized by their surroundings, oblivious to but seemingly respectful of their neighbors. One woman is dressed as a butterfly. Another guy is wearing a space suit. Sometimes they're in sharp silhouette. Sometimes, when the light show cooperates, they're so garishly lit you'd think they were paid entertainers.

They're amazing to watch, better than a band, maybe because they're just a slightly more extroverted fraction of the rest of us—a kind of rave focus group in whose galloping bodies and delirious expressions it's actually possible to see pure, unmitigated happiness, like the kind cartoon characters feel. The music speeds up, slows down, speeds up. The light show flutters through its insane narrative. And I leave, fried, around four AM, pissed at myself for being such a wallflower, and wondering why my friends and I are so unwilling to really and truly relax.

Joel, whose previous rave experience gives him more access to the subtleties, chose the Rainbow Gathering, again an annual event, this year held a couple of hours south of Yellowstone Park. The Gathering, whose existence long predates rave, has traditionally been a kind of weekend-long campout and convocation for hippies and Deadheads, but it's become a popular place for ravers to meet and exchange ideas about the future of their movement.

The Rainbow Gathering, Wyoming: Last year the twenty-third annual Rainbow Gathering took place among the hills, meadows, and forests of the Bridger-Teton National Forest in western Wyoming. It's about forty-five minutes from the only thing close to civilization, a town called Big Piney, whose population I'd estimate at about 550.

The Gathering has always been an annual retreat for hippies, counterculture advocates, and nature lovers. But recently it's begun to draw some of the earthier members of the American rave movement, myself included. In fact, this year the Zippies made the event even more appealing by scheduling one of their parties just adjacent to the Gathering. True to form, they wind up arriving at the site too late to entertain anyone but the stragglers. Nevertheless, at its height, almost fifteen thousand people are in attendance.

Like a rave, the Rainbow Gathering involves so many sights, sounds, and activities that it's difficult to experience them all. I've been here for five of its scheduled seven days, and I'm far from exhausting it. We live in camps, each of which has its own kitchen serving ever-changing meals. Food is cooked in clay ovens that are constructed from materials gathered on-site. There have been group discussions on religion, relationships, philosophy, politics, and issues related to the Gathering itself. Attendees craft candles, pottery, weavings, and carvings. In an area my friend and I have dubbed the Rainbow Spa and Salon, you have the option of bathing or having your hair washed in solar-heated water. Showers are available, but someone has to hold the hose for you.

Alongside the physical similarities between the Gathering and a standard rave, there's the ever-present rhythm that characterizes them both. It doesn't matter whether it's forty beats per minute with laser accompaniment or ten to fifty flame-lit drummers in the middle of a two-hour, fireside percussion marathon—you develop an intense relationship to the rhythm. At raves, from the moment you arrive until your exhausted departure, you are surrounded by the beat. At the Rainbow Gathering, you fall asleep and wake up to drumming. The universal rhythm is constant.

But there are differences between the Gathering and a rave, especially in the attitude toward technology. Many Rainbow family members take pride in their shunning of the technological advances of contemporary culture. Some consider them aspects of "Babylon," a term they frequently use to disparage modern-day society. While it's certainly admirable to live without relying on the sometimes destructive advances wrought by science and chemistry, it makes me sad to think of the limitations these people could be placing on themselves. Maybe by consciously ignoring the outside world they've managed to achieve an ignorant bliss, but they're also missing out on the limitless possibilities that technology affords, which inspire so much hope in ravers.

Thankfully, most Rainbow Gatherers, whatever their beliefs, are here for a greater purpose. The Gathering is a break in time, an opportunity to enjoy what the earth has to offer outside the world of the man-made. If there's a message here, it's a simple one, and it applies to hippies and ravers alike: We must use modern life to keep these natural spirits alive, and make room for the unknown spirits that await us.

London, England: It's several months later and we're in a London hotel fighting off jet lag's weird high. Maybe we can pick up some pointers from these raver old-timers. Rave was born here. Actually, if you want to get technical about it, rave was probably born in Chicago on the day Genesis P-Orridge of Psychic TV noticed a record-store bin marked "Acid House," and mistakenly thought it meant acid as in LSD—it really meant acid as in the corrosive liquid. Anyway, P-Orridge took a slew of these records home to London, and, when the music wasn't as wild as the tag had implied, he set out to record what he'd heard in his daydreams. This new, tweaked-out, vaguely psychedelic dance music sounded stunning on Ecstasy, the drug of choice among trendy young Londoners. And it was extremely influential in both the rock and dance scenes, which have been traditionally less separatist than those in the States. When club DJs started adding this new acid house to their playlists, and rock bands like Happy Mondays, Stone Roses, and Charlatans ran with the ball, they kick-started a musical genre that would eventually filter overseas and lead people like ourselves starry-eyed to the source.

We'd heard rave was essentially dead in England. As far as we can tell, it is and it isn't. Certainly English rave has gentrified over the last few years. As we walk down Camden High Street—a kind of scruffier Melrose—techno blasts from most storefronts. On TV, corporate advertisers like Coca-Cola and Hyundai use it to audio-wrap their products. Even the BBC—establishment central—intros and outros their newscasts with weakling techno instrumentals.

What is all but dead are the large, illegal outdoor events that were British rave culture's early meat and potatoes. The government here is famous for its semi-fascism toward countercultural behavior, and ravers appear to be its current enemy number one. The Criminal Justice Bill, aimed in part at eliminating rave from the landscape, became a law at the end of last year, despite protests and demonstrations. The bill allows police to shut down any public gatherings of more than a couple dozen people.

And there are serious problems within the scene itself. Just a month before our arrival, a young Scottish raver sold some bad Ecstasy and was literally cooked alive on an Edinburgh dance floor, inspiring the hysteria-prone English tabloids to call for a crackdown and instigating a fierce debate within the pages of rave-oriented magazines such as *Mixmag* (e.g., "Do we need to be self-policing our drug use?").

Chris Campion, a London-based freelance writer, is a friend of a friend of Joel's. One night early in our visit, he offers to guide us through Megatripolis, a weekly indoor rave hosted by Heaven, one of the city's largest dance clubs. Campion, a wiry twenty-five-year-old with big, perpetually spooked brown eyes, is enthusiastic about the music, but—and here he echoes virtually every British rave aficionado we come into contact with—he feels rave is all but spent as a social force in England. He doesn't go out to events much anymore, preferring to hole up at home with his headphones. The last time he set foot in Megatripolis, it was years ago when the crowds were smallish and ultrahip.

Tonight the club is packed, and there's a decided "bridge and tunnel" non-look to most of the assembled. The dance floors are packed, but the energy is weird. Across one of the rooms is a bar with a thick fringe of thirsty people. Maybe that's the problem. In the States—and this was apparently the case during the early, heady days of English rave—alcohol is considered anathema to the transcendent nature of the rave experience. But now, with the government on rave's tail, and the move to safer quarters indoors . . . well, pollution was probably inevitable.

Our hopes for English rave are raised later in the week, when, scouring *Time Out*, London's popular weekly entertainment magazine, we notice an ad for something called Megadog. Megadog turns out to be a real mindblower on the order of Narnia and other large stateside events. Set in the sprawling auditorium and courtyard of a disused-looking university complex, it features several different environmentally distinct areas, and a flux of entertainment, from an extraordinary light show to berserk circus acts. This being England, the assembly seems a bit more reserved than we're used to, but there's that same tangible, indefinable feeling of mutual comfort and kindly interactions. Joel suddenly merges with the dancing horde, his face so blissed it's almost unrecognizable. Dennis watches Joel from the sidelines, then loses sight, and eventually he's just as high on all the beauty as everyone else.

Part of that beauty has to do with the absence of sexual tension. People are sweaty and shirtless. Bodies are moving in ways that would normally inspire, well, hormones. But nobody's cruising, or not that we can pick up on. Maybe it's the drugs. Unlike alcohol or coke, pot and Ecstasy do something sweet to the brain that seems to outbalance whatever lust incidentally arises: pot induces self-involvement; Ecstasy spins its cocoon of well-being. Everyone at Megadog seems kind of spaced and contentedly alone, despite their proximity. Maybe the asexuality is influenced by techno, which tends to be rather cerebral. Maybe it's a reaction to AIDS. Probably it's all of the above and more.

Techno doesn't get any more cerebral than the electronic music of the Future Sound of London. Their 1994 CD, *Lifeforms*, is so far advanced in every way from the work of even their most adventurous peers that it's impossible to characterize in a word. ("Progressive," maybe? Is that term safely disassociated from '70s pomp merchants like Yes and ELP?)

One day near the very end of our visit, we make a pilgrimage to FSOL's recording studios/second home in the north London suburbs, hoping to hear a less embittered read on the current state of rave. Garry Cobain, a stylish intellectual, and Brian Dougans, his painfully shy cohort, respond to our inquiries with a shrug and a very slight mist about the eyes. FSOL's plans have nothing to do with dance events. They talk about wanting to transgress every tradition of the pop music world, and build instead an extremely high-tech relationship between their music and whoever wants to listen. When they perform live, it's here in the studio, linked by telephone lines to an international array of radio stations and concert venues. They're in the early stages of starting their own television station, hoping to reformat their increasingly far-flung sound investigations.

FSOL may be idealists in desperate need of a reality check, or they may have just put their collective finger on a practical way to translate rave's extraordinary goals into cultural realities. Time will tell. In the meantime, they make an amazing noise. Just think, continues Cobain, gesturing wildly, the more the government tries to regulate art production, the more sophisticated FSOL's mode of communication will become. Dancing, drugs, record companies, MTV, governments . . . artists don't need to be tied down by any of them. "Just fucking imagine it," he enthuses. Joel and Dennis share a glance, and our trip sort of flashes before our eyes. Okay, cool. We can.

DRUG FICTION
(April 1997)

DOPE BOOKS: THE UPS AND DOWNS OF DRUGGED-OUT FICTION

Literature has always had a cozy on-and-off relationship with drugs. Back in the late nineteenth century, when cool people sat around in Parisian cafés drinking absinthe, Rimbaud, Verlaine, and Baudelaire were there to transcribe the results. More recently, such novelists as J. G. Ballard, Jack Kerouac, and Alexander Trocchi have dedicated their careers to making mind alteration seem romantic. In fact, every generation since Shakespeare has produced writers who explore drugs to heighten the effect of the standard narrative. Where would American literature be without Poe, Burroughs, Philip K. Dick, and Tennessee Williams, and where would they have been without their respective stashes?

So while it seems like every other book on the market lately is either some ex-junky's roman à clef or a designer drug–related tome, there's nothing to be either alarmed or overly hopeful about. These druggie and pseudo-druggie books are no more or less numerous than they ever were, and no better or worse. The only difference lies in the nature of the drugs that tend to capture writers' imaginations these days.

Take heroin, a drug that purportedly sends users on an almost religious experience, yet seems to give every writer who's tried to describe it the same grim down-and-out story. The more social drug Ecstasy has inspired some extremely lively prose, but with a few exceptions, it's also made for a rather banal, lovey-dovey worldview. Then there's crystal meth, a drug so anti-contemplation that it's doomed never to produce a related literature. Considering these drugs' creative limitations, and the fact that getting stoned is currently seen as more self-destructive than shamanistic, it's no shock that contemporary drug fiction hasn't been as groundbreaking as its historical forebears.

Drug literature first became a media phenomenon in the '60s, when drugs moved aboveground and their specific names entered the popular vocabulary. It was the era of psychedelic literature, and giddy hallucinogenic novels such as Thomas McGuane's *Ninety-two in the Shade*, Richard Brautigan's *Trout Fishing in America*, and Hunter S. Thompson's *Fear and Loathing in Las Vegas* (to name but a few) sometimes sold like Grisham potboilers. Readers too timid to actually partake in illicit substances experimented instead with these novels, and literature had its healthiest cutting edge ever.

In the '80s, novelists, like their contemporaries, were mostly into cocaine. Since coke users are a sneaky, sociopathic bunch, it's only natural that their novels reflected that behavioral mode. The most obvious example would be the Brat Pack, who, in a very few cases, perfected a clean, almost yuppified style that mostly betrayed its coked-up origins (simulated or otherwise) through a zigzaggy pace, a paranoid demeanor, and a severely clipped attention span. Bret Easton Ellis was and remains the god of this style, though the Brat Pack's general influence is apparent in the sincerely ironic (or is that ironically sincere) cyber–New Age novels of Douglas Coupland and others.

The '80s were also interesting for introducing a new kind of younger novelist who was clearly influenced by drug literature—especially the psychedelic novels of the '60s—yet who seemed not to have experimented with drugs on a personal level beyond a little requisite dabbling. William T. Vollmann, Mark Leyner, Rick Moody, and the late Kathy Acker are just a few of the writers whose work produces a disorienting effect while making only cursory, and in some cases rather derogatory, mention of drug use itself. They and other writers like them—most notably David Foster Wallace, a self-confessed recovered speed freak—have become a kind of new avant-garde for the Sober Generation, their books a collective testament to the peculiar power of the unaltered mind.

Still, in the past year or so, there have been a scatter of terrific drug-obsessed novels, most of which have gotten lost in the pack. Lee Williams's *After Nirvana* takes on post-grunge kids without a cause, nailing their plight with a curiously deadpan yet wicked style. Todd Grimson's *Brand New Cherry Flavor* is an exquisitely overripe tale of pill popping alt-rock scenesters. And Barry Graham's *Before* is a tender, sublimely economical study of young stoned Brits in love.

Drug fiction, however, has gotten much of its strongest reanimation from the much-talked-about Scottish writers, specifically a half dozen or so thirtysomething novelists based in and around Edinburgh. Their work represents the first cohesive, grassroots literary movement to hit English-language fiction since possibly the Beats. But unlike the Beats, to whom they've often been lazily compared, Irvine Welsh, Duncan McLean, Gordon Legge, Alan Warner, and others are incredibly good. There's not a Harold Norse among them, so far at least. Apart from Welsh, however, who lucked into fame thanks to the film version of his first novel, *Trainspotting*, the Scots are more talked about than read. Critics have been very parsimonious with their ink, and divided their opinions, for understandable but unfortunate reasons.

Part of the problem is the Scots' tendency to write in Scottish slang, which makes suspicious sorts worry they're being sold counterfeit goods. Unable to negotiate this style, critics seem afraid to commit, as though the movement were little more than a clever, antiestablishment prank. An even bigger problem is the Scots' subject matter—namely, the lives of people for whom Ecstasy, sex, and clubbing are serious business: in other words, youth culture, which has never been considered a proper literary topic, and worse still, rave culture, which remains a largely European phenomenon. In terms of American readership, the snag isn't so much that the novels are too hip, but rather that, in a time when young Americans are absorbed in the exploration of cyberspace, and occasionally will buy novels set in or around the Internet, the Scots' passionate computer illiteracy doesn't seem to register.

Of this rather consistently brilliant group, Alan Warner may be the most brilliant. A less show-offy writer than Welsh, Warner creates savage, meticulous back-worlds full of accidental violence, furious lust, unchecked drugging, and hopeless love. His second novel, *These Demented Lands*, out this month, is more refined than his first, the bone-crushingly great *Morvern Callar*, to which it forms something of a sequel. The setting is a remote island, apparently off Scotland's northeastern coast, where a death-obsessed investigator of airplane crashes, an aspiring rave promoter, and dozens of other mysterious, exquisitely half-drawn characters with names like The Devil's Advocate get stoned and think deeply about their circumstances, mostly in and around a decrepit honeymoon hotel called the Drome and its neighboring airstrip.

"I took off my clothes and climbed into bed. I let the CD music run on; it was some young-sounding band, moaning on with real enthusiasm. These young pessimists; what a joke—all day long they lament the darkness of the universe then drink all night and at six A.M. you can bet they won't be shitting a peptic ulcer out their still-tight arseholes. They want everything—even the right to pessimism; they won't accept it's a pleasure reserved for those of us over thirty."

An excerpt can't possibly do justice to Warner's rangy, compulsive, seismic prose, which not only knocks one out sentence by sentence but whose narrative builds and compounds itself like a ticking bomb. *Lands* is such a luscious read that Warner might just win over the snobs this time, although I suspect that, like most of the Scots' novels, it's doomed to gather dust in bookstores until either critics loosen up or thrill seekers realize that novels can be a source of major kicks again.

As unfamiliar as Warner and his fellow Scots' work may seem right now, theirs is actually a classical and even old-fashioned pursuit— trying to vivify fiction with mind-altering chemicals as their guides, counterpoints, and nemeses. In this they have greater ties to visionary writers like Rimbaud than they do to most of their contemporaries. In the end, the Scots don't just talk beautifully about the ups and downs of being high, they turn their readers into armchair day-trippers.

OPENINGS
Six Young Artists
(1994–2004)

RYAN TRECARTIN

When the choice between lingering in front of a video projector or hitting a half dozen other galleries is increasingly a cinch, the jolting energy, nerve, and intricacy of twenty-four-year-old Ryan Trecartin's work in the medium comes as no small shock. An abiding interest in indie rock, goth, psychedelia, and other hot topics won't distinguish his practice from that of other artists of his generation. But everything aesthetic about his videos—from the baroque screenplays that polish flippant teen slang into cascading soliloquies to the dueling fascinations with profound loneliness and extremely affected behavior to the swarming, jumbled, yet precisely composed shots that pack each frame to the rafters with visual stimuli—displays a near obliviousness to what's going on in his field, whether it be the clichés of current video art or the signature styles of past experimental films. Trecartin does, however, share a penchant for full-frontal gayness and a love of extravagance with the movie directors his work most immediately brings to mind: Kenneth Anger, Jack Smith, and early John Waters.

Trecartin was "discovered" last spring when a student at the Cleveland Institute of Art showed the visiting artist Sue De Beer a few minutes of a crazy video he'd found on the dating/networking Web site Friendster (www.friendster.com). Upon her return to New York, De Beer told the writer and former New Museum curator Rachel Greene about her find. With only the artist's first name to go on, together they searched Friendster's database until they found Trecartin's profile, then wrote to ask if he would send them a copy of the video in its entirety— a forty-one-minute work titled *A Family Finds Entertainment* (2004). Floored by what she saw, Greene began showing the piece to enthusiastic artists, curators, and gallerists. Several months and much buzz later, Trecartin's first solo show opens in January at the Los Angeles gallery QED; the J. Paul Getty Museum, an institution not exactly known for supporting young, unproven artists, has commissioned a new work that will be exhibited this spring; and *AFFE*, the video that started it all, will be in this year's Whitney Biennial.

All of these *Pecker*-like details aside, Trecartin is not your classic recontextualized outsider. Raised in rural Ohio, he designed costumes and stage sets in high school before picking up his first camera at the Rhode Island School of Design. While there, he made a number of short films, including *Yo, A Romantic Comedy* (2002), a messy, hypergay exercise in genre, and the heartfelt, bratty *Valentines Day Girl* (2001), and helped form a multidisciplinary art collective called Experimental People. After graduating in 2004, he moved to New Orleans with the group, whose members were among the huge cast appearing in *AFFE*. Then Hurricane Katrina destroyed Trecartin's elaborately painted, decorated home (featured prominently in the video) and with it virtually all of the nondigital artwork he'd ever made. Following a period of drifting and homelessness, Trecartin now lives and makes art in Los Angeles, thanks to the support of an admiring collector.

If *A Family Finds Entertainment* can be reduced to a thumbnail description, this might be it: Trecartin stars as Skippy, a clownish but terrifyingly psychopathic boy who has locked himself in the upstairs bathroom of his family home during a wild party. Ignoring his siblings' and friends' pleas that he come out, he paces the little room, cutting himself with a knife and musing opaquely on his existential dilemma in a kind of King Lear–style delirium. Downstairs, the partyers are experiencing wild mood swings and having complex, disassociated conversations (mostly about him) that are constantly interrupted by bursts of visual effects and animated sequences that disorient the cast of characters like so many lightning strikes. Eventually Skippy emerges, borrows money from his creepy, sexually inappropriate parents, and heads outdoors, where he runs into a documentary filmmaker who decides to make a movie about him—but then Skippy is immediately hit by a car and, apparently, killed. Back inside the house, a hyperactive girl named Shin, also played by Trecartin, gets a call on her cell phone with the bad news. She spends twenty or so hysteria-filled minutes trying to focus and construct a sentence linear enough to tell her friends what has happened. When she finally does, a band plays music that seems to magically raise the young man from the dead, and everyone runs outside and sets off fireworks. Then everyone runs back inside before the police show up.

A wonder of Trecartin's videos is that his approach seems as intuitive and driven by a mad scientist–style tunnel vision as it is rigorous and sophisticated, grounded in his expert editing and inordinate gift for constructing complex avant-garde narratives. For this reason, his movies resist the kind of deconstructive analysis through which one normally manages to strip new, challenging art down to its nuts and bolts. It's early yet, but the great excitement of Trecartin's work is that it honestly does seem to have come from out of nowhere.

FRANCES STARK

The day I walked through "The Power of Suggestion," LA MOCA's recent survey of drawings by young American artists, there was a pack of high schoolers on a field trip. They moved from room to room, gathering in campfire-like semicircles around each piece. Their teacher, a balding gent with a mildly cultured air, would ask them what they thought so-and-so was attempting to convey, and they would mostly try to come up with elegant ways of saying, "It's weird but kind of cool," over and over. All except for a handful of artsy teens near the back, who maintained a tightlipped nonchalance. Then the group reached Frances Stark's *Untitled (Goethe)* (1995), four interrelated works on paper consisting of text fragments from Goethe's novel *The Sorrows of Young Werther*, lightly traced out in purplish-blue carbon. Although the drawings were as prim, cryptic, and seemingly adult as the other art in the show had been bouncy, explosive, and seemingly youthful, the artsy clique suddenly came to life, rhapsodizing and gesturing in a way that seemed to flummox their teacher and fellow students. Their buzz of "amazing" and "I know what she means" had a rapt sincerity so at odds with their grooveball demeanor that it made me wonder.

"Maybe they responded passionately," says Stark, "because that's what I'm doing in a lot of my work—having a kind of love affair with an artist's voice. I'm not interested in the texts I use necessarily. . . . I'm not a fan of Goethe or *Werther*. When I first read the novel, I thought it was boring. I'm just fascinated by the construction of interiority. And maybe those kids were responding to the work's touch, because it's not creepy or ironic."

Stark is part of that sparkling group of relatively recent Art Center College of Design graduates who are just now coursing through the art world—Sharon Lockhart, T. J. Wilcox, and Joe Mama-Nitzberg among them. Art Center is a school famously smitten with French theory (i.e., its recent sponsorship of the ravey Baudrillard "Chance" conference), and Stark, like the best of her fellow alumni, is a reluctant disciple. Formally, the visual patterning of her work is so reduced that it seems to require an instruction manual, until, that is, one notices its reference points—Goethe, Emily Dickinson, the Beatles—whereupon her tight lines and seemingly precious arrangements become almost unbearably tender and parochial, and the field of emotionally magnetized pop-cultural particles organizes into a radiant code. At heart, she is the sadder, wiser descendant of every grade-schooler who ever mindlessly emblazoned her or his notebook cover with stars' names and rock lyrics. She has merely clarified the impulse—and refined the practice into an art so obsessive and fragile that it seems to emanate all the wistfulness in the world.

"Like in the pieces I did about the Beatles," Stark says, referring to her characteristically spare drawings, some gigantic, some tiny, in which a timeline of the band's career that Stark found in a press kit for the film *Backbeat* was meticulously traced with carbon paper, cut up, and arranged in lonely-looking blocks of text. "To me, the Beatles are the definition of modern fame, and that's about it, as far as what they mean at this point in time. I wasn't thinking about them really. I was thinking about the typist sitting at a computer in some office hurriedly typing out the same Beatles timeline that had been printed a zillion times before. It was full of the kinds of mistakes that you could only make on a computer, and I loved that. The sloppiness, the reduction of something that had once been the biggest, most sexualized, hottest, craziest fucking thing in the world into this chronology that didn't even mean anything anymore. I think of those lines as brushstrokes in a way. I repeat some of them just because they have awesome typos."

Like a good many Los Angeles artists past and present, Stark likes to have a number of media at her disposal. She is a writer of lush experimental fiction that has appeared in a number of anthologies and journals. She has sung and played in rock bands, including lo-fi cult favorites Palmetto and Layer Cake. She is the anonymous rotating "model" in Charles Ray's *Fashions* film, and stars as Yoko Ono in Raymond Pettibon's forthcoming feature-length video, *The Holes You Feel*. She even makes a medium out of fandom; Xerox copies of her dense, needy, verbose letters to favorite rock stars like Pavement's Steve Malkmus and Sebadoh's Jason Loewenstein have appeared in both her visual art and her fiction. It's telling that when she speaks to artists whose work means the world to her, she can only go on obsessively about herself, but when she deals with the work itself, she can barely even alter the originals. Stark is a kind of respectful customizer, tweaking assembly-line typefaces until they become disembodied, secondary manuscripts in which her admiration, envy, and romantic projections fuse with her heroes' genius.

"In a way," says Stark, "I'm trying to re-create that feeling of how you can stare at five hundred pictures of George Harrison or Jason Loewenstein or whoever, and you can feed so close, but then so far. It's just that I'm interested in working with language, not with visual images. . . . I just love how literature can be mimetic and revealing at the same time." Stark's work makes that love visual and wholly remarkable.

TORBJORN VEJVI

Why is it that when you're a kid, you can imagine perfect things, but you can't make them, and when you're an adult, you can make perfect things, but you can't play with them? This deep if unlikely question is brought to mind by the work of Torbjorn Vejvi, a twenty-seven-year-old Swedish artist based in Los Angeles.

In a series of small sculptures produced in 1998 and 1999, Vejvi selected pictures from the pages of old *National Geographic* magazines and glued them to foam core, creating complex, three-dimensional objects that treat the images' reality the way a chandelier treats light. Each picture is cut into pieces and reorganized around the shape of a witty architectural model, such that the image splits apart, like child's clothes forced onto an adult's body. This transformation of the picture into sculpture instantiates an investigation of the image, refocusing its dramatic emphasis, modulating its tone, and reshaping even its depicted space—in effect transforming the image into a crime scene, in which its original purpose is simultaneously degraded and magnified in meaning, à la trace evidence. Sometimes the effect is severe, as in *Between races* (1998), in which a nondescript shot of jockeys playing pool is weirdly dislocated. At other times, the interest lies in Vejvi's reverence, as in *Old house* (1998), where an image of a rickety mansion has been rebuilt as a tiny (somehow flatter) movie set, while the group of people dancing around it meld into the façade as if decorative elements in a mural. Vejvi's genius lies in his ability to translate his emotional response to each image into a unique, diagrammatic form whose empathic yet wary build causes one to think about the ways emotion can be distanced, which, in turn, inspires an unsettling intellectual disquiet.

Vejvi grew up in a remote forest in southern Sweden. One night, his parents took him to the city of Goteborg to see a major theater production. Vejvi was entranced, less by the play itself than by the elaborate sets. He began to build little theaters in his bedroom, first writing plays to justify the sets, and finally designing sets that suggested an accompanying narrative. Encouraged by his parents and teachers, he continued to draw, paint, and make objects without really thinking of himself as an artist. Eventually, he enrolled in the graduate program of one of Sweden's most respected art schools, Malmo Art Academy. At that point, he was painting and making sculptures and short videos, which he began to show in Malmo and Stockholm. In 1997, he was offered the chance to study at UCLA for a year. After he settled in Los Angeles, his work was quickly recognized and championed by local artists, critics, and curators. In a fortuitous coincidence, the LA art community's current, intensive dialogue around formalism's growth potential (through aesthetic decision-making that is less conscious than hallucinogenically intuitive) facilitated the decoding of Vejvi's brilliantly original attempt to turn advanced sculptural notions into workhorses for ideas traditionally relegated to photography and painting, and his success inspired him to remain in Southern California.

Having devoted himself to art at such a young age, and in relative seclusion, he cites few major influences, though the painters Sigmar Polke, Luc Tuymans, and Peter Doig are among his favorites. Emotion and memory being his subject matter, Vejvi has sought out a variety of ways to control and minimize their "chaos" through a balance of "abstraction and realness," and he mentions a crucial point in his development when he discovered that "space can be not just a volume, but a place of tension, too, and that negative space can be used as a point of contact." In fact, it is characteristic of Vejvi's work that its meaning is to be found in the spaces in between. Although known for working small, his newest, larger pieces, such as *10 feet up in the air* (1999), an impeccably messy pile of inoperable paper airplanes, are even more impressive, as he seeks to create work that "demands a physical response equal to its cerebral one."

To that end, Vejvi has recently abandoned found imagery to build an extraordinary series of boxlike sculptures that utilize emotionally charged material in an emblematic way. Too tender and impractical to be architectural models, and too bemused and poignant to qualify as minimalist sculptures, these extremely attenuated memorials to Vejvi's childhood incorporate simplistic, resonant iconography into optical illusions that simulate the tricky, doomed negotiations between past experience and memory, as though art's rarefied process were a kind of magical force capable of reconciling them. In *Untitled* (1999), two rows of trees made of contact paper bracket a white box, seeming to diminish forever into two of its sides, only reaching alignment along the walls of a narrow hallway that bisects the sculpture. The shadowed interior of the passageway is illuminated by a precious, melancholy beam of natural light that falls through a circular hole cut into the ceiling. In another box piece, also *Untitled* (1999), eight decals depicting a generic boy and dog face off across a closed hallway that circumscribes the sculpture, serving as portals to the conflicted nostalgia at the heart of the work, while a blank, open-ended hallway bisecting the box's interior conveys a faint, disjunctive loneliness. Like the sublimely nonsensical images in the best of Robert Wilson's theater productions, these spare, perfectly symmetrical juxtapositions of emotive signage and suggestively empty space create an atmosphere at once personal and so reduced and essence-free as to seem abstracted from the collective unconscious. As in all of Vejvi's work, an almost childlike idea of perfection is balanced by a mature acknowledgment of the limitations of materiality, resulting in objects that long to be explored, and which inspire an equivalent longing, even as their very configurations signal that impossibility.

The tendency in contemporary art is to gild an existing genre with some stylistic idiosyncrasy that extends its life span in a surprising fashion. Vejvi is that rare artist—like Joseph Cornell, Paul Thek, or, to cite a contemporary, Vincent Fecteau—whose work has such profound needs of its own that the painstaking process of divulging them in formal terms creates a bond with art that seems to destandardize it. Vejvi has found a way to convey feeling so unmistakable, yet so meticulously withheld, that the beauty of its absence is almost unbelievable.

VINCENT FECTEAU

Young artists tend to be 90 percent nerve and 10 percent whatever else. They rise and/or flop depending on the complexity of their cleverness. Vincent Fecteau is different—not that he's not exceedingly clever, etc., but he seems strangely unsure of himself. So unsure, in fact, that unlike other "Slacker" artists, such as Sean Landers or Jack Pierson, he doesn't flaunt his feelings of inadequacy. Instead he fumbles, nitpicks, and beautifies away, lost in a blissful if nerve-racked daydream. Fecteau makes art the way kids build backyard spaceships, with meticulous attention to detail, a grudging respect for the trash he works with, and no real hope of re-creating what he sees when he closes his eyes. He's shooting for the sublime, albeit in a backhanded way. His collages and sculptures are exquisitely calculated, goofily designed, emotionally weird low-tech containers for the ineffable, whatever *that* is. He's not sure what he's getting at, or even how best to express his confusion, which is why his work constantly shape-shifts.

Fecteau's obsessive search for meaning (or whatever) takes him to some unlikely places—cat calendars, *E.T.*, content-free celebrities like Dan Aykroyd—but he can't quite translate the unusual effect these things have on him. Actually he's not even sure his art is the right place to try to manifest his private search, but it's not like he has any choice. All he can do is fine-tune his ambivalence and hope that if he's enough of a perfectionist on the surface, the work will communicate what he can't. A strange unfocused beauty, specific but indefinable, radiates from his art's cautious comedy of errors, as scarily familiar as it is tingly on the eyes as it is amusing to deconstruct. "For me, art is all about frustration," says Fecteau. "It comforts me to think of my pieces as models or diagrams for other pieces . . . not artworks in and of themselves. But they suggest the possibility of other artworks. That makes me feel better. Otherwise I'd feel like I was trying for something that's impossible. It's like the thing in pop music that's so intangible yet magical. There's something there, and I can't figure out what it is. And I'm trying to look for it in all these different places."

Fecteau's work has similarities to that of other artists/foragers of pop culture, like Richard Hawkins, John Miller, Jessica Stockholder, and Nayland Blake, all of whom he admires. But his art has just as much if not more in common with self-consciously modest visionaries like Vija Celmins and Richard Tuttle. Incorporated in his witty toying around with abstract forms and found imagery is both a kind of awe at people's ability to find meaning in the banal and a melancholic resignation to the peculiarity of his task. "My continuing struggle is that I want to express this cheesy emotion that I know isn't cheesy," he says. "And I don't know how to do it."

When Fecteau was an undergraduate, he interned for one intense summer with the late Hannah Wilke. Though there's little evidence that her work directly influenced his, her contentious relationship to the art world opened his eyes. "I was doing these drawings that were really bad. Hannah used to say, 'Don't be an artist. It's no fun. Go into interior design or something.' And I saw how difficult it was for her, just on a day-to-day basis. She was a real artist—she had this conceptual basis she was working from. But she did all these other things that were coming from her narcissism and whatever else she was going through. So I think she did influence me in the way she structured things, and in other ways." Wilke's process provided a sobering contrast to the agenda being promoted at the time in Wesleyan's art department: "Talk about p.c. The conceptual work being done there was really emotionally vacant. And whenever I'm confronted by something like that, I just want to do something horrible."

Fecteau moved to San Francisco on graduating, and soon thereafter he had his first one-person show, at that city's late great renegade gallery Kiki. For "Ben"—the show's title was lifted from Michael Jackson's love song to a pet rat—he lined the walls with silly, eerie photocollages, mostly made of cats' heads scissored from magazines and organized into towering piles of various sizes and shapes. Some of the cats' eyes were both emphasized and partly obscured by a layer of glue, simultaneously paying tribute to the creatures' mysteriously monotonous stares and parodying—with Fecteau's characteristically strict yet reticent delicacy—our tendency to project meaning and reciprocal interest into things that are essentially functional. The cats became advertisements not for their own indecipherable needs but for our neediness; they remained harmless and innocent even as our projections crystallized on their surfaces.

Other works combined Fecteau's own photographs of cats with appropriated images of *E.T.*, that universal-by-default symbol of sanitized horror. One of these pieces grouped the images in a circle that seemed at once decorative-wreath-like and defensive, like a wagon train geared for enemy attack. On the floor were small sculptures resembling comically inept rat traps or pet hamster houses built out of shoe boxes. Again, Fecteau's designs emphasized the touching and ridiculous ways in which we salve our terror of the unknowable by attempting to capture and disempower it in its most palatable forms.

Fecteau's newest pieces broaden the range of his references and reveal an even more poetic formal approach. They are deeper and more mysteriously comical, and the relationships they create between found imagery—including such complicatedly resonant items as *Jonathan Livingston Seagull*, the Anne Frank house, and liquor bottles—are simpler, less overtly theatrical, and capable of housing greater indecision. Physically, they're increasingly insecure and vague, as though they longed to exist in a form somewhere between the second and third dimensions. Even more than in his previous work, one feels Fecteau's inordinate complicity with the objects of his fascination. As the work loosens, its mazelike internal world materializes, and the artist's touch grows ever more enigmatic and inconsolable.

RICHARD HAWKINS

There are at least two pieces of correspondence missing from *They Call Him Mr. Gacy*, C. Ivor McClelland's 1989 collection of letters to and from convicted serial-murderer-turned-painter John Wayne Gacy. In 1987 a recent CalArts graduate named Richard Hawkins wrote the infamous criminal a letter. Did Gacy, it queried, experience feelings of confinement and hopelessness in the presence of beauty? And, if so, did his torture-murders of some thirty-odd boys help him feel better? Hawkins, who often incorporates celebrity memorabilia in his work, hoped to gain Gacy's participation in his installation in progress—a multimedia study of unrequited sexual fixation, with the actor Tom Cruise as its *objet fixe*. But the questions he posed were intended neither as jokes nor as the usual lurid countercultural curiosity. For Hawkins honestly saw in Gacy an alter ego of sorts, someone with extreme sexual fantasies who happened to be trapped in a shy, insecure person's body. Was the only thing that differentiated them the fact that Gacy had had the courage of his convictions? Hawkins was relieved if inexplicably disappointed when an unsympathetic Gacy, who strenuously denies his guilt, responded with a tirade of homophobic abuse.

The works of the Los Angeles artist Richard Hawkins document his schizophrenic interest in male beauty. Witty, poised, and seductively artful, yet explosively lustful not far under the surface, they propose a kind of ominous dream date between his repressed self—the man he'd imagined Gacy to be—and cute, unreachable pop-culture stars, such as Cruise, Sebastian Bach of the rock band Skid Row, and the actors Kirk Cameron, Matt Dillon, and Billy Wirth (all of whom figure prominently in his work). His photos, paintings, collages, texts, and sculptures are self-consciously inadequate souvenirs of this wet daydream, constructed out of items he's bought in tourist and heavy metal shops along Hollywood Boulevard, and altered until they reflect in equal measure his intense desire and the embarrassed attempts to conceal it. Take *Trixter* (1991), a piece about Hawkins's favorite member of a current heavy metal band. It involves a Halloween devil mask, shredded into a rubber pasta and paper-clipped with pictures of the band's sweet-faced singer, Pete Loran. This wad of things is draped over a single nail and obsessively fussed with, almost as if some anal-retentive priss had tried to discover a folk-art treasure among the ruins of some teenage boy's trashed bedroom.

A similar piece, *Slaughter* (1991), which replaces the devil mask with one of Freddie Krueger and the Loran pics with ones of the drummer Blas Elias, was included in "Situation," a recent survey show of contemporary lesbian and gay art at New Langton Arts, curated by Nayland Blake and Pam Gregg. There, amidst works by peers like Cary Leibowitz, G. B. Jones, Donald Moffett, and Catherine Opie, the squeezed-sponge-like intensity of Hawkins's piece made a particularly fierce impression. As is often the case with his best work, *Slaughter*'s deceptively simple juxtaposition of two dichotomous elements discloses a veritable maze of little emotional conflicts, from the self-consciously insecure attempt to pay tribute to a bona fide idol, to the overly neat approximation of a display of temper. While other artists in the show, such as Clifford Hengst, Connie Samaras, and Steven Evans, refer to pop-music figures and products as a way of grounding their oddball formalism in the overly familiar, Hawkins's fetishizing of a heavy metal band's drummer is colored by his fannish admiration of that band's treatment of themes close to his heart—suicide, demonology, and sexual power. Even when his work's reference points stray outside the pop firmament, as in a recent series of pieces in which favorite books are altered by the autographs of incongruous celebrities—Rob Lowe's in *Psychopathis Sexualis*, Keanu Reeves's in Goethe's *Italian Journey*—there is always the sense of desire outweighing intellect. Thus the scribbles of people whose value lies in their youthful attractiveness take ownership of works that have been proven to be timelessly great.

In the last few years the art world has grown accustomed to openly lesbian and gay male work. But just as younger homos of both sexes have recently begun rebelling against what they see as the assimilationist politics of earlier generations, it's possible to see Hawkins as one of a growing number of postgay artists who are fervently studying such politically incorrect turf as the eroticism fueled by overcompensating homophobes like the aforementioned Bach or the Guns N' Roses guitarist Slash. Hawkins is far less interested in claiming gay ownership of a corner of contemporary art than he is in using his art education to devise perfect Trojan horses for the bedrooms of heavy metal aficionados. But unlike Pruitt-Early's condescending beer-can sculptures, which assume teens to be sensation-starved morons, period, Hawkins's approximations of what rockers might like if for some wild reason they decided to investigate the art world are, for all the embarrassed irony of their presentation, deeply respectful of the tastes of these sexually repressed and emotionally inarticulate young men. While his attempts to find delicacy in the fallout from their brutish rituals always wind up resembling art, the works are often so interfered with by his horniness that they exude intentionality in spite of themselves, like bunches of roses sent to the wrong address.

JASON MEADOWS

A horse goes into a bar and sits down. The bartender asks, Why the long face?

That joke is beautiful and not merely dumb because, for an instant, it coerces you into picturing an insane simultaneity—a generic horse's head merged with a sad-sack human face to create something eerily incongruous. The punch line is contingent on that disorienting and ultimately futile mental task, and its pleasure lies in this futility. Jason Meadows's sculptures inspire a similarly puzzling reverie, asking you to second-guess his odd decisions to wed efficient, Home Depot–esque lumber, particleboard, and the occasional fluorescent light fixture to an entirely wacked notion of the hallucinatory, producing work that is at once elegant and user-friendly.

"The hallucination is a unique window, and then it's also very slippery," says Meadows, a tall, bespectacled twenty-five-year-old. "My work is something very simple disguised as something very complicated. Hopefully I can make complex gestures that have a time release. So you might look at the work and only see the way it's held together on a formal level. But later you might only remember its presence, and what you were feeling when you were in the room with it."

Meadows grew up in Chicago, the son of antique and curio enthusiasts. In high school, he began taking weekend art classes at the Art Institute of Chicago, and he later got his BFA there. He moved west to do graduate work at UCLA partly because he'd been galvanized by the catalogue for Paul Schimmel's once-notorious "Helter Skelter" show at MOCA, which showcased so-called transgressive Los Angeles artists like Mike Kelley, Chris Burden, and Raymond Pettibon. In Meadows's first year at UCLA, he made his breakthrough piece, *Brown Canyon Module* (1996), a king-size, packing-box-like object containing criss-crossed wooden tiers casually lit by clip lamps, which so impressed the faculty and created such a buzz in the LA art scene that he became one of the city's most talked about and showcased young artists—despite the fact that he won't actually graduate until this spring.

Meadows's sculptures are the product of intensive research into the ways in which principles of plane geometry are used in engineering and architecture, followed by, in his words, "really loose decision making." This combination of elaborately justified, polished structure and aesthetic impulsiveness creates a kind of mild strobing effect, which is almost but not quite neutralized by the work's tossed-off but finessed wit. The comical tone is both the first thing you notice about the work and the last thing you remember about any given piece. The cleverest example of Meadows's ability to equalize the sublime and the goofball is *Untitled* (1997), which looks for all the world like a tilted, upside-down picnic table perched atop a pair of intersecting cartoony hill shapes. The longer you look at the piece, the more you find yourself thinking about the table's not literally precarious yet entirely impractical angle—an angle that seems to result from an intuitive decision so lacking in sense, yet so sound, that it leaves you feeling both becalmed and lost.

"I'm very interested in the idea that something you know really well, something domestic, could suddenly flip-flop and become something different and alien," says Meadows. "There's this Borges story I love where sort of out of the blue you get to the bottom of a staircase and you can see everything in the entire universe at once. I'd like to create a way of looking that can give you an infinite view or picture of something. I guess I'm talking about the paranormal, but on a less ridiculous level than UFOs and ghosts, although I love that stuff."

Asked to mention like-minded artists, Meadows lists a weirdly disjointed array that includes Brancusi, Charles and Ray Eames, Liz Larner, and even M. C. Escher, whose oblique yet corny way of working he finds enthralling. Tony Smith, Charles Ray, B. Wurtz, and Richard Artschwager also spring to mind, as do a number of Meadows's fellow UCLA grads (among them Liz Craft, Evan Holloway, and Brandon Lattu). But Meadows says it's contemporary electronic music—particularly techno, break beat, and trip-hop—that truly inspires him. He describes his work as "a three dimensional representation of musical ideas. I always get a kind of psychosomatic reaction from music that has to do with the logic of the patterns and systems of rhythm, and I aim for that in my work."

It's popular for young artists to reference techno these days, but in Meadows's case it seems a legitimate point of comparison. Thinking of his work as mixed visually along musical lines, rather than built in a traditionally sculptural way, helps explain its strange, carefully imbalanced combination of high-minded abstraction, furniture-derived imagery, druggy misshapenness, and school-yard sincerity. Take *Untitled Collaboration Sculpture* (1998), a tall, lean tower that vaguely resembles a spinal column, which Meadows created with the artist Jorge Pardo. Operative only when viewed as a kind of materialization of sound, or a visible pulse, it, like much of Meadows's work, has more in common with recent recordings by misfit visionary techno artists like Aphex Twin and Luke Vibert than with anything you see around in galleries today.

Still, the most extraordinary thing about Meadows's work is that—for all his spacey aspirations and well-honed intellectual self-justification— it's an easy and pleasurable thing to be around. Imagine a playground designed by a particularly soulful particle physicist. It's hard to picture, but there's something about Meadows's low-key yet forward-thinking sculptures that toys innocently with your mind while, at the same time, making you think unusually hard and well about the great unknown's possible discrepancies.

KING JUNK
R.I.P. William Burroughs
(August 1997)

Why is the death of William Burroughs such a curiously uneventful event? Despite a superficial resemblance to his friend Allen Ginsberg's recent passing, the two deaths couldn't feel more different. Like Burroughs, Ginsberg was both a writer well past his prime and a spotlight addict inclined to interlope on passing youth cultural movements as a way to life-extend his legend. Nonetheless, Ginsberg remained a force to the end, an artist with a sincere political and spiritual agenda who saw his fame as a way to effect cultural change. His presence never stopped mattering to some faction of society, however small their number or offbeat their cause. His death was a surprisingly powerful blow, even to people who'd long since turned their attentions away from his poetry in embarrassment.

Burroughs, on the other hand, was essentially an active relic who had exploited the mystique around his early work for so long that I suspect even he didn't know why he was famous anymore. While he continued to write, he was less an artist than a retiree who dabbled at his former craft. Despite the omnipresence of his name, he himself had ceased to participate in our world decades ago. He was an old man living quietly in the middle of nowhere, invisible apart from the occasional cameo, attached to us only by that famous visage and voice, and by the patented anecdotes and crackpot theories that he respun endlessly for any interviewer willing to make the trek to Kansas. The Burroughs whom most of us know and love is an echo, and, thanks to the miracles of sampling, that echo will continue unimpeded for as long as there are young rebels in need of a transgressive figurehead.

In a way, Burroughs died in the late '70s when he was resurrected from relative obscurity and repackaged as a kind of outlaw comedian/philosopher. Victor Bockris's influential 1981 book, *With William Burroughs: A Report from the Bunker*, a collection of transcribed dinner conversations and photos, presents him as a cranky, befuddled living legend who, when not putting on clownish displays of outré behavior, was propped up in front of a passing array of rock stars who seemingly meant nothing to him. It's a well-known secret that beginning with his "comeback" novel *Cities of the Red Night* (1981), Burroughs's prose was a product of partial ghostwriting, and that his involvement in his books diminished steadily to the point where there seemed to be nothing but textual smoke and mirrors. Perhaps this is not a bad thing in and of itself, as he was an amusing character to have around, and everybody's got to pay the rent somehow, but the result is that his death feels almost completely abstract. The effect on me, and on most of the people I've spoken to in the last few days, is a kind of cold fascination to see what his work will look like once the atmosphere around it has cleared of marketing shenanigans.

Don't get me wrong, Burroughs was an important figure, but for several specific reasons. He perfected (though did not in fact invent) the cut-up technique, one of the touchstones of postmodernism, and an influence on innumerable writers, artists, and filmmakers, not to mention most of the important rock/electronic bands since the '60s. He accidentally popularized the idea of experimental writing by being such a presentable, grandfatherly kook that people bought his novels because they were amused by his personal style. Before heroin addiction stunted his talent, Burroughs wrote a handful of brilliant novels, basically everything from *Naked Lunch* (1959) to *The Wild Boys* (1969). Along with Jean Genet, John Rechy, and Ginsberg, he helped make homosexuality seem cool and highbrow, providing gay liberation with a delicious edge. Those were his gifts to contemporary culture, and they are not insubstantial. The rest of the Burroughs mystique—the gun toting, the belief in UFOs, ghosts, and elaborate CIA conspiracies, the cheerleading for heroin—was pure showbiz. Not that he didn't actually love dangerous weapons, do drugs into his eighties, and sit in orgone boxes daydreaming of enlightenment, but the mythic status of those oddball personal habits had everything to do with the contexts in which they were placed.

Gus Van Sant, in whom Burroughs found an unusually thoughtful and sympathetic collaborator, is the exception. But to most of the plethora of rock bands, filmmakers, and advertisers who dropped Burroughs's trademark exterior into their product, he was a signifier of their own daring, and little else. And in allowing this indiscriminate dispersal of his image, Burroughs the artist became Burroughs the simplistic and rather meaningless icon, less a living, breathing figure than a detachable touchstone of any wild kid's notion of dangerous intelligence. So is it any surprise that his death seems to bear more relationship to the retiring of Joe Camel than it does to, say, the loss of a valuable cultural presence like Ginsberg?

I suspect it will be years before those of us who didn't know Burroughs personally know what we're missing. At the moment, his death mostly raises the possibility that a lot of long-standing questions about him might finally get honest answers. Like was he really a genius or just a very clever concocter of literary hocus-pocus? Why did he allow himself to become the poster boy for junkiedom when heroin addiction had decimated his talent and killed slews of his friends and fans? Did he really think, as he was often quoted as saying, that women were an inferior species that should be wiped off the earth? And, more important, why didn't more people call him on shit like that? What does it mean that he got away with the manslaughter killing of his wife? Until these and other questions are resolved, Burroughs himself, and by extension his work, will continue to be hidden behind the walking-talking logo who may or may not have died last Saturday.

BALE BONDS
The Christian Bale Interview
(December 1997)
Cowritten with Joel Westendorf

Enter the image-based Hollywood world of the Hawkes, Baldwins, and O'Donnells. You see the flashes pop, the emotionally unremarkable lauded, and the future plans for "slacker-esque" movies dancing in the eyes of these so-called stars. Yet you will witness the sensitive and shy, less worldly types we see on the silver screen usually having to settle for a position of less grandeur. High-profile is something that Christian Bale definitely is not. He is managed quietly by his father, an ex-pilot with scant Hollywood connections, he has no publicist, and has never been the focus of a major American magazine article. These elements would seem to be a drawback here. Yet his "in-the-biz-not-of-it" stance may just have been the key to his "performance rather than profile" popularity.

His fans are a vocal bunch who flood their idol with mail, particularly e-mail. He was more than a bit shocked earlier this year when America Online informed him that he is the third most popular subject of conversation in its "Hollywood Online, Talk about Actors" forum. Being just behind Brad Pitt and Keanu Reeves, and way ahead of more visible figures like Tom Cruise, Leonardo DiCaprio, and Hugh Grant. He has large, active fan clubs in such unlikely places as Harvard, Yale, and Stanford universities. And Bale's official, Toronto-based fan club raised thousands of dollars for charity this June in an online auction of items he wore or used while making the bizarrely popular film *Newsies*. Not bad for one still paying his dues.

A tall, lanky, big-boned twenty-two-year-old with a broad, childlike face, sensual lips, and prematurely wise eyes, Christian is unconventionally handsome. And apart from the odd burst of hesitant laughter, he maintains an impassive, thoughtful expression, occasionally bending his mouth slightly to accommodate a mildly bemused smile. Why the excitement over someone so low-key?

In 1987's critically acclaimed Spielberg film *Empire of the Sun*, Christian delivered an incredibly stellar portrayal of twelve-to-fourteen-year-old J. G. Ballard in the story of his experience as a young prisoner of war. Remarkably, at thirteen, Bale got the role despite his film inexperience and lack of formal training, and to this day he has only participated in a couple of workshops, when he was roughly twelve. The merits of his do-it-yourself method became especially evident in last year's *Little Women*. With his natural talent and charm, he stole most every scene he was in. While his experience between those two films included some box-office failures (*Swing Kids*, and Disney's failed attempt to repopularize musicals, *Newsies*), Christian's realness and nonpretention shines through in what would be considered his weaker roles. He has never given less than a solid and touching performance, and has never gotten a bad review.

So now he's got *Little Women* and the vocal role of "Thomas" in last summer's *Pocahontas* under his belt, and his two upcoming films include Christopher (*Carrington*) Hampton's screen adaptation of Joseph

Conrad's *The Secret Agent*, as well as the long-awaited Jane (*The Piano*) Campion project *The Portrait of a Lady* (set for release this spring and fall, respectively). Seems the world may be witnessing a larger stride being taken by Bale.

Normally very wary of publicity, Christian has given very few (if any) in-depth interviews. However, he agreed to give us a rare look into his experiences. Possibly to do his share of the necessary publicity for both films, but more likely because of the fact that we've recently become friends as well.

A very knackered Christian had just returned to London after four months on location in England (*Secret Agent*) and Italy (*Portrait . . .*) when we managed to snag him for an interview at two A.M. his time.

Joel Westendorf: So are you up to answering a few questions?
Christian Bale: Yeah. [*chuckle*]
JW: Okay.
CB: All right (self-convincingly). This is an ordinary conversation. Let's just start.
JW: Right.
Dennis Cooper: So what's the plot of *The Secret Agent*?
CB: It's set in the 1890s in Soho in London in an earlier porn shop, which is very tame by our standards. In fact, we had to do two versions. One for the cinema, and one for television. One where they scan the racks and there's loads of dildos. Then they scrape all the dildos off and do it again for TV.
DC: With troll dolls instead.
CB: [*laughs*] Exactly. No, that's even more indecent, isn't it? So, Joseph Conrad's novel *The Secret Agent* was one of the first thrillers in the style that we know them today. I heard that it inspired people like Graham

Greene and John leCarré. It's a lot of characters, all up to no good basically. And they all end up dead. That's the short of it.

JW: Could you give me an idea of your character "Stevie"?

CB: Well, most of the characters are caricatures. But I mean, very subtly done. My character is "innocence" basically. He's the only one who's completely innocent in the whole thing. He's like nineteen or something with a mental age of let's say seven or eight. So, he's in his own little world, and he's sort of fascinated with trying to solve the wrongs of what is going on in the world. And he has the advantage of his *lack* of perception really, he can see things as either purely good or purely bad. Whereas all the others have become quite mixed up, especially with Bob Hoskins's character, who's amoral. He just doesn't seem to have a grasp of good or bad at all. So you've got this complete innocent trying to live in this world and he just can't.

JW: What are the other characters like?

CB: Well, there's Winnie, who is Patricia Arquette. In the film she's my sister, my mother, she's everything. Nobody else takes care of me. My mother, played by Elizabeth Spriggs, has gone a bit batty and isn't in any state to look after a handicapped kid. So Winnie is sort of his whole world. She's the only one he can talk to. Verloc, who is the secret agent, is Bob Hoskins. Because Winnie is married to him, without thinking too much about it, Stevie believes that Verloc is a good man. It's one of the lines in the film that I always say. "Good man, Mr. Verloc."

JW: What's Bob Hoskins like?

CB: It was quite funny with Bob. My character is so submissive when he's around, and treats him with such awe and respect—not to say I don't have that for Bob at all, I've got an awful lot of respect for him—but I couldn't just be me sitting there talking with Bob. When Patricia, Bob, and I met out in Los Angeles for the first time, we had lunch and had a few drinks and got a bit drunk and everything. And I really couldn't see us doing that again once I had started playing my character. It would have felt a bit odd.

JW: How about Patricia Arquette?

CB: Of all the people on *The Secret Agent*, I sort of felt most comfortable with Patricia. Because with Stevie, she is the only one that he really chats with. She sort of adopted the sister attitude with me, and beat the shit out of me as soon as they shouted cut, doing kung fu kicks on me and shit, you know, in period costume.

DC: You told us a funny story about something that happened on the set . . . having to do with a bomb?

CB: Yeah, we were on Greenwich Hill in London, by the Observatory. I was doing a scene where a bomb went off in my face. It was a public place, and we cleared everybody out because there was this bomb and they could get hurt. Now I didn't actually see him, but there was this guy who was hiding in the bushes taking a piss when this frigging bomb went off. And he came running out of the bushes afterward, I don't know in what state of undress.

DC: How did you get on with Gerard Depardieu?

CB: Well, the first time I met him I was lying asleep in my dressing room, and I woke up because there was such a loud belch, and I sort of sat up and there was Gerard Depardieu standing there in his shorts sort of scratching himself. [*laughs*] And he said to me [*adopting a French accent*], "It's okay? I can come in?" And he came in and we had a chat for ten minutes, and he was off again. We didn't talk much during the filming. Mostly leering at each other. He'd come up and go [*makes blubbery noise with his lips*], "Christian!" And I'd sort of go [*same noise*], "Gerard!" And that was the extent of it really.

CB, JW, DC: [*laughter*]

DC: You've had no formal training as an actor, right?

CB: That is true! I did a couple of workshops when I was like twelve or something, but I've been able to work so, um . . . I just haven't needed to. I thought about going to drama school for a bit. I just started to think, "Hm, this seems to be happening a bit easy." I was in Kenneth Branagh's film *Henry the Fifth* when I was fourteen, and Kenneth's mentor is Hugh Cruttwell, the ex-head of the Royal Academy of Dramatic Arts. So I spoke with him about it, and he said wait until you're older because you get a lot of people, they go along, they don't really have any of their own ideas, and so they come out being identical to each other. When I did *Newsies* I spoke with Robert Duvall about it as well, and he said essentially the same thing. So that basically decided me.

DC: You had to inhabit some pretty terrifying emotions in *Empire of the Sun*.

CB: I think what actually worked in *Empire of the Sun* was the fact that I didn't have any sort of preconceptions about acting or what it should be or what I should be doing. I just got out there and did it. I really wasn't a film fan at all, and Spielberg just makes everything incredibly easy.

DC: Your grandfather did some acting and stuntwork.

CB: Yeah, both of my granddads. You're talking about the one on my dad's side. He was John Wayne's double for a while. I haven't actually seen any of the films, but my dad watched one recently. I can't remember which one it was, but it was set in Africa.

DC: *Hatari!*?

CB: It may have been. I keep wanting to say *Uhuru*, but that was somebody on *Star Trek*, wasn't it? My dad says you can actually make out my granddad's face in the shadows at some point, which you shouldn't be able to do, but you could.

DC: Did you know him as a kid?

CB: Not at all. I went to South Africa at the end of '92 to meet him. He had cancer, and he was basically hanging on to meet us. So only that one time.

DC: Was his being an actor an inspiration to you?

CB: Well, he wasn't exactly an actor. His brother was. All of them on my dad's side are enormous. They're like six feet four, six feet six, and built like brick shit houses. So my dad's uncle Rex, who I met, though I don't remember it because I was so young, was an actor. I think he tended to play heavies all the time because he was so big. But I've never seen anything that he did. My granddad was more like . . . what do you call it, a white hunter, which just means he was a park ranger in South Africa.

JW: When you did *Empire of the Sun*, were you aware how big of a deal it was to have a lead in a Spielberg movie?

CB: When you're thirteen . . . It's not as if I was running around banging on doors at that age. I didn't really care too much if I got the parts or not. Just sort of coincidences had happened and I was lucky. So I didn't have an idea of the whole "big picture" of it. I mean now, when I've decided that I *do* like acting, and I'd like to continue doing it, you start to get slightly more self-conscious, and *realize* what on earth you're doing. But when you're just . . . doing what's in front of you, you don't think of that, you know?

DC: It was such a dream role. It was so expansive and involved such a range of emotions. Did it spoil you? Did it make it hard to take on roles that didn't have that incredible room to move in them?

CB: It did spoil me, yeah. When I did it, I remember a lot of people saying that no matter what I did, no matter how much work I did later, no matter how much work I managed to get, this was going to be one of the best roles I'd ever have. And that you hardly ever get any roles like that one coming along. But I've really enjoyed doing . . . whatever, small parts, it didn't matter. You can't keep on competing with yourself all the time. Doing that, it's going to get a bit boring. After *Empire of the Sun* I didn't work for almost two years. I'd be getting a bit worried now if I did that.

DC: Why was that?

CB: I went back to school. I think it was quite good really because it seems sort of sad when you see young kids starting that young and they're considering it their career already.

JW: Do you think that you were expected to think as an adult at an early age? And do you think you had to grow up too fast?

CB: No. I don't know who would've expected that. I mean certainly I might have thought it.

JW: Do you appreciate the fact that you were respected as a kid?

CB: Um . . . I'd have been a little power-mad thirteen-year-old kid if I'd walked around saying, "I want a little bit of respect around here!"

JW: But I mean looking back.

CB: Certainly.

JW: Yeah, seeing as my dad's a pastor, I had to go to a lot of church functions as a kid. People expected me to be super-polite and intelligent, and looking back now I can kind of appreciate that they encouraged my intellect and didn't treat me like aww . . . silly little kid.

CB: But that's only looking back on it. You probably wouldn't have cared too much at the time, would you?

JW: Right, not at the time.

CB: I mean, it can be a pain in the ass if people are sort of not expecting you to be a kid, which you gotta be.

DC: Hey, now that we're back in this period of your life, do you want to talk about your date with Drew Barrymore?

CB: [*laughs*] Well, I was thirteen and I'd just done *Empire of the Sun*, and I was a young impressionable lad. She was quite a well-developed girl, and I was standing playing the arcade at Amblin, and suddenly this voluptuous figure arrived beside me, and I thought *Bing!* I was quite stunned, and she asked if I wanted to go see a film, so I did. We went to see some bloody awful horror film, and that was the end of it. She never called again.

DC: Did you know her from *E.T.*?

CB: Yes, I had seen that. But she was quite a different girl.

DC: Yeah, she went through some changes.

CB: Yeah.

JW: Any*way*, I get the feeling that either you've been typecast or you've found a particular type of character that you feel comfortable with.

CB: Like what? Give me . . .

JB: The classically thoughtful, handsome lad, period type.

CB: Well, everything I've been in has been period. I think the most recent thing, the most modern thing I've done was like 1940s. But I don't have a thing for period at all. I'd love to do something contemporary.

DC: There's a continuum to your characters. Laurie in *Little Women*, Jack in *Newsies*, Thomas in *Swing Kids*, even Jim in *Empire of the Sun* . . . they all seem to have very deep private emotions. It's as if the characters have a hard time expressing their feelings. You get the sense of a kind of a reservoir of confusion in them. But at the same time all of those characters are kind of rowdy and playful and goofy.

CB: It's funny, I've never heard anybody say that before. I suppose it's easier for you to look at it and say, "Well, he's doing that and that and that," than it is for me. Certainly I wasn't ever planning . . . on all of that. I don't believe that any actor can become their character. It sounds like bollocks really. You've gotta be comfortable for it to be any good. Nobody can be that comfortable if you're playing a completely alien character to what you know. So there's always going to be something of you there.

JW: I watched *Little Women* again recently, and I couldn't recognize *you* at all. Your face, yes, but it didn't seem like you.

CB: The manner.

JW: Yeah.

CB: It's really only tiny things that make the difference. You can't get away with enormous things, because it has to feel comfortable to yourself, regardless of how different a character is from you. Otherwise you wouldn't be able to do it. So it's the tiny adjustments which have a big effect when you're watching.

JW: It's kind of creepy. In a way.

CB: Yeah.

JW: Not to say your acting is creepy.

CB: But doing something like *The Secret Agent* . . . you would think it's a massive leap to play a mentally retarded person. The thing I was mainly concerned about was not wanting to overdo it. And it really only becomes comfortable once you've thought about it a lot, and rehearsed by yourself. There shouldn't be a huge jump between how you feel walking on the set and how you feel once you've switched into character. The whole point is to pretend that you're not performing.

JW: I'd be curious to know if your approach has changed much from film to film.

CB: I think it changes with everything I do. Let alone from film to film, from *day to day*. I have to change my approach because something that I've been doing one day may have been working, but then the next day I'm in a whole different mood, the atmosphere on the set is completely different, and it just won't work anymore. So you've got to find a different way of approaching it to be comfortable and to make it believable.

If I picked it apart and analyzed it I'm sure there would be things that I do every single time to make myself feel comfortable, but I like not analyzing it.

JW: That must be a cool thing to do. To adopt another persona for a while. A lot of the theory books I read . . . well, a book called *Quantum Psychology*, and some chaos theory books highly recommend paradigm shifts, which is to completely change your point of view and act in a way that you normally never would. Doing it in day-to-day life can make waves. But you can do it as a job.

CB: I think everybody does it, don't they really? You know, whether you're just walking down the street or whatever thinking to yourself, "Oh, I'll be like this for a bit. See what happens," you know? Especially when you're having a bad day or something and just nothing's going right, and you think, "Christ, I've got to change this somehow. All right, I'll be a different person." The nice thing about acting is that you get to do it, everybody wants you to do it really well, and everybody else is doing it as well.

JW: I can imagine that depending on how deep you get into a character, you might experience some sort of out-of-body sensation.

CB: I think the best way of describing it is like a trance really. I mean, obviously we're talking about the best situations. What I try and do is purposefully forget everything that's going to happen in the scene. Obviously there are marks to hit and the lines, and you've had rehearsals. But once you've done all of that, hopefully it's in your brain enough that you can just forget it. For me the best thing is to just hope that it's not all going to go wrong.

JW: That reminds me of gnosis, a trancelike state where the conscious mind is still, and the subconscious comes forward. Direct access to the things you've placed in the "back" of your mind.

CB: Yeah, that's the ideal really.

DC: To change the subject slightly, did it bother you that *Newsies* and *Swing Kids* weren't that successful in the theaters?

CB: I was out of the country when *Newsies* came out. I would have liked it to be more successful, for the sake of the director really. But it was just a very difficult thing that he was trying to do. You know, kick-starting or re-kick-starting musicals is . . . is . . . bloody difficult. I mean, in my lifetime I've never been to see a musical, and to be honest, I'm not really interested in seeing one. *Newsies* actually started off just as a drama, and then Disney decided they wanted to try musicals. And they changed the script into a musical, but I'd read it before that. I really didn't fancy the change, you know. I didn't really want to sing or dance for it. I actually sort of thought for a while that I could get out of singing and dancing, that somehow I could be the lead in a musical and not have to sing or dance, but, uh, heh heh, yeah, they caught up on me with that.

DC: What do you think about the fanaticism around *Newsies*? Do you know that a bunch of your fans have written the script for a sequel and that they want to make it?

CB: What, *Newsies Take Tokyo*? No, I didn't know about that. I know there's a guy who changed his name to Jack Kelly [the name of Bale's character in the film]. Maybe he's going to star in it. *I* won't be in it.

DC: You *won't*?

CB: No. My musical days are over. I don't want to be Julie Andrews any longer.

DC: But what do you think of the whole *Newsies* cult? Do you just think it's strange?

CB: Well, *Newsies* is a good-time film, isn't it? I don't have a computer so I haven't looked at all the things that are going on on the Internet, but it's true, of all the films I've done, it has the most constant interest.

Most of the letters I get are about *Newsies*. I guess there are an awful lot of musical fans out there. They do exist.

DC: What do you think of your huge popularity on the Internet?

CB: Well, I've been really disorganized up until now about fan letters and things like that. Just recently a friend has started a fan club thing on the Internet. I've seen it on a friend's computer. There were some messages there for me, and we just had to look at some of them and uh...we had quite a laugh. It's very odd, all those people out *there*, on computer terminals discussing you.

DC: I mean, they really take apart the films. We saw a discussion about how in one scene in *Newsies* it was obvious that your suspender accidentally got caught on something, and how brilliantly you rescued the moment by pulling the suspender back in place.

CB: [*laughs*] That . . . that was it! I was in New York staying at a friend's place and both of us were fairly hungover at the time. And we just decided it would be a laugh to have a look at some of the messages. And I don't know what on earth they were talking about, but there were two people having a discussion about me and the *tongue thing*, and the *spit thing*. And we didn't have a clue what they were talking about!?!

JW: Whatever.

CB, JW, DC: [*raucous laughter*]

DC: We saw *Pocahontas* with you. Did you have any way to judge your performance in it?

CB: Not at all. I didn't even have a sensation that it was me at all. I don't think I felt any different from you guys watching it.

DC: Thomas wasn't based on you physically, was he?

CB: No, they already had a character when I went in. But he was about thirteen and Irish. Originally I was doing an Irish accent, but either I've got a crappy Irish accent and they were just polite or they decided why bother, and they made him cockney. So I did cockney for a bit, then they said, "Well, we're not sure that Americans will be able to understand a cockney accent." So we lightened it until they said, "We just like your own voice basically. Can you stop acting and doing all these little turns?" I'd thought I was going to have to be really hamming it up for a cartoon. But I really didn't have to do anything. I didn't do much more than what I'm doing now. They did film me while I was doing it, and they base little mannerisms on yours, and they have an artist drawing your mouth so the words fit.

JW: The more well known you get, the more people are probably gonna start comparing you to actors around your age like Chris O'Donnell and Leonardo DiCaprio.

CB: It's inevitable, isn't it really. And you know, meeting people for auditions and stuff, you tend to see all the same people again and again, and you're always hearing about Leonardo DiCaprio at the moment, because, you know, he's sort of the . . . top-drawer bloke or whatever. It's inevitable that I'm going to get put in the same brackets, and I don't mind at all.

DC: Are there any actors you'd really like to work with?

CB: There are an awful lot of people that I would go and see a film for. The only person I've ever sort of been a fan of and whose videos I used to collect and all was Steve McQueen, but he's been dead for like fifteen years, so not much chance of working with him.

DC: You were referred to as "a little Steve McQueen" by Steven Spielberg.

CB: I think Steven said that just to please me.

JW: Does the prospect of fame make you feel uncomfortable?

CB: I'm sort of a paradox because I want to continue doing films. I want to be an actor, but . . . I suppose it's a personal preference, but I don't tend to want to know anything about an actor. Because then you go along to a film and you've got all these other things that you're thinking of when you're watching them instead of just being able to, uh . . . pretend that they're a particular character. I'm not very good when on rare occasions I do get recognized. It's fine if I'm on a film set. But if I'm just walking down the street and somebody recognizes me, I'll . . . feel a bit edgy.

DC: Do you feel any responsibility to your fans at all?

CB: Well, that's the horrible thing about it. You can't help but feel that a little bit. And of course you have no obligation to remain the same for their sake. You have to be free to change. But yeah, there is that feeling when somebody is very intelligent and he's written to tell you what he likes about what you do, and you think, "Well, I'm not gonna do that in this next thing, or I don't want to do that anymore." Yeah, you do feel a little bit bad about it.

DC: We just saw *Total Eclipse*, in which Leonardo DiCaprio and David Thewlis get pretty hot and heavy with each other, and I suppose that inspires this question. Is there anything that you *wouldn't* do in a movie?

CB: Well, I was just sitting and watching the film *Priest* with my sister and her husband. And you know, there are quite explicit sex scenes in that. And a fair amount of snogging going on. At one point they turned to me and said, "What would you do?" [*laughs*] And my reply was, "Well, I think I would do it, you know?" I would do it. I would have a reservation about tongues, I think. Otherwise, without having been put in the genuine situation, I would, yeah. I really don't think I would have a problem with it at all.

DC: Aside from nudity and sex, what if you hated a character you were asked to play?

CB: Oh, I thought you were talking about things where my grandparents would say, "Ooh, why'd he do that?"

DC: I was. But is there a character you just wouldn't want to inhabit?

CB: No, as long as I liked the film. I read something where Gary Oldman said he always has to like a character to play it. But I don't know really. I think you just make it so the character can live with himself no matter how self-hating he seems.

DC: It's a bigger challenge to play a monster.

CB: I suppose it is. And characters like that are more interesting to people. You don't want a lovely nice boy who's never done anything wrong in his life. You don't want to watch him, do you?

DC: How monstrous is the character you play in *The Portrait of a Lady*?

CB: Well, he's a drama queen basically. He's been a bit of a fop all his life, making sure he wears the right clothes, making sure he's very in fashion. He collects little antiques and bibelots and things like that. He suddenly finds himself in love, and he doesn't care about those things anymore. And the girl's father, who's played by John Malkovich, sort of bans him from seeing her. So in all my scenes I'm sort of huffing and puffing and pulling a strop.

DC: Was it interesting to reconnect with Malkovich? You hadn't worked together since *Empire of the Sun*, right?

CB: We really didn't have any scenes together. One scene starts with me standing next to him and as soon as the action starts I walk off in a huff. And that's the extent of it really. There's a lot of flaring nostrils going on in that one.

DC: You did *The Secret Agent* and *The Portrait of a Lady* back-to-back. Was that a mind-fuck at all?

CB: I was filming *Secret Agent* whilst I started rehearsing for *Portrait of a Lady*, and I found myself changing from day to day. If I was rehearsing I would go in with one attitude and then have to change it completely for my next working day because of the two characters.

JW: Is there a mental residue left over from playing a character?

CB: There can be. For instance, I never sit with my legs crossed. But for my character in *Portrait of a Lady* I decided he would sit like that. And while I was doing the film I just found myself sitting cross-legged a lot of the time. I still do on occasion. I'll be sitting somewhere smoking a cigarette the way I imagine he would be doing it. And I'll suddenly recognize what I'm doing and say, "Actually, this isn't like me, is it?"

JW: I understand that Jane Campion likes actors to get into their characters long before the actual filming. In fact, I heard that Valentina, the actress who plays your love, was given a photograph of you to keep on her bedside table, sort of to get her in the mood.

CB: Actually, I don't know if Jane told her to do that or if she just did it on her own. I know she had the picture.

JW: How does it feel to be "helped" into your character?

CB: It's fine as long as it's only a starting point. I don't want to have to be told what to do for anything. But yeah, with Valentina, we were asked to write little love letters to each other beforehand in character. It sounds incredibly stupid, but it's part of the whole immersion into the film, and you just sort of have to kid yourself into the whole thing.

JW: Did the love letter trick work?

CB: If anything, for me it was just in the actual writing of the letter. I wouldn't even have had to give it to her necessarily. It was just the fact that I was writing as him, trying to think of his mind-set, and therefore writing my own dialog. But it was nice getting the letter back from her and keeping it in a secret place and doing all of that.

JW: What was your reputation on the set? Do you think that the cast and crew knew what to expect from you?

CB: I really don't have a clue. I was talking with Valentina, and we both said that on different days when the other one of us wasn't working we'd thought we might sort of casually mention one another and see people's reaction. It would have been quite interesting, but I never got a chance to do it.

DC: One of the few actors that we know you're friends with is Winona Ryder.

CB: Yeah, she's helped me out an awful lot. It was her idea to bring me in to audition for *Little Women*. And it was that film that's gotten me the work I've done since. So I owe a lot to her. She's a nice gal.

DC: You're chums.

CB: Yeah.

JW: Do you have any hobbies?

CB: That's quite an interesting question actually. Um, I go around collecting money and raising awareness for various charities. [*laughs*] No, I don't know. I play arcade games. I do all sorts of nonsense things which aren't going to benefit me at all later on. Oh, I started rock climbing. Actually it's more something I would like to call a hobby than actually is a hobby. I've done it so rarely. But I've got the shoes! Does that count?

JW: Sure. It's the thought that counts.

CB: Oh, it's the thought that counts? I've got hundreds of them! Yeah, just put that I waste my time in arcades. I don't have a bloody hobby. Christ. Uh, I love to sleep. I get up to some wonderful things in my dreams. I'm sort of a jack-of . . . nothing.

JW: Jack-of-no-trade?

CB: Yeah.

JW: Well, one trade.

CB: Jack-of-no-trades . . . Master-of-bugger-all!

JW: Not to tell you what to do, but . . . You should get a hobby!

CB: I should, shouldn't I? Actually, those kids in *To Die For* . . . I'm like them, aren't I? They were asked, "So what do you do?" And they go, "Uhhhh . . . I dunno." Joel, I don't have a hobby.

JW: Well, we have to find you one.

CB: Yeah.

JW: Out of all of your films, which would you say was the most satisfying experience all around?

CB: I think I've got to exclude *Empire of the Sun* because I was a whole other person basically. Like I said, what was so good about that is that I didn't have any ideas about acting or filmmaking. And I was working with Spielberg, who is known for getting these fantastic performances out of kids. But if I keep harping back to *Empire of the Sun* I'm never going to be able to move forward. I was thirteen when I did that. Suddenly you go through your teenage years and the whole self-conscious thing starts coming into play, you know. And I've done some bloody terrible performances since then.

JW: Like what?

CB: Um . . . Well, I never like to say actually because it's rude to the people I worked with.

JW: If it means anything. I think you were better in *Newsies* than you were in *Treasure Island*.

CB: Well, I actually did something in *Newsies*. I think I felt differently doing *Little Women*, *The Secret Agent*, and *The Portrait of a Lady*. I suddenly found sort of more confidence in what I was doing, which obviously has to do with my personal life, and with the people I'm working with. So I'm going to have to say the three of them together.

DC: If someone said you could have ten million dollars to spend on any film project you liked, how would you spend it?

CB: I wouldn't want to direct it. I'd certainly want a part in it. There's this book I love, *The Moon and Sixpence* by W. Somerset Maugham, and I'd always thought that it would make a good film, but actually Christopher Hampton is going to make it next year. Right now I just want to act. I'm not really interested in getting into the production end of it. So maybe I'd just pocket the money. And then I could do whatever job I wanted for the rest of my life, couldn't I? I'll go do artsy-fartsy shows in a tent in someone's backyard. [*laughs*] Probably not, actually.

DC: So—

CB: Wait, maybe I'd make *Borstal Boy*, the Brendan Behan book. I like that book an awful lot.

DC: With you playing Brendan Behan?

CB: I'd love to, but . . . He looked such a brawling sort of drunken lad. And he had that sort of face that looked like it had been punched a number of times. He was short and stocky. I'm tall and lanky.

DC: Maybe you can get extremely tall actors to work with you. Then you can stuff your cheeks with cotton—

CB: And then go and have some people beat the shit out of me beforehand.

JW: When I picture you in the future, I see you as a Gary Oldman, or a Tim Roth, or a Jeremy Irons.

CB: That's a big compliment. I like all of them.

JW: I can't see you being a "big star," in that old-school actor kind of way.

CB: You know it always sounds a bit prissy when you . . . Basically most interviews with actors are incredibly prissy, aren't they? It's incredibly tedious hearing actors talk about their techniques and all that. I like to hear gossip as much as anybody else. I'll pick up the tabloids and go ooh and ahh and have a laugh at somebody else's expense on occasion. And I understand about publicity surrounding a film. You've got to get people in to see it, so you've gotta do it. But I think it's nice to stay as invisible as possible. Being an actor is the complete opposite of being a rock star or something where everybody wants to know you. With rock stars, it's you writing and performing. It's just you, isn't it? But an actor shouldn't be bigger than the film he's in. I wouldn't want to be above that really. I'd lose a lot of interest and a lot of the enjoyment of making films if that was ever to happen.

JW: I just envision you sticking to these smarter films.

CB: But sometimes it's great to see an action flick, isn't it? You don't always want to see little character films. If they were all like that we'd be bored to tears. We'd be dying to see someone blown to bits. But with the action things, it's only as effectual as reading a comic book when you see somebody get shot. You're not thinking that's real because you're not caring for the characters in the first place. That doesn't sound too cold, does it?

JW: No. I mean, think of *Pulp Fiction* and then think of *Once Were Warriors*, which we saw together. *Pulp Fiction* has a more shallow effect because you don't really know the victims, whereas in *Once Were Warriors* you feel like you know the victims, and the violence involves domestic abuse, so you actually feel touched in that case. Anyway, it sounds like you're going to kind of roll with the punches.

DC: So we want to finish off with a couple of . . . well, possibly rather silly questions, okay?

CB: Uh . . .

JW: Okay, you know how New York delis sometimes name sandwiches after actors? What would your sandwich consist of?

CB: It would be a whole roast chicken. And forget the bread.

DC: And now a quick round of word association.

CB: Oh, God, I hate these things. What is it exactly?

DC: I'm going to say a word. It could be a name, place, or whatever, and I want you to say the first word that comes to mind.

CB: Okay, let's give it a go. But can I change my mind later, if I don't feel . . . ?

DC: Sure. Okay, Shelley Duvall.

CB: Uh . . . Ditsy.

DC: Rome.

CB: Italian women with long dark hair.

DC: Is that a hyphenated word? Never mind. Uh, Guinness.

CB: Black, lovely.

DC: Mojo [Christian's Jack Russell terrier].

CB: Potato. Mojo potato and shagging everything in sight. A little randy bugger peeing on anything that's black and plastic and technical.

DC: Publicity.

CB: [*long pause*] Absolutely nothing comes to mind. Actually, public bar came to my head really. A pub. Maybe I want a drink whenever I hear publicity mentioned.

DC: Los Angeles.

CB: The desert, the beach, and all that. Which is what I like about it really.

DC: Charlton Heston.

CB: Guns.

DC: Religion.

CB: People wailing. I mean, I just watched *Priest*. And I just bought a leather-bound Bible as well.

DC: ABBA.

CB: My first crush was on the dark-haired one.

DC: Frida.

CB: Was that her name? It's a nasty little story. I sound like a real sick little twisted kid. I remember thinking one time, what if ABBA had a car crash outside my front door? And it was her, and she had a really bad head injury. And I sort of nursed her back to health while she had a big bandage around her head.

DC: How old were you?

CB: About six.

DC: Okay, Claire Danes.

CB: Angel. I think to do with the Soul Asylum video she was in. But she is also quite angelic to look at.

DC: Death.

CB: All I can think of is bloody Becomes Her.

DC: You're deep, man.

CB: Duh . . .

DC: Television.

CB: *Baywatch*. I apologize for this.

DC: No, no. It's very revealing. And lastly: heaven.

CB: [*long pause*] Well, I'm thinking of the club in London called Heaven.

DC: I knew you were going to say that.

CB: You knew I was going to opt out of any philosophical comment.

DC: Okay, you're finished. That wasn't so bad. I mean, that's printable, isn't it?

CB: Yeah, I think so. You're allowed to reveal that.

SPOOKY HOUSE
(October 1998)

All the great holidays are geared toward children, but most adjust reasonably well to the slowing of one's metabolism. Halloween, arguably the most genius of them all, is a depressing exception. Horror movies, goth clubs, and select theme-park attractions are Halloween's simulacra, doing for its refugees what porn and strip clubs do for the sex-starved, but, unless you develop a taste for the paranormal, the world will never feel that extravagantly and safely haunted again.

That said, Bob and Dave's Spooky House is a brilliant compromise. Originally designed and built by Bob Koritzke, the owner of a local advertising and marketing company, and Dave Rector, a software engineer, the Spooky House is essentially a walk-through, special-effects-laden, supermarket-sized maze built annually on the parking lot of a San Fernando Valley mall. (Dave dropped out a few years back, and now it's just called the Spooky House, though it's still popularly known as Bob and Dave's.) It materializes three weeks before Halloween, and has basically the same lifespan as a Christmas tree lot. The Spooky House has taken many physical forms over its eleven-year history, but like a Ramones song, it's a masterwork of several endlessly reiterated ingredients— "scary" props and lighting effects, a fog machine, a noisy soundtrack, and a gorily costumed cast of volunteer and low-paid performers whose job is to activate the milieu in much the same way that actors at Gettysburg turn a plot of grass into a shadow of the Civil War. In this case, the goal is less to jog memories of the act of trick-or-treating itself than to upgrade the original, eerie experience into a kind of wild dream of what Halloween could have been had one of the houses whose doorbell you'd rung actually contained some evil, irresistible world inside. The Spooky House is that fantasy made flesh, rendered to the harmless specifications of a child's fears, but in an adult-oriented tone and at an all-ages scale.

For some reason, Los Angeles is the kingdom of the spooky house. Every year, in addition to Koritzke's attraction, there are literally hundreds for connoisseurs to choose from, ranging from obscure shoestring versions known only within the neighborhoods in which their proprietors live to multimillion-dollar makeovers of major entertainment centers. But where in most spooky houses, great and small, the house is almost entirely abstracted out of the equation (loosely signified by the homey narrowness of the mazes and corridors, plus the occasional appearance of thrift-store beds and couches), the Spooky House strikes a chord somewhere between full-scale house and scaled-down playhouse. It's an old Disney trick—to make kids feel like adults, and vice versa—but, either by design or by accident of budget constraints, the place looks seriously run-down.

Despite its sobering asphalt location, the Spooky House errs on the side of realness in a way that Disney would be far too lawsuit-phobic to allow. Rather than abandoning the pretense of homeyness at the front door, the attraction's interior is designed to suggest a kind of dismembered corpse of a home whose rooms have become separated through some violent attack from within the architecture itself. They're connected by a segmented maze that forms a set of black wooden guts, as though the walls, in subdividing, had revealed a fourth architectural dimension. The secret to the Spooky House's broad appeal lies in its quality of the private made public. The materials are beyond low-tech—plywood, cheap fabrics, and maybe three shades of house paint; makeup jobs and costumes so grab-bag and amateurish that no amount of fake fog can revise them into plausible images. Like *The Blair Witch Project*, its power lies in the feeling that you and your friends could have made something exactly like it in your own backyard or basement.

All spooky houses milk that vibe, but Koritzke's art provides an unusual complement to this idea, keeping things homemade and formulaic, with tweaks that misshape the house into a puzzle of positive, homelike spaces and negative, sketchily home-related spaces. Its ramshackle construction, experimental floor plan, and gleefully overacting cast of high schoolers and aging nerds only hold your attention for so long before they're double-exposed with your own corrective flights of imagination, and become a kind of three-dimensional map to the things that used to go bump in your night. It's an experience that strums rather than rattles your nervous system, less putting you at the scene of some unsolved mystery than transporting you, mind and body, into every horror movie that ever gave you nightmares as a kid, and giving you a few moments to explore its sets and look its monsters right in the mask.

Visitors in small, unsupervised groups take this elongated tour of the house, encountering inhabitants who appear to be confined by some inexplicable force to the rooms themselves. Seeming at first oblivious to their visitors, these half-slaughtered, crazed adults and children in slightly upscale Halloween garb act out short skits that describe their ongoing domestic horror, then inevitably turn on their uncaring intruders, chasing them with axes and screeching chain saws into the relative safety of the maze itself, whose static effects—ranging from the inevitable strobe-lit displays of carnage to the inevitable psychedelic visual washes designed to confuse one's sense of direction and scale—suggest a cycle of poems, related to the rooms and one another via tenuously associative props and decorations. These poetic spaces are interspersed throughout the attraction's otherwise coherent, slasher-film-derived narrative. The overall effect is at once traditionalist in the thrills and chills department and formally avant-garde in a way that, at the very least, makes this particular spooky house a weirdly sophisticated work of folk art. "Postmodern" is too pretentious a term for such a populist contraption, but it's no coincidence that its devotees have included such well-known Los Angeles–based pomo visual artists as Charles Ray, Mike Kelley, Richard Hawkins, and Cameron Jamie, whose photographic and video work partially involves documenting the spooky house experience.

While the Spooky House is unique in that it both allows for egg-headed interpretations and provides cheap, forgettable thrills for those who ask only to shriek giddily at carefully appointed moments, its appeal is basic—a longing to feel afraid of that which is most familiar to us. It's impossible to decorate or even daydream our homes into haunted houses, because we know our own limitations too well and true horror is unimaginable by design. Bob Koritzke has not created a satisfactorily utopian equivalent. The whole premise is too silly, and a feeling of silliness outweighs the possibility of terror or death, even in such a refined example. Still, to walk warily and giggling through this twisted "house" on one night a year is probably as spooky an experience as adulthood can contextualize, honoring reality with a stratum of childlike spookiness that, at the very least, seems to raise Halloween from the dead in the form of a confoundingly sweet and successful non sequitur.

THE ANTI-LEO
The Brad Renfro Interview
(October 1998)

Brad Renfro is best known as a kind of teenage Marlon Brando, beloved of the Hanson crowd. Like River Phoenix before him, Renfro
glares from the pages of magazines like *16* and *Bop*, seeming every
inch the high school outsider forced to attend the prom. The thousands of boys and girls who clog online newsgroups with Renfro-
related posts love him exactly for this contentiousness. Well, and for
his looks, which are as cute in freeze-frame as his on-screen behavior
is moody and implosive.

The more Renfro the actor ignores the needs of this fan base—
choosing roles in R-rated fare like *Sleepers* and in indie-circuit films like
Telling Lies in America—the more his young admirers long to mother,
date, and save him. Unlike Leonardo DiCaprio, who also straddles the
worlds of puppy love and serious acting, Renfro has yet to toss his more
innocent fans a *Titanic*-size bone. You get the sense that he doesn't have
it in him. His favorite word is *real*, and you can feel that in his work.

Born in Knoxville, Tennessee, Renfro was discovered while performing in a local public-service announcement. Beginning with his first
film, Joel Schumacher's *The Client*—made when he was just eleven—

and continuing with his new film, Bryan Singer's *Apt Pupil*, in which he costars with Ian McKellen, Renfro has turned in consistently fierce, willful, deep, and increasingly nuanced performances that make it easy to forget that he only turned sixteen this past July.

But in person, he's unequivocally sixteen—a not-especially-hip, not-quite-square, polite, jokey, intensely emotional young guy forced to give an interview in his agent's LA office and visibly weirded out by the prospect. Having been intrigued enough by Renfro's looks and style to name-check him in my recent novel *Guide*, I find him interesting and discover that while he's as disorientingly well put together as I'd imagined, my urge to gawk is outweighed by caution in the face of his awkwardness. It doesn't help that Renfro's handlers seem worried that he might say something a little *too* real. At several points, we're interrupted by office workers: One woman takes Renfro into the hall, and later, a wary-looking man plants himself in the room, his ears so perked they're practically vibrating.

Dennis Cooper: Your agent said you're not feeling well.

Brad Renfro: It's just stress. Being in LA does this to me.

You live in Knoxville, which looks very nonstressful in pictures.

Yeah, it's cool, but it's getting violent these days.

What's up?

Well, this guy got shot last week outside a club, and he died. A friend of mine works at this café right by there. Luckily, she wasn't there at the time, but the café's windows got shot out. So it's not too scary to live there yet, but for such a small town, that seems pretty hard-core.

So where would you move, if you moved?

Not *here*, that's for sure. You can be young and stupid anywhere, but staying in Knoxville keeps me away from the business itself, the whole grind—everybody going out to eat and such. It keeps me real. 'Cause out here, there isn't much reality. There really isn't. That's why Tennessee Williams stayed in the South.

So you don't have any Leonardo DiCaprio envy?

No, no. He's a great actor, and now he can't do anything. It used to be I'd see him all over the damn place, and he wouldn't get too bothered. But now, phew. Man.

Talk about demystifying fame.

No shit. I don't know if the money would be worth it, either. Because he does make bank. He makes a lot of money. Hell, I haven't even made a million dollars. But is twenty million dollars worth no life? I don't think so.

You and he are both top dogs in the *Tiger Beat* scene. Does that have any value for you?

No. I'm quite flattered, but I don't know what to think of it. I don't strive to be a teen idol, you know? But the teen-idol thing is probably why I'm able to pick and choose the movies I want, because I have those fans.

Who says those teens don't have the right idea? You're always going to have those who look at you because you have interesting looks or whatever.

It's not like your films cater to that audience. For the most part, they're fairly heavy. I guess Tom and Huck *is kind of the oddball in your oeuvre, as it were.*

Yeah, well, I don't regret making that movie, because my little sister loves it. It's just that I thought I was making an American classic, and it was very Disney family. If you really watch, you can see that I'm not in the same damn movie as the other actors. I'm all hard-core and shit, and it seems like I'm bigger than the rest of them. There's an edge there that doesn't really fit, but to me, that was Huck. Who's to say it was tobacco in his pipe, you know?

Disney didn't want a hard-core Huck?

Not at all. It was constant friction. I just did it and got through it, because it was my job. But, you know, I maybe showered six times the whole damn shoot. That's where I got this bad reputation, you know. How I'm, like, whatever . . .

Trouble.

Yeah, trouble.

But you're not?

No, I'm not. I'm *real*. Real only seems like trouble if you're not real yourself. Honest to God.

You seem drawn to characters who have moral dilemmas.

As in, like . . . ?

I think I've seen all your films, and from *The Client* through *The Cure*, *Telling Lies in America* and now *Apt Pupil*, you seem to play the wide-eyed kid with a secret dark side.

Well, that's me, but that's also mankind. Someone asked me about *Apt Pupil*—you know, "Brad, are you saying people are evil?" And I go, "All people have evil natures." And they go, "What about babies?" And I go, "What about when babies turn two and start fighting in the crib over a toy?"

Babies are purely selfish beings.

Exactly. They *are* purely selfish. I love children, but . . . It's human nature to constantly be in a fight with your own being.

So *Apt Pupil* must have played into your interests.

Definitely, definitely. I was really excited to get that part. It was the only really cool film at the time. Well, there was that and *American History X*, as far as what was available to someone my age. And Bryan Singer's great. Ian McKellen's a genius to me.

Your styles are so different, though. His acting is so capital-B British, really organized, and—

I'm so off the wall? Yeah, I learned so much from Ian McKellen, but it wasn't like I could learn the craft of acting. I'm sure you've heard of doing something and not knowing how you do it? That's pretty much where I come from. What interested me about him was how he handled people. He makes everyone feel so comfortable. I tried to learn that from him, because that's something I need to learn.

How do you approach acting?

Just saying the words and believing them. I literally believe what's going on is really happening.

Is it like fantasizing?

Pretty much. I'm a person who doesn't show a ton of emotion until it's time. I ball too many things up—to the point where I cry for no reason. And I have to sit down and go, "What the hell is this for? Oh yeah, *right.*"

So I guess I have to ask you about the whole *Apt Pupil* shower-scene controversy.

I was there.

A number of the extras, who are basically your age, said they were ogled by gay crew members during the shooting of that scene and consider it a form of molestation.

I was there. I didn't notice anything.

So you don't support the boys who brought the lawsuit against the film?

No. As far as I know, it got thrown out of court anyway.

Are you into politics?

No. I don't care.

So you have nothing to say about the whole Clinton-Lewinsky thing?

Oh, I can say a little something about that. I think the only place where Clinton went wrong was in being married. I just think he's a man of the times. Fuck it. If I put myself in his shoes, I would have lied like a motherfucker, too. And there's the whole "If she only swallowed, none of this would have happened" jokes. But I shouldn't get into that, I guess.

Are you religious?

I'm a firm believer in God. I wouldn't be where I'm at if it wasn't for God.

You never question that?

Okay, here's a great Bible verse. Jesus is sitting and eating with politicians and sinners, you know, one of them asks one of his disciples, "Why does Jesus sit there and eat with sinners and such?" And Jesus turns and says, "He who is not sick has no need for the physician, and vice versa." I think when we're all at our rock bottom, there's nothing else but God. But I think all Christians have questioned Him at one time or another.

Did you ever investigate Buddhism?

I think any religion's okay, except Satanism. I can't think of anything in Satanism that could benefit you.

But there's something flashy about Satanism, don't you think?

I think it's more powerful in the short term. That's the trick that the Devil plays on you. It's like, cocaine's great the first couple of times, you know? I think that's just the Devil. That's how he works. I'm as firm a believer in the Devil as I am in God. I'm just not a supporter.

So do your musical tastes run to Stryper and that sort of thing?

Fuck, no. I'm into blues and jazz. Wes Montgomery, Buddy Guy, Electric blues and old-school, too. You got your Blind Boy Fuller, Robert Johnson, Sonny Terry, and Brownie McGhee. And I still like punk, of course. Anyone who ever liked punk will never *not* like punk. It's very easy to like. Being punk rock means not caring what people think of you. At one point, I did have green hair when I was thirteen or so, but I thought it was more punk rock to be just kind of normal than to go and pierce my dick or nose.

Are you into old-school punk or new-school punk?

I can't stand new-school punk. It's so poppy, like Offspring or Green Day or whatever. I'm more into the D.C. bands—Fugazi, the Teen Idols, shit like that. And the LA late-'70s scene stuff—Descendents, Black Flag, Germs.

At one point, you wanted to make a film about the life of Darby Crash of the Germs, didn't you?

Yeah. It's funny. I didn't get to do that. Some other guy's doing it, I guess. It would have been cool to play a totally reckless punk. I think I could do that pretty well, but fuck it. Right now, I'm wanting to write and direct a film about a boy in a mental institution. He doesn't speak, and the film's about his theory that dogs are superior to humans and how there's really no need for conversation in a perfect world, because everything would be about unconditional love. You wouldn't have a need for verbal communication. I haven't written it yet, but I have the thought.

Do you write?

I write poetry and stuff but not scripts. I just have to sit my ass down and do it. It seems a bit overwhelming, like writing a book of haiku or something. It's a weird form.

Do you have favorite actors?

Steve Buscemi, definitely. I love him, because he just does his thing. Jack Nicholson, Chris Walken. Those cats are cool. I'd love to work with them. But, hell, I'd even work with Ann-Margret, you know? Who's to say she's not a genius? You never know.

Do you ever approach actors or directors you like and ask to work with them?

Just the normal shit. I mean, I don't go, "Hey, I want to work with Stanley Kubrick. I'm going to chase his crazy ass down." I don't send fan letters. I don't make picture collages and shit, like little strips from a magazine. "I'm Brad. I want to work with you." No.

I guess I'll end this by clearing up a really common rumor about you. Did Joel Schumacher adopt you when you were making *The Client* with him?

Fuck. That's not true whatsoever. When I was eleven, I made a joke that he was going to adopt me, or some shit, but that's all. I think I liked the idea back then, 'cause my life was kind of hard or something. I live with my grandparents, pretty much always have.

A lot of people think the rumor's true.

What a bunch of dipshits. These rumors, man. I'm like the [rumor] magnet; I don't know fucking why. Supposedly, I'm doing some movie with Natalie Portman and Liv Tyler called *The Little Black Box*. I've never heard of that in my life. I think Milos Forman is directing it. It would be fucking cool as hell, but it isn't real.

I heard you were in the *Star Wars* prequel, too.

Oh, yeah. Go. I'm all over the place. That's cool. Wait a second. Ouch.

What's wrong?

Shit, I'm getting a stress cold sore. [*pulls out his lower lip*] Look at this.

Charming.

Exactly. I'd better go do whatever with this.

Well, thanks.

Yeah. Have a good day, sir.

NICK DRAKE: THE BIOGRAPHY
(June 1999)

By the time Nick Drake died in 1974, he was twenty-six, zombified by depression, and a recording artist so obscure he makes Smog seem like Smokey Robinson. A protégé of the legendary British producer Joe Boyd, he was the oddest man out among English art-folk stylists of the early '70s, a genre-mate of the more spotlight-savvy Incredible String Band, Fairport Convention, Ralph McTell, and Steeleye Span. He made three increasingly great, decreasingly popular albums, and was tentatively admired by a few renegade critics for a sound that, in retrospect, suggests a cross between a more opaque Leonard Cohen and a less anal Sade. His lyrics reflect the preoccupations of the late hippie period—nature, myth, soft-focus mysticism—but, unlike the "Jollie Nellie jigging round the maypole"–style verse promulgated by his contemporaries, Drake's words are a charged mumble of half-baked imagery crabbed by intense, myopic despair. The rivers and moons and fields that run through his songs are so at odds with the lush yet stricken tone of his voice that the space in between might as well be outer space. It's no surprise that his tuneful dislocation makes more sense as a progenitor of weakling, downcast lo-fi rockers like Cat Power, Palace, Sebadoh, and Belle and Sebastian than it did as a quirky example of prog-archivilism.

Patrick Humphries's *Nick Drake: The Biography* is a curious book. The degree to which Humphries has delved into Drake's life is impressive—bordering on obsessive—and while he manages to almost dispel some common myths about Drake's mode of death and sexual preference, as well as semi-explain the artist's ethereality as undiagnosed bipolar disorder, the story of Drake's life remains fragmented, repetitive, and constructed of guesswork. The through line goes something like this: A sensitive, popular, upper-middle-class boy gets hip to the headiest rock of the late '60s, takes up the guitar, experiments with pot and acid, becomes less personable, gets a recording contract, quits college, moves to London, makes three albums that don't sell and get so-so reviews, becomes increasingly remote, moves in with his parents, and overdoses on antidepressants. He appears to have had very few friends, and even they were more like intrigued acquaintances. Their memories are the substance of this book, and, to a one, they claim not to have understood him in the slightest. The typical encounter with Drake involved him showing up at someone's house unexpectedly, sitting for several hours without saying a word, then leaving unexpectedly. Since he left no diary, and wrote few letters, his life consists of a series of such sightings, sometimes with months in between, which essentially leaves those who called him Nick and we who speak his name in hushed tones in the same boat. Was he too brilliant for this lame-ass world? Was he a self-absorbed, tiresome, yet talented wimp? They never knew, so we never will.

What Humphries has done is replace several specific myths about Drake with a larger, more generalized one. It has been commonly thought that Drake killed himself because he was a heroin addict who couldn't deal with his latent homosexuality. Nothing is for certain in this biography, but Humphries makes a persuasive case that Drake's death was rather something in between suicide and accident—a recklessly self-induced overdose by someone so desperate to get some shut-eye that he didn't care what he took. The homosexual thing seems to be a revisionist explanation for the fact that a beautiful man never had a girlfriend, serious or casual. Apart from a couple of innocent "cuddles" with the folksinger Linda Thompson, and rumors of girlfriends here and there, there's not much evidence that he ever had sex with anyone. Still, pretty, sensitive, and asexual don't necessarily add up to gay, and there's not a hint here that he ever fancied his own. Heroin addiction also seems more likely a knee-jerk diagnosis of his passivity. There's lots of evidence that he stood and stared, none whatsoever that he nodded off.

In a way, for all the new information Humphries unearths, he winds up making Drake more of an enigma than the misinformation suggested. Drake's was a life free of juice and tidbits—no blowouts with friends or colleagues, no gossip, no peaks or valleys. His life doesn't tell us anything about the time he occupied. He might as well have lived in the Dark Ages. He left no live recordings, no film recordings, and only a few undiscovered songs. In the handful of extant photographs, he looks weirdly uncomfortable for such a handsome guy, and that's it. In other words, he's nothing more or less than a person who wrote beautiful songs with some abstract, undecodeable wrong at their center. Only one thing's for sure—he was one amazingly screwed-up young man whose death was less a promise short-circuited, à la Kurt Cobain or Richie Manic, than a slow, silent fade to a logical black. That may not say much about an artist whose songs absorb some of the best contemporary artists and listeners, but that's apparently all he wrote.

ODD MAN OUT
David Wojnarowicz
(October 1999)

I remember when word spread that the (pre-groovy) East Village was brandishing an art scene. If memory serves, an influential tagline in one of the now-defunct neighborhood weeklies described this scene as consisting of "art that wakes up and smells the audience." Living in the East Village in the early '80s, as I happened to be doing, I perceived the beleaguered area as a kind of pocket of hard truth in Manhattan's gridlocked reality. So it was inviting to believe that the bohemians, druggies, and artist types who called the Village home were people too rough-hewn and economically challenged to suffer the intellectual pretenses that seemed to have hypnotized contemporary art into a state of numbed, polished cleverness. Of course, "East Village Art" ended up being just another inflationary term that overrepresented a hodgepodge of recklessly sincere artists, but that's the future talking.

David Wojnarowicz was one of the first of the scene's few crossover stars. Unlike other name East Village artists—say, Rodney Alan Greenblat, Rhonda Zwillinger, and Keiko Bonk—he was not just distinguishable from the hordes because he manifested the goofily personal with a conventional-seeming finesse. His fierce, politicized, multidisciplinary art was the embodiment of East Village Art's grandest ideals, and, in retrospect, an almost single-handed justification of its hype. His sculptures, installations, paintings, and photographs from the early '80s are deeply felt and formally worked out to the point where they resemble what we think of as contemporary art, yet remain crass enough and conceptually clumsy enough that they fail to make the grade. That passing resemblance nevertheless got Wojnarowicz, and by proxy the East Village aesthetic, into the 1985 Whitney Biennial, and into some notable collections, but it's not why his work continues to be debated while the works of most other East Village artists are trinkets that escape even the art world's memory.

Before the East Village scene's make-believe art world attracted galleries of a more explicitly commercial intent, it provided Wojnarowicz with the opportunity to sell his work without appearing to sell out. Till that point, he was best known as a mysterious perpetrator of some obtuse graffiti—an omnipresent barring cow's head stenciled on random sidewalks; some hard-nosed, elusive literary phrases spray-painted in and around popular gay cruising areas. In his free time, he performed with the band 3 Teens Kill 4. Apart from the oft-published photo sequence of a young man shooting up, masturbating, and wandering the streets in a Rimbaud mask ("Arthur Rimbaud in New York," 1978–79), Wojnarowicz's output was less the work of an Artist than that of a creative misanthrope on a mission to assert the particulars of his disenfranchisement by disrupting others' occasions. Whereas Basquiat's and Haring's graffiti works were developed, artistic gestures that transferred smoothly to galleries, Wojnarowicz's was rather a kind of poetic tagging: Lawrence Weiner with a furious punk touch. With his first proper shows at stalwart East Village galleries like Civilian Warfare and Gracie Mansion, his work filled out conventionally, and became less an opaque "fuck you" than an illustration of a fuzzy new art movement. It was no longer at odds with its context, per se. It was the most ambitious float in a parade celebrating the Downtown sensibility, a fact that was not lost on the artist.

I'd known Wojnarowicz since the late '70s, when I published some of his Rimbaud photos and a few pieces of his fiction in *Little Caesar*, a magazine I was editing at the time. But I hadn't seen him for a few years when I ran into him in 1985 while making the rounds of the East Village galleries. He was a hot young artist by then, lionized as a home-town hero by the *Village Voice*, and name-checked by most of the major art magazines. I had mixed feelings about the sculptures and themed installations he had begun exhibiting. While it was heartening to see a true iconoclast rewarded, it seemed to me that Wojnarowicz's work had beefed up interestingly but, in doing so, had lost the quality of complete and pure alienation that had given his talent its bite and specificity. He seemed to have subsumed his weird range of ideas into a generalized, somewhat obvious political cartoon and begun using standard art-making techniques to make classic, even hippie-ish, anarchist statements against the usual powers that be. The riveting fuzziness of his graffiti had been replaced with overly clear-cut attacks (say, in his well-known sculptures and painting/collages in which sharks, burning children, and kissing men were given world maps for skin). Anyway, I expressed my concern, half expecting one of his famous bursts of temper.

Instead, Wojnarowicz sat down with me on a stoop and launched into a tormented, self-righteous, hour-long harangue that has, ever since, struck me as definitive of East Village Art's brief moment, for better or worse. He said that his success was destroying him because he couldn't reject it in good conscience. He'd dreamed of this kind of recognition and had even fantasized about exactly the kind of black-sheep art world that the East Village scene encompassed in theory, a situation where art could be anything at all, and where walking into a gallery would always involve a disconcerting, confrontational experience with an uncompromised, individual vision. But this belief had been contingent on the idea that New York was secretly full of artists who had as clamorous a sensibility as his own. Instead, he found himself surrounded by peers whose talent was merely raw, and raw only by virtue of economic hardship, but whose sensibilities were as coddling and self-indulgent as those of the Salles, Fischls, and Longos who populated the official art world. As a consequence, similar delusions of greatness had settled over the scene. In response, he'd rebelled against his peers by giving his work a social conscience and physical grandiosity, both to counteract the ongoing romanticization of the homespun and to embody what he imagined an "East Village Art" should be. But his rebellion had backfired. The political sheen had given critics and curators a way to pigeonhole his work and had led them to misdiagnose his personal rage as the spearhead of a movement with which he felt no camaraderie whatsoever. He said he was going to quit making art, and stormed off.

Of course, Wojnarowicz didn't quit, and he never stopped exhibiting his work in galleries; in fact, it's generally thought that his post–East Village shows at SoHo's P.P.O.W. gallery were the best of his career. That improvement has been fatuously attributed to his lucid response to testing positive for HIV in the mid-'80s: He could express his horror unreservedly knowing that the politics swirling around his illness would do the job (ham-fisted or otherwise) of ascribing social meaning to his personal battle. It might also be true that the SoHo context provided a more inappropriate and therefore more fruitful locale for the contentiousness that underscored his best work, although, if anything, his later works were art with a capital A—discreet, Conceptual, and object-oriented. I'd argue that while the East Village scene made Wojnarowicz a proper artist, it also reinforced his interest in writing, leading ultimately to the publication of his memoir, *Close to the Knives: A Memoir of Disintegration* (Vintage, 1991), one of the more significant volumes of contemporary prose. It's as though the particular privacy of the act of writing allowed him to work with greater care and complexity in the same sneaky, solitary way he had done when decorating deserted sidewalks. By contrast, his visual art seemed to have devolved into something of a part-time job, an interesting way to pay the bills.

Whereas Wojnarowicz's art is probably doomed to an eternity spent in gay- and/or AIDS-themed group shows, his writing is far more likely to be remembered. Falling into loose association with similarly self-taught, self-absorbed geniuses like Jean Genet, Celine, and his beloved Rimbaud, Wojnarowicz's poetic, ranting prose translates his life story, fantasies, and outrage at society's imbalance into something that bears little stylistic resemblance to other writing, but rings as natural as any diaristic jotting. Where most of his visual artworks have a slight staginess problem, and tend toward the illustrative and agitprop, his inventive yet direct use of language encompasses his deeply contradictory nature without the least sign of strain. It's telling that in the last year or so of his life, Wojnarowicz wrote continuously, made almost no art that didn't illustrate some text, and, according to some reports, had plans to write a novel. It's not a huge surprise that in his recently published journals, *In the Shadow of the American Dream* (Grove, 1998), there's almost no mention of his visual art, much less his career in the art world, East Village or otherwise.

The various successes and failures of Wojnarowicz's visual art illustrate the problem of the East Village scene. Unlike, say, punk or the rave scene, two vaguely similar grassroots cultural movements, it failed to have any impact whatsoever, either on art itself or even on the way we think about art's presentation. It was a poignant blip, a retarded, well-meaning art world–ette that not only didn't have enough evidence to prove its case but didn't have much of a case to begin with. For all the meaning that could potentially be attributed to its pseudo-populism, it seems in retrospect to have aspired to be a grittier Chelsea, albeit with more entertaining openings. If Wojnarowicz was its truest and most hard-core product, his work's endurance says nothing about the half ton of East Village art entombed in the far reaches of some very embarrassed collectors' storerooms. If the East Village scene proved anything, it's that a gallery is always and only a gallery, regardless of where it happens to be located and irrespective of the occasional artist who passes through its doors on his or her way to meaningfulness.

MORE THAN ZERO
Mary Harron's *American Psycho*
(March 2000)

In an interview given around the time that "Walk on the Wild Side" became a fluke hit single, Lou Reed was asked how it felt to achieve mainstream fame after years of cult notoriety. He jokingly replied that at least he'd no longer be known as the guy who was in the weird band that did the song "Heroin." Reed couldn't have foreseen that, more than twenty years and innumerable songs later, most contemporary pop music fans know him as the guy from that weird band who also sang "Walk on the Wild Side." Americans' memories are famously short, except when it comes to the infamous. But while controversial subject matter tends to stick in the mind, one decade's mindblower can easily be the next's casual reference point.

Bret Easton Ellis's first novel, *Less Than Zero* (1985), can't exactly be called his "Heroin," but (for all the digits in its sale figures) its youthful indiscretions were such that respect came largely from the fringe literati. *Less Than Zero* also pegged Ellis so squarely as an '80s icon that he must have felt some relief when his third novel, 1991's *American Psycho*, caused a stink that rendered *Less Than Zero*'s impact antique. Dropped prepublication by Simon & Schuster, and eventually released to 'Namlike protests from the Left (and massive, ongoing popular success), the novel's title will undoubtedly be Ellis's other middle name no matter how many times he outdoes it. Still, *American Psycho* was finally beginning to win grudging acceptance as an influential, even classic American novel, when word came that the director Mary (*I Shot Andy Warhol*) Harron was giving it the cinematic treatment. Now, with the movie nearly in theaters (it premiered at Sundance in January and opens nationally next month), the aspects of Ellis's novel that so infuriated the self-appointed censors are again potential fuel for the same old fire, albeit in a far more shockproofed culture.

Like every first-rate novel, *American Psycho* functions in a way that is entirely literary. It may be driven by standard narrative devices that, in and of themselves, are at home in any genre, but its originality is so language-based and unfilmable that one can assume the movie rights were bought on something like a dare. And the transfer of Ellis's supposedly misogynist text into Harron's hands is an inherently curious notion, she being a woman, a self-described feminist, and the director of a low-budget film about another shocking cultural moment—Valerie Solanas's attempt to murder Andy Warhol. But even if Pasolini himself had risen from the grave to make this Reagan-era *Salò*, the problem would remain that fiction is a special code that can coax readers' imaginations into constructing mental imagery that would blind their eyes, and even the most adventurous film won't make viewers see what they can't, no matter how artful the approach. The list of disturbing literary works turned into artsy, retarded films is ever lengthening—*Querelle*, *Naked Lunch*, *The Sheltering Sky*, *Fight Club*—and even the few successful translations are a matter of debate (maybe *Satyricon*, maybe *Trainspotting*, just maybe *Crash*). *American Psycho* the movie had its own medium's cards stacked against it from the outset.

In a recent article in *Harper's Bazaar*, Bret Easton Ellis looked back on his original *American Psycho* experience and revealed that the novel was his response to the stranglehold that political correctness had on late-'80s culture, which "may have nudged me into exploring the repressed, darker side of Patrick Bateman to an even more gruesome degree than I initially thought when I began the book." In fact, that nudge, and Ellis's tangible excitement, fear, and shock as nudge skids into psychosexual free fall, mixed with his ability to maintain equilibrium via the distanced, ironic, quasi-superficial prose style that is his trademark, is not only the novel's genius but its raison d'être. It might be difficult to imagine the bravery this novel required in a culture subsequently glutted with gangsta rap, "Sensation," reality TV, and so on. But it's impossible to imagine an *American Psycho* 2000 that could effectively simulate Ellis's kamikaze plunge into now-declassified taboos like serial murder, racism, misogyny, and graphic violence. Those paradises are now parking lots, leaving Mary Harron with few respectable angles on the material that weren't purely devotional, à la Gus Van Sant's *Psycho* remake, or purely technical, à la Sherrie Levine's gender-switching co-optations of the work of male artists.

Given all that, Harron's *American Psycho* is as successful as could have been expected. It makes no attempt to boldly go where no film has gone before; neither does it denude, misinterpret, or leech off Ellis's novel. The director's tongue-in-cheek aesthetic is ultimately flattering to the coked-out, soft Republican antics that Ellis was parodying, with cinematographic claustrophobia standing in for the novel's linguistic tunnel vision. Harron houses the story of Patrick Bateman's transformation from Wall Street snot to frighteningly wacked serial killer in a linear strobe of period lofts, clubs, and restaurants, all lit to make the actors look alternately like products in a showroom or mockdebauchees in a Helmut Newton ad. She signifies Ellis's speedy, pop-cultural chatter by filling her sets with art by Longo, Prince, Bleckner, et al., and by dressing all but cops, whores, and the homeless in a wide price range of defunct fashions that, to production designer Gideon Ponte's credit, register as '80s detritus without seeming merely kitsch. The film's irony is so advanced—and laid on so thick—that it makes even a heavily quotation-mark-enclosed comedy like *Happiness* seem like *Patch Adams* in comparison. Even its psychological life is designer suave, such that Bateman's eventual collapse into hysterical self-disgust serves principally as an indicator that the meticulous fabric of the film is under duress. His tears make you realize that irony is a more flexible and operatic tone than it's normally acknowledged to be, but, as in the novel, Bateman's personal misery, let alone that of his victims, is mean-ingfully unaffecting. Even *American Psycho*'s feminism is underplayed, and will matter or not depending on whether you think the startlingly broad comedic handling of the murders is counterproductive by reason of politics, as one might well argue, or just one of the film's many curi-ous formal devices, applied to keep things hyperkinetic within its own strict, mannered guidelines, as seems more immediately the case.

One thing seems relatively certain: Whatever content-related fuss *American Psycho* the movie incites will more than likely resemble that which greeted last year's "Catholic-bashing" *Dogma*, meaning that un-less Harron wants to go the Kevin Smith route and help publicize the chanting of a few uninformed wackos, her movie is probably in the clear on that front. Whether by default or by design, *American Psycho* has covered its potentially offensive ass. It's an unusually intelligent, self-reflexive, refrigerated comedy whose buff, shimmering body—not to mention the daredevil performance by the actor Christian Bale as Bate-man—should impress all but the most timid, lamebrained critics. Still, its hopes for more than a brief, blurb-adorned life rest on an unlikely consensus among the kind of sophisticated moviegoers whose word of mouth got the ball rolling on *American Beauty* and those smart, extreme-seeking kids who occasionally ignore their PlayStations long enough to see *The Blair Witch Project* or *The Matrix* on multiple occasions. But unlike those films, or previous, high-concept serial-murder comedies like *Man Bites Dog*, *Henry: Portrait of a Serial Killer*, and *Serial Mom*, which have a quasi-immature dastardliness that offsets their deconstructible artfulness, *American Psycho* is grown-up to the max. Trickier yet, it's the kind of remote, sociopathic, blatantly perverse adult (think *eXistenZ*, *Eyes Wide Shut*) that most kids would consider creepy, and even weird adults would prefer to admire from a considerable distance. Ellis's novel will outlive its moment long enough to achieve respectability, but it'll always diagram its own dangerousness in a way that can't help but trigger conflicting passions. In the case of Mary Harron's *American Psycho*, the question is who'll feel passionately enough about the art of filmmaking to revisit the topic of serial murder one more time and melt this admirable movie's cold, cold heart.

FIRST COMMUNION
Robert Bresson
(April 2000)

In the early '80s, a friend invited me to a screening of Robert Bresson's *Devil, Probably,* on the condition that, no matter what, I not say a word about it afterward. He claimed that Bresson's films had such a profound, consuming effect on him that he couldn't bear even the slightest outside interference until their immediate spell wore off, which he warned me might take hours. He was not normally a melodramatic, overly sensitive, or pretentious person, so I just thought he was being weird—until the house lights went down. All around us, moviegoers yawned or laughed derisively; some even fled the theater. But, watching the film, I experienced an emotion more intense than any I'd ever have guessed art could produce. The critic Andrew Sarris, writing on Bresson's work, once famously characterized this reaction as a convulsion of one's entire being, which rings true to me. Ever since, I've imposed basically the same condition on those rare friends whom I trust enough to sit beside during the screening of a Bresson film, and I'm not otherwise a particularly melodramatic, sensitive, or pretentious person.

Bresson isn't just my favorite artist. There's a whole lot more to it than that, though the effect he has had on me is too enormous and personal to distill. On a practical level, his work constructed my sensibility as a writer by offering up the idea that it was possible for an artwork's style to embody a kind of pragmatism that, if sufficiently rigorous and devoted to a sufficiently powerful subject, would eliminate the need within the work for an overt philosophical or moral standpoint. Every artist tries in some way to find that least compromised intersection of planes where his or her ideas meet and slightly exceed the world's expectations, but I don't think anyone has found a more perfectly balanced style than Bresson. His work communicates an unyielding, peculiarly personal vision of the world in a voice so sterilized as to achieve an almost inhuman efficiency and logic. The result is a kind of cinematic machine whose sets, locations, narrative, and models (Bresson's preferred term for actors) function together as an unhierarchical unit so perfectly self-sufficient that all that is revealed within each film is the disconcerting failure of the models to fulfill Bresson's requirements. Their emotions resonate, despite a conscientious effort on Bresson's part to make them move about and speak as though they have none. The fact that the actors, unlike any other aspect of Bresson's films, are driven by individual feeling draws attention almost by default, and creates a relationship with the audience so intimate that it's almost unbearable in its aesthetic restrictions.

A full appreciation of Bresson's work requires moviegoers to approach his films as though starting from scratch. This is a huge thing to ask of an audience, which is why Bresson's films will always select their admirers with care and infrequency. But the films earn that degree of commitment because, despite their intensive demands, they ask almost nothing for themselves. They're too plain to be considered experimental or avant-garde, and require no suspension of disbelief. But they're antitra-ditional as well, although their respect for the tradition of storytelling borders on the fanatical. They're neither difficult nor easy to watch, at least not in the usual senses of those words. Instead of flaunting their difference, or feigning modesty by deferring to the conventions of Hol-lywood film, they offer up an art so unimpeachably fair, so lacking in ul-terior motivation, that the effect is a kind of mimicry of what perception might be like were one capable of simultaneously perceiving clearly and appreciating the process by which perception occurs. The only thing these films ask is that one share a fraction of Bresson's single-minded concern for the souls of young people whose innocence causes them to fail at the cruel, irrevocable task of adulthood.

Apart from his first feature, the comedy *Les anges du péché*, and per-haps the curiously terse if fascinating *Une femme douce*, Bresson never made a film that's less than sublime. For whatever reason, his early, black-and-white films, like *Pickpocket*, *Diary of a Country Priest*, and *Mouchette* are the most celebrated. But, if anything, his later, less widely circulated color films—*Four Nights of a Dreamer*; *Lancelot du Lac*; *The Devil, Prob-ably*; and *L'argent*—are the masterpieces among his masterpieces, to my mind. Many of the aforementioned stylistic tropes for which Bresson is alternately reviled and admired reached their full significance in this latter part of his oeuvre, as the lapsed Catholicism that gave his early, doomed characters the remote possibility of redemption and allowed viewers to interpret his work's introversion as a metaphor for religious self-erasure loses ground to an even more thoroughly hopeless notion of fate as the random and godless chain of events that structures a life. In Bresson's earlier films, the protagonist's almost inevitable suicide is a tragic segue into the comforting delusion of heaven; in the later films, suicide is the inexorable outcome, given the bleak circumstances; and the staggering numbness induced by Bresson's cold, mechanical witness to these deaths forms the least opinionated, and therefore only accurate depiction of, suicide's consequences that I've ever come across.

When I first saw *The Devil, Probably* at the age of twenty-eight, I wrote Bresson a number of long, desperate, worshipful letters offering to do anything, even sweep the floors of his sets, to assist him in his work. At the time, I would have given up my life, my friends, even my dream of being a novelist in order to help him create films that, to this day, are for me the greatest works of art ever made. It's an unjustifiable, perhaps even irrational claim, but I'm not alone in my devotion, which might also explain why my pleas went unanswered. Perhaps I was just one of many depressed young people who'd confused Bresson's stylistic perfection for a perfect solution and my letters went straight into the trash. In any case, I've now lived longer than any of the Bresson characters whose hopelessness I once took as a reflection of my own, and I credit his films, whose effect on me remains indescribable, but whose consequence to the novelist I eventually became is simply put: In my own dark, idiosyncratic art, I continue to do everything in my power to carry on a fraction of Robert Bresson's work.

MYSTERY MAN
Denis Johnson's *Name of the World*
(August 2000)

Denis Johnson is a new-fashioned fiction writer schooled in old-fashioned narrative ways and means, damaged by psychological forces unknown, and saved from both mainstream popularity and cult obscurity by his knack for exhuming suggestive fragments from disenfranchised male psyches, not to mention a great if slightly conservative curiosity about what the standard American sentence can and can't do. Technically, his work is most comfortable in the company of books by similarly youngish, mildly experimental realist writers like Steven Wright, A. M. Homes, and Ricky Moody, but there is a lonesomeness in his voice that makes his shape-shifting body of work seem less calculatedly versatile than strangely all over the place, fueled in unpredictable directions by some honest-to-God restlessness whose origin and aim are hard to pin down. His oeuvre's resulting mystique inspires devotees as far afield as the *New York Review of Books* and *Punk Planet*, possibly because, in the classic tradition of American iconoclasts from John Huston to Stan Ridgway, he's inarguably skilled, well-intentioned, and such an irrepressible fuckup at the same time.

Among his six previous books of fiction, only *Jesus' Son* has the vibe one associates with the term "minor classic." It's also the work most indebted to a specific literary convention. *Jesus' Son* is craggier, prettier Raymond Carver minimalism without the sentimental false notes and trick endings. The rest of Johnson's books are problematic, but, apart from *Fiskadoro*, a stiff-jointed, modernist riff on the psychedelic machismo that Thomas McGuane built, and *The Stars at Noon*, an uncomfortable, Eurpeanesque art novel and Johnson's one completely misguided effort, they are sporadically brilliant works of fiction kept from actual greatness by internal battles between Johnson's talent for simple, emotionally jarring sentences and his dogged need to reconfigure the novel itself.

Already Dead, Johnson's previous novel, was set in a rather magic, realistically drugged-out, cultish, violent California. An epic by his usual standards, it suffered from a case of gigantism that left him cranking out mechanical and inspired sentences at about a 100-to-1 ratio. *The Name of the World* is a case of him biting off slightly less than he can chew. It's a short, polished novel with a small, containable cast of characters, written in a self-consciously dull first person that prioritizes accumulating incident and interceding memory over any grander narrative schematic. The setting is, as always, a new one for Johnson: this time, the life, past, environs, and thought processes of a beleaguered university professor and sometime journalist, Michael Reed, who is mourning the death of his wife and child in a car accident, and facing the possible early end of his career.

The turf and related dilemmas are familiar ones, covered in recent decades by writers as diverse as Philip Roth and Michael Chabon, and *The Name of the World* follows the now tried-and-true formula: Life-scarred, middle-aged man with stunted artistic aspirations decays in academia, then is revived through a role-reversing, sexual-tension-fraught relationship with an ambitious student, in this case a cartoonishly drawn, Karen Finley–ish performance artist named Flower Cannon. Reed stumbles into one of her on-campus performances, then comes across her in a series of unlikely situations; he's smitten and intrigued by her artsy, confrontational ideas. A flirtation fizzles, but he comes to admire her fearlessness, and eventually returns to his life as a journalist with Cannon as an unlikely role model and muse.

Johnson's contributions to the advancement of this growing canon of academia-centered literature are negligible. He essentially does the usual in his unusual voice, and the pleasures here are mild and almost entirely literary. There are well-placed, effective epiphanies signaled by sudden pileups of short, anxious sentences that temporarily and beautifully flush emotion to the novel's elegant, blasé surface. As Reed's mind enlivens, the novel's long, meditative paragraphs break down into an invigorated quasi-journalistic style—all attentive, jotted dialogue that effectively allows the world to come flooding into the novel without derailing its hermetism. Johnson's voice functions perfectly at this newly muted volume. Gracefully efficient in mind and body, with occasional ripples of originality, *The Name of the World* resonates exactly as a novel of this sort should, making it one of his more successful books, if not his most memorable.

So the Denis Johnson mystery continues, and adjectives like "luminous" and "poetic" will undoubtedly dot the blurbs on the back of this novel's paperback edition, as they do his older books. Whether by accident or design, Johnson's work is and will remain an enigma as long as he proves himself almost incapable of standing still long enough to nail a particular narrative form and set of characters. As strange as the comparison might appear, with every book he seems more like a kind of Madonna (or, if you prefer, Bowie) of contemporary fiction, his talent equally divided between a gift for up-to-the-minute, authentic gab and an ad man–like ability to recycle the same basic content in a seemingly endless array of Zeitgeist-savvy forms.

It may be an imperfect marriage in most cases, but the result is that his books are eventful enough to cause a considerable amount of initial excitement and happy head scratching. By the time the buzz wears off, and each book's weaknesses become apparent, his work has moved on. Johnson isn't the only contemporary novelist whose talent and ambition are weirdly at odds. The overly schematic conventional is practically a genre unto itself. But in his case there's something ongoing and indefinable that makes his predictably unpredictable missteps haunting and slippery.

FLAILING VISION
Lars von Trier's *Dancer in the Dark*
(October 2000)

It sounds good on paper. Lars von Trier, the bold, gifted, iconoclastic Danish director, completes his long, tantrum-filled mission to win the Cannes Film Festival's—and serious filmdom's—award of awards, the Palme d'Or, and is cemented as one of the greats. But this isn't the '70s, and taking first prize at Cannes last May doesn't automatically make *Dancer in the Dark* a classic or assure von Trier's position in the pantheon. Those who've seen his shape-shifting oeuvre as proof that European avant-garde film survived the senility, retirement, and death of its postwar masters were understandably champing at the bit. Fresh off cofounding the better-than-nothing film movement Dogma '95, directing the shockingly-good-in-parts crossover hit *Breaking the Waves* (1996), and bombing his future in Hollywood with the ferocious, controversy-baiting Dogma entry *The Idiots* (1998), von Trier seemed ready to fulfill his long-standing potential and, in so doing, meet Cannes's relatively highbrow if weathered standards.

Until you actually lay eyes on *Dancer in the Dark*—which opens in theaters this month on the heels of its U.S. premiere at the New York Film Festival—it has everything going for it. Von Trier's preproduction announcement that the Dogma manifesto contained heretofore unacknowledged loopholes, plus his proven talent as a quick-change stylist, left the film's form enticingly in question. His decision to make a musical suggested that he might be ready to address the sloppy, indulgent structures that can misshape even his best work. The Icelandic pop star and songwriter Björk, who is cast in the lead, has as much talent and integrity as anyone in the music biz, not to mention a Liza Minnelli–like charisma that could easily fill a screen. No matter how huff-and-puffed-up von Trier's reputation, odds were good that the film would be an event, if not quite a divine intervention.

Dancer in the Dark concludes von Trier's gradual evolution from poete mauditto quasi-documentarian. Early works like *Medea* (1987) and *Zentropa* (1991) laid the cinematography on thick and backpedaled narrative into a rumpled sketch. This lavish murkiness was an acquired taste, but von Trier's borderline-pretentious imagery was juiced with a complex tonal weirdness, at once operatic, self-absorbed, spiritual, and blackly ironic. Severe auteurial self-consciousness battled severely grim subject matter to a curious stalemate, leaving the work so overwrought yet absurdly refined that most critics, both pro and con, were left debating how seriously his seriousness should be taken. With *Breaking the Waves*, the visuals were deemphasized and the story line forefronted, but the director's moody prankishness remained in full operation. Seen by some as a real breakthrough for a new, less artsy and ironic von Trier, the film was in fact a kind of audience-friendly remix of his familiar pomp, archness, and soul searching. *Breaking the Waves* may have amped up the realism, but style continued to function as a pervasive if ambient qualifier. That final image of a heavenly, computer-animated ringing bell struck some as an extraneous, postmodern smirk, the last vestige of von

Trier's old, bad habits; but in light of *Dancer in the Dark*, it's clear that he can't go very far without them.

Dancer is being sold as a musical tragedy, and von Trier himself has characterized the film as an attempt to merge his love of compatriot cineast Carl Dreyer's sublime starkness with his love of the iconic American musical *West Side Story*. In the context of von Trier's work to date, it's tempting to take *Dancer*'s sappy, amateurish, over-the-top melodrama and sub–*Music Man* song-and-dance numbers for a poker-faced scam. But everything else about it—the cast's flawlessly sincere performances, von Trier's rough-hewn, attentive camerawork, Björk's characteristically emotive, poetic songs—suggests that viewers should be reaching teary-eyed for the Prozac. If the intent is tongue-in-cheek, *Dancer in the Dark* is one of the most transparent, pointless, and ugly-spirited formal exercises in memory. (Unless, of course, you buy the argument that, at this point, we can only experience genuine sentiment under the self-protective cover of parody.) But if von Trier really is going for a more traumatic, grittier *Dead Man Walking* meets *Norma Rae* with a handful of joyous musical interludes, then the film is such a miscalculated mess that it's hard to know where to start picking it apart.

Rather than abandon or transcend Dogma's anti-Hollywood strictures, von Trier merely cheats a little, adding a score, credits, in-camera visual effects, and a hoary, sentimental plot, making the film feel a little like Martin Ritt goes avant-garde, minuscule budget and all. In short, Björk plays Selma, a Czech factory worker who lives in some small American town in the Pacific Northwest (shot, as it happens, in Sweden). Secretly going blind, Selma works double shifts in order to raise money for her son, who's also going blind, but doesn't know it, and needs an operation to save his vision. (It's too late for Mom.) Occasionally, Selma drifts into daydreams wherein life is a Hollywood musical (if only for the duration of a dance number), and she its beloved star. One of her friends is a depressed cop in financial straits. He steals her money; she confronts him; he asks her to kill him; in order to get her money back, she does it. She's arrested, tried, convicted, and sentenced to death. She won't save herself by testifying about her son's impending blindness, since the stress of knowing he's about to go blind might worsen his vision and ruin the chances of a successful operation. (Presumably, her execution is no biggie.) Her down-to-earth best friend, Kathy (Catherine Deneuve), finds out the truth just in time, but the only way Selma can get a retrial is to use the money for her son's surgery to pay for a lawyer, so she chooses to die.

Björk acts her heart out, and while it's quite odd to see her cry hysterically and fire a gun, she is never anyone but the winsome, opaque pop star of such established intrigue. Von Trier would have us believe that Selma's quirkiness derives from a nostalgic love of old musicals, but you don't buy it for a second. Deneuve's performance is Catherine Deneuve in method actor–ish quotation marks. A variety of American character actors do their best to seem quintessentially American, while cameos by von Trier regulars like Udo Kier and Stellan Skarsgard keep reminding you that the film was actually shot in Europe without providing any commentary whatsoever on von Trier's mishmashed, uninflected, outsider image of American culture. Everyone just seems lost in the film's jagged, pseudo-honestly visualized drift, and it doesn't take long to realize that nothing the actors could possibly do will keep the astonishingly implausible story line from concluding with an ambiguous pan into the meaningful nothingness of the heavens, this time sans ringing bell. The apparent point? Reality is a cold, cruel place; dreams will get you nowhere, and then you die—and then whatever. In other words, duh, boohoo, and maybe wink wink.

One thing you could always say on von Trier's behalf is that he's a nervy artist with a lot of visual flair—a bona fide enfant terrible. But with *Dancer in the Dark* he has accidentally exposed a huge problem in his work overall, which may help viewers exorcise the haunting, elusive quality that gave his earlier films their genius-esque vibe. The guy has no heart, and he was very lucky that *Breaking the Waves*'s Emily Watson has such a big, uncontainable one. The French are welcome to differ, but von Trier might be wise to leave plaintive realism to someone who cares (say, Dogma teammate Thomas Vinterberg) and stick to doing what he evidently does best—pulling new wool over the wool that he has already pulled over our eyes.

A CONVERSATION WITH WILLIAM T. VOLLMANN
(November 2000)

Could there be a more appropriate interviewee for this "No New York" fiction section than the West Coast author and meta-individualist William T. Vollmann? One of the most respected and well-published contemporary writers, he's also the great undomesticatible iconoclast of American fiction. From his mysterious and complex first novel, *You Bright and Risen Angels* (1987), to his ferociously direct and still complex new novel, *The Royal Family*, Vollmann's dozen novels and collections of short stories constitute as brave, unpredictable, and wholly original a body of work as the American literary establishment is capable of celebrating. Even so, his career has not been without controversy. Vollmann's 1993 journalistic piece for *Spin* about his efforts to kidnap an underage Thai prostitute caused some to question his morality, and his habit of firing a blank pistol during his readings has contributed to the mistaken impression that Vollmann is a man prone to the violent acts his work so frequently and brilliantly describes. A resident of California's obscure, all but uncultured capital city of Sacramento, the polite and surprisingly gentle Vollmann spoke with me by phone during a brief downtime between picking up his children from school and heading off on an East Coast book tour.

Dennis Cooper: Early on in your career, your novels and stories were compared to metafiction maestros like Pynchon, Gaddis, and Barth. But in reviews of *The Royal Family,* names like Steinbeck and Dos Passos keep popping up—a radical shift in the perception of your writing. Does it make sense?

William T. Vollmann: Sure. When I was first writing, I had this feeling of power in my fingers. There were all these words wanting to come out, and it was an extremely exciting and pleasurable process, almost like automatic writing. I'd just sit there at the computer and start writing away, and I wouldn't know what I was going to write or what was going to happen. It was really thrilling. I'm forty-one now, but right when I turned thirty, I started getting carpal tunnel syndrome, which made it impossible for me to type quickly. With every keystroke, there was a certain amount of physical pain. So that changed the writing process for me. Instead of riffing and creating the most beautiful sentences that I could, I found that a lot more of the writing was going on in my conscious mind beforehand. So there was a shift to subject matter, I guess, whereas before I'd been interested in form. And I really, really do admire Steinbeck. I think he has such a fine heart. So much of writing doesn't have heart in it. I want to write about people with problems, and try to help them, or, if not help them, make other people understand.

Don't you think Steinbeck's writing can get a little rigid? I sometimes think that even though his subject matter is emotionally explosive, his voice is so stiff that the war doesn't always break out.

Everybody has faults, and, even with Steinbeck, there are a lot of failed experiments. But *The Grapes of Wrath* and *East of Eden* are really interesting and have a strong experimental quality as well.

How is this change in the way you write fiction going to affect your novel cycle in progress, *Seven Dreams*? At least a couple of the novels predate your bout with carpal tunnel, and the series concerns itself a great deal with issues of form, structure, and style.

Well, within that septology, there's a lot of room for variation, so it won't be a problem. I basically just want to tell the same story seven times in different ways: There's an indigenous culture, and a European culture comes in and destroys it. I just finished the next one, about Pocahontas. It's called *Argall*, and it will come out next year. Argall was the man who kidnapped Pocahontas, if you know your history. He was responsible for a lot of terrible things. He introduced black slavery to Europe, and was involved in a lot of violence. It's a pretty violent book.

Books like *Whores for Gloria, The Rainbow Stories,* and *The Royal Family,* where you chart and reinvent your own personal experiences, have a rawness and immediacy that aren't in the historical novels like *Fathers and Crows* or *The Ice-Shirt,* for instance.

I hope that's true. With the *Seven Dreams* books, I try to create a sentence structure that corresponds to the prose of the European protagonist of each volume. So *Fathers and Crows* has a glorious, pseudo-French style, and in *Argall*, the approach is sort of similar. That does create a certain amount of distance. With *The Royal Family* and the other books you mentioned, they're written in more or less current idiom, so the language seems to come more naturally to the people who are talking, and it comes fairly naturally to me. It will be interesting to see how readable those books are in a hundred years, though. Did you ever read Gide's novel *The Counterfeiters*?

Sure. That was a major book for me.

I remember reading it in French when I was in college, and I thought it was amazing, but I had a lot of trouble with it. My French teacher said that the slang has changed so much since it was written that a lot of French people have difficulties with it now. So I would think that some of the stuff in those particular novels of mine will be tough for people in the future. I think about that a great deal, so I give a lot of consideration to making the idioms seem hard-won and necessary.

You're a forebear and something of a hero to younger, experimental writers like Mark Z. Danielewski, Dave Eggers, and Tristan Egolf. Do you feel a kinship with these so-called post-metafiction guys?

I'm really a loner. I live out here in Sacramento, where hardly anybody has a bookshelf. When I do get together with writers, I talk to them about their taxes or something like that. That's about it. I used to live in San Francisco, and wanted to live there again, but my wife got a job here. I don't drive, but it's only two hours by Greyhound bus to San Francisco, so I go down there a lot. But I don't know writers, even there. My best friend there is a house painter, and my other friends are a stripper and a photography student and a Sheetrocker. Do you have a lot of writer friends?

Surprisingly not. Most of my friends are visual artists. One of the things I find inspiring about them, as a writer, is that they think and talk a lot about nonart things like physics, science, and math and try to apply those principles to their artworks. Whereas most writers don't seem to let their minds wander very far afield when they think about writing.

I know what you mean. I'm working on a book of stories right now about Europe during World War II, and one of my characters is the composer Shostakovich, and the more I listen to his stuff, the more exciting it is to me. I'm trying to learn more about music, partly as a way to affect my writing. Take the way one of Shostakovich's symphonies is structured. I'll think, How can I express that in words? I'll study it, and figure out the fundamentals, and realize that I can repeat certain phrases and get a certain effect. And the way his music takes off from the chromatic scale and becomes abstract. I can try to create the same effect in my prose. I'm finding that it really works.

It's strange that the conventions of the traditional novel remain so securely in place, and that the worlds within the contemporary novel often end up seeming so lifeless and restricted. It's like fiction continues to move through time on this old train track, when there are so many modes of transportation available. But even at their most formal, your novels are almost overwhelmed with life. How do you do that, or does it come naturally?

Well, one thing I kept thinking about when I was writing *The Royal Family* was that the social circumstances of the world I was describing—the world of prostitution, essentially—were very, very different from mine. People interacted more. They'd lived in the same tenement for most of their lives, and they knew their neighbors well. They didn't have television or video, and they weren't very mobile, so they were more focused on change over time. Most Americans aren't so close to their neighbors or family, and their lives are strangely more static than the lives of these people who do and see and experience a lot less. I consciously tried to represent that in the novel.

What is it about prostitution that keeps pulling you back as a writer? It's the only chorus in your otherwise varied body of work.

In the world of street prostitutes, there's a sense of community, and also an absence of community. There are a lot of dead-end relationships, which sometimes both parties want. And then there can be a certain amount of tenderness and trust involved over the long term, too. The wisdom of middle America is that the john has the power, and the prostitute is powerless, but it's a lot more fluid than that. The prostitute can give the john purpose. The prostitute can fall in love, or the john can fall in love. There are all kinds of things like that. The power really does go back and forth. It's very complicated, and that interests me.

Your passionate treatment of subjects like prostitution seems to cause a lot of confusion among the literary establishment, as evidenced by your review coverage, at least. It's as though you're acknowledged as an important writer, but, at the same time, one gets the feeling that they wish you'd behave.

Maybe so. I'm always really surprised by that. I don't set out to shock people. I'm not shocked by the stuff I write. It's just that what interests me is sometimes very depressing. But I think it's so important, and that's why I want to write about it. People think that writers can just write well about anything, and they don't understand that the force in the prose comes from the writer's personal fascination with what he's writing about. That makes it hard sometimes, and people misunderstand. But I don't know if it would be better or worse if it were otherwise. For me, the most important thing in terms of my career is if I can persuade my publisher to take the next book, and if I can somehow make ends meet. The reviews aren't so important. I really try to write books that will last and will interest people in the future—not just my writing, but the people I write about, whom most of the world doesn't know or care about. It would just make me so happy to think that in a hundred years from now someone could go read my books and know that the people in them were alive.

LIKE A VIRGIN
Henry Darger in the *Realms of the Unreal*
(January 2001)

When eighty-one-year-old Henry Darger died in 1973 and his secret trove of art and writings was unearthed by his nosy Chicago landlords, the term "outsider art" was new, having been proposed only the previous year by the art historian Roger Cardinal as an English alternative to *art brut*. At the time, the work of artists like Adolf Wölfli, Simon Rodia, and the Rev. Howard Finster, to the extent that it was known at all, was effectively stigmatized as a form of arts and crafts practiced by unusually creative religious fanatics, conspiracy theorists, and the mentally ill. But the discovery of Darger's epic and unschooled but aesthetically rigorous project, which happened to use contemporary art techniques like appropriation while paying equal respect to the kind of sentimental illustration that passes for art among grandmas and Republicans, gave outsider art a fresh exemplar of unimpeachable grandeur and potentially massive popular appeal. Still, there remained the tricky problem of what to make of those naked, penis-sporting, underage girls who populate *The Story of the Vivian Girls, in What Is Known as the Realms of the Unreal, of the Glandeco-Angelinnian War Storm, Caused by the Child Slave Rebellion*, the fifteen-thousand-page illustrated novel to which Darger devoted his adult life.

It's taken thirty-one years for someone to figure out a way to position Darger as the new Grandma Moses, but in filmmaker Jessica Yu (who won an Oscar in 1997 for her nonfiction short *Breathing Lessons*), he has been afforded an enormously effective ambassador. *In the Realms of the Unreal*, Yu's Academy Award–short-listed documentary feature (which recently opened in New York and San Francisco), is a cozy, ingratiating introduction to Darger, yet it doesn't shortchange the peculiarities that permitted such a free fall of fascinating aesthetic decisions in his work. Yu's inspiration would appear to be the great documentarian Errol Morris, and her film has the voluptuous, flower-bed-like palette and quickly paced, wandering construction of his recent work, in particular 1997's *Fast, Cheap & Out of Control*.

Yu's multifaceted film is at once a recounting of Darger's threadbare biography, an intelligent but plainspoken analysis of his achievement, and a cinematic adaptation of his oeuvre. Darger's life story, which follows a classic Depression-era narrative from a lonely, underprivileged childhood spent in orphanages, boys' homes, and a hospital for the "feeble-minded" through a wanderlust-filled early adulthood to his now-familiar late life as a grizzled, unassuming janitor and clandestine artist, is delineated in bits and pieces throughout the film via a handful of photographs, stock footage, and interview snippets with acquaintances. Simultaneously, Yu lays out the far more elaborate, ultraviolent, and emotionally traumatic narrative within Darger's massive body of interconnected artworks. In a nutshell, *The Story of the Vivian Girls* depicts a long and bloody war between seven heroic, prepubescent sisters and the evil Glandelinians, a race of warlords who practice child enslavement. In what amounts to an animated fiction featurette within the larger nonfiction film, Yu crops, pans, and introduces motion into several dozen of Darger's paintings while the voice of the classy child actress Dakota Fanning (a Vivian girl stand-in) narrates. The animations themselves are quite slight and mechanical—imagine a more inert, twitching episode of *South Park*—but their effect is surprisingly lovely and hip. Bleeding through this elegant, parsed-out cartoon are shots of the period magazines and newspaper clippings that served as Darger's source material—a tactic that successfully adds a rich, compensatory inner life to the artist's rather static, ho-hum, day-to-day existence and makes a solid case for Darger's work as an enterprise as complexly connected to popular culture as any present-day Yale MFA's.

Interestingly, while falling short of answering the question of why an apparent nonpedophile would give his androgynous girl protagonists so many nude scenes, Yu does deactivate the presumption that a grown man drawing naked kids automatically implies a lurking eroticism. If never quite substantiated, the film's argument that the super-religious and possibly lifelong virgin Darger was simply unfamiliar with female anatomy tempers certain suspicions, and evidence presented from his diaries that he was a constant self-incriminator who sought God's forgiveness for sins as minuscule as failing to set down a drinking glass properly will likely serve as satisfactory penance for all but the most sex-phobic contingent of the Christian Right. *In the Realms of the Unreal* configures Darger as a kind of weirder, crankier Lewis Carroll or J. M. Barrie—a man whose fetish for children is untraceable enough to be deemed an acceptable fuel for the controlled blaze of his imagination. With that hot spot in his otherwise fanciful work rendered as lukewarm as possible, and with his vision in the sympathetic, gifted hands of Jessica Yu, a collaborator as heaven-sent to Darger's work as Peter Jackson was to J. R. R. Tolkien's, this strangest and most ambitious of outsider artists may well follow the likes of R. Crumb and Norman Rockwell into popular lore and leave the admiring but standoffish contemporary art world in the dust.

FUCK THE CANON
A Conversation with Clive Barker
(August 2001)

Clive Barker might just be our most versatile contemporary artist, not to mention among the most prolific. Sure, others have had their art reconstituted in forms they haven't themselves mastered, but I can't think of anyone who has worked so directly and successfully in as many media. He's a respected novelist, short-story writer, screenwriter, movie director, painter, photographer, and hands-on mastermind behind products ranging from video games to action figures, to theme-park attractions, to a forthcoming DVD created in collaboration with Jonathan Davis of the band Korn. Through it all, he has remained an amazingly consistent auteur whose explorations of the metaphysical and erotic have had a profound influence on popular culture. His effect on the contemporary horror novel and film is self-evident. But when you consider that such artists and entities as *Buffy the Vampire Slayer*, Marilyn Manson, Chris Carter, goth culture, the "edgy" rock video, and virtually all original programming on the Sci-Fi Channel would not exist in their current forms without Barker's groundbreaking work, his impact becomes astonishing.

At the center of it all are Barker's books. His dozen novels and short-story collections include best-selling cult classics like *Books of Blood*,

Cabal, Weaveworld, The Damnation Game, and *Imajica.* Fiction remains Barker's primary medium and the springboard for much of his work in other fields. His new novel, *Coldheart Canyon,* a seven-hundred-page epic that pits a group of thinly disguised Hollywood figures against the ghosts of their silent-film-era counterparts, will be published by HarperCollins in early October. The "Abarat Quartet," a cycle of four interrelated novels, will begin to appear next year, and the rights have already been purchased by Disney, which plans to develop the cycle into a major motion-picture franchise and theme-park attraction. Next year will also see the release of *The Dark Fantastic,* an official biography of Barker by the writer Douglas Winter, and, possibly, films based on his novels *The Damnation Game* and *Weaveworld.*

Barker is no stranger to media coverage, to be sure, but he has rarely been given the opportunity to speak in an extended and serious way about his writing and art. Knowing Barker lives in Los Angeles, I thought interviewing him seemed like a great opportunity to right this wrong. I should also say that Barker and I have been admirers of each other's not-un-like-minded work for many years, but had never met before. Unexpectedly, the interview took on the character of a conversation at times. While Barker's tendency to make comparisons between his work and mine creates a discomfiting situation for me as an interviewer, he seemed genuinely interested in defining the similarities and dissimilarities between our respective books as a way to define his own process. So I've let the least embarrassing of these exchanges stand.

At forty-eight, Barker is no longer the ethereal-looking, shag-haircut-sporting waif so familiar from his early publicity photos. He's a muscular, youthful, crop-haired, cigar-smoking, almost tough-looking man, but without the slightest quality of menace or aloofness. Raised in Liverpool, he retains a strong, mellifluous English accent only slightly coarsened by his recent decades in the company of slang-spouting Angelenos. The interview took place in one of his several homes, this one in the eastern heights of Beverly Hills, where Barker lives, works, and supervises the activities of his production company, Seraphim Films. We sat at a long, medieval-looking wooden table in an otherwise deserted and unfurnished house whose every wall was covered from floor to ceiling with eerie, wildly colorful paintings destined for the pages of the "Abarat Quartet."

Dennis Cooper: In your novels, you use the taut, conventional, domino-effect-like structure that thriller fiction requires, but improvise a lot within it. In *Coldheart Canyon*, for instance, the story will suddenly slow down and obsess on something that seems very personal to you, but not particularly important to the story line itself, on the surface at least. It makes the work feel very alive.

Clive Barker: I think that's true. I have two completely different kinds of models for what I do. One is a populist model, and I think it's very important that we make our work available and accessible. But then there's got to be room for associative storytelling. You of all people know what I'm talking about, although you break down the narrative much further than I do.

In some ways, your work is almost traditional, and your sentences almost utilitarian, yet in all the work of yours that I've read, I don't think I've ever come across a detail that was clichéd or lazy or lacked some kind of poetry. That's an amazing feat.

Maybe the best way to talk about that is by talking about *Coldheart Canyon*, because in some ways it's my most dangerous book for that. Hollywood has been written about so much. There's so much capacity for cliché. That's, of course, what drew me to add my two cents to it. What was new for me was to write about a world I live and work in, and know through friendships with people in the movie business, and through my experiences as a producer and director of films. So it was very interesting for me to write about my own despair about the movie industry, but it took me much longer to do—twice as long as usual. I should also say the novel owes a lot to Roddy McDowall. Did you know Roddy?

No.

He used to have these Friday dinner parties, and I got to be part of that and meet legends. I think the very beginning of this book was one of those dinner parties. Ray Bradbury, whom I adore, was there, and Gore Vidal, whom Ray did not like at all, and Dominick Dunne, and Maureen O'Sullivan, and Dennis Hopper—I know this gets surreal, but I swear it's true—and Elizabeth Taylor. Now, I may be forty-eight, but I can still be a fan boy about that kind of stuff. I can still be totally fascinated by how this group of demigods operates on our collective consciousness, but also on our individual consciousnesses, and how we secretly try to match up to them. And what I wanted *Coldheart Canyon* to do, in part, was address what a crock of shit that was. By transferring our appetite for the transcendental to those tatty remnants from a freak show—which is what many of the people we attach our attention to are—we do two terrible things. We advance people who are just regular human beings and set them up for falls, and we take that sacred appetite and put it where it can be of absolutely no use whatsoever. One of the things I'm interested in all through my books is what we do with our appetite for God in a world that seems to have taken Him, or It, away. Over and over and over again, my characters attach themselves to unworthy divinities.

It's curious that your feel for the powerfully erotic aspect of violence is so well known, yet your interest in subverting contemporary notions of religion is rarely discussed, even though the two themes are indivisible in your work.

It is curious, isn't it? To me, apart from Zen and certain strains of Buddhism, religion is all about rigor. It's about there being only one way. But the idea that we should be able to play with the relationship between what we worship and what we think worthy of worship is something I want to get at. You know, that the movie stars we worship are just fuckups like us. Obviously, sex lies underneath our appetites for all these people. We think what it would be like to go to bed with X or Y, yet mainstream American cinema remains remarkably sexless. Spielberg, who is the genius of that system, deals with sex not at all.

He dabbled in S/M with *A.I.*

Well, that was just weird. He had to deal with that because of Kubrick, but his discomfort is palpable. But take the new Antonio Banderas film, *Original Sin*. That's remarkably sexy.

And it's a big flop.

Is it really? I saw it last week, and I said to myself, "That is going to fall on its face." It's just too fucking sexy. But interestingly, horror movies have always been a place where you can get sex in. Coppola's *Dracula* was an incredibly sexy movie. I mean, those creatures climbing over the wall and biting Keanu's dick. That was pretty strong stuff. Sex is what always drew me to horror movies. I mean, the horror, I didn't care. But I loved the issues of the flesh and control in horror movies. To control and not to control the libido, or to be controlled or not by the libido, is a fascinating problem for me.

Is it a different problem for you depending on the form you're working in? You work in so many media.

For me, painting is the ideal place to put eroticism. I think the eruption of eroticism in photography and pornography has not in any sense devalued the painted image. In fact, what pornography has done is reinvigorate it, because you can see what the photograph cannot do. If you want to jerk off, yeah, you pick up a video. But if you want something to investigate, paintings and short fiction are still the place to go. I don't think long erotic novels work, with one or two exceptions. Frank Harris's *My Life and Loves* is one exception.

De Sade.

But have either one of us ever sat down and read one of his novels from cover to cover?

Well, I have, but I'm a freak. But I admit there are parts I read more carefully and parts I sort of edit in my head. Do you rewrite and edit your work a lot?

I always do huge amounts of rewriting, but in *Coldheart Canyon* there was lots and lots and lots. For one thing, I lost my dad a week after I started the book. I'm a good Boy Scout in the sense of wanting to deliver a book when I've promised I will. But it was a stupid thing to do, because I was carrying, and am still carrying, a lot of completely un-felt-through feelings about my dad. So I kind of went and hid in the narrative, and you can't hide from those feelings. They come and get you wherever you are. So what happened was the first draft was this clotted, stupid pass where I wasn't dealing with anything about my dad. So I took a few weeks off and had some long conversations with myself and my husband, David, and then started the novel over using rather than avoiding my unresolved feelings.

Do you write novels in a linear way, from beginning to end?

Yeah. I think it's an indulgence to do it the other way. I think it's a kind of cowardice. There are places in anyone's books that are going to be easier than other parts. And if when you come to a part that's difficult and think, "Hm, I'll skip that," all you're doing is lining up these problems that are going to wait for you and kick you in the ass. So I'm very rigorous with myself. I won't allow myself to go on to a fun bit, like the sex. I think if you write big books like I do, and don't write in a linear fashion, something inevitably gets screwed up in the emotional flow. In *Coldheart Canyon* there are many characters, and each character has its own arc. The arcs start at divergent points, but they converge at roughly the same point. So what you try to do is induce in the reader an incredible feeling of excitement, because everybody's arcs are resolving because they're encountering one another, right? It's not that they're resolving in an abstraction. They're resolving because A meets B meets C and so on.

Which explains its length, I guess.

Yes. But this will amuse you. I proposed it as a short story. You've had this problem?

I have the opposite problem. I just finished a novel that I proposed would be 400 to 500 pages, and it wound up being 160 pages.

Maybe we can help each other. [*laughter*] Listen, I need to ask you something. I know it makes this more of a conversation, but . . . how are you able to make your novels so compact? It's very foreign to me.

Well, in my work explanations are beside the point. That might be why. I'm interested in a suggestive approach. My work's so internally chaotic that the surface has to be as impeccable and barren as possible to communicate at all.

Hm. Let me offer you this. Why do you take pleasure in books like mine, which, by your own self-directed aesthetic, are surely flabby books?

But that's exactly why your books interest me. I know how to do tight, but I don't know how to do what you do at all. And partly because your work and my work have so much in common, in terms of their horrificness and interest in psychosexual violence and so on, this fascinates me. I think to myself, "How the fuck does he do that?"

I had a conversation with Pete Atkins, who wrote *Hellraiser II*, *III*, and *IV*, and several novels as well. I've known him since I was eighteen. When he started writing novels, he said, "I get bored with bits in between the action bits and the big set pieces." And I told him that if you don't have those, the big set pieces don't have any foundation. Also—and this is absolutely the reader's experience, though it might not be the writer's experience—sometimes a sentence which might not be particularly interesting on the page says something completely vital. So I think a lot of what I do comes out of wanting to tell the story the best way I can. The lyricism comes out of a hunger to have prose aspire to the condition of poetry, as yours does. I think one of the reasons that you and I have a certain kind of fan who will love us to our dying day is because there's a richness in what we both do. It's layered. We both have the erotic and violent thing, and a poetic way of dealing with it, but you are in your work, whereas I am not in mine. I think that's the major difference between your work and mine. The most populist thing I do is to not be in my work.

Well, your work and my work are about the imagination. So in that way, you are in your work. Certainly, I feel you there, and I imagine that personalized quality of your work is partly what inspires such devotion among your readers.

Yet I don't think my readers feel the kind of intimacy with me that your readers feel with you. There's much more of a sense that the world I create belongs to them.

Well, it's that balance between what's yours and what's theirs that's so remarkable. For instance, my favorite film of yours as a director is *Lord of Illusions*, partially because the eroticism in it is so scarily pure. I thought it was a very personal film, much more than *Hellraiser* or *Nightbreed*.

Right. It was also my least successful film. [*laughter*] In *Lord of Illusions*, I got to do all kinds of shit that I wanted to do. The bondage stuff in there, the girl and the ape, all kinds of shit. It's very funny because Frank Man-cuso was head of MGM/UA at that time, and he didn't like the movie at all. There was one shot of a dead child on the floor, and he said, "This shot will never appear in an MGM/UA movie." As it turns out, it did, because I took it out, and then when he wasn't looking, I put it back in. I knew he'd never bother to see the film again.

My understanding is that writing and painting are the two media over which you exert total control, whereas the "Clive Barker" films you don't direct—like the *Hellraiser* sequels and the *Candyman* movies, the video games, the action figures and so on that bear your brand name—are more a matter of delegating creativity under your general guidance. Is that true?

Well, that depends.

Okay, for example, I'm a great devotee of the "spooky houses" and "spooky mazes" that pop up around town every Halloween. The Clive Barker Maze at last year's Universal Studio's Halloween event was one of the two or three best I've ever seen. It managed to be innovative in a form whose strengths are generally about tradition. I wondered at the time how much you had to do with it?

I had lots to do with it. My husband, David, has really introduced me to this. In England, we don't have a lot of this. When Universal asked me if I'd be interested in doing one, I said, "Sure, I'll give it a crack." I saw it as a four-minute piece of theater that loops. David and I went through it and talked to the actors, and gave them their motivations. So I took it very seriously. You know, the Halloween maze is a very American form. It's interesting to me that you're free enough to take them seriously. [*laughter*] That takes a certain amount of courage.

To me, they're like sculptures in a way. In fact, the people I know who are most interested in them are visual artists and writers. We go around in gangs every year seeing as many as we can, and we study them.

When I started doing mine, people would say, "Why are you doing that?" They thought it was silly. But there are a lot of things you can do with them. To me, they're like what you thought horror movies would be like before you saw a horror movie. You know, "They're coming after you— they're coming after you, and you won't be able to stop them." Their inter-activity is interesting, too, and their density.

I wonder, then, if one of the more attractive things about Disney buying the rights to your forthcoming "Abarat Quartet" books is the fact that they're going to develop a theme-park attraction based on them?

That's absolutely one of the most attractive aspects. When they offered me that, I just said, "Yes." The fact that they're planning to create a film franchise based on them didn't hurt, of course.

They bought it before you'd written it, right?

Right. They bought it based on the word "Abarat," on about 350 paintings I'd done as illustrations for the books, and on a rough idea I had for the narrative. They'll get the first book in about four weeks.

Has the Disney aesthetic been on your mind while writing the books? Did you feel that you had to conform to their code?

[*laughs*] I don't think that would even be possible. Even if it was, that would be a disaster. To be honest, it would have seemed preposterous to me. If someone had said to me, "You should do something for Disney," I would have said, "Forget it." It's quite strange, really. No, I'm going to write a cycle of what I think will be four novels that will include about five hundred to seven hundred paintings as illustrations, and then they will go do their thing. Their thing is brilliance. When Disney is on, nobody else can come anywhere near. The chance to play in their territory, using the Imagineers, is awe-inspiring. I'm a very simple creator. I handwrite everything. I paint on canvases that I buy from the art store.

People are referring to the "Abarat Quartet" as your *Harry Potter*. Is that a lazy comparison?

It's my *Harry Potter* in this sense: *Harry Potter* has been incredibly successful because adults read that stuff. The magnitude of its success is predicated on that fact. So I don't think it's a lazy comparison. The difference is me. [*laughter*] The fact that they could come in and look at the paintings, which are Boschian and dark and intense, and say they want it was an exciting surprise.

It's not a stretch to guess that there will be a segment of the Disney audience who will freak out at the fact that they're working with you.

I know. I'm the *Hellraiser* man. I'm the *Candyman* man. But I have to believe that at the upper echelon of Disney they know they need a guy with some edge. And while I'm not planning to make any more *Hellraiser*s anytime soon, I am planning to make horror movies, and one of them is with Disney/Touchstone, and those will be tough movies.

I was also thinking about your last novel, *Sacrament*. I wonder what will happen if the Christian types get wind of that. It might be your least quote-unquote horrific novel, but the gay sex in there is pretty unflinching. I mean it didn't shock me, but . . .

[*laughs*] Yes, I don't imagine it would have. You know *Sacrament* sold about 50 percent of what my other books have sold.

Really? Because it was so gay?

Yeah. It's interesting to me that the numbers haven't been as strong on that book. You can go online and very easily find pods of very dedicated Clive Barker fans who really object to that novel. There's almost an audible sigh from those pages. They say, "Well, I suppose he had to get it out of his system," and that kind of thing. There are scenes in that book that are really strong sexually. It's not a gentle introduction to gay sex. But I always need to write the most intense thing I've ever written, whatever the subject matter.

Does it frustrate you that your books tend to be marginalized or condescended to by the literary establishment? You're not the only important writer to be denied a place in the canon, but you're a glaring example. Your popularity and your influence on culture are undeniable, yet it's hard to imagine that, say, the *New York Times Book Review* or the *New York Review of Books* et al. will ever acknowledge your work's significance.

That used to bother me a whole heap, but now I figure that there's an anti-canon falling into place. The likes of our work is in it. I think what we have to realize is that the scope of literature is changing again. I think the charge of my work is its saving grace, and it's also the problem for mainstream literature. If you look at the Booker Prize and all that, there's a lot of little old lady and Oprah's Choice literature out there. My heroes, like Bosch and Goya and Poe, are to some extent still marginalized. I'm not sure I would like it if it were any other way. The alternative is that this stuff be embraced.

Which would make you cringe?

God, yes. I'd think, "What have I done wrong now?" Besides, being marginalized creates passion in my fans and makes me feel very loyal to them. I believe very strongly—for myself, and for you as well—that there will be a reassessment of what the old canon was. For example, you know there was this incredible hue and cry last year when the British public was polled and asked to name the most important book of the century, and the winner by a vast margin was *The Lord of the Rings.* That entertained the hell out of me. So you had all these literary types saying, "No, no, no, you can't have this in my canon. I refuse." The fact of the matter is that our books are being read by far more influential minds than the books of writers who are being properly positioned by their publishers and by the reviewers they sleep with. Fuck the canon.

You never worry, "What if they're right and I'm wrong?"

One of the things I've learned as an artist, as my life has gone on, is to stop saying "right" or "wrong." My behavior pattern has been to do whatever I wanted to do, and deal with the consequences afterward. In fiscal terms, the consequences have been negative more than positive. There were a lot of decisions I could have made that my bank manager says I *should* have made. But I just couldn't, because I felt like a prisoner.

A prisoner of Pinhead?

Yes. Of *Hellraiser*, for instance, and the phenomenon it inspired. But I've actually escaped quite well. And after "Abarat" comes out, I think the rest of that will go down in the dust. And I don't think I'll direct any more films. They're too time-consuming. I'm forty-eight. My dad was seventy-three when he died, and my granddad was sixty-three. The Barker men don't tend to last long, and there are all sorts of projects I want to do in what time I have. Like I have a huge metaphysical book in my head.

À la *Weaveworld* or . . . ?

It will make *Weaveworld* look like Nancy Drew. A huge, huge, huge metaphysical book. I want to investigate the erotic at its most profound, in forms that I think we possibly begin to see in Burroughs, but which haven't been pursued as a consistent thesis. We're talking my Bible. I want to write the Bible. [*laughter*] So there's a lot to do.

WE'RE DESPERATE
The Punk Photography of Jim Jocoy
(January 2002)

When the inevitable documentaries on American popular culture of the early twenty-first century begin to appear, future generations will no doubt find plenty of opportunities to scratch their heads. We can't really know what will instigate the snickers, any more than our fore-bears could have seen the silliness in duck-and-cover drills, leisure suits, and bouffants. But it doesn't take Nostradamus to predict that cultured Americans' rampant, puppy-dog-like fascination with the whims of the fashion industry will doom most of the things we take seriously to the fate of serving as eternal examples of how much superficiality we were willing to embrace in order to avoid actual meaning.

How did we end up like those European peasants who chose lives of oohing and aahing at the luxuries of the ruling class over blowing their peers' privileged, idling brains out? What is it about pretty, va-cant models and the guys who design their outfits? What isn't it about poor, embattled Middle Easterners and the guys in Washington who design their misery? Twenty-plus years in which there has been mini-mal pressure within popular culture to judge things through the filters of politics or philosophy certainly hasn't helped. But it will probably take clearer, less easily entertained minds than ours to find the real reasons.

As hard as it is to believe at the moment, there have been times in recent decades when fashion was the art of average Joes and Janes with skinny wallets, personal ideologies, and no interest in getting feedback from a bunch of wealthy artistes and sycophants in Milan, Paris, and New York. Back when rap music was the invention of people with issues larger than what brand of champagne they drank, popular brands of clothing were co-opted by rap aficionados and retrofitted with a fresh, ground-roots symbolism. In the early days of rave culture when dancing, drugging, and utopian politics commingled, the infantilized outfits and accoutrements of that scene's denizens signaled their belief that a considered naïveté could form the basis of a viable new philosophy. Then there's '70s punk-rock fashion with its provocative, clashing amalgamation of virtually every trendy style of clothing that came before it. Hip-hop and rave styles have been pretty much assimilated into mainstream fashion, but the punk look remains unfazed by the fashion industry's attempts to borrow and upgrade fragments of its edge. It continues to evolve and thrive among those who want to show off their dissatisfaction with the societal structures that marginalize people whose lives center around the notion of a principled emotional truth.

Jim Jocoy's portraits of punk rockers from the Los Angeles and San Francisco scenes of the late '70s are a modest, beautiful testament to the voracious outfits and characters of the period. Although it's as much a book about history as about fashion, *We're Desperate* is nonetheless a great reminder that the fashion photograph can be both simpler and heftier than the quasi-candid, moody visual erotica that fills the pages of almost every current magazine with a circulation greater than five figures. The young models/designers in his pictures—a few of them still recognizable (Darby Crash, John Doe, Iggy Pop, Lux Interior), all of them unidentified and shot with minimal preparation in hallways, bathrooms, and parking lots in and around defunct clubs like the Masque in LA and Mabuhay Gardens in SF—display the outfits they happen to have devised for that particular evening filtered through a range of classic punk-rock attitudes. No matter what poses they strike or which strain of punk style they've chosen to individualize—quasi-hoodlum, surly tart, freaked-out businessman, disheveled geek, gritty mod, etc.— each person and his or her clothes are unified and specific to a degree that's startling given contemporary scenesters' preference for dressing to emblematize the ideas of their favorite designers.

The long-lost punks in Jocoy's sweet and inspiring photographs remind us of a fact that most contemporary Americans seem to have successfully wished away: that clothes are just clothes unless they're so uniform that they function as a statement of personal dedication or their wearers are confident and creative enough to outshine them.

NAKED YOUTH
Bill Henson
(February 2002)

Until recently, being an American admirer of the photographer Bill
Henson was a lonely and rather painstaking chore. Apart from a small
survey of his work at the Denver Art Museum in 1990 and a few photographs included in a 1984 Solomon R. Guggenheim Museum exhibition of Australian art, he has been almost impossible to find in the
United States, less unknown than anti-known—a sub-subcult figure
even within circles devoted to contemporary photography. Given that
his work has been a staple of the European art world since 1981 and that
it occupied an entire pavilion at the 1995 Venice Biennale, Henson's invisibility is bizarre enough. But when you consider that his photographs
of the '80s and '90s predict and arguably outclass much of the personal,
edgy portraiture currently in fashion and ubiquitous in galleries, you
have to wonder (or at least I do) whether Henson's effect on contemporary art isn't much larger than his reputation in the States reflects.

My own discovery of the forty-six-year-old Australian photographer
was a weird stroke of luck. While house-sitting for an art critic friend in
the late '80s, I fished a thin catalogue of Henson's work from the shelves
of art books and gave it a scan. At that time, auteurish, confrontational

photographers with a taste for the fucked-up and taboo were near the center of the critical dialogue, as well as the hippest things going. Not only did the dozen or so images in Henson's catalogue hold their own against the work of better-known artists like Robert Mapplethorpe, Larry Clark, Nan Goldin, and Bernard Faucon in terms of their refined transgressiveness, but just as interestingly, their plush, cinematographic look and romantic, almost melodramatic tone had a radically old-fashioned gorgeousness that raised fascinating questions about the strengths and limitations of his contemporaries' lower-key, sketchier— or, in Mapplethorpe's case, serenely rigid—styles.

Just prior to the appearance of that catalogue, a permanent realignment had taken place in Henson's work. In the '70s and early '80s he was known for his black-and-white, mock-candid, quasi-daguerreotype images of self-absorbed individuals lost in crowds or striking solitary expressive poses in gloom-shrouded voids. In the mid-'80s he began to produce color photographs focused almost exclusively on introverted, compellingly beautiful teenage outsiders and the abandoned buildings, vacant lots, and deserted back roads that formed their turf. The catalogue featured a then fresh series of diptychs and triptychs that juxtaposed portraits of naked, dirt-smudged teens looking almost like coal miners with images depicting the interiors of palatial homes filled with antiques and old master–ish paintings. The teens appeared to be addicts, prostitutes, and runaways snapped at moments of intense self-mourning. Unlike the subjects in Clark's or Goldin's similarly populated work, Henson's figures were approached with such unreserved empathy and preserved with such an artfully impersonal, elegant visual luster that they became strangely interchangeable with their lavish architectural counterparts. The dichotomy between luxurious empty decors and undressed tormented characters was over the top, to be sure.

Yet there was a purity of intention that turned these heavy-handed gestures into acts of moving, even desperate complicity, the way an opera's rigorously expelled emotion can turn its overstated musical phrasings into profound instruments.

The experience of being haunted by reproductions of contemporary artworks, with no real hope of comparing them to the originals, or investigating the work's context, or having even a small library of criticism against which to check one's opinions, constitutes an odd and not unpowerful dilemma—one that living in the art-importing center of the world normally prevents. In 1995, there was a rare Henson sighting in the form of another catalogue for the photographer's aforementioned Australian pavilion exhibit in Venice. By then, his work had phased into something more sexually explicit and emotionally diffuse. In place of the multipanel photographs from the '80s there were autonomous, single-frame images containing pictures, violently cut up and then collaged, of young, pale, faceless bodies fucking, sometimes in large groups, in dark, apparently cavernous locales. It was as if the orgy in Antonioni's *Zabriskie Point* had gone on past the point of exhaustion and into some posterotic realm where sex was the only cure for unquenchable loneliness. Again, as in Henson's almost too blatant parallel between the superficial spoils of the privileged and the ruined internal lives of the young and disenfranchised, his aggressive cuts and reassemblages bordered dangerously on a dumb-ass, obvious way of signifying his subjects' interpersonal agonies; yet some depth of understanding and level of finesse at which the reproductions could only hint left an almost addictive longing to search out these pictures and deconstruct their effect.

Despite the Biennale exposure, it would be another six years before I would see Henson's work in America. And by the time he had his long-delayed solo gallery show in 1999 at Karyn Lovegrove in Los Angeles, the experiments with collage and multipaneling had given way to large framed photographs that engaged even more unobtrusively with the psyches of his young subjects. In this recent work, boys and girls stand, sit, and lounge around alone or in seemingly romantic couplings, their averted faces revealing emotions so deep, mixed-up, and masked in achy casualness that one searches the photographs' compositions and patina for the aesthetic system that makes such intimacy possible. What becomes apparent when you see Henson's work in person is the importance of the almost pitch-black darkness that, in whatever formal context he has devised over the years, always cloaks his forlorn, defiantly unneedy subjects, giving their run-down urban environments the look of remote desert outposts. It's a black that seems both to be caked on the surface of the photographs, like tar or centuries of soot, and to recede infinitely into the background. It looks as solid as lead, a physical threat to the teens it blankets, and at the same time it's as if the blackness were exuded by their bodies, forming a kind of paranormal manifestation of some feeling too intense and guarded to register in any other fashion. In its own peculiar way, Henson's black is as unique an achievement as, say, Robert Ryman's white. It gives the similar impression of an idea refined to a point of such complexity that it can only be communicated through a suggestion of its absence. Were it not for Henson's primary, almost devotional need to elicit empathy for his troubled human subjects, there's a feeling that nothing would prevent that black from completely absorbing his attention and extinguishing the work.

Bill Henson's photography is far too reclusive within the world of its own concerns to fit comfortably into the kinds of categories that make a writer's job easy. Characterizing it as a forebear of the new portraiture practiced by younger artists like Anna Gaskell, Tracey Moffatt, and Collier Schorr is helpful in distinguishing its more forceful, less attenuated pursuit of emotional truth, just as viewing it in light of Henson's transgressive contemporaries' work puts a useful emphasis on the unabashed classicism and painterliness of his style. While these associations flatter him and create a reasonable introduction to his work, the map they form gives only the vaguest directions into the matter of Henson's achievement, which lies not so much in the twist he gives to the subject of disenfranchised youth but in the almost premodern beauty he conjures from such a familiar and clinically post-postmodern source.

BACK IN NO TIME: THE BRION GYSIN READER
(September 2002)

If you're like me, the name Brion Gysin evokes a time, a crowd, and an aesthetic, but it has little gravitational pull. From the late '50s until his death in 1986, Gysin's name and craggy, exotic face were omnipresent bit players in literate America's ongoing infatuation with the Beats. Credited by William S. Burroughs and Paul Bowles with having invented the literary "cut-up" technique, and celebrated as a visionary wordsmith by the fringe alternative press, Gysin produced an output so skimpy that most of us could only assume the hype around him had a point. To the faithful, Gysin's wishy-washiness was a key element of his image; he was the nomad Sufi maverick, the Nowhere Man of American letters, the mysterious provocateur rumored to have turned the Rolling Stones psychedelic and quasi-satanic. But for the less impressionable, there was little hard evidence. Apart from authoring two Beatesque novels, cowriting a book with Burroughs, and dreaming up (with Ian Sommerville) the "dream machine," a revolving lamp shade emitting stroboscopic pulses, which he promoted as a mind-expanding drug alternative, Gysin seemed less like an artist than like a famously peculiar, artsy friend to the countercultural stars.

Jason Weiss, a Brooklyn-based writer and editor, hopes to put some meat on Gysin's charismatic bones with this collection of published and unpublished writing spanning forty-four of the author's seventy years. Included are big chunks of his two novels, *The Process* (1969) and *The Last Museum* (1986), and a slice of his and Burroughs's *Third Mind* (1978). But the bulk of this 364-page volume is taken up by odds and ends—poems, song lyrics, magazine articles, autobiographical snippets, bits for artists' catalogues, even a piece intended for a cookbook—which, with a few exceptions, only bolster the impression that Gysin's legendary status was writ in dope smoke. He may have been the first person to take a pair of scissors to a typewritten page, but, as evidenced by the doodles he produced using the cut-up method, he was no Thomas Edison. *Back in No Time* suggests that Gysin was an intelligent, restless, and admirably adventurous person. It even hints that he was a terrific and underrated painter. But it proves only that all the paper, ink, and determination in the world can't turn an intriguing character into an interesting writer.

Even at its most radical, Gysin's writing drags under the weight of its mystical pretensions and/or fills page after page with witless gibberish. His poems in particular tend to read like mental cash register receipts ("I AM THAT I AM / AM I THAT I AM / I THAT AM I AM / THAT I AM I AM / AM THAT I I AM / THAT AM I I AM . . . ") or drivel penned by a stoner student majoring in world lit ("The city, the city of your dreams of whom I said / Are ye he whom my soul loveth? / But I found him whom my soul loveth / and every fair from fair some time declines"). There's a reason why Burroughs was credited with creating the cut-up technique. Comparing his brilliant early cut-up experiments of the '50s and '60s to his buddy's simultaneous efforts, it's apparent that Gysin primarily used "the novel" to demonstrate his methodology. The results, like this example from *The Process*, mix meandering, travelogue-like narratives with jolting diaristic asides that read like giddy, conspiratorial winks:

> They can all be rubbed out by the *zikr*, of course! *Wow!* The minute
> I typed those last words to YOU, I knew what had to be done: *Wow!*
> *Anything* to get myself out of that trap in Tam. I paid the lady gladly;
> the Emerald for my UHER, cheap at any price. It was a simple matter,
> then, to record the *zikr* on a loop of spliced tape; playing endlessly
> over and over, again and again and again.
>
> Such is the process: . . . Be as careful about inserting your finger in
> the running loop of words as you would be about plunging your finger
> down your own throat. Abrupt word-withdrawal can be a shattering
> experience. Taken cold-turkey, it can cramp you with chills of panic
> as the seasick words swirl around in a long ring-a-rosy like a vomit of
> alphabet soup. The nymph Nausea grabs you by the gullet, throwing
> you into severe anti-orgasmic spasm while Pan, the dumb little brute-
> god, attacks you along with his goats.

Gysin's mishmash of Eastern-religion-derived hocus-pocus, co-opted
bits of Greek mythology, drug references, and chilled-out existentialist
narrative drift à la Sartre and Camus could only have seemed convincing
within a culture so engrossed in expanding its collective consciousness
that any old stab at it would suffice. That his work managed to maintain
a following beyond the hippie era speaks to his heavily publicized influence on Burroughs and to the durability of the Burroughs myth. No one
who admires Gysin wants to limit him to mere footnote status—editors
and blurbers continue to maintain that he's a "seminal" figure—which
indicates an affection for the guy that is intriguing in and of itself. Nonetheless, it's telling that the only artist specifically named by Weiss (aside

from footnote-y mentions of David Bowie, Iggy Pop, and the filmmaker Antony Balch) as a beneficiary of this influence is Burroughs, and maybe it's to be understood that influencing Burroughs is tantamount to affecting all cutting-edge art of the late twentieth century. Certainly the best works in this collection are Burroughs-related: the provocative *Third Mind* collaboration and Gysin's *Naked Lunch*–inspired screenplay (1972), which far surpasses David Cronenberg's botched effort. But the fact remains that Gysin's value as a writer is almost entirely dependent on the relative value of Burroughs's accomplishments. To be charitable, reading Gysin provides an unusually consolidated tour through some of the wackier excesses of an important bygone literary movement. But unless you're looking to justify the risk-free goals of most contemporary American writing, *Back in No Time* is the bookworm equivalent of a CD box set by some obscure experimental rock band whose claim to fame is that they vaguely influenced someone more important.

'80S THEN
Mike Kelley Talks to Dennis Cooper
(April 2003)

Dennis Cooper: The early '80s were hugely formative for LA art. It was, for instance, the first time that CalArts graduates started to stay in the city, rather than moving to New York. Yet on the surface, the local art world was still pretty dull and provincial.

Mike Kelley: Most activities were taking place in alternative spaces like LACE [Los Angeles Contemporary Exhibitions] and LAICA [Los Angeles Institute of Contemporary Art] rather than in galleries. I don't think LA was any more provincial than other art centers of the period. Artists here were mirroring the various international phenomena; for example, LA had its own version of neo-Expressionism with painters like Andrew Wilf and Roger Herman and Gronk. Like everywhere else, there was a lot of attention on painting, which led to an assortment of artists bonding together.

I credit you, as well as the video artists Bruce and Norman Yonemoto, with creating what was a very multidisciplinary art scene. You were both collaborating on projects with artists and writers and musicians. Artists would hang out at the literary center Beyond Baroque, and the writers would hang out at LACE. We all went to see pretty much the same punk and experimental music.

I graduated from CalArts in 1978 and moved to LA. The first artists I met were Bruce Yonemoto and Jeffrey Vallance. Also, there were the artist/musicians, like John Duncan and Tom Recchion, who were associated with the LA Free Music Society. Through Benjamin Weissman and Tim Martin, who went to CalArts with me, I got to know writers associated with Beyond Baroque, like you and Bob Flanagan and Jack Skelley and Amy Gerstler. I also got to know some LA artists of the previous generation: Chris Burden and Ed Ruscha and Alexis Smith and James Hayward were all extremely supportive early on.

John Baldessari and Douglas Huebler were teaching at CalArts at the time, and they're often cited by artists of your generation as key influences and mentors. Was that true for you as well?

I was very close with David Askevold, who was also on the faculty. We did projects together very early on. Huebler, sure, though we didn't really hang out much. Baldessari was a very central figure even though he was busy with his career; a lot of artist gatherings and parties took place at his studio in Santa Monica. I was definitely influenced by some of the visiting faculty at CalArts, especially Laurie Anderson, Jonathan Borofsky, and Judy Pfaff.

When I first met you, I thought of you as a performance artist first and foremost.

That's what I was doing primarily, really because there was no gallery scene. There was no place to show my static works. The only gallery for young artists in the very early '80s was Riko Mizuno's in Little Tokyo. I had a show there in '81. A lot of artists of my generation, like Jim Isermann and Jill Giegerich, showed there, as well as older artists like Chris Burden and Alexis Smith. When Mizuno closed her gallery, soon after, these artists moved to galleries like Rosamund Felsen and Richard Kuhlenschmidt and Fred Hoffman. I guess that was the beginning of my groups of younger artists becoming known.

Ulrike Kantor's gallery on La Cienega was a funny place. It was a serious gallery, but it attracted a heavily punk-rock scene.

All the neo-Expressionists showed there, the locals as well as some Germans. Her gallery was very "East Village." For a while it was right next door to Rosamund Felsen, where Chris Burden, Jeffrey Vallance, Alexis Smith, Lari Pittman, and I showed. A lot of the artists at Felsen had some kind of link to Conceptual art.

When did you first show in New York, and how did that happen?

My first New York solo show was in '82 at Metro Pictures. Helen Winer brought me into the gallery. Before Metro Pictures she had run Artists Space and became familiar with my work through there, I believe. John Miller, Tony Oursler, and I all went to CalArts together, and we were very close. John and Tony moved to New York right after my graduation, and through them and other CalArts connections I met artists on the East Coast like Erika Beckman, Matt Mullican, and Jim Welling. At that time I didn't feel like there was a coastal separation. It wasn't until the market boom in the mid-'80s that I started to feel the return of regionalist prejudices. Before that, I felt that my generation of artists, like the Conceptual-ists, was very much international in orientation. Allegiances were based on aesthetic connections, not regional ones. But by the mid-'80s, the rise of the huge art stars brought with it a rise of certain biases. However, I don't think these regionalist biases were based on any true difference; they were the outcome of resentments related to economic competition.

I remember your work being poorly received in New York throughout the '80s.

Very much so. There was a strong bias against West Coast art in general that was the result of the economic success of painters like David Salle. In 1983 LACE did an LA/New York swap show with Artists Space. Younger LA artists including Mitchell Syrop and Lari Pittman showed in New York, and LACE presented New York artists of the same generation, like Jeff Koons and Charles Clough. There already was by that point a strong back-and-forth connection between the coasts, but because of the New York artists' financial success, the West Coast artists were suddenly viewed differently. It really adversely affected Mitchell Syrop's career. People started saying he was emulating Barbara Kruger, when in actuality he had developed his own combination of photography and text independently.

To me, Tim Ebner is a great or rather horrible example. In New York, his interest in systematic abstraction caused his work to be contextualized with neo-geo artists, but the romantic, "surf and sand" aspect of his art was never recognized. So when neo-geo became old news, his work went out of favor without ever having been understood in the first place.

Artists like Jim Isermann and I had a hard time. Our work was too outside the kind of Pop and Minimalist references that were in favor in New York, too overt in its adoption of material referencing mass-cultural tropes. For similar reasons, it took forever for Jim Shaw to be shown in New York. He even had a hard time in LA; his work just didn't look like "art" to people. The same with Paul McCarthy; he didn't have any gallery affiliations at all until very late in the '80s, when Rosamund Felsen started showing him. Raymond Pettibon was still considered a punk artist, a guy who did album covers, essentially. In LA, the punk/art scene was somewhat equivalent to the East Village scene in New York, but without the attendant commercial success. Raymond and Jim Shaw entered the "real" art world through that scene. They both had shows at the Zero One Gallery, which was more of an after-hours club than a gallery. Even in LA it took a while for people to recognize that some of the artists showing in that context were sophisticated.

When did you stop being seen as an underground performance artist and start being seen as a serious visual artist?

In LA, my work always received a good critical response. Luckily, there were some good critical writers on the West Coast at that time, writing for the *LAICA Journal*, for example. Howard Singerman, Christopher Knight, and Colin Gardner all wrote seriously on my work. I was being written about, but I didn't have any gallery success until the stuffed-animal show in New York in 1990. Before that I was sometimes labeled a neo-Expressionist or a funk artist because of the crudeness of my drawings. People in New York just didn't know what to do with my work. I think the big change happened when I started showing in Europe in the late '80s and became acquainted with artists like Martin Kippenberger, Georg

Herold, Albert Oehlen, and Franz West. I felt a strong connection to the work they were doing; it struck me as similar to what I and other artists I respected in the United States were doing. In New York people had a hard time distinguishing between artists who use regional imagery in a nationalistic way, like the neo-Expressionists, and artists, like the ones I just mentioned, who played with that a little more critically. I felt a real kinship with them, so I ended up bypassing New York and associating myself with the German artists. I had had a consistent presence in New York since the beginning of the '80s. I've been in the Whitney Biennial six times, but I was still always depicted as an outsider. This struck me as funny, since I never thought of myself as a West Coast artist. I grew up in Detroit, and my early aesthetic training was rooted in East Coast art. West Coast art, except for "finish fetish"—some East Coast writers still can't get past that cliché—is a relatively recent invention. "LAX" in Vienna and "Helter Skelter" initiated the idea. That's when artists like me and Pettibon and McCarthy and Pittman became more commercially acceptable and defined as '90s artists, which is funny because we had all been working seriously since the late '70s.

I think of the time before "Helter Skelter" in the early '90s as a kind of grace period. After that, the work of a lot of LA artists had a name that was actually quite reductive.

"Helter Skelter" fixed the idea that my generation of LA artists are all obsessed with negative aesthetics, and this image is only now starting to dissipate. One of the main things that drew this group of artists together initially was that our art was busier, more maximal than what was in fashion in '80s New York. So an artist like Lari Pittman and I had a lot in common in that sense and because of the psychosexual aspects our works shared. But by the '90s, as identity politics became a bigger part of art discourse, Pittman's work was increasingly discussed in terms of gay identity, and we were no longer grouped together. In the early '80s, we were all eccentrics and outsiders united by our mutual exclusion. There was no art market at that time. We weren't thinking about sales. The '80s changed that forever. That was the major shift in art practice in my lifetime.

I remember when you had your retrospective at the Whitney in the early '90s and you did a talk. A number of younger artists I knew in New York attended, and they were confused and kind of outraged that you characterized your work in terms of your blue-collar background. They had a very specific, "Helter Skelter"–derived idea about your work, and your bringing in issues of class completely threw them.

Well, such issues were really out of fashion at that point. By the mid-'80s there were inklings of what's happening now, which is a kind of complete art-world embrace of popular art and mass culture, but with no critical intent. Anything that was too "intellectual" was looked down upon, and that's even more the case now. That attitude has flowered into a dominant trend. I'm amazed that so much contemporary art in New York galleries at the moment could be said to have its roots in the "LA aesthetic." Of course I think the similarities are only surface ones.

To understand the work of LA artists of our generation, you'd really have to look at the visual art, literature, and music of that period in context.

A lot of writers associated with Beyond Baroque were exploring mass culture in a manner I found new and inspiring. I think the intermixture of

writers, musicians, and artists and video makers in LA then was remarkable. Really, the main damage resulting from the rise of the '80s art world
was that it reintroduced genre distinctions that had dissolved in the '70s.
Suddenly a sculpture was different from a painting, which was different
from a book, and that was different. Ultimately, the most important thing
for me about the '80s was that for a short time in LA in the early part of
that decade, those distinctions were nonexistent.

THE JOHN WATERS INTERVIEW
(April 2004)

Under normal circumstances, introducing John Waters would be a pure formality. He is easily the world's most famous icon of cultural outrage and transgression. As a filmmaker, he has created a body of work that is widely recognized as one of the great treasures of American movie history, and he has inspired a degree of reverence in his admirers that few if any other directors can claim. Early classics like *Female Trouble* and *Pink Flamingos* remain among the most quoted and name-checked movies of all time. Mid-career films like the Broadway-anointed *Hairspray* and Waters's comedy masterpiece *Serial Mom* launched the aesthetics of younger directors like Wes Anderson and Todd Solondz. Recent movies like *Cecil B. DeMented* and *Pecker* are easily his most daring and impressive films to date. Waters is that rare creature, a great artist whose oeuvre has achieved not only critical respect but also massive international popularity. Still, Waters's visual art, in which he photographs old, low-budget movies playing on his TV set then combines select freeze-frames into witty pictorial narratives, remains relatively unknown and uncelebrated outside the contemporary art world, and even to some degree within it. Just as it took many years for the film community to acknowledge the genius in Waters's unique, iconoclastic movies, the art world has taken its sweet time in giving his equally original and daredevil visual art its due. Now, after close to a decade of being exhibited in galleries around the world, Waters's photographs and photographic collages are receiving an official stamp of approval in the form of a retrospective at the New Museum of Contemporary Art in downtown New York. Cocurated by Lisa Phillips and Marvin Heiferman, *John Waters: Change of Life* opened in February and runs through late April.

Dennis Cooper: Would it be fair to say that you think a facial expression is more interesting than a brushstroke?

John Waters: A facial expression?

Let me put it this way. A painting is constructed of brushstrokes. Your visual art is constructed of freeze-frames, and most of them involve people's faces, so in a way, the facial expression is your art's equivalent of the brushstroke.

I see it more as my material. I don't think that it's my paint, because I think my work is about writing and editing more than it's about photography or color. I love to take color pictures of black-and-white films transferred to video off the TV monitor because it looks so sickly and bad. The images I use tell a story in a different kind of way than the source material intended. That's what I mean when I say it's more about writing. Maybe the facial expressions work like subtitles: they tell you how to read the work's narrative. Because my pieces are like storyboards, many of them. They're storyboards that I don't have to turn into a movie. I'm taking a movie and turning it into a storyboard.

One of the great innovations of your work both in the visual arts and in film is the way you present personality as a serious artistic subject. There's your interest in personality—capturing it, arranging it, depicting it. And then there's the overriding personality of your art. Is editing, selecting, and combining images a matter of finding balance between your personality, which informs all your art, and the personalities of your subjects?

It's a matter of refining it, to me. And hopefully reducing it to what people in the film business call a high concept. It's that one moment that delights me for some reason, and that I hope can delight others, or rather horrify others—or get them to see in a different way. Most of my source material is from failed movies or forgotten movies or movies from the bottom of the $1.98 reduced bin that no one cares about anymore. If I use an image from an epic movie, it's always to destroy it in some way: as in *Hair in the Gate*, the money shot from every big movie but with a hair in it. Personality is certainly important. Personality is what interests me in writing, in art, in movies, everything. So if I can make my photographs have a new personality, it's giving them new life.

I started doing this because I wanted stills that were not available. I wanted publicity photos that no newspaper would print. The work is about show business and about an insider kind of thing. The whole art world is about insiders. You have to learn how to see and all that. So that's there and important, but at the same time, I'm delighting in personality. And that's why I'm never bored. I mean, I can sit on a corner or go into a 7-Eleven, and I can make up a story about every single person I see, a really complicated story, instantaneously, almost, as they walk by. And that's good practice.

In your stories, there's outrageous and even juicy stuff, yet there's a sincerity and a respect for the character that's very different from how, say, E! television or *Access Hollywood* goes for the juicy but reduces it to the palatable and banal.

Well, that's a different thing because they're trying to appeal to everybody. We know the delightful, wonderful, great thing about the art world is that you have to appeal to about three people. Which is such a relief to me. And the three people you have to appeal to are especially moody and snotty. I love that. I'm so for that. So, it's the exact opposite way of seeing. I'm not against E! entertainment. I think they actually did a great biography of Divine. I'm not against what they do, but I don't see the connection in any way. But then I watch television almost never. I mean the only time I ever turn on the television is to take pictures of it for my artwork, or to watch porno. Turning on the television is something that's very hard for me to do.

You see personality as an art form. Warhol was interested in personality and depicted it in his work, but while he would erase himself, your personality is the fabric of your art. Your art is your personality, and within that personality there are layers of other personalities. It's quite complex.

I'm so glad you say *art*—I can't say that word out loud because that's up to others to decide. I would never say I'm an artist. I hate when you ask people what they do, and they say, "I'm an artist." I believe I'll be the judge of that. Saying somebody's work is art is a good review. But what was the question? Oh, about my personality. It's completely in my photo shows because I'm still the one telling those twisted little narratives. I'm telling them in a different context and in a different world, but as in the films, I'm making fun, in a way, of something that I really, really love. I think that is the personality of all my work, no matter if you like it or not.

It's the way your personality and the personalities of your subjects collude and collide and mix that's so interesting. How much fine-tuning do you have to do to make sure your personality doesn't interfere with or override their very distinct personalities? Is it second nature to you, or is that balance a very deliberate and labored-over thing?

Does it come easy? You know, I have a studio, and that's the only place I really ever think of ideas for my photographic pieces. So when I'm going to have a new show, I go over there, where I have envelopes full of photographs I've taken for possible future pieces. I fine-tune them by putting them all out on the floor and editing them. It's like pitching a movie in a way. I only have three stills to tell you a whole story. The movie pitch is the ultimate high concept of the motion-picture business. You know the joke: studio executives have the attention span of gnats, so you have to tell them the whole thing in one sentence. Well, I'm making fun of that process in a way; I'm reducing all movies to the one second that I think you really only need to remember. But is it my personality? Whenever I put my own image in it, I try to annihilate my celebrity. I did a piece using all these glamorous Greg Gorman head shots of me. I defaced each one of them in a unique way: rubber stamps, Wite-Out, press-type patterns, rubber roaches glued to my face. . . . I autographed one of them one hundred times to obliterate the image. Or there's one called *Self-Portrait*, in which I turn into Don Knotts. Well, that's just about low self-esteem. Everybody in the art world and show business secretly does have low self-esteem. That's why we take the risk every day of having to worry if strangers like us. That's what reviews are. I mean, you put yourself on the chopping block for the rest of your life. I'm just trying to make fun of my weaknesses and celebrate them.

That kind of self-examination is one of the many things that distinguish your visual art from your films.

My films are about people who would never win in real life. They always win in my movies.

You never annihilate them. In your visual art, there is plenty of annihilation going on.

I'm annihilating my own celebrity. That's a very, very different thing. In the art world, I believe my celebrity as a filmmaker is the source of great suspicion. I know that. I'm recognizing it. It's the only thing I can't change. So I like to make fun of it. That's mental health, isn't it? In your own life, if you can't change something, you make fun of it, and you learn to live with it and accept it. That's maturity. If you can make fun of your worst night, you will survive everybody.

[*laughter*] I'll remember that.

It's true. [*laughter*] Think of the worst thing that's ever happened to you. If you can think of a humorous way to tell somebody that story, nobody can get to you. You can't be blackmailed.

You're one of the few artists where if someone announces him- or herself as a fan of yours, it's a way for them to identify themselves. To define oneself as a John Waters fan is to announce one's way of looking at the world.

Matthew Marks said the best thing. He said, "You are the best kind of celebrity there is. The only people who recognize you are the ones you'd want to." And that's true. People say the nicest stuff to me. And the people who say nice stuff to me are nice people, you know? They aren't people clutching at you and lunatics. So what was the question?

The question was going to follow that statement. [*laughter*]

Then I butted in.

What I was going to get at is that there is a lot of preconception and pre-judging of what you do because you have such a strong image. People have a preconceived notion of what you do. They'll glance at your work and think they can judge it.

Well, I've always thought that, physically, I'd never have to go on a diet. If you're my age, and you have something weird on your face, my mustache, and you wear strange shoes, no one looks in the middle.

[*laughter*]

That's the secret, really. I just want to share that with middle-aged men.

I guess what I'm saying is that as a massive admirer of your work, and of your recent work in particular, I feel like your fame and reputation create a situation where your newer work doesn't get the intricate attention it deserves.

I sort of disagree.

Really?

I think the press has always been pretty fair to me. You know, I made my first movie forty years ago. So I think I've had a fair shake. There has been some very, very intelligent criticism about my work. Of course, like every-body, I can remember the ones that really hurt me. But I never answer my critics. That's the sign of a true amateur, I believe. So I would disagree with you. Basically, I have done what I set out to do in my life, yes, and I feel I have been adequately rewarded, I do.

Okay, then do you take your fame into account when you construct your work? Are you consciously dealing with the positive and negative impact that your fame has on the perception of your work?

I make fun of it in the photographs. But I have completely stopped put-ting myself in my movies. I do twenty to thirty John Waters performances around the country every year. I'm certainly not hiding from my fame. I recognize it. I think it's part of my work. We're talking about a trailer for my new movie that maybe will be just me introducing it, like William Castle used to do. I can't say I'm innocent. I can't say my fame happened without my participation. It happened with my participation from the very beginning because I'm a carny, and publicity is free advertising. When we started, I didn't have any money for ads. So the only way we could get people to know our work was to make up some kind of persona to sell it. It wasn't a lie, the persona, but, yes, I get dressed as John Waters some days. I admit that.

Knowing you as a friend, I am fascinated that you're interested in so-called high art, but you're also interested in art that functions strictly as a souvenir of a certain kind of sensibility. Say serial-killer art. Low art, in other words.

Well, that is true, but I have never bought serial-killing art in my life. I have a John Wayne Gacy painting that was a very welcome Christmas present from a friend, and I had it way before anybody had one. I do have a portrait of a serial killer, too, that was made for me by friends maybe twenty-five years ago. But I do not collect things like that. People always seem to think I do. I mean, a fan sent me a glass of dirt from John Wayne Gacy's basement, and I wasn't going to throw it out. Yeah, I recognize the horror of that little tchotchke. And I do have it in my house. But it was sent to me. I do not see things like that and art as the same thing. I consider them weird collectibles. When I have my art collection listed for insurance and stuff, they're not listed there.

So how did your interest in visual art begin? Were you a kid?

Yeah. Well, I've told this story, but when I was about eight I went to the Baltimore Museum. My aunt took me there, and I saw this little Miró print, and I bought it and took it home. And when I had it home, all the other kids went, "Ooh, that's the ugliest thing, you're an idiot." I felt this great power from it. So it was really an early way to rebel. And I still like work like that, that is kind of artless and inspires contempt in people who generally hate contemporary art. It's the first thing I embrace.

Did you make art as a kid?

Well, my parents told me this story that I don't remember. They said I always came home and told them about this kid who was so weird in school. All he did was paint with black crayons. They said I talked about him all the time. My mother said she talked to my teacher and my teacher told her that kid was me. A child psychologist can probably figure that one out.

You didn't make paintings at home?

Yes, I did a little bit. When I was a teenager I loved Marisol. And of course Andy Warhol. Pop art was a great, great influence on me. And when I was in high school, my girlfriend—it's that long ago—gave me a Warhol print of Jackie in 1964 that I still have. It's in my dining room. It's a Silver Jackie and I believe it cost a hundred dollars at the time, which is like a thousand dollars today. It was a really big, great gift.

I was trying to think of a contemporary artist whose work bears comparison with yours. I suppose there could be quite a number, but the first artist who came to mind was John Baldessari.

Really? I think Richard Prince would be the one who's closest. I talk about redirecting, and using that term is sort of kidding about what Richard did, which was rephotographing. If you got a portrait done by him, he would say, "Well, show me a few pictures that you like yourself in." And then he'd take a picture of them. I think that's so great. I'm a big fan of Richard's. And of John Baldessari's also, but his work is put together in a different way from mine. Maybe he added more art than I did. So certainly, of course, they both led to what I do, and Warhol led to what they do. I'm also a fan of Elaine Sturtevant now.

Everybody who ever used appropriation in any way has certainly led to what I do.

The first artwork I loved when I was a teenager was a Baldessari. It was this large silkscreen photograph of him standing in front of a pole, and it said *WRONG* across the bottom.

[*laughter*] Yeah. It's so liberating when something like that speaks to you, and you think, Oh, God. When you can use it for defiance. And certainly every artist that you and I like uses defiance and destruction of what people thought of as art as a very, very important part of their work. Even the name of this magazine. Would you start a magazine called *BOMB* today? No. Already it's a politically incorrect title. Imagine raising money for a magazine called *BOMB* after 9/11. And in show business, God, we could never have a magazine called that because it means something very, very different. It means flop!

[*laughter*] They were trying to force that rock band Anthrax to change their name after 9/11, but I don't think they ended up doing it.

Well, remember AIDS diet candy? I mean talk about putting someone out of business overnight. They had that whole ad campaign: "Lose weight with AIDS." Jesus.

Well, back in the late '70s, my friend the poet Tim Dlugos and I always used to say about a boy we were attracted to that he had "the ass of death."

AIDS ruined everything and it will never get back to right.

Okay, enough of that. Maybe I'm wrong about this, but when you re-contextualize your own films in your visual art, you only use your early films. Why?

Because the bad technical aspects of the early work lend themselves very well to contemporary art. With the later work, I've tried, but it looks too slick. See, if you primitively photograph badly photographed movies, it becomes a new kind of rawness that I believe can work in the contemporary art world. I'm not saying that I think my older films look better than my newer ones, but they work better for what I'm trying to do on the contemporary art scene because they look more distorted. The one that works best for me is *Mondo Trasho* because with that one, you know, I cringe. It's completely overexposed. I mean, believe me, this was no choice in style. I didn't know what I was doing.

Oh, you're being too modest.

No, I'm not being modest. I literally had no idea, because I never went to film school. I didn't know what to do. I didn't know how to turn on the camera, you know, basically. Somehow my incompetence ended up right in the year 2004 in the contemporary art world.

In my conversations with you over the years—

Which we can't print.

No, no.

I'm kidding because we always gossip in them.

If we talked like we normally do, it would be like one of those gruesome *Interview* magazine things. You know, actors who worked together on some film cracking each other up with behind-the-scenes anecdotes.

I love gossiping with you, because we can gossip about books and art and stuff.

Okay, one *Interview* magazine moment. I always tell people the story of when we first met. You invited me to lunch when I was on the *Frisk* book tour, and you did this really witty thing. You served me raw meat.

Oh, but I didn't know you were a vegetarian.

I know, and I was horrified because I didn't want to ruin the wittiness of the gesture, but I couldn't eat it. So I saved the day because I told you if it was River Phoenix, I would eat it. He was still alive at the time, of course.

[*laughter*] You were against eating meat, but not against cannibalism. I can understand the difference. That's the misconception that you must get your whole life because of your work. I mean, that was my stupidity. People used to send me dog shit in the old days. Just because I did a scene where someone eats it does not mean that I do. But I am sure that there are people who are scared of you.

Not so much anymore, because people take me more seriously now. But yeah, I used to get a lot of people asking me where they could get snuff movies or telling me how I could get snuff movies. Anyway, what I originally wanted to say was that in my conversations with you, it often seems to me that, particularly when it comes to movies, you prefer work that's serious or dramatic to work that's comedic. You seem much more picky about work that has comedic intent.

It's harder to be funny. It's really hard to be funny.

Is it because there are more surprises for you in work that's entirely serious?

Maybe because I try to make comedies, it's harder for me to like one. I always want to laugh when I go to a movie. But I guess I do like serious things better sometimes, and that is probably a misconception that people have of me. They think I like just gross stuff, you know? I am always shocked by that question because to me, yeah, I had those kinds of sight gags, certainly. *Pink Flamingos*, you have to remember, asked the question, What could be illegal anymore? What could bad taste possibly be when everyone thought the revolution was going to happen? Which is such a hilarious idea when we look back on it. But we did think a revolution would happen in a weird way. It's so amazing, and that's because of LSD, which, you know, I'm not at all against. But it's hard for people today to imagine that anyone could have really thought the way we did. I don't know if that's answering the question.

It's interesting, so it doesn't matter. But about comedy and your relationship to the standard comedy film, I'm hoping to draw out a distinction. For instance, it's hard to imagine that you would be interested in working with, say, Adam Sandler, or even with a comedic genius like Bill Murray.

First of all, I have worked with Bill Murray. Bill Murray sings uncredited on the sound track of *Polyester*.

Oops, well, there you go.

Adam Sandler I thought was quite good in *Punch-Drunk Love*.

I agree, but would you cast him?

I'm never against the idea. I mean Johnny Knoxville is the star in my new movie. I don't think that's a surprise, do you?

No, but that's a different kind of comedy. He's not a quote-unquote comedian.

Well, I used to be against hiring comedians, but I did this time. I hired Tracey Ullman for my new movie. I will never say I won't hire comedians again because she was great and funny and wonderful to work with. I was always afraid that if I hired a comedian, that would mean that I didn't have enough faith in my own dialogue to be funny. But after this experience I don't agree with that anymore, because she brought a great timing and dignity to this movie. Before you know that the movie's funny you know what the tone is going to be just because she's starring in it. Which I think is important. But it's true that what you think I'd like and dislike aren't always quite as predictable as you might think.

Well, I've learned over the years of knowing you not to say that I like this or that comedy film because you tend to go, "Oh, I hated that."

[*laughter*] Yeah, I guess the comedies that I have the most trouble with—although some of them are good—are the fifty-million-dollar Hollywood comedies. It's really hard to be funny with that much money.

Buddy movies.

There are some good buddy movies. I like *The Incredible 2-Headed Transplant*.

[*laughter*] **Can you talk about your process as a visual artist? For instance, do you say, Okay, I think I'll make some art now, and sit down in front of the TV with your camera cocked?**

First, I'll have the ideas for like twenty pieces before I even begin to search for the images. And then I look for them. I have a friend, Dennis Dermody, who helps me a lot because he has an incredible film knowledge. I might say, I need fifty movie stars sitting on the toilet, and he knows where they are. But I think my pieces up long before I do them. Then I take the photographs and make the pieces. Most of them don't make the cut. So let's say I'm going to try to do thirty pieces, which is more than one show. Maybe half of them will work, and half of that half become something different from what I'd intended. A lot of times the pictures I took for one piece that doesn't work will end up four years later as part of the narrative of a completely different piece. So I have an endless number of shots available. They're all stock footage to me now. Most of my time is spent on the floor of my studio going through all those shots and arranging things.

You always send out great Christmas cards, which I guess could be described as special versions of your visual art in card form. But this year,

you sent out this amazing transparent Christmas tree ornament with a fake dead roach inside. No doubt there are a slew of them for sale on eBay right now.

I haven't looked. Yeah, I wonder who will be the first jerk who tries to sell one.

So does this signal a new foray into sculpture for you?

I'll be honest: it did enter my mind to do the Christmas balls a little fancier and bigger and make them a little sturdier and sell them as art, but I decided to go low-tech. By the way, eBay people, that Christmas ornament was a *very* large edition.

Lastly, I want to ask you about your movie *Pecker,* whose protagonist is a kind of accidental artist who makes a brief splash in the art world. I've seen *Pecker* referred to as your most autobiographical and personal film. I've also seen it referred to as your revenge on the contemporary art scene's pretensions and cliquishness.

It's really neither of those things. It's a love letter to the contemporary art world, I think. No one I know in the contemporary art world was at all mad about the movie. I don't remember any pissed-off art review about it. We got a lot of bad reviews of the movie, but not from the art world. And there's one big, big difference between *Pecker* and my own story. Pecker was naïve. I started reading *Variety* when I was twelve. I was anything but. New York certainly didn't come clamoring to see my early work like what happens in *Pecker.* I wished New York had come and seen my underground movies back when I was showing them in a church in Baltimore. I knew about New York, and when I was fifteen I would run away and go see movies at the Filmmakers' Cooperative. I wasn't naïve about art. And fame happened to Pecker accidentally. It did not happen to me accidentally at all. In fact, it was a long time before anyone outside Baltimore noticed what I was doing, and it was frustrating. At the time, New York was incredibly chauvinistic about the underground art world. Oh, another difference is, unlike Pecker, I didn't grow up blue collar. I gave Pecker the most wonderful, understanding family. My family was also understanding. So there are certainly auto-biographical things in *Pecker*. I used to push my little sister around, and give out flyers like Pecker. I did take pictures of my friends and turn that into whatever I did. So, that was certainly autobiographical. And by the time I made *Pecker*, I had been in the art world awhile. I was a collector, and I'd had shows. I'd been to a million art shows and artists' dinners. Pecker didn't know about the art world when he was discovered. In real life, Pecker would have been an outsider artist, and I certainly was not. As we know, outsider art is an entirely different world than the world of contemporary art.

So *Pecker* is not particularly close to your heart. It's not your special film, your personal or vulnerable film?

Oh, yeah, I love it. All my movies are close to my heart. There's not one scene in any of my movies, including the new one, *A Dirty Shame*, where you could ask me where that idea came from and I couldn't tell you about something in my life that caused it.

Is that true of your visual art as well?

Well, I'm a collector, and I appreciate the vocabulary of contemporary art and enjoy all of that. So, in that way, sure. Honestly, you know the only time I ever relax is when I go to galleries. I go to a lot of them, obsessively, like forty in one day. So I guess you could say my photographs come from that part of my life. Because that is my real life, too, you see.

Is your visual art as important to you as your films?

Yes, it is, actually. It certainly is a big, big part of my life and very important to me. In a way it's even more delightful because it's a newer experience for me.

The art crowd is very different from the film crowd.

They're even cuter.

LOONY TUNES
Ondi Timoner's *DiG!*
(September 2004)

Art history has long maintained a church and state–style separation between naïve, unsophisticated work by so-called outsider artists and work whose construction and style are unmistakably savvy and sociable. Henry Darger, the Chicago janitor who spent his downtime secretly making obsessive paintings, is a good example of the consequence of these distinctions, remaining an honored guest of the art world rather than a bona fide star.

In rock music, this prejudice is reversed: The outsider is the ultimate insider. Rock's history has been one of constant reinvention by artists too crazy or ignorant to understand the rules, and its canon is top-heavy with the music of weirdos, drug addicts, and idiots savants. Young musicians who aren't inherently out of their minds go to great lengths to cultivate *Beverly Hillbilly*–like personas and create the impression that their only influences are nonmusical—say, the rustling of trees or the yells of their alcoholic parents. Rock fans and critics are so attentive to signs of wildness that a musician need only share a foul mood or two to have their CDs scrutinized for evidence of genius.

DiG!, a documentary directed by Ondi Timoner that chronicles and compares the career trajectories of two West Coast bands, the Brian Jonestown Massacre and the Dandy Warhols, is steeped in the notion that, for a rock musician, psychological problems are solid proof of artistic significance. The tormented genius in question is Anton Newcombe, the songwriter and leader of the primarily Los Angeles–based BJM, who spends the film doing drugs, throwing tantrums, and obsessing about Courtney Taylor, his well-behaved and better-groomed counterpart in Portland, Oregon's, DW (Taylor is also the film's narrator). Both bands practice a kind of edgy, left-of-mainstream pop rooted in late-'60s psychedelia and delivered in a ramshackle '90s alternative-rock style. They begin the film on equal footing as buzzed-about underdog acts with requisite hard-core followings and obscure, critically acclaimed recordings. But where the nerdy, grizzled BJM grab hipsters' attention with their riotous, self-destructive live performances, the cuter, more professional DW draw a slightly more middle-of-the-road college crowd who think they smell the next Matchbox Twenty.

Newcombe and Taylor are at first friendly and mutually supportive due to their shared influences and high self-regard, but they're quickly revealed as very different kinds of artists. Newcombe takes an unassailably romantic, purist approach to his music and sees taxing his health and destroying his personal and professional relationships as heroic measures to ensure his work's originality. By *DiG!*'s conclusion, he has lost a long-suffering girlfriend ("Heroin makes him evil"), BJM's devoted manager of six years ("Anton is a great songwriter, . . . but he is so horrible in so many ways"), and most of his band, including key member Matt Hollywood ("I would rather think of [Anton] as dead and miss him"), not to mention innumerable brain cells and several golden opportunities. Taylor, by comparison, is more a Paul McCartney type who sees popularity as the ultimate determinant of what is and what isn't great. While he shares Newcombe's love of the retro and experimental, he's essentially a clever guy with a knack for writing quality **pop** hooks. As the DW happily manicure their sound and image, sign with a major label, and earn a spot in MTV's rotation and the BJM self-annihilate in the name of integrity, the bands' comradeship devolves into an ugly, if entertaining, one-sided feud. Newcombe's anti-Taylor antics escalate from the slightly embarrassing (when the DW have a minor hit with their song "Not If You Were the Last Junkie on Earth," BJM record an obtuse response, "Not If You Were the Last Dandy on Earth," and pass out copies at a high-profile DW gig) to the downright creepy (after a show in San Francisco, Newcombe gives DW a gift containing shotgun shells and other sinister, symbolic items). The bulk of *DiG!*, which will premiere on the Sundance Channel and arrive in theaters this fall, juxtaposes scenes in which Newcombe acts out his frustration at Taylor's success with scenes illustrating Taylor's alternately smug and guilt-stricken responses.

DiG! feels like what it is—a documentary initiated as a shapeless, home movie–like project only to stumble onto a theme rather late in the game. Its vibe of intimacy and casualness is absorbing, and its strengths lie in a wealth of lucky-break moments: a stoned, disheveled Newcombe trying to torture a Phil Spectoresque masterpiece from his cheap four-track recorder or brawling with his bandmates onstage; Taylor preening for the camera and racking his brain for reasons why he might deserve his ex-friend's abuse. The film grows less interesting when it seeks to justify Newcombe's erratic behavior and commercial failure as upshots of his genius and infers that Taylor's success is a result of his relative inconsequence as an artist. Part of the problem lies in the fact that the snippets we're given of the BJM's music present nothing that sounds particularly remarkable. Its artsy, lo-fi tenor and traditional, stretched-out song structures are entirely familiar. There's a frustrating disparity between the film's idolization of Newcombe's talent, driven home by a series of talking-head interviews with smitten peers and admirers, and its fixation on his extreme behavior. By comparison, the DW's music sounds equally unamazing but no more or less successful in its attempt to infuse the once groovy with a contemporaneous coolness.

Perhaps inadvertently, *DiG!* suggests that Newcombe's integrity may in fact be an illusion created by the medium in which he works. Take away the nobility of indie rock and Newcombe's cult status in that genre and he starts to seem a lot more like a haywire underground celebrity— say, post-Hole Courtney Love sans the paparazzi—than 2004's answer to tortured visionaries like Syd Barrett or Brian Wilson or Kurt Cobain. The same could be said of *DiG!* Notwithstanding its novel subject matter and muddy air of studiousness, the film is essentially reality TV on a subculture safari with rock stereotypes substituting for ideas and Newcombe and Taylor as its dueling Anna Nicole Smiths.

ACKNOWLEDGMENTS

The author is very grateful to Michael Signorelli, Carrie Kania, Ira Silverberg, Joel Westendorf, Peter Schjeldahl, Lane Relyea, Amy Gerstler, and Sander Hicks.

This book's title is taken from the song "Smothered in Hugs," composed by Robert Pollard and recorded by Guided by Voices for the album *Bee Thousand* (Scat Records, 1994).

"Homocore Rules" appeared in the *Village Voice*, 1985.

"Placebomania" appeared in *Art Papers*, 1989.

"The Keanu Reeves Interview" appeared in *Interview Magazine*, 1990, and the book *All Ears* (Soft Skull Press, 1999).

"No Mo' Pomo" appeared in the *LA Weekly*, 1991.

"The Queer King" appeared in the *LA Weekly*, 1992.

"Burden of Urban Dreams" appeared in the *LA Weekly*, 1993.

"Beauty and Sadness" appeared in *Spin Magazine*, 1993, and the book *All Ears* (Soft Skull Press, 1999).

"Love Conquers All" appeared in *Spin Magazine*, 1994, and the book *All Ears* (Soft Skull Press, 1999).

"Grain of the Voice" appeared in *Spin Magazine*, 1994, and the book *All Ears* (Soft Skull Press, 1999).

"Purplish Prose" appeared in the *LA Weekly*, 1994.

"Larry Clark's *Perfect Childhood*" appeared in *Bookforum*, 1994.

"Too Cool for School" appeared in *Spin Magazine*, 1994, and the book *All Ears* (Soft Skull Press, 1999).

"Real Personal" appeared in *Spin Magazine*, 1994, and the book *All Ears* (Soft Skull Press, 1999).

"Phoner" appeared as the liner notes to the Geffen Records CD re-release of Sonic Youth's album *Sister*, 1994.

"Junkie See, Junkie Do" appeared in *Spin Magazine*, 1995, and the book *All Ears* (Soft Skull Press, 1999).

"Minor Magic" appeared in *Artforum*, 1995.

"AIDS: Words from the Front" appeared in *Spin Magazine*, 1995, and the book *All Ears* (Soft Skull Press, 1999).

"The Ballad of Nan Goldin" appeared in *Spin Magazine*, 1995, and the book *All Ears* (Soft Skull Press, 1999).

"Hipper Than Thou" appeared in the *LA Weekly*, 1995.

"Flanagan's Wake" appeared in *Artforum*, 1996, and the book *All Ears* (Soft Skull Press, 1999).

"King of the Jumble" appeared in *Spin Magazine*, 1996, and the book *All Ears* (Soft Skull Press, 1999).

"Inside the High" appeared in the *LA Weekly*, 1996.

"Ice Nine" appeared in the *LA Weekly*, 1996.

"Rebel Just Because" appeared in *Detour Magazine*, 1996, and the book *All Ears* (Soft Skull Press, 1999).

"Letter Bomb" appeared in the *LA Weekly*, 1996.

"Why Does Herr F. Run Amok?" appeared in the *LA Weekly*, 1997.

"A Raver Runs Through It," coauthored by Dennis Cooper and Joel Westendorf, appeared in *Spin Magazine*, 1997, and the book *All Ears* (Soft Skull Press, 1999).

"Drug Fiction" appeared in *Spin Magazine*, 1997.

"Openings: Six Young Artists" appeared in *Artforum*, 1994–2004.

"King Junk" appeared in *Spin Magazine*, 1997, and the book *All Ears* (Soft Skull Press, 1999).

"Bale Bonds," coauthored by Dennis Cooper and Joel Westendorf, appeared in *Detour Magazine*, 1997.

"Spooky House" appeared in *Nest*, 1998.

"The Anti-Leo" appeared in *Time Out* (New York), 1998.

"*Nick Drake: The Biography*" appeared in *Bookforum*, 1999.

"Odd Man Out" appeared in *Artforum*, 1999.

"More Than Zero" appeared in *Artforum*, 2000.

"First Communion" appeared in *Artforum*, 2000.

"Mystery Man: Denis Johnson's *Name of the World*" appeared in the *LA Weekly*, 2000.

"Flailing Vision" appeared in *Artforum*, 2000.

"A Conversation with William T. Vollmann" appeared in *Bookforum*, 2000.

"Like a Virgin" appeared in *Artforum*, 2001.

"Fuck the Canon" appeared in the *LA Weekly*, 2001.

"*We're Desperate*" appeared in *Bookforum*, 2002.

"Naked Youth" appeared in *Artforum*, 2002.

"*Back in No Time: The Brion Gysin Reader*" appeared in *Bookforum*, 2002.

"'80s Then: Mike Kelley Talks to Dennis Cooper" appeared in *Artforum*, 2003.

"The John Waters Interview" appeared in *Bomb Magazine*, 2004.

"Loony Tunes" appeared in *Artforum*, 2004.

ALSO BY DENNIS COOPER

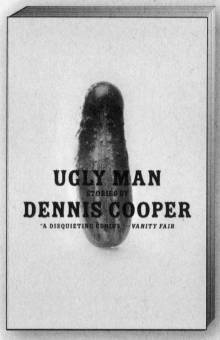

ISBN 978-0-06-171544-0 (paperback)

"Potent and humorous. . . . As always, the need for connection—even if experienced at the level of unspeakable yet intimate violence—as well as the need to expose what lies underneath are Cooper's main preoccupations."
—*New York Times Book Review*

"*Ugly Man* has a lightness that Cooper hasn't achieved elsewhere . . . it is certainly this highly talented author's most accessible work to date."
—*Time Out* (New York)

"This is classic Cooper: explicit, unconventional and, to the uninitiated, alarming." —*Publishers Weekly*